"Marisa?"

Slowly, as if in a trance, she pulled her attention from the fire and allowed her eyes to meet his.

"Let me love you, Marisa."

In two strides he was before her, his mouth capturing whatever words she might have uttered. She struggled at first, but then realized she was no match for his strength. As his mouth worked its magic over hers, her lips parted under his, wave after wave of shocking tremors rippling through her innocent, newly awakening body . . .

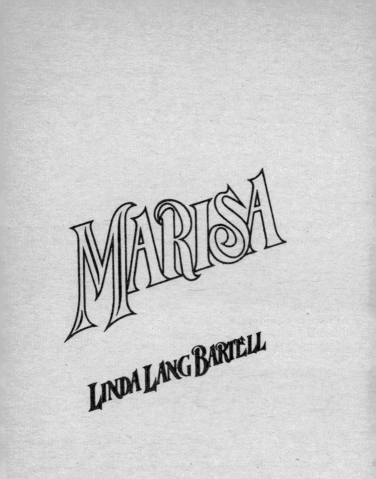

MARISA

LINDA LANG BARTELL

AVON
PUBLISHERS OF BARD, CAMELOT, DISCUS AND FLARE BOOKS

MARISA is an original publication of Avon Books. This work has never before appeared in book form. This work is a novel. Any similarity to actual persons or events is purely coincidental.

AVON BOOKS
A division of
The Hearst Corporation
105 Madison Avenue
New York, New York 10016

Copyright © 1988 by Linda Lang Bartell
Published by arrangement with the author
Library of Congress Catalog Card Number: 87-91619
ISBN: 0-380-75380-4

First Avon Books Printing: January 1988

AVON TRADEMARK REG. U.S. PAT. OFF. AND IN OTHER COUNTRIES, MARCA REGISTRADA, HECHO EN U.S.A.

Printed in the U.S.A.

K-R 10 9 8 7 6 5 4 3 2 1

To my intrepid little daughter,
Heather Lauren,
who fills my life with joy.

I would like to express my gratitude
to my editor, Ellen Edwards,
for sharing her expertise;
and to her assistant, Nancy Yost,
for her cooperation and thoughtfulness.
Also, many thanks to M. Knowles, D.V.M.,
for kindly answering my questions
regarding poisoning.

Invictus

Out of the night that covers me,
    Black as the Pit from pole to pole,
I thank whatever gods may be
    For my unconquerable soul.

In the fell clutch of circumstance,
    I have not winced nor cried aloud:
Under the bludgeonings of chance
    My head is bloody, but unbowed.

Beyond this place of wrath and tears
    Looms but the Horror of the shade,
And yet the menace of the years
    Finds and shall find me unafraid.

It matters not how strait the gate,
    How charged with punishments the scroll,
I am the master of my fate;
    I am the captain of my soul.

—William Ernest Henley

Cowards die many times before
    their deaths;
The valiant never taste of
    death but once.

—William Shakespeare

Prologue

"They come."

The softly spoken words died away on the breeze even as they were uttered. Only the muffled sound of approaching horses' hooves dominated the charged stillness.

In the deepening dusk a small number of men stood waiting, lined up across the far bank of a steep ravine, rallied from their hiding places within the forest behind them by Brand Ericson.

"Then let them come." Brand's words echoed the turbulent emotions roiling within him in the wake of the gargantuan battle he had thought ended—and lost. Lost as surely as the lives of his father and two brothers. Yet once again the Normans, it seemed, were attacking the defeated Anglo-Saxons, this pitiful but determined band of men hoping to trick the mounted knights in the rapidly approaching darkness.

And so they waited, exhausted, for what seemed a brief eternity, the cloying, metallic stench of gore and death hanging in the cool evening air like a miasmic pall. One last stand for their late King Harold and their beloved England. Who knew what would happen next? Who knew if the Normans, under a relentless William of Normandy, could be stopped before all of England was overrun in the wake of the death of the courageous Harold and his most loyal leaders?

1

A group of horsemen appeared at last and, misjudging the steepness and depth of the gorge, rode straight into it, preparing to cut down those defiant English on the opposite side. But their horses began to plunge uncontrollably into the treacherous ravine. Pitched to the ground, their riders became fair game for the waiting Anglo-Saxons, who mercilessly swooped down upon them and quickly dispatched the confused knights.

Once again the sounds of men grunting with exertion, crying out in pain, the screams of injured horses, the *clink* of sword and dagger against chain mail, the thud of metal against unresisting flesh and cartilage . . . all distorted the twilight stillness in an eerie cacophony.

"En avant, encore!" bellowed a voice that could only be the Bastard himself, and another wave of mounted Normans was thrown headlong into the waiting arms of their enemy. As this new charge met the same fate as its predecessor, the Anglo-Saxons knew they had won this small victory. For within moments of the second charge someone shouted again in muffled French, and the remaining Normans, not daring even to try to assist their doomed comrades, withdrew and disappeared into the night.

"Take the uninjured horses," advised Brand as he grabbed the reins of one such agitated beast and fought to bring it under control. "They are battle-trained, and if you can learn to use them to advantage, so much the better for you."

As his men emerged from what the Normans would later name "Malfosse," or "Evil Ditch," Brand quietly advised them to go to their homes—to warn any Anglo-Saxons they might come upon to be prepared for the worst, for the Normans had taken the major battle and England was now in mortal danger. "God go with you," he finished bleakly.

He leaped to the back of the huge, blood-streaked Norman war-horse, twice the size of an English pony, and headed northwest, stopping now and then only to slake his thirst at a stream or to snatch a few hours' rest before continuing on at a breakneck pace. As he left the battle site farther and farther behind, his thoughts turned pragmatically to his son. If William overran England, the English nobility would lose everything. Griffith would become a virtual slave to the Normans, the brutal, war-loving descendants of the Viking chieftain Rollo.

You cannot think 'tis over yet, a voice warned. A nagging sense of foreboding hung over him like a dark, ominous cloud and forced him to consider his boy's future. If William succeeded in his devil's work, then there had to be a way for Brand to strike some bargain with the duke. Some way to ensure that his only son would receive the holdings Brand had planned to pass down to him, not to some Norman mercenary as reward for his part in subjugating the English.

Brand was prepared to do anything to secure Griffith's future.

December 1066

Brand had been to London only once before—when he'd hurried south with Harold Godwinson from the Anglo-Saxon victory at Stamford Bridge, and the unlucky King had tried to catch a few days' rest and regroup his tired army for the march to Hastings to meet William of Normandy. Brand hadn't been positively impressed then with the town once known to the Romans as Londinium, its narrow, labyrinthine streets winding through the city, their center drains running with waste, filling the air with the stench of human excrement and garbage. Now, he couldn't believe the utter chaos that reigned in the old city.

He'd had to circumvent the charred ruins of Southwark at the southern end of the London Bridge to enter the city itself. Among other changes, he'd noted that William had obviously sent in Norman carpenters and stoneworkers and hastily erected a wooden citadel at the eastern end of the city—a fortress dwelling outside the old Roman wall on the riverbank. Bewildered Anglo-Saxons, many homeless now that their lords had been either killed or imprisoned and expropriated of their lands, lived in makeshift dwellings or even out in the open, struggling merely to survive. Normans, ever on guard, swaggered through the filthy, refuse-littered streets, lording it over the unfortunate English population.

Brand had sought lodgings the night before the coronation and had had to settle for a tiny, airless room in a small, shabby inn so close to the Thames that he could hear the lapping of the water as it licked at the banks in a steady rhythm with the ebb and flow of the tide. And he'd had to pay an outrageous sum to stable the huge gray destrier he'd taken in the aftermath of Hastings—the use of a stolen Norman war-horse a defiant gesture that he knew was reckless.

The many ships and seagoing vessels, which had caught his attention once before, held little interest for him now as he considered his own fate and that of his son. He'd hoped that by attending the coronation on Christmas Day, he could curry enough favor to aid him in getting a quick audience with William—a thing so abhorrent to him that he'd had to ruthlessly squelch the urge on more than one occasion to return home and prepare to fight to the death when William sent some mercenary knight or Norman baron to claim his spoils.

Caught between the pent-up frustration to which he was easy prey in the cubiclelike room, and the alternating anger and melancholy he experienced whenever he ventured outside the inn, Brand was relieved when Christmas Day dawned and he made his way to Edward the Confessor's abbey at Westminster, where the Bastard was to be made King of England. Mounted Norman guards swarmed outside the abbey, and the crowd inside was a mixture of Norman and English.

"A sly one, he is," mumbled an Anglo-Saxon standing next to Brand. "Look how he uses the Archbishop of York to crown him instead of Stigand of Canterbury." At Brand's puzzled frown he elucidated, "Aldred of York crowned our Harold as well."

Brand nodded, realizing more than ever how clever a strategist was the Duke of Normandy. As the congregation was asked to declare its approval twice—once by a Norman bishop in French and then by Archbishop Aldred in English—shouts of acclamation went up, echoing throughout the abbey and reaching the Norman guard outside. The guards in turn, interpreting the din from within to be a sign of trouble, began to set fire to the city in response. Noise and smoke from outside filtered through the doors, and the increasing uproar sent the spectators inside streaming out of the abbey in panic. The Norman guard stormed in to defend the duke.

It was impossible to fight the panic-stricken throng, and Brand found himself being carried along on the tide of humanity flowing in confusion out of the church and spilling into the smoke-filled street. He tried to shout to the Normans atop the plunging, screaming chargers, but to no avail. Glancing around, he was tempted to retreat into the abbey and safety, but rebuked himself for being a coward.

As he stood in momentary indecision, debating how best to help the Normans and English, who realized what had happened and were trying to establish some semblance of order, an ancient wooden building nearby went up in flames with a loud *whoosh*. Brand's first reaction was to turn and flee the burning thatched roof, as it scattered sparks and burning straw everywhere, large chunks separating and crashing heavily to the ground. Then he noticed a well-dressed Norman shouting orders to people streaming by and Brand joined him in directing everyone away from the growing inferno.

Engrossed in his efforts, he failed to see the burning beam falling toward them until the roar of the structure collapsing alerted them both. But it was too late. Brand saw the flame-eaten joist coming at them and gave the Norman a mighty shove to the side. The move cost him. Unable to follow the man to relative safety in time, Brand instinctively threw up his arms to protect himself and caught the red-hot timber across his left cheek and side of his neck before his hands could stop its advance. With a cry of pain, he heaved it away and staggered toward the Norman. As he fell to the ground, the last thing he remembered was the man wrapping his gold-embroidered mantle around Brand's body to smother the flames.

When Brand came to, he was disoriented at first. The fact that he was lying on a comfortable bed, in a more spacious and well-appointed chamber than his own tiny room on the waterfront, with a strange youth sitting watching him, did nothing to clarify matters.

He raised himself to one elbow at the sight of the page's clothing . . . Norman dress. Slowly the events of the coronation ceremony filtered back into his mind, the dull, burning sensation coming from his cheek and neck confirming it had not been merely a bad dream.

"You must lie still and try to sleep." The youth looked slightly uncomfortable, and Brand could guess that the page was mentally deducing from Brand's clothing and manner that he was not a peasant. The building frown on the Norman's face, however, told Brand the young man was also taking into account that his "guest" was of a conquered people now. Surely the youth could detect the hostility that shone in Brand's eyes and warned him to tread carefully, conquered or no. The boy continued to speak in halting English. "You are to rest, my lord, until your strength returns."

Brand raised a skeptical eyebrow. "But my strength never deserted me—and the burns will heal." He looked down at one hand, thankful for the thick calluses that had shielded the tender skin beneath from the brunt of the burn. And it was his left hand, not his right—not his sword hand.

He sat up and gave the youth a stiff smile. "I must leave, but I would bid you thank your lord—whoever he may be—for saving my life."

Osbern shook his head. "My lord Geoffrey said 'twas the other way around. He said you saved his life and tending to your hurts is small enough recompense."

Brand pictured the blazing beam hurtling down upon them and then deliberately blocked out the gut-wrenching image. He shook his head. "We are fortunate, both of us, to have escaped so lightly. . . . I take it the fire was brought under control?''

"Aye, my lord. William is now King of England.''

Instantly Osbern bit his lower lip, seeming to regret his words as Brand's lips tightened into a hard line, his topaz eyes glittering with suppressed anger. A sense of utter hopelessness, of bitter despair, struck Brand like a physical blow and threatened to overwhelm him. The youth examined the burns on Brand's cheek and neck once more in an effort to hide his awkward regret. "I think you need no more ointment, but I beg you stay until my lord Geoffrey returns, for he wishes to thank you himself.''

"Where is he?''

"He stayed to see the coronation finished.''

"I see." Fighting the urge to rudely rise from the bed and stalk from the room, Brand asked, "And just who is this Lord Geoffrey?''

"Count of Brionne." A matter-of-fact masculine voice with a heavy French accent answered his query from the doorway. Its owner strode into the room with all the confidence of one who knows his place in life and is well-satisfied with it.

Brand stared for a moment, taking in the bright crop of fair hair, cut short and high in back in the Norman fashion; the rich silk tunic with gold-embroidered hem, neck, and sleeves to match the cape with which de Brionne had enfolded Brand.

"Fortunately for you, my lord, only your clothing was singed and naught else save where you touched the burning wood." He moved to the bed and reached out to lift Brand's hand, turning it over to inspect the blistered palm. "Your sword hand?''

"Nay.''

"Good. A man needs his sword arm at all times." A smile played about his mouth. "I thank you for my life, er—?''

"Brand Ericson of Wessex, Thane to Harold Godwinson—while he was Earl of Wessex and then King of England.''

Rather than taking offense at the hint of defiance in Brand's lengthy pronouncement, Geoffrey de Brionne merely nodded. "A good man. But not ordained to rule England, unfortunately for him."

Brand opened his mouth to speak, then thought better of it. *Save your anger,* a voice said, and he bit back a scalding reply.

"Now, Brand Ericson, what can I do to repay you for my life—although I realize naught but the saving of yours can ever equal so valorous a deed."

Brand realized a golden opportunity lay before him. He would be a fool to ignore it. "Can you get me an audience with Wil—with the King?"

De Brionne's eyes narrowed thoughtfully. "An audience with William, is it?" He was silent for a moment, watching Osbern clearing off the small table beside the bed of its medicines and clean white linen strips, some of which he'd just used to lightly bind Brand's hand. "I can intercede for you, Brand Ericson, and mayhap get you in to see William, but I cannot promise anything beyond that. Whatever your business with him, 'tis your own."

Brand nodded curtly. "I ask nothing beyond an audience, my lord. My proposition is for William and William alone. No one else can help me."

Inside the wooden motte and bailey keep, erected so hastily for William's safety, there was pandemonium. The absence of the calming, organizing influence of Norman women in the stronghold was blatantly conspicuous. And the waiting . . . It seemed to Brand that he'd been waiting for an eternity, all the while surrounded by foreign, hostile Normans babbling in their own language, of which Brand understood only a smattering.

The pain from his burns added to his irritability, yet he found his thoughts turning to Geoffrey de Brionne. It was a stroke of uncommon luck for Brand that it had been the Count of Brionne whose life he'd saved, for the man was obviously of noble character and compassion. It could never hurt to have a good man—even a Norman—on his side.

His thoughts were put to rout as the discomfort from his injuries intruded, and just when he thought he could wait no longer, Brand found himself alone with Geoffrey, Count of Brionne, and William, Duke of Normandy.

"Stay, Geoffrey," William ordered when the count made a move to withdraw discreetly from the room. "I would have you hear what this heroic Anglo-Saxon has to say."

Brand stiffened at the sarcastic ring of the King's words. Hatred welled up inside him with such force that he felt he would choke from it. "If you imply that I saved my lord's life as a way of getting into his good graces, then I assure you, my lord King, that I have less dramatic ways—though equally as effective—of manipulating people."

Brand stared the King straight in the eye, waiting for the imminent command to remove Brand from the room for his audacity and incarcerate or kill him. But William knew a brave, intelligent man when he saw one, and his instincts told him that Brand Ericson, one of the few surviving members of English nobility, could possibly be of use to him.

They silently took each other's measure, Brand struck by William's tall, broad-chested form as he strode around the room like a caged animal with a wealth of pent-up energy. Dark hair, piercing eyes, and a jutting jaw gave the King a belligerent look, but Brand knew much about his cunning and shrewd administrative abilities, as well as his unquestioned courage in battle. He'd seen at least three different chargers cut from under William at Hastings and each time the duke had grabbed another mount, even removing his helm when once again astride to identify himself to his men, shouting encouragement to them and brandishing his sword high in the air.

Indeed, Brand thought, this was no man to take lightly— in any situation.

"Geoffrey tells me you were thane to Harold before he became King. I would guess you are here to request the

retention of your lands.'' He stopped pacing and faced
Brand. ''Tell me, then,'' he continued, without waiting
for Brand to answer, ''why I should allow you to retain
your holdings when you supported an unlawful king and
fought against me when I came to claim what was rightfully mine?''

Brand fought to keep his expression schooled, ignoring
with difficulty the slurs cast upon the dead Harold Godwinson. *Do not waste words with him,* the sensible side
of him cautioned. *Harold is dead—you cannot defend him
to this usurper. Tell him exactly why he should allow you
to keep that which is yours.*

''Because my stronghold is near the northwestern border of Wessex and Wales and I—and my father before me—
have managed to keep relative peace in that area.''

''Ah, yes. Camwright? It is known to me. But, Brand
Ericson, tell me why the Welsh would not welcome an
alliance with their new Norman neighbors, when all the
world knows of their constant bickering with the English.
Did not Harold Godwinson lead the contingent who killed
the Welsh Prince Griffith ap Llewellyn?''

Brand suspected that, statesman that William was, he
must be aware of the situation in Wales, yet he answered
with hard-pressed patience, ''The Anglo-Saxons have always had their differences with the Welsh, but I can tell
you that without a doubt the Cymry will deal more willingly with an Anglo-Saxon than with a conquering, foreign
Norman.''

At William's frown, Brand added, ''I was wed to Rhiannon, kin to Prince Bleddyn. I am not without personal
influence.''

William's penetrating dark eyes kindled at this bit of
information. ''Indeed. But you said 'was.' ''

''She is dead.'' The words were clipped, torn from him
as they were every time he had to utter them.

Geoffrey de Brionne had been studying Brand as he
stood proudly before William, and now he watched Brand's
eyes darken with a personal agony that had nothing to do
with his injuries. There had to be a way to erase the pain

in the Anglo-Saxon's eyes—such a valiant heart as his deserved comfort and newfound love. The image of his beautiful daughter flashed before Geoffrey's mind's eye in that split second. Perhaps Brand Ericson was exactly the challenge Marisa needed to mature and face life as it really was—to reach her full potential as a woman.

The words came out before Geoffrey even realized he was speaking. "Begging your pardon, my lord, what of a Norman-English alliance right there on the Welsh border? What better way to ensure the continuing stability that Ericson has already helped to establish, while fusing the blood of a noble Norman house with that of an Anglo-Saxon?"

Brand's heart stumbled in its steady cadence at the implication of his words. *You will do anything necessary to ensure Griffith's future.*

"An alliance? A suggestion worth considering, Geoffrey. But who would wed this taciturn Anglo-Saxon who burns with hatred even as he stands before us?" Brand caught the hint of mockery in the thickly accented English.

William eyed his count expectantly, since he'd been the one to verbalize the idea. "Who would be courageous enough to come to this place before I have made it safe for even the ordinary citizen, let alone for a Norman woman?"

Geoffrey said nothing for a moment, his eyes assessing Brand critically. Then, as if satisfied with what he saw before him—satisfied with what he'd witnessed that morning, with what he knew of this stranger who'd saved his life at peril to his own—he said simply, "Marisa."

William looked at Geoffrey as if he were undone. "Marisa?"

"Oui."

William walked over to a sideboard and poured himself a goblet of wine from an ornate ewer. "Surely you are mad, de Brionne!" he declared, as Geoffrey politely waved aside refreshment. Brand also declined, betraying none of his surprise at this hospitable gesture. "Marisa is one of the most beautiful women in Normandy—in France!—and one of the most eligible. She can have her pick of any nobleman, yet you would shackle her to—'' He stopped, realizing he was voicing his very uncomplimentary thoughts aloud. Here, after all, stood a man of high birth, who'd offered to help him ease his tremendous burden, even though this man would personally profit from it. God knew he would need all the help he could get—even from a resentful Anglo-Saxon.

Geoffrey de Brionne stepped into the breach. ''Marisa is beautiful, my lord King, and highly eligible. However she also needs a strong hand—yet one that will not crush her zest for life.''

''And Brand Ericson is that man?''

''She has refused many offers, to my dismay. Her brothers take her side, saying there is no hurry, but I believe 'tis past time. She will not refuse my command to wed the man of my choosing, nor will she object overmuch to leaving Normandy.''

William narrowed his eyes calculatingly, weighing the advantages of such a union in the long run, though he was mystified as to why Geoffrey would suggest his own daughter for this former thane who made his home in the wild region that bordered Wales.

Then the shrewd gaze moved to Brand. He could not correctly gauge Brand's thoughts, the struggle he silently waged to honor his secret vow to his son back in October in the aftermath of a great battle. No one could ever take Rhiannon's place, Brand was thinking bleakly—loving, soft-spoken, tolerant, sweet-tempered . . . He did not deserve personal happiness, not after Rhiannon. With an arranged marriage to a foreign woman he would get exactly what he deserved—misery. Yet he must keep a clear head and not let his emotions interfere. This was evidently the only way he could keep his lands—if the look on William's face was any indication. And keeping his lands was of the utmost importance, not the fact that he was on the brink of being forced to take a wife—a Norman wife.

''What say you, Brand Ericson? In exchange for your

present holdings and your continued influence on the Welsh—in our favor, of course—you agree to wed Marisa de Brionne.''

''And,'' added Geoffrey quietly, ''you will show her the same consideration you would any English woman.''

Brand smiled without humor. ''You think me an ogre, my lord Count? Why did you just offer me your daughter if you fear for her?''

''Just a warning, Ericson. I pride myself in being an excellent judge of men. What you did for me this day was instinctive—something only a very selfless man, one of exceptional character and unquestionable honor, would do.''

Brand acknowledged the compliment with a nod. ''Then I agree to the bargain.''

''Good,'' approved William of Normandy. ''Now come and pay homage to me.''

As Brand knelt in obeisance before the new King of England, he felt as if he'd just sold his soul to the Normans.

Chapter 1

"Just think, Adela—to be a man and fight battles . . . to ride a mighty destrier and wield a sword! How exciting is a man's lot compared to that of a woman!" Marisa de Brionne's deep amethyst eyes glowed with vicarious thrill, her color heightening with her excitement.

"You should be thinking of wedding and birthing babes, *cher enfant*, rather than wishing for something that can never be."

The admonitory note in her beloved servant's voice did nothing to dampen Marisa's enthusiasm. "Draw your sword, Saxon swine!" she cried, stooping swiftly to grab a wrist-thick bough from the pile of kindling in the corner behind her.

"Frivolous child, you will have all the hounds abaying with your foolish play," warned the older woman as several of the wolfhounds dozing lazily before one of the great hearths bounded to their feet to join in the play.

"Back, Rollo, before I skewer you where you stand!" Marisa commanded her favorite dog. He crouched back on his haunches and leaped gracefully into the air, grabbing the end of her makeshift weapon. The branch twisted sharply, the rough bark scraping her tender palm, before it went swishing through the rushes on the floor as Rollo proudly trotted off with his prize.

"Oh," she cried in mock consternation, ignoring the blood that threaded over her small palm. "Bested by a mere beast!"

14

Adela smiled in spite of herself. It never ceased to amaze her how easily her young mistress could change from a poised and capable chatelaine, when the occasion necessitated, to a fun-loving, cosseted child. How she would one day miss this woman-child who'd been like a daughter to her these past ten years. "That is precisely why you should stick to your embroidery and lute playing, child.'Tis time to stop your useless imaginings and consider your future. Even your father and Eustace will take a firm hand with you if you do not decide on a husband soon."

The light in Marisa's slightly almond-shaped eyes dimmed briefly at the thought. "*Eh bien,* if Richard and Raoul were only here instead of in England awaiting their share of the spoils, *they* would take my side, to be sure. Eustace is even starting to hint of marriage and babes and—Oh, 'tis only because he is betrothed to Rohese and cannot see beyond her great brown eyes." She put her hand to her mouth to stanch the lazy trickle of blood.

"Rohese and her great brown eyes will soon be lady of the manor and *you* will still be here. Eustace is the only one who finally shows some wisdom where his sister is concerned." Adela expertly finished stitching the border on a silk bliaut, the same blue-violet hue of Marisa's eyes. "And perhaps, too, my lord Geoffrey will come around soon."

Marisa sighed in temporary resignation. The thought of the disdainful Rohese as lady of the keep of Brionne was like a thorn in her side. Attractive and very much aware of it, the girl had always been puffed up with self-importance—or so it seemed to Marisa—especially now that she had bewitched Eustace into a betrothal. The keep of Brionne was one of the largest in Normandy and one of the few made of stone—an invaluable added prize to accompany the hand of the eldest son of the Count of Brionne. With a shake of her head Marisa dismissed the untenable thought of living under the same roof as Rohese and relinquishing her own authority. She knelt to hug the huge wolfhound who'd returned with his trophy and dropped it at her feet. "You see, Adela, how eagerly males seek to win my favor? When my husband-to-be comes along, I will know him on the instant and only then will I consent to wed."

"I only hope you are not too old and bent with age to win over this prince of a man," Adela remarked wryly, putting down her embroidery for a few moments to hold out her hands to the warmth of the roaring fire in the hearth. "How can you forget, Marisa, that most marriages are not love matches—especially those of the nobility? Would you not accept your father's choice of a husband to increase his holdings or form an advantageous alliance?"

Marisa put her nose to Rollo's and imitated his growl until his tail switched back and forth and an answering vibration rumbled up from within his chest. "Father would never do that to me." She pushed away from the hound and stood, brushing her woolen skirts free of rushes, when suddenly the image of Robert de Lisieux flashed before her mind's eye. Robert, who had courted her patiently and made her laugh with his good humor and sweet nature . . . and whom she had spurned for no particular reason except that she had not wished to marry at the time. Now it was too late. "I must see how the evening meal fares," she announced to Adela with unnecessary brusqueness. At the woman's raised eyebrow she added, "Young Judith has much to learn in the kitchen and—"

"Marisa!"

The rush of cold January wind from the opened portal at one end of the great hall swept over Marisa like a premonition of doom, and she shivered, wondering for the first time in her seventeen years what it was like to possess the Sight. . . .

She turned slowly at Eustace's call, almost afraid to face him. But no trace of alarm marred his regular features as he strode toward her. In fact, a broad smile curved his lips before he began shouting orders to several servants in the hall.

"What are you about, Eustace?" Marisa asked her eldest brother, relief wafting over her in the wake of his good humor.

"Father is coming home, Marisa!"

"Father?"

"Aye. He bade me ride ahead and prepare for a celebration. I met him while on my rounds and he—"

"Raoul and Richard? Are they with him?"

He shook his head, removing his mantle and stepping toward the fire. "They have been granted holdings, each of them, in England, and may not return."

Crestfallen, Marisa ran to him and grabbed his arm. "Never to return?"

Eustace smoothed her disheveled, silver-blond curls, so like his father's, as one would a child's. "Indeed. Did you not know that when they left, *chère?*"

"Oh, Father hinted at such things, but I—I could not bring myself to believe I might not see them again." Her eyes misted and Eustace hugged her to him with brotherly affection.

"Take heart, *ma sœur,* for indeed you may see them on occasion. Father has come to escort you to England himself."

"To England?"

"Indeed, to England."

Marisa whirled around at the sound of Geoffrey de Brionne's voice. He'd come in quietly, hoping Eustace had broken the news of her impending journey, all the while silently cursing himself for being a coward.

"Father!" She ran to him and buried her face in his heavy wool mantle. "Is it true?"

Though her voice was muffled, Geoffrey understood her query. *"Oui, chère.* Are you not excited? And is this any way to greet your sire after nigh on five months' absence?"

Marisa shook her head and raised her face to look into his gray eyes. "I—I am sorry, Father, but I am eaten up with curiosity! Why—*why* am I to go to England?"

Geoffrey guided her by the elbow toward a hearth and

took a proffered cup of wine from a servant. Eustace joined them and beckoned Adela into their intimate little group. "This concerns you, as well, Adela."

Again, a grim foreboding seized Marisa as she stared up at her father, her eyes questioning. He drank deeply, feeling the strong red wine begin to warm him from within. His determination began to stabilize as well.

"Marisa, I have found you a husband."

As the import of his words registered, a look of disbelief flickered across the exquisite features. "A—a husband?" she whispered.

At the look on her face Geoffrey took another draught of wine, and Eustace came to his rescue. "Oh, come now, Marisa. You are well into the marriageable age and surely you've known that you would be wed one day. 'Tis only natural."

Rohese will soon be lady of the manor and you will still be here.

Ire rose in Marisa's arresting eyes at her brother's glib rebuke as she marshaled her defenses. "I assure you, *frère,* I am no lackwit." She mustered a smile for her father, not wanting to spoil his homecoming. "Well then, my lord Father, who is this prince of a man?" She glanced at Adela, a shaky smile curving her lips in an effort to appear insouciant. "Is he wealthy? What is his name and what does he look like?"

Geoffrey was struck dumb for a moment at her seeming capitulation. "Indeed, daughter," he answered truthfully when at last he'd found his voice, "I believe him to be a prince of a man, for he saved my life."

Marisa's smile strengthened at this commendable deed after Geoffrey explained the circumstances that had resulted in his brush with death. "Tell me then, *mon père,* what he looks like—where he hails from in Normandy and what new lands he has acquired in England. Surely he is held in great esteem by my lord William?"

Geoffrey looked over the top of his daughter's bright head at his eldest son, then at Adela. No help from that quarter—neither one of them had ever seen Brand Ericson nor did they know he was Anglo-Saxon. Yet.

"His name is Brand Ericson and I think—speaking from a man's point of view, of course—that he has a good face, and is tall and well-formed. He is young enough to make a fine husband." He remembered Brand's stern, brooding countenance and decided the Anglo-Saxon was probably only slightly older than Eustace. "His character is unimpeachable and, in maintaining his holding near the Welsh border, he will be doing the King a great service."

"Well, if I must wed him, then I am glad he is young and pleasant to look upon."

She unexpectedly hugged her father in gratitude—and relief—determined to be a good daughter and make the best of the situation. Eustace asked, "Is not the name 'Brand Ericson' Anglo-Saxon?"

Instantly, he could have bitten his tongue at the look that crossed Geoffrey's features. Marisa recoiled from the embrace as if struck and looked up at her father, her face chalk-white.

In the booming, expectant silence, all eyes came to rest unwaveringly upon Geoffrey de Brionne. And in that moment, the Count knew himself to be a fool for ever allowing his daughter to have wound him around her little finger over the last ten years. He was actually more afraid of telling her the truth than facing an opponent on a battlefield. Three pairs of eyes remained riveted to his face, awaiting his reply.

"An Anglo-Saxon name? Indeed it is, for Brand Ericson is Anglo-Saxon."

The brisk April wind over the Channel whipped the blue-gray waters into spume-crested waves and sent them dashing against the side of the bark that carried Geoffrey de Brionne and his daughter to England. Foam scattered on the breeze, shining crystalline in the sunshine and reminding Marisa of whisper-light snowflakes flying before a frigid winter wind. The lone sail of the small vessel snapped smartly as it caught the breeze as they headed for Dover. Marisa tried to immerse herself in the beauty of the vast panorama of water and the arch of azure sky above them; the warm, golden sunshine; and the exhilarating feeling of skimming across the waves in a boat—something she'd never done before. Anything was preferable to dwelling upon what was to happen upon their arrival in London.

Something nudged her thigh and pulled her gaze away from the fathomless aquamarine depths below her to the questioning brown eyes of Rollo, looking piteously up at her. A smile lit her features and she knelt down to put her arms around the seasick wolfhound. "Poor Rollo," she murmured against his warm, gray fur. "You have never been on a boat, either, have you?" The dog pulled back from her embrace and his lolling tongue made a feeble attempt to touch her cheek.

"One would think you—both of you—were traveling to your execution instead of merely to a new land." Geoffrey de Brionne's voice turned his daughter's attention away from Rollo and she stood up. "I told William you were the woman to journey to England so soon after the conquest—that you were courageous enough to wed an Anglo-Saxon for the first significant union of English and Norman, but here I find you obviously commiserating with that lop-eared beast over your future."

Marisa's mouth tightened in annoyance. "I was not commiserating with yon hound about anything, Father. He is unused to sailing over the water, as am I, and while I admit I have been trying to forget for a while what is to happen when we reach England, Rollo is only a dumb beast who needed my assurances."

She turned away, the wind catching long, pale strands of her hair that had escaped her braids and tossing them about her face like gossamer threads in the sunlight. Geoffrey studied her profile, thinking how beautiful she was—just like her mother, except for the color of her hair, which was his own legacy to her. He had spoiled her shamelessly, as had her three brothers, since the death of his wife half a score of years past. In an attempt to make up for the loss—for Geoffrey could never bring himself to wed another—he'd always given her everything her heart could desire and his sons had followed suit. Now it was time she shouldered the responsibilities of life, and, not for the first time since he'd offered her in marriage to Brand Ericson, he wondered if he was expecting too much from Marisa and too suddenly. Well, it was too late now and the only thing he could do was try to prepare her, even if he could not find the words to tell her of Brand's previous marriage.

"What of your desire to do those things a man can do—to see England and—"

"And submit to an arranged marriage?"

"And what of Brand Ericson? He is a man of noble blood, and he submitted to having a marriage arranged for him. This does not only happen to women, *chère*."

She turned to meet his regard. "I will wed him, Father. I have already agreed, have I not? But an Anglo-Saxon? The enemy? And one who considers us the enemy, as well? Who no doubt harbors as much hostility toward us—toward *me*—as I toward him? What chance has a marriage like that to be happy?"

"I do not consider Brand Ericson my enemy. He saved my life—without hesitation he flung me to safety, nearly sacrificing his own life in the process. There was no time for thought of Norman or English—only the lightning reflex of a man of unquestionable courage and honor." He put a finger under her chin and turned her face to his. "Do you think I would give you to just anyone? To an Anglo-Saxon who would mistreat you in any way?"

Tears welled up in her eyes and spilled over onto her cheeks, to Marisa's dismay, and she shook her head, the wind scattering them like so many droplets of rain. "I thought not."

He hugged her to him then, squeezing her tightly with the force of his emotion. "You will be treated well—I have his word, and I do not doubt it. You are in a position to help begin the healing process necessary to assure peace and prosperity in England, to begin the merging of two cultures peaceably, something which I believe will take years to achieve, for not all of England has submitted yet to William's rule.''

Marisa drew back to look into his eyes. ''I will try, Father.'' A long sigh escaped her lips and was swept away by the breeze.

He smiled at her and added, ''There is one more thing, Marisa, that you should consider. Ericson stood to lose his lands and his title before he agreed to wed you. He is one of the few surviving English nobility and had approached William with the intention of preserving his holdings in return for his part in keeping peace with the Welsh. I believe he saw that the King might not have accepted his proposition had he not agreed to take you to wife. I doubt that he would make life unbearable for you if he wishes to keep that pact secure.'' He was silent for a moment, giving her time to digest his words. ''And,'' he added in an attempt at levity, ''aside from his word that he will learn our tongue to ensure that there's less chance of misunderstanding between you, he personally admitted to me that he is no ogre.''

Marisa nodded and looked out to sea once more, the silvery tresses catching and reflecting the sun's bright rays like a mirror of polished metal. Indeed, he may be the most honorable Anglo-Saxon in England, she thought, but to *wed* him? To wed and live side by side with him—to bear his children? A long-haired, barbaric Anglo-Saxon? *''Dieu me sauve,''* she whispered to the uncaring wind.

Butterflies flitted through Marisa's midsection, and her palms were cold and damp, her mouth dry. She had declined to meet her husband-to-be before the wedding mass, deciding it would only be worse to meet him before they were wed and rail uselessly against her father and the King—and Brand Ericson himself. If she were to be disappointed, it would be when she was joined in matrimony and not before—a proud, stubborn streak demanded it be that way.

Adela, who was to remain with Marisa in England, helped her mistress dress in her wedding finery with love and pride. "He will be dazzled by you, *petite*," she assured Marisa as the girl obediently raised her arms to allow the pale peach silk bliaut to slide over her head and down over the ivory undertunic.

"From what I have heard tell, one such as he would be dazzled by anything female—and clean and sweet-smelling into the bargain."

Adela's expression became troubled for a brief moment at Marisa's uncharacteristically unkind remark. "You are just unsettled, *chère*. Every maiden is so before her wedding." She smoothed the apricot stitching around the neckline and edges of the wide, three-quarter-length sleeves proudly, for she had put all her skill into this work of love for the girl who was like a daughter to her. The embroidery also decorated the hem of the long bliaut and matched the cream-colored undertunic or chainse, with its higher neckline and wrist-length, snug-fitting sleeves.

"And now your hair." Marisa sat on a low stool in her father's room and submitted to Adela's attentions. "I will use the darker ribbon instead of the peach, Marisa, for it will stand out to better advantage with your hair color." And she deftly braided the shining, shoulder-length tresses and wound them into a coronet atop the small head, weaving the bright apricot ribbons throughout.

For once Marisa was not concerned about her appearance, for her thoughts were on the man she was to wed. Perhaps she should have met him first. Perhaps he would think her rude in her refusal to see him beforehand. After all, did not her father think highly of him?

" . . . your shoes?"

"Hmm?" Marisa unthinkingly slipped her feet into the beautifully tooled leather shoes that matched her dress, thinking that her father always saw the best in everyone. He was not one to judge a man by his birth or station in life. If Brand Ericson were bald, toothless, and missing one leg, Geoffrey de Brionne would have found his attributes—no matter how insignificant—and extolled them to her. Especially because the Anglo-Saxon had saved his life. Not that he would have deliberately lied to his daughter, but he would have looked beyond outward appearances, even though to a girl who was about to wed—a carefree, untried girl who could have had her pick of the handsome bucks in her native Normandy—looks and bearing were of utmost importance in the man she was to marry.

"Marisa, 'tis time."

Geoffrey's voice broke into her ruminations, and she stood up, her finely arched brows drawn together in a thoughtful frown. Adela swung a lightweight mantle over Marisa's shoulders for the ride through London's muddy streets to the abbey at Westminster—the same place where William had been crowned, Geoffrey had told her. It was an honor to be wed in the grand Westminster, built by Edward the Confessor, and the King was even to attend. But Marisa felt only a growing numbness as her father led her outside and helped her mount her horse.

"*Eh bien*, Marisa," said a voice in her ear. "You must smile and hide your doubts." It was Richard de Brionne.

Geoffrey's second youngest son, Raoul, rode on her other side and added, "Indeed, *ma sœur*, you must do the de Brionne name proud, mustn't you?"

Marisa couldn't help but smile, for the one comforting thing about this entire affair was that she would be able to see these two siblings to whom she had always been so close, for they had been granted holdings in Wessex. She did smile then, first at one and then the other, the light challenge in both pairs of gray eyes striking a chord in her as nothing else had thus far.

She was lifted down from her palfrey before the great church by her father, who guided her into the dim interior and toward the front of the assemblage. As her eyes adjusted, Marisa noted that there were quite a few people present, including William himself, who smiled at her. The absence of women, however, was very obvious and brought home all the more powerfully the great step she was taking as one of the first gently born Norman women to come to England.

During the long mass, a myriad of sounds and smells assailed her senses—the occasional scrape of a dress sword; the muffled, masculine clearing of a throat; the sibilant hiss of flambeaux placed along the walls at regular intervals. Her nose caught the smell of resinous pitch and hot, melting wax, the odor of sweating human bodies in close quarters, a whiff of her own scented bathwater that still lingered, and the clean aroma of sandalwood from her father and brothers as they surrounded her almost protectively. Marisa concentrated on the few Anglo-Saxons present and, especially, on discovering which man was Brand Ericson, for she knew he was somewhere close by. But within the ranks of the small crowd, she had a hard time distinguishing anyone except her family, the Norman bishop who presided, and the King. She turned her head slightly to the side several times and covertly glanced from beneath the dense shield of her lashes, but from her position, she had no clue as to who Ericson was. The differences in hairstyles and clothing still did not single out her husband-to-be, and, Marisa ruefully admitted to herself, he did not owe her the courtesy of making himself known to her after her rebuff only hours before.

Then Geoffrey was guiding her forward toward the altar, and Marisa espied a tall, dark-haired man, who had evidently been standing near the front of the church, move to stand before the bishop. As she walked toward him, all her deepest misgivings surfaced once again, causing her to pale with apprehension as Brand Ericson slowly turned to watch her approach him. In the muted light of the church, Marisa at first could distinguish only his tall stature and the chestnut hair that rode low on his neck, the ridges and hollows of his face shadowed from her curious gaze. But as she came closer his features became clearer and her pulse skipped erratically at the stern cast to his countenance. No, she amended, not stern but grim. He looked as unwilling as she felt, and this fact did not sit well with her. *He* was unhappy with *her*.

Her vanity and her female pride both battled and overcame her trepidation, and Marisa felt, in spite of herself, the corners of her mouth curving softly in a smile, as that part of her that was utterly feminine attempted to take up the gauntlet and wipe the bleakness from his features. But there was no answering smile, no reassurance in the topaz eyes, nor the least bit of understanding or empathy as his gaze locked with hers. Then she reached his side and he was turning toward the waiting bishop.

Marisa heard none of the marriage blessing, nor did Brand. He could think only of how breathtaking beautiful she was—and how undeserving he was of so lovely a creature. Like an ice goddess, she had hair the color of raw silk arranged atop her exquisitely wrought features like a pale crown—and alabaster skin, and soft, ripe lips that smiled guilelessly at him. She looked like a marble madonna, the large eyes deeply violet in the smooth perfection of her face. He felt the beginnings of relief in the wake of his unwilling admiration. Perhaps he hadn't put his neck in a noose after all. . . .

Surreptitiously he watched her sandy-hued lashes lower as she bowed her head to receive the bishop's blessing. Brand felt such a tumult of emotions inside him that his hands fisted at his sides. The scent of roses that drifted up from her—for she reached only to his shoulder—served merely to further ensnare him in her sweet lure, and he set his teeth together in self-disgust. Surely the girl was not perfect. There had to be something drastically wrong with her that she was this paragon of beauty—the daughter of a Norman count, no less—and still unwed. In his desperation to hold fast to his late wife's memory, to find fault with the young woman at his side, Brand was prepared to grasp at anything that would prove her to be less than she appeared.

He received the kiss of peace and turned to bestow it upon his bride. As Marisa raised her face expectantly to his, she caught sight of what she had thought to be only a shadow before—or perhaps she had not really noticed in the flickering candlelight. . . . Part of his left cheek and neck were blighted by a pink, newly healed burn scar. Her eyes widened in shock and she drew back slightly when he bent to kiss her. For a fleeting moment Brand read what he interpreted to be revulsion in her eyes and kissed her so quickly, his anger and pride wiping clean the slate of her attributes, that her soft lower lip was bruised against her teeth from the unnecessary force and swiftness of it. Marisa tasted the salt of blood.

Gripping her none too gently by the elbow, he turned her to face the throng waiting to congratulate them, failing to see the ire that replaced her initial surprise and darkened her irises to purple before she mustered a smile for the others before them.

There was a celebration feast in the King's quarters, but while it was all Brand could do to be civil, considering his new wife's rejection of his scarred face—surely her father had told her of his burns?—Marisa was artificially gay. The sweet strains of her laughter floated through the hall with such frequency that Brand wanted to strangle her for her seeming frivolity. He could not know that her forced gaiety was not only for her father and brothers' sakes, but even more so for his. Let him think what he would—she would not let him know how he had hurt her with his reluctance to give her the kiss of peace, his roughness with her after the marriage blessing. She would die before she would admit to defeat, though. One day Brand Ericson would sorely regret the humiliation he had caused her.

Marisa succeeded so totally in her charade that, as his eyes kept straying to her in spite of himself, Brand became convinced that he had wed a spoiled, uncaring wench who was hardly the type to accept his people, let alone care about them as he did. And he would have wagered that neither would they take to Marisa. *She will make my life a living hell,* he thought darkly, *but 'tis too late. The bargain is sealed.*

Only the thought of Griffith's secure future kept Brand from leaving the banquet for Camwright—alone.

Chapter 2

Despite the crowded conditions of the hastily thrown-up keep, a small room had been prepared for the bridal couple. In the absence of other women, Adela accompanied Marisa to the tiny chamber and prepared her for her husband's arrival.

"You must smile and anticipate your new husband's coming, Marisa. Do you not think your father made a good choice?"

Marisa listlessly stroked Rollo's rough fur, for she had insisted that the hound be admitted to the room. "How can you think one whose face is thusly marred can be a good choice? And if that weren't enough, the man never smiles! He surely is nothing more than I expected of a crude Anglo-Saxon."

Adela unbraided Marisa's hair and ran an ivory comb through the satiny mane. "You forget, *chère,* that he is of a vanquished people, still possessed of his pride yet surrounded by his conquerors, and that surely makes his lot even harder to bear. As for the scars—they do not detract overmuch from his looks, and even more importantly, you must remember he sustains them from having saved your father's life." At Marisa's suddenly pensive frown, she added, "I also believe if you can eventually persuade him to smile, he will look not only younger, but will surprise you with the beauty of his features."

After Adela had quietly withdrawn from the room, Marisa thought about her words. Adela was wise—and

29

she had been right in chiding Marisa about her comment concerning Brand's burn scars. But Adela hadn't been the one to bind herself to so saturnine a man, to receive a travesty of the kiss of peace rather than a gentle sign of union. Her cheeks burned with mortification as she sat upon the bed, her feelings churning within her, when suddenly the door was flung open and Brand was handed through it by a host of tipsy well-wishers, her father and brother among them and as exuberant as the others.

The door slammed shut, ribald comments and laughter echoing through the keep, slowly dying away as the crowd dispersed. Brand remained unmoving before the closed portal, trying to appear at ease after consuming enough Norman wine for two. Marisa de Brionne sat before him like a vision upon the bed.

Before he could make a complete fool of himself, however, Rollo, who had dived under the bed in the midst of all the commotion, emerged from the far side and padded stealthily around it. He came to a halt before Brand, his teeth bared, a low growl of menace coming from his throat.

Brand looked from Marisa to the huge wolfhound and back again. "You thought perhaps to hold me at bay with the hound? Or is this the custom in Normandy? I must get past him to claim my bride?"

Had Marisa not been so caught up in her resentment of his treatment of her in the church, she would have seen the humor in the situation—and, the flash of rare amusement that flickered briefly in the golden-brown eyes. But she was in no mood to interpret his words as anything but a threat. "I do not need a hound to keep an Anglo-Saxon rabble at bay—husband or no."

Instantly she regretted her harsh words, for Brand's cheeks flushed a dull red, his mouth compressing, his eyes narrowing slightly. He advanced upon her, ignoring Rollo, who growled once more and glanced from Brand to his mistress in indecision.

"Easy, Rollo," Marisa warned in a feeble attempt to make up for her insult.

"So 'tis 'Rollo,' is it?" Brand stopped short of the bed and held out a hand to the dog. "Come, Rollo. Let us show your gracious mistress how animals take to this Anglo-Saxon rabble." The dog sniffed at Brand's fingers, tentatively at first, then, glancing up at Brand and obviously sensing he meant no harm to Marisa, began to bathe the Saxon's entire hand with his long, gritty tongue.

"The very name 'Rollo' conjures up images of death and devastation for which your Viking ancestors were notorious," Brand continued. "While we Anglo-Saxon rabble were living peacefully according to our laws, your forebears—and only one hundred and fifty years removed—were plundering their way through sleepy towns and shires, innocent monasteries and abbeys, on both sides of the Channel."

Taken aback by his knowledge of Norman history, Marisa had the grace to blush in the face of the truths he'd uttered. "I regret my poor choice of words, my lord," she murmured.

Now it was Brand's turn to be surprised. He studied her in the glow of the braziers and the several candles that had been placed about the chamber, noting the hectic color that swept across the high cheekbones, matching that of her sweetly molded lips. . . . The cascade of her fair hair shone like palest gold in the shadowed room and gently framed her face. His eyes dropped to the sheer linen night rail, delicate ribbons lacing across one another at the neckline, hiding from view the treasures beneath. Brand quickly raised his eyes, caught between her implied reluctance to consummate the marriage when he'd mentioned the dog, the disloyalty he felt toward Rhiannon in feeling a yearning for another, and his own deepening needs, for he hadn't had a woman in months.

Grabbing on to anything that would take his mind off his new wife's disturbing desirability, he noticed the slight swelling of her lower lip. "What happened to your mouth?"

"I was kissed by a man so eager to have done with it that he was less than gentle."

Of its own volition, his hand reached out to cup her chin, tilting it toward the taper on the table beside the bed. "And mayhap he was less than gentle because of the revulsion in his bride's eyes." He spoke his thoughts aloud, having been unaware that he had caused her physical harm—no matter how slight.

Marisa jerked her face away, her frayed emotions finally gaining the upper hand as she thought of how unfair it all was. Here she was, young and—so they said—beautiful, and she'd been wed to a stern-visaged, scarred Anglo-Saxon, a man who by all rights was her enemy because he and his kind had fallen before the might of William of Normandy. He was now reduced to bargaining like any common serf, with his superiors and obviously against his will, and here she was *wed* to him.

"Did you fight at Hastings, Brand Ericson, or did you fear excommunication and hide at Camwright?"

His look changed from contemplative to mocking. "What do you think I did, Marisa? Nay, tell me first what you would have done had you been in my place."

"I should have fought for the land of my birth—no matter the threat."

"Ah, then 'tis a great loss that you do not number among the men in this world, for we could use many more like you."

"You make mock of me!"

He began to remove his clothing, to Marisa's shock, as he spoke, turning away from her. "And *you* imply that I hid in my stronghold while my king and countrymen spilled their blood in defense of England. And then, I gather, you are assuming I rushed to London in order to curry favor with some Norman of consequence—like the Count of Brionne—in order to strike any kind of bargain possible to retain my wealth and holdings."

"I only asked . . . I implied naught." But Marisa was hardly aware of what she said, for her eyes were trained in fascination upon the unclothing of his splendid form. She had obligingly bathed important guests in her father's home, but this was different. This was her husband—the

man who was going to . . . She averted her face as he
tackled his hoselike chausses and cross-garters.

He doused several candles before turning toward her,
and Marisa scrambled under the covers like a rabbit scurrying before a pack of hounds. Before she could even
pull the pelt-covered blanket over her, Brand was on the
bed beside her. Rollo's head was on his knee, his brown
eyes imploring the Anglo-Saxon to stroke his head. *Traitor!* Marisa thought fiercely.

Brand's face was so close to hers as he leaned upon
his arm toward her that she felt compelled by some
strange force to turn to meet his gaze. She could see the
brown flecks that made his golden eyes look like deepest
amber, could feel his warm breath on her face. And she
could see the outline of his newly mended scar branded
across his left cheek.

For the second time she shrank away and averted her
eyes. ''Do what you will,'' came her martyrlike words
of surrender.

In the silence that held sway for long moments, the
words seemed to echo off the very walls in insult to a
man who had swallowed every last shred of pride in accepting a Norman woman for his wife. ''Do what I will?''
His bitter laughter sounded all the more harsh for the
quiet of the room. ''I *will* retain my lands by virtue of
having taken you to wife. There was never talk of taking
you to my bed, Marisa. I vowed I would not abuse you—
but there was no promise of aught else.''

He reached over to snuff out the last candle and
stretched out beneath the covers, the warm length of his
body only inches from hers.

''If you must act the injured party, Marisa, then you
need never fear I will so much as touch you. . . . Sleep
well, *wife.*''

Marisa remained awake until far into the night, acutely
conscious of the man who slept beside her. When she
awoke at last after a fitful sleep, a damp chill penetrated
the dark, windowless room. The braziers burned so low

they gave off little light and even less heat, yet she was warm.

To her mortification she discovered the reason why. She was cuddled up to Brand Ericson as trustingly as a newborn pup to its bitch. In the split second before she bolted upright, Marisa caught a glimpse of his shadowed features. His eyes were open and staring straight ahead, his brow furrowed with thought, his expression stern, the angry scar across his cheek a mere blur in the dim light.

Though he hadn't exactly pushed her away from the heat of his body, he certainly was not reciprocating her unconsciously intimate entwinement.

She withdrew an arm and a leg from him, her cheeks flaming at what he must be thinking, and turned toward the edge of the bed. She threw back the covers only to meet Rollo's wet greeting as his cool nose touched her bare leg.

"Good morningtide, *madame*," Brand greeted her tonelessly as her awakening triggered his rising from the bed to stir up the dying embers of the braziers. "I wondered when you would rouse yourself. We have a long journey ahead and I am eager to get home."

As he studiously occupied himself with the two braziers and lighted several tapers, Marisa dressed with alacrity. If she worried about his viewing her disrobed, she realized that his interest lay elsewhere. He produced what looked like a small pig's bladder, which had evidently been stitched to the inside of his tunic. "I trust you slept well, my lady?"

The tinge of sarcasm was not lost upon Marisa. "Indeed, my lord," she answered sweetly with a covert glance at his profile. Her eyes wandered to his powerful arms and chest, for he was clad only in braies. "And you?"

He grunted without looking at her, producing a small dagger and piercing the sac as he held it over the bed.

"What are you doing?" she asked in spite of herself.

His eyes met hers. "They will ask to see the bedclothes, *wife*. Although I had anticipated no need for such deception, it seems my precautionary measure will now serve me well. . . . I must keep them content with proof of the consummation."

How could she be so stupid? Annoyance bubbled through her at his action. "So you spoke truly last night. You never intended to deflower me, did you?"

His eyes seemed very dark and very distant as they remained locked with hers in challenge. "As far as I am concerned, I have kept my part of the bargain: I have made you my wife. If you have any objections, voice them now."

I believe him to be a prince of a man, for he saved my life.

At the memory of her father's words, Marisa swallowed the biting retort that rose to her lips, turned her back to him, and walked over to the basin of cold water. As she freshened up, she heard him say, "I will see to the preparations for our journey."

When she turned around, he was gone. She returned to her ablutions, rubbing a hazel twig dipped in salt against her teeth with a vengeance. So he expected her to voice her objections, did he? Well, his hints had fallen on barren soil, as he would discover, she vowed. The daughter of the Count of Brionne would not be intimidated by his dour edicts.

A knock at the door made her jump; she expected the object of her thoughts to have returned. Her mixed feelings as she uttered, "Come in," turned sour as Adela entered the room with a tray laden with bread, cheese, and wine. "Please set it down there," she directed with an attempt at blitheness that she suspected did not fool Adela for a moment. "Then leave me. My lord will be returning betimes."

After Adela withdrew, a frown darkening her brow, Marisa ate enough to satisfy her empty stomach, and spitefully fed Rollo every last morsel. She took great satisfaction in watching the wolfhound devour the fresh bread and tasty cheese intended for her new husband. Let him find his own food if he refused to break the fast with her—their first meal alone together as man and wife. She even gave the unsuspecting hound some of the wine, pouring it in a puddle on the floor and laughing aloud as he lapped it up tentatively at first, shaking his muzzle at the odd taste, then finishing it eagerly and looking for more. "Ah, you do your namesake proud, Rollo," she said, laughing, and naughtily obliged the begging dog.

Just when Marisa was ready to leave the room and go searching for someone, anyone, Brand entered after a peremptory knock. "I regret I was kept so long . . ." His eyes lit on the empty tray, then narrowed in comprehension. "I see you wasted no time in assuming me thoughtless enough to leave you here alone until—"

"Well, what did you expect me to think? You left without a word of your return and—"

Just then Rollo came around the bed and staggered toward Brand in greeting, his hind legs bringing his back end around in an attempt to catch up to his forelegs. He failed utterly and plopped down on one haunch halfway to Brand, the other back leg sprawled out at right angles to his upright head and chest.

Marisa suddenly felt contrite at the animal's condition, but Brand's contemptuous voice lashed her far more effectively than her own sense of guilt. "I see how you care for your animals, Marisa. Knowing the dog will have to run full-tilt to keep up with us when we leave shortly, you couldn't have done him more of a disservice short of cutting off his legs."

Marisa's head snapped up, her eyes wide at the impact of his words. She knew immediately he spoke the truth— that she'd been childish and inconsiderate in her desire to hurt Brand for what she'd interpreted as a slight to her. Tears burned the back of her eyes and she knelt down to bury her face in the inebriated dog's neck.

"When you are through sniveling, you can drag him down to the courtyard, where all is in readiness for our departure."

* * *

The leave-taking was heart-wrenching for Marisa. Even knowing that Richard and Raoul would be living in Wessex did not ease her reluctance to leave her father, especially in view of the poor beginning of her marriage and her guilt over Rollo.

Then her gaze alighted on Brand's horse.

If Geoffrey noticed the gray, he gave no indication, but Marisa went absolutely still as she studied the warhorse, recognizing the animal as one raised and trained by her father, one that had once belonged to Robert de Lisieux. Her heart lurched beneath her ribs at the implications of Brand's possession of the destrier. If she was correct, then Robert de Lisieux was dead . . . and her husband had killed him.

"What happened to the hound?" asked Geoffrey, mystified by Rollo's erratic behavior.

Marisa pushed her churning thoughts aside and turned reddened eyes to him. She opened her mouth to admit her foolishness, but Brand unexpectedly interceded. "The flask of wine overturned and he lapped it up before aught could be done. I doubt he will be so eager to tangle with anything but water again." Though Marisa knew the hidden meaning behind his last words was for her benefit, she was surprised and grateful that he'd covered for her. Geoffrey was studying Marisa's face, noting the misery etched thereupon. "Marisa feels she is to blame because she overset the wine," Brand added.

Somewhat mollified, Geoffrey hugged his daughter with bone-crunching force and swung her up onto the palfrey. Her brothers were already mounted, having agreed to escort Marisa, Brand, Adela, and Brand's four men-at-arms until their paths took a different direction to their own holdings. "God go with you both," Geoffrey said, staring up at Marisa and then Brand in the fine mist of rain that fell from the dingy gray sky.

Soon they were proceeding through the clamorous, dirty confusion that was London and. northwest toward Camwright.

Marisa was aware of little for the first hours of their

journey. Robert had suggested they tie Rollo to Marisa's mount until he was capable of running at his normal lope, and Brand obligingly agreed. With every graceful movement of the palfrey's canter, Marisa felt for the dog, who was trussed up like a prize stag behind her.

When Raoul and then Richard had gone their separate ways with several of their own men-at-arms, Marisa swallowed her pride and asked Brand if Rollo could be untied and set free.

Brand slid down from the gray and undid the cords that firmly bound the dog. With a strong pull he hefted Rollo from his ignominious position and allowed him to stagger about until he got his bearings. The overjoyed animal bounded about within moments of being set free, and Brand bent down to murmur something into the dog's ear. After receiving a vigorous switch of the gray tail, Brand vaulted atop his charger again without a glance in Marisa's direction.

"Your lord has a soft spot for animals, *chère*," Adela said quietly as she pulled up even with Marisa. "I suspect he is not heartless where you are concerned, either."

Before Marisa could reply, the servant dropped back once more and Marisa frankly studied her husband, who often turned his head to speak to a man he called Morgan. Marisa gathered that Morgan was close to his thane, a friend as much as a man-at-arms, and that he was Welsh. His hair and eyes were black as sea-coal, and he was of a slighter build than most of the men Marisa knew.

Morgan rode on Brand's right atop a small, shaggy pony that made him look too big for the animal, his long legs dangling close to the ground. Thus was Marisa afforded an unobstructed view of Brand's right profile, unmarred by the livid scar. *Adela spoke truly,* she admitted grudgingly to herself. *He is not unattractive in his own fashion.* When a rare burst of soft laughter drifted back to her, Marisa also admitted that he was not without a sense of humor, though he refused to display it to *her*.

That first night they stopped at a primitive inn outside

Oxford. Brand slept wrapped in his cloak on the floor with Rollo stretched out beneath his head—to Marisa's annoyance. When she tried to thank him for deliberately changing the story regarding Rollo and the wine, he shrugged it off, saying only, "Ofttimes the guilt over a misdeed is enough punishment for a spoiled child."

Yet he treated her deferentially in front of his men and Adela, or as deferentially as was possible for him, she thought darkly. When they were alone that first night, he was cool and distant, his attitude that of mere tolerance toward a bothersome, willful child. Marisa seethed inwardly, secretly building up her anger at Brand Ericson until it was like the banked coals of a dying fire, needing only a spark to burst into incendiary flame.

The second day Marisa noticed that the peaceful green valleys and wooded pastureland, the rolling meadows and low hills, were giving way to rougher, higher terrain. About midday Brand dropped back to inform her that if all went well they would be at Camwright by nightfall.

" 'Tis most considerate of you to inform me, my lord," she answered sweetly, then hated herself for being unable to bite back her next question. "But tell me, do you expect to sleep on the floor of our chamber for the rest of our married life?"

He turned his gaze from the view before him to her face and studied it for so long that she felt heat rise in her cheeks. "I was not aware that you wanted it any other way."

Well, maybe now she didn't, she mused, in light of the possibility that he'd killed her friend and suitor.

Marisa continued to meet his regard head-on. He'd tied a narrow leather thong around his forehead to keep his almost shoulder-length, wavy brown hair out of his face in the wind, and unbidden the word *barbarian* came to mind. He did not wear chain mail, but rather the lighter-weight boiled leather jerkin that the Welsh favored for fighting in their mountainous land.

Seized by a determination to find fault with him, Marisa did not hide the acute distaste that sprang into her eyes. "Tell me, my lord husband," she said, ignoring his invitation for a comment concerning their sleeping arrangement at the inn, "if you are Welsh or Anglo-Saxon. By your dress, you look remarkably like yon Welshmen of whom you seem so fond."

He turned to scan the horizon ahead, seeming to choose his words carefully. "I am pure Saxon, my lady, of the line descending directly from the House of Alfred, called the Great. Yet the Welsh are near and dear to me. They are wily, savage fighters and in some ways more civilized than we are. But you shall discover that for yourself in good time."

"Riders from the south!" bellowed Morgan as he wheeled his pony around to face that direction, the other three men-at-arms following suit in the wink of an eye.

Brand reached for his great sword as he swung the gray about, yet he remained protectively before Marisa and Adela, the latter having reined in beside her mistress. "Be still—say naught, do you hear?" he commanded in a low voice.

"Oui," whispered Marisa, suddenly filled with trepidation at the size of the party that was charging toward them on hulking coursers, the links in their chain mail reflecting the sun like webs of pure silver. They had to be Norman.

Once it was determined that they were, indeed, Norman, Brand's men formed a protective circle around the two women, their swords displayed menacingly, and waited with seeming calm for the newcomers to approach them.

The leader moved forward, leaving the others slightly behind him, a solid wall of steel mail and horse flesh. "Who are you and what is your destination?" the chevalier demanded in heavily accented English.

"I am Brand Ericson of Camwright, bound for my home by writ of the King."

The Norman leader lowered his sword in a move calculated to demonstrate his absolute confidence in the men who backed him, and removed his helm. The sun picked

up the blond highlights in his thatch of short sandy hair.
Even from where she sat behind Brand and Morgan, Marisa could see that his face was handsome and arrogant—
as if chiseled by the finest stonecutter. Yet there was also
surprise for a moment on the attractive, sneering features, for Brand had answered in French.

"Which King, English dog? Yours is dead."

Marisa stared in fascination as the knuckles of Brand's
right hand whitened around his sword hilt, the only visible response to the taunt he understood so well because
of his newly acquired knowledge of the Norman tongue.

"King William, Norman. Now, I would advise you to
let us proceed without interference. I have more important matters to attend to than verbal fencing with a hostile
warrior itching for a fight."

*And that is exactly what you will get if you do not mind
your tongue,* Marisa thought with rising alarm, despite
the fact that the "hostile Norman" was one of her own
countrymen.

The sneer turned into a black frown. "Mayhap *you* are
the one who itches for a fight, Saxon, as you sit atop a
stolen war-horse, hurling insults at a chevalier of William's." He motioned to the men behind him and two
rode up to him, one on either side.

"My horse Goliath was a gift from the King," Brand
lied. "And now, if you will get on with your business,
we will get on with ours."

The Norman shook his head. "Not so fast, my haughty
friend. I would see this writ given you by King William."

"Do not give in to the swine!" Morgan hissed under
his breath. "We can take them!"

"You know better than that," Brand countered softly.
"Let him come with only those two beside him, for we
are still five to their three. Let him see the writ—if he
can read—and then we will deal with him in the face of
our proof of safe conduct.

"You may approach, Norman, but only with the two
men now at your side."

There was a brief hesitation while the three Normans murmured to one another before riding forward as one. When the leader stood before Brand, he held out his hand and Brand reached inside his tunic to procure the rolled parchment. "I trust you can read as well as fight?"

"Enough to understand William's mark."

After he studied the document for a moment, he let it curl up again in his palm and closed his fingers around it, causing Marisa's heart to bounce spasmodically within her chest. He wasn't going to return it.

"If you wish to keep your hand, do not even consider it."

The only way to discover the truth behind Brand's warning would have been to tangle with the five English, and the Norman knight was not quite prepared to do that in light of the unmistakable challenge in Brand's narrowed eyes.

He gave the parchment back to Brand, his gaze alighting on Marisa behind the Anglo-Saxon. "I do not know how you came to acquire a Norman bride—and a beautiful one at that—nor how you managed to persuade the King to allow you to retain your lands, Saxon, but I will accept your 'proof' and permit you to proceed. This time."

Without a backward glance, he swung his horse's head around and returned with his cohorts to the rest of the group.

Brand's party remained where it was, refusing to scurry away like frightened rabbits, until the Normans were out of sight. Marisa caught the glow of triumph in Brand's clear eyes as he glanced back at her to make certain she had weathered the storm. There was no trace of fear in his gaze—nor had he displayed any in his voice or actions.

As they began to canter toward Camwright once more, Morgan let out with a bellow of laughter, and the others joined in. Marisa decided that she had just caught a glimpse of the valor her father had so admired in Brand Ericson.

Chapter 3

Twilight cloaked the land, mauve and coral striations sweeping across a pale aqua evening sky in a palette of breathtaking hues, as the travelers approached Camwright itself. Behind the stronghold and village stood the majestic mountains of Wales, deep purple against the magnificent play of color behind them.

Marisa took in the wild, vibrant beauty with her breath caught in her throat, for she had never seen the like. Rolling hills, yes, but never mountains such as these. "I see you are impressed with the land of the Cymry," said a deep, musical voice beside her.

She pulled her eyes away from the scene to meet the dark gaze of Morgan ap Dafydd. She mustered up a hesitant smile for him, for it was the first time he had addressed her in the two days of their travels. "Indeed, my lord—"

"Morgan."

"Morgan, then. Indeed, I think the mountains are beautiful. I've never seen such a sight."

The awe in her voice made him give her an answering smile, and for the first time, as he reached up to take her down from her horse, she noted the fine features and the hidden fires in his black eyes. The top of her head reached to just above his shoulder, but she would later learn that he was tall for a Welshman.

Brand's voice broke the spell. "I see you've managed to make her smile, Morgan." If he did not sound quite sarcastic, neither did he seem pleased with Morgan's success where he had failed. "Come, I know Edyth has prepared a sumptuous feast in celebration of our return and will be anxious to meet you, Marisa."

With a proprietary hand on the small of her back, he turned her toward the wooden gatehouse that flanked the double gates of the stockade surrounding his estate, and guided her toward the wooden stronghold that dominated the settlement. Villagers swarmed in after them, pitch torches held high so as to view their thane's new wife. Marisa blinked in the bright, wavering light, still puzzled by Brand's seeming irritation with her and Morgan.

They continued toward the great hall, a mammoth, timbered structure with sides that bellied outward, the huge wooden doors strengthened with metal bands opening from either of the long sides. It was a far cry from the great stone keep at Brionne, but warm, welcoming light beaconed from the door on their side and a woman appeared in the doorway. Before she could emerge and come forward to welcome the newly returned party, however, an old crone stepped out of the crowd and appeared on Marisa's other side.

"So, 'tis the Norman bride come to usurp the place of my Rhiannon!" she half crooned, half accused in her strange-sounding, Welsh-accented English.

Marisa shrank back instinctively against Brand, whose arm slid around her waist. Though out of obstinacy she'd pretended to understand little English, she caught the gist of what was being said.

"What do you here, Angharad? I thought you had returned to your people." Brand's voice was low, but it nonetheless held a threat.

"My people are here as well, Brand Ericson, or have you already forgotten my grandson?" The silence around them was suddenly deafening, and Marisa felt all eyes on herself and this toothless, wild-looking hag. She dared to glance around, only to see dark-eyed Welsh mixed in with blue-eyed Saxons—perhaps even Danes—and noted that none of them were smiling in welcome now.

"Indeed, I have not forgotten, old woman, but I will have no trouble from you. You are free to come and go as you choose, but unobtrusively and with a civil tongue in your head."

Angharad shot a look of pure, triumphant comprehension at the silent Marisa. "She does not know, does she? *She does not know!*" Her laughter sang out through the buildings and then died away on the brisk evening breeze. Marisa was so unnerved she shivered involuntarily and wondered why Brand did not just walk away from this woman, why he did not take her inside and away from this Angharad.

"I did not think the time was right, Angharad," he said. "There was never any disrespect intended. Surely you of all people know how I felt. Now, if you—"

"Bring the boy, Edyth!" she shouted in her singsong voice. "Bring the proof of their love—a love that transcends even the grave!"

A presentiment of disaster descended upon Marisa like a smothering shroud, and she did not even notice Brand's arm tighten around her waist as she followed all eyes to the open portal of the great hall. The woman silhouetted in the doorway disappeared for a moment and then reappeared with a small boy at her side. She bent to say something in his ear, and he ran eagerly through the crowd, searching for someone.

"Here, Griffith!"

Like magnet to metal, Griffith found his way to Brand's side, stopping short of throwing himself at the adult, his dark eyes suddenly puzzled at Marisa's presence and Brand's arm around her.

"Behold, childie, your father brings a pale-haired one from across the sea to take your mother's place!"

The little boy stood rooted to the spot, bewildered, before Brand gently disengaged his arm from Marisa and bent to scoop the child up into his embrace. " 'Tis known you have the Sight, Angharad, and other powers as well," he said. "But you do not—nor have you ever been able to—frighten me. Now, you will leave Camwright until you can accept my wife. You have already turned my homecoming into a travesty, frightening Griffith and revealing things to Marisa that I would have told her myself.'' He turned toward the hall, grasping Marisa's arm with one hand to take her along with him.

''You can banish me forever, Brand Ericson, but 'twill not change the future. You have brought evil with you this time. You will bring the Norman scourge down around our ears with your bargaining as surely as I stand here. Remember my words this night and all the others hereafter as you take that pale-skinned foreigner to the bed you shared with my daughter!'' Then she turned and disappeared into the silent crowd like a wraith.

Fear slithered down Marisa's spine at her words, but before she could digest all that she'd heard, a voice from the hall came to them and the woman who'd been standing frozen in the doorway limped forward, a welcoming smile on her pretty face as she stepped into the circle of the light.

''Go home, my good people,'' she ordered gently, a smile on her angelic face. ''Angharad still mourns her only daughter and would frighten you out of spite and anger. Go to your homes and fear not. She cannot harm you and yours.''

She came up to Brand and Marisa just as Morgan reached them. Marisa, still stunned by what she'd just witnessed, stared unabashedly at the clubfoot that hindered the woman's otherwise graceful gait. ''Welcome to Camwright, Marisa,'' she said warmly and took Marisa's free hand. ''Please come inside. You can wash the dust of your travels from you, and we can show you the hospitality for which my brother is known.''

Brand bent down to plant a quick kiss upon his sister's forehead and then allowed Morgan to escort the two women into the hall while he spoke softly to his son.

Marisa, vaguely conscious of her rudeness at staring at Edyth's misshapen foot rather than into her shyly smiling face, dragged her eyes upward and managed a weak smile. ''My thanks, my lady Edyth.'' The words sounded

hollow and false in her ears, but shock was still richo-
cheting through her at the old woman's pronouncement—
*my grandson . . . the bed you shared with my daughter
. . . a love that transcends the grave . . .*

Brand Ericson had been wed before.

All the pieces had fallen into place when Marisa had
looked upon the little boy's face . . . dark eyes and midnight hair—Welsh coloring. Brand Ericson had been married to a Welsh woman and had a son by her.

She stumbled up the single step into the hall, and only
Morgan's hand at her elbow prevented her from falling.
Her legs felt like jelly, yet she knew not why this knowl-
edge would affect her so startlingly.

"He did not mean to deceive you, my lady," Morgan
was saying, his dark eyes roaming over her face intently,
searching for some sign of recovery in the stunned blue
eyes. "He thought Lord Geoffrey had told you—"

"I will attend to this, Morgan," Brand interjected
warningly from immediately behind them.

At the sound of his voice, Marisa stiffened, a purging
anger sweeping away the crippling bewilderment that had
briefly held her in its grasp. The look of concern in
Edyth's eyes only increased Marisa's sense of betrayal.
What a fool she'd been! Small wonder he'd spurned her
physically after their marriage . . . he was still in love
with his dead wife!

"Marisa," Brand said, "I will tell you everything after the meal—all that I thought Lord Geoffrey had told
you until—"

"Until what, Saxon?" Her eyes glittered with suppressed anger and humiliation. "Nay, do not answer that.
You owe me naught—this is a marriage of convenience,
is it not?"

He nodded curtly, his expression shuttered as he
handed Griffith over to Edyth. "I trust you will hold a
civil tongue in your head as befits your station now. As
my bride, you will act every bit the thane's wife and
preside at the head table this night. You can hurl your
abuse at my head later in the privacy of our chamber, but

for now . . .'' His eyes held hers for a long moment, the same words he had said to the crone Angharad ringing in her ears in a taunting litany.

She finally jerked her gaze away and countered with soft vehemence, ''I know naught of thanes, Saxon. I am Norman, remember? But I do know of the proper behavior for a Norman count's daughter, and I will teach you and your people a thing or two about dignity and gentility.''

With a queenly lift of her chin, she addressed Edyth, who was speaking in low, earnest tones to Adela. ''My lady Edyth, will you be so kind as to direct me to my chamber? I wish to freshen up after our journey.''

Adela took one look at Marisa's glacial expression and said a silent prayer for all of them, then followed her mistress and Edyth to the other side of the hall and out the door to the smaller sleeping bowers outside.

Marisa did her father credit as she obligingly shared Brand's trencher and goblet at the board before his retainers and servants. Several times she fought back the childish urge to bite the fingers that held the choicest tidbits of food to her mouth. Later, she would not be able to say what she had eaten—whether it had been boiled meat or raw, cheese or mudcakes, bread or sand. But the potent mead, to which she was unused, warmed her from within and not only brought roses to her pale cheeks, but also helped her keep her vow to be gracious to Edyth, Morgan, and the others to whom she had been introduced.

She found her gaze wandering frequently to the little boy Griffith in spite of the fresh waves of betrayal that swamped her anew with each glance. He was about six or seven years of age, and had beautiful features, she had to admit. He resembled Brand and yet he didn't. Marisa loved children, but her feelings were so mixed, so tumultuous every time her eyes alighted upon Brand's son that she wondered if she would ever be able to hug him or give him the love a motherless child needed.

Later, as Adela readied her for bed, Marisa allowed

her facade to crumble. She sat obediently, staring into nothingness as the older woman unbound and brushed her hair. Adela finally set down the brush and took up the girl's hand. "Child, your hand is like ice. Let me stir up the braziers. . . ."

"Back home we had great stone hearths to keep the chill at bay, not a puny iron brazier or two in a bedchamber set away from the hall." She sighed resignedly and raised dull, lifeless eyes to Adela. "Everything is so primitive here. Mayhap I will catch a chill and—"

"Do not think such a thing! What would Lord Geoffrey think if he could see his daughter thusly?"

"Father deceived me. 'Twas bad enough to give me in marriage to an Anglo-Saxon, but far worse to sell me off to one with a son and an enduring fidelity to a dead woman."

"What do you mean, *chère*? Has he not . . . ?" Adela knew it was not her place to ask such a thing, but it was a calculated query meant to bring out Marisa's anger in place of this uncharacteristic dejection. Then, too, she suspected that, had Brand made Marisa his wife in every sense of the word, the news of a previous marriage would not have affected her so strongly.

As if on cue, Marisa came to life at the half-formed question. "Nay! I will see him in hell before I will allow him to touch me. Let him dream of his Rhiannon, let him dwell upon that which can never be again. And let him rue the day he ever dared bargain for my hand!"

When Adela had removed herself from the bower, Marisa remained seated upon an embroidery-covered stool near the brazier, brooding. Though she was dimly aware that she was acting more like her dour, brooding husband than herself, the thought was not enough to rouse her. She was naturally ebullient, with a zest for life typical of youth, yet she was also set back by the discovery of Brand's late wife and his son, and the accompanying suspicion that Rhiannon was the reason he'd not claimed his conjugal rights. *I'll end up a shriveled, cackling crone like Angharad*, she mused.

Rollo's cool nose nudged her knee, and Marisa turned her gaze from the fire to the dog. "You!" she exclaimed, her spirits lifting at the sight of the beloved pet, who'd taken to the object of her enmity with maddening eagerness. "You deserve to be trussed up behind me whenever I go ariding!"

His ears drooped at her accusatory tone and his tail switched tentatively as if in mute apology. She scratched him behind the ears and, out of the corner of her eye, noticed the great bed that dominated the bower. Against her will Marisa studied its embroidered coverlet and somehow knew that her predecessor had done the intricate stitching that depicted beautiful figures and designs spread out over the width and length of it. Her mind conjured up visions of Brand and his first wife entwined upon its soft, feather mattress. Without warning, the image of Robert de Lisieux's face flashed before her and Marisa knew she could not sleep with his murderer.

She stood up suddenly, the decision made. "Make your choice, Rollo," she declared. "I'll not sleep in that bed. You can come with me"—she grabbed her cloak and swung it around her shoulders—"or you can—"

The door was flung open without warning, and Brand stood before her, tall and forbidding. At a glance he took in her mantle-draped figure, her night shift and bare toes peeping from beneath, the pale curtain of her hair shimmering in loose abandon about her shoulders, and demanded harshly, "What are you about *now?*"

With an imperious tilt of her head she met his stare head-on. "I choose not to sleep in *that* bed. Therefore I will seek another place to—"

"Perhaps among my men, Marisa?" He arched a brow, as if at an exasperating child. "Or mayhap among the hounds?" Uncertainty flitted across her fine features before he added, "There is no other place."

"The servants' quarters will do." She started toward him, hoping to bluff her way past, but he merely stepped into the room and closed the door behind him with a soft *click*. They stood less than a yard apart, and Marisa felt her ire stir to dangerous heights at his overbearing manner.

"You will sleep in this room, Marisa. You will not shame me before my household by sleeping elsewhere."

Her eyes narrowed ominously, unexpectedly reminding Brand of a spitting cat. "*I* will not shame *you?* What do you think you did only hours ago? By not telling me of your—"

"Your father was at fault there, not I."

Marisa had to admit that he spoke the truth, but her anger was too far gone now to back down. "You have made a mockery of our marriage, Saxon, but I will not run back to my father yet!" At his dark frown, she rushed on. "Oh, do not think for a moment that I would remain here under these—these abominable conditions if I did not wish to. Remember this: the union can be annulled and there are others in Normandy who would jump at the chance for my hand in marriage. Believe me, Brand Ericson, I have no need of a husband who acts like a sheep being led to slaughter when we are alone together."

"*You* implied you wanted naught to do with me on our wedding night, Marisa. I was willing to make the best of things, but *you* looked upon me with revulsion and *you* made it clear that you were less than eager to commerce with Anglo-Saxon rabble."

She was silent a moment, her chest heaving with anger. Brand watched in unwilling fascination as a pulse worked in the hollow of her throat as she fought for control. It was true, but that fact did not erase the humiliation she felt . . . to discover that he still loved his first wife, according to that woman's own mother. "If you truly wanted me, you would have taken me on our wedding night. I think 'tis more a matter of your feeling disloyal to your first wife. And if that is the case, the marriage to me already contained the seeds of destruction! Tell me, Brand Ericson, just why you agreed to wed me, after all. 'Twas not only to preserve your holdings, was it?''

He seemed to struggle a moment with himself—as if he were loath to tell her—but in the end he bluntly revealed all. ''I made a vow to myself after the great battle . . . that I would do anything to secure Griffith's future. Anything, do you hear, Marisa? The price I had to pay for preserving my son's heritage was wedding Lord Geoffrey's daughter to form an alliance between Anglo-Saxon and Norman on the border of Wales and England. That is why I agreed to the marriage.''

She swung away from him, fighting her anger and frustration. Yet some little imp prompted her to delve into her darker side, searching for words to wound him. ''I know now why my father made no mention of your previous marriage, Saxon.''

''And why is that, Marisa?''

''He knew that since I could have any man in Normandy, although I would perhaps take an Anglo-Saxon for a husband by his decree, I would never settle for the leavings of another woman.''

The stillness swirled around them, charged with tension, bonding them together in antagonism.

Hating herself for the calculated cruelty of her words, but hating Brand even more, Marisa marched over to the clothes chest at the foot of the bed, almost tripping over Rollo in the process. Flinging open the lid, she immediately spied exactly what she sought—a fur-lined blanket folded neatly on top. Dragging it out, she spread it on the floor well away from the bed and removed her mantle.

''Just what do you think you are doing now, wench?'' His anger was replaced by exasperation and made his voice impatient. He stepped toward Marisa as if to stop her.

''Why, I am making my bed, my lord,'' she said with deathly calm, her red-rimmed eyes affecting Brand more than any stinging words she could have flung at him. The beautiful, smiling girl who'd so trustingly come to him in holy matrimony at Westminster was gone. And he was to blame. Her homecoming had been abominable, and those directly responsible were Geoffrey de Brionne and Angharad . . . and himself.

Running a hand through his nape-length hair, he allowed a heavy sigh to escape his lips. "You cannot sleep there, Marisa. There is a storm abrewing in the mountains. Already the air is chill and the wind picks up. You'll catch your death."

She faced him, unaware that the brazier behind her outlined the slim, gentle curves of her body. Brand felt something in his chest constrict at the sight. "I am not to leave this room, by your wish," she said, "nor can I sleep in that bed, by mine. Therefore this seems to be the only alternative.

"Rollo!" The dog obediently approached her. "Down." She pointed to the pelt on the floor and he obeyed. Marisa, using his head for a pillow, wrapped herself securely in the heavy coverlet and closed her eyes. "I think I am truly the more fortunate of the two of us this night, Saxon. You see, I have my living, breathing Rollo beside me to keep me warm, while you have only a memory to do the same for you. May your dreams meet all your needs, my lord husband."

Thunder roared around the bower and rain slashed against its timbered sides. Rollo raised his head and whined softly, but Marisa was already awake—had been since the storm had begun. The dampness had penetrated the room and the cobblestones beneath her felt slick with moisture when she tentatively reached a hand out from her warm nest to feel the smooth stones.

Her teeth began to chatter. "Shhh, Rollo," she soothed softly. " 'Tis all right." She sat up and unwrapped the blanket from her body. Rising, she walked to the nearest brazier and picked up a poker to stir up the embers and add more wood. From the even breathing that came from the vicinity of the bed, Marisa guessed that the storm had not disturbed Brand. She was wrong. He had dozed only fitfully, the bitter words they'd exchanged earlier

having stirred up the banked passions that still burned
within him, the poignant memories and futile longings
that had plagued him for over two years—until he'd met
a girl with arresting violet eyes and a vivacity that made
his gentle, loving Rhiannon seem meek in comparison.

*Fool! This one is spoiled, willful. She will be your
nemesis yet!*

He started from his doze at the sound of wood being
added to the braziers. Quiet though Marisa tried to be,
the sound she made was different from nature's discor-
dant orchestration outside the bower.

He watched her silently, enjoying the way the growing
fires limned her slender form, leaving very little to the
imagination. What would it be like to hold her in his
arms? To kiss those pink, beautifully molded lips and
caress her slender waist and then—

The brazier closest to the bed spat a glowing spark
from its red-hot interior, arcing it outward and directly
toward Marisa. Before Brand could react, she dropped
the poker with a soft cry as the burning projectile hit her
chest, right below her collarbone. As Brand bounded
from the bed, the smell of burning cloth assailed his nose,
and he felt an unexpected and ridiculously overprotective
concern.

"Marisa?"

She was reeling backward, away from the brazier, and
he caught her in his arms, lifting her to his chest. Unthinkingly laying her upon the bed she'd shunned so vehemently earlier, he lit a taper close by to better inspect
the damage. A hole the diameter of his thumb had been
burned through her gown and, as he gently pulled the
cloth from her skin, he saw the angry red patch beneath
that was already beginning to blister.

But Marisa was more shocked than in pain and, as he
drew away to get some ointment, she clutched at him.
"Nay, just get me down from here, please!"

He stared down at her, wondering at her dismissal of
the pain. He was well familiar with that kind of hurt.

"Put me down," she demanded with less force than

she'd intended, for of a sudden she felt her gaze caught and held by the thick-lashed, golden eyes above hers, anxiety reflected in their brown-flecked depths. They were beautiful eyes, came the thought unbidden.

He will surprise you with the beauty of his features.

Caught up by intense, unexpected emotion as the elements raged around them, they were mesmerized in that tautly stretched moment.

And then his lips were upon hers, softly at first and then more forcefully as he tasted the sweet contours of her mouth. At first Marisa was shocked, but as his warm, firm lips brushed over hers, for a long, rapturous moment she forgot the bed, and Rhiannon, and her burn—everything but the wonderous response she was feeling deep inside her as his tongue teased the line where her lips met and coaxed her mouth to reveal the honeyed delights therein. The kiss was like no other she'd experienced in her awkward experiments with smitten swains. His tongue boldly entwined with hers and made her melt inside as the fierce flame of passion ignited and radiated outward, rendering her weak and breathless.

Then she remembered where she was. If someone had doused her with a bucket of icy water it couldn't have been more effective. *He* had done this with *her* upon this very bed . . . the very bed Marisa had sworn she would never lie upon. She pushed him away and sat up, still shaky and confused over the sensations he'd created with a mere kiss.

"But your burn, Marisa. Let me attend to it, at least." He'd be damned if he would apologize for kissing his wife.

"It can wait until morning." On somewhat unsteady legs she returned to her makeshift pallet on the floor and curled up against Rollo's warmth.

Neither Brand nor Marisa slept soundly for the remainder of the night, each one acutely aware of the other's presence.

Chapter 4

Voices passed in and out of Marisa's dream-drugged mind, hazy images and echoing fragments of dialogue, disturbing her sleep. She tossed restlessly, twisting from side to side as if to escape them, but in the end, she had to emerge from her slumber to free herself from their disturbing presence.

Her lids were weighted with lack of sleep, and it took her a few moments to recognize her surroundings. The braziers burned brightly, warming the bower in the cool April dampness, and several wall sconces held flaming flambeaux that cheerily lighted the room and scented it with the aroma of hot resin.

Marisa pushed herself to a sitting position, brushing the hair from her eyes in a slow, lethargic movement, before she realized that an added pelt atop the original cover had contributed to her cocoonlike warmth. No wonder she'd slept right through Brand's leaving, she thought ruefully as her gaze took in the empty bed nearby. Stroking Rollo under the chin, she contemplated the kindness that had prompted her stern-countenanced husband to see to her comfort. Had it anything to do, she wondered, with that briefly tender moment they'd shared in the hours before dawn, that first intimate encounter in the few days since they'd spoken their vows?

Nay, she decided as she pushed the dog away and began folding her bedding and replacing it within the chest. *'Tis no more than he would do for one of his own villag-*

56

ers or even the beasts that serve him. Whatever purpose she was to fulfill, she could not do so if she were indisposed. Or worse.

If nothing else, Marisa did not want to be a burden to Brand Ericson. She would perform that which was expected of her as would a de Brionne. Since her mother's death, she had been chatelaine of a keep far larger, more complex, and more sophisticated than the primitive stronghold of Camwright at the base of the Cambrian mountains. She would rise to the task.

She let Rollo outside and freshened up with warm water from a basin left on the corner of a brazier, wondering if Brand had thoughtfully put it there. A discreet knock sounded upon the door, and Edyth entered bearing a tray of tidbits of roast meat, bread, dried fruit, and mulled wine.

"Good morningtide, Marisa," she greeted shyly, as she set the tray on the oak table beside the bed.

"Good morningtide to you, Edyth." She smiled at her sister-by-marriage, wondering how such a sweet, soft-spoken creature could be the sister of so grim and taciturn a man as Brand Ericson.

"I've brought some ointment for your burn. Brand said you'd been struck by a hot cinder."

Surprised, Marisa allowed Edyth to guide her to the chair and untie the ribbons of her shift, exposing the small blister. As she deftly applied the ointment—which smarted at first and then slowly began to numb the area—Marisa said with an all but imperceptible flinch, " 'Twas kind of you to be concerned about so small an injury."

"Not at all, Marisa. You have Brand to thank for telling me of it. In fact," she added, replacing the stopper on the small clay pot and glancing at Marisa through the camouflage of her dark lashes, "Brand was going to bring it to you himself, but I thought it best that we got better acquainted and . . . talked."

Marisa nodded, relieved that Edyth had been the one to come to her rather than her enigma of a husband. "Will you share a bite with me?" she asked politely. At Edyth's shake of her head, Marisa moved the tray from the bed-side table to the carved, straight-backed chair near one of the braziers. "I hope you know I do not expect you to act as a servant to me, Edyth. You should have had one of the others watch for signs of my awakening. Or better yet, why did you allow me to sleep so long at all?"

Edyth sat upon the great bed and smoothed her fingers over the embroidered coverlet. "I did not sit by idly while you slept, Marisa, and Griffith was only too willing to wait for Rollo to appear. He loves animals, you know, like Brand, and is fascinated by your pet." Even as she uttered the words, childish laughter floated through the partially open door where boy and dog cavorted in the late morning sunshine. "And then Brand said you were not to be disturbed—that you had not slept well during the storm."

In the face of this unexpected revelation of yet another not unpleasant facet of her husband's character, all the tenderness displayed in his treatment of her when she'd been burned during the night swept back over Marisa in an overwhelming rush. To cover her confusion, she said, "Well, you must not worry about Griffith. Hulking beast though Rollo is, he is as gentle and lovable as a lap dog."

"I saw that from the moment you rode through the gates of the manor yard." She frowned a little, and Marisa wondered if Edyth's words had brought to mind Marisa's bizarre welcome. "Marisa. What a lovely name. What does it mean?"

Marisa swallowed a mouthful of freshly baked bread. " 'Tis from the Latin meaning 'from the sea.' I do not know why my mother chose it, except that Father said she was always whimsical, a dreamer. Or perhaps she was thinking of my Viking ancestors who came from the sea, as your brother so thoughtfully reminded me on our wedding night."

At the distress in Edyth's eyes, Marisa was instantly contrite. "Forgive me, Edyth," she said gently. "How ungracious of me. You give me a compliment and I insult one of your family." She was quiet a moment, watching

Edyth adjust her disfigured foot beneath her skirt, then added, "He said to me exactly what I deserved, for in truth, I insulted him far worse with my spiteful tongue." Her eyes filled with pained remembrance at the thought of what she had said to him in a burst of unthinking temper. To cover the awkward moment, she remarked, "The embroidery on yon coverlet is exquisite."

Edyth's gentle features lit up at the compliment. "Thank you. It seemed as though I worked on it forever."

"*You* did the stitching?"

"Aye." If she noticed the cloud that seemed to dissolve over Marisa's fair head, she gave no indication. "Marisa, I would have you know that we are, all of us, very sorry about the events of your arrival. Angharad has always been a mischiefmaker, and she exaggerates—as you no doubt noticed—almost everything she says. Many of our villagers fear her, for she is purported to have the Sight. And also"—she looked up into Marisa's startled eyes for her reaction—"to possess powers obtained from the old pagan gods."

"And she was mother to Rhiannon?" Marisa asked in disbelief.

Edyth shook her head. "She was the half sister of Rhiannon's mother Efa. When Efa died in childbed, her husband went mad with grief, so they say, and disappeared. Angharad took their only child away to raise her. As you may have guessed, she worshiped her adopted daughter. But some say she is mad."

Marisa nodded, sipping the mulled wine and grateful for the courage it seemed to impart as she phrased the next question softly. "Theirs was a love match, as Angharad implied?"

Edyth stood and walked over to the door to watch Griffith romp with the huge, gentle wolfhound. The sun touched her profile with its benign rays, and her voice had a faraway, wistful sound to it. "They were playmates as children, and despite the fact that they were of two different cultures, everyone expected them to wed. Sometimes . . . sometimes they seemed more like brother and sister, for Rhiannon could run and dance and do all the things with Brand that I could not." A fine etching of pain marred her features as she turned back toward Marisa and limped into the room once more.

"I regret I've caused you sadness, Edyth. I have no right to question you about anything that does not directly concern me."

Edyth smiled once again, chasing away the shadows. "The least I could do was explain a few things, Marisa, after Angharad's thoughtlessness and unnecessary cruelty last night."

Rollo came trotting into the bower—alone. "Where is you new friend, boy?" Marisa asked, but a cant of his head and then a curious nose poking into her tray of leftover breakfast was her only answer.

"Griffith is painfully shy—much as his mother, except when Rhiannon was among those few who were closest to her. Griffith lost her two winters past, and he is now almost seven. He still pines for her and has withdrawn more and more since her death, despite my best efforts."

Marisa nodded thoughtfully, suddenly oblivious of the remnants of her meal, which began to disappear with admirable speed and canine stealth. Her heart naturally went out to the small child who'd lost his mother so early and suffered still. Despite the fact that he was not hers, that he belonged to the woman who still claimed Brand's heart, she would at least attempt to befriend him. If eventually more could come of the simple friendship, so much the better.

"Marisa?" Edyth's voice interrupted her thoughts and Marisa raised her eyes to meet those that were much like her husband's. "Brand is very bitter, as are all of us English. He still feels guilt over Rhiannon's death, but it runs even deeper than that. His is a festering, debilitating wound that is eating away at his very soul. He was close to Harold Godwinson—to all the House of Godwin. He saw our father and two brothers perish as they fought beside the King at Stamford Bridge and then at Hastings. Harold was killed and two of his own valiant brothers while Brand watched, unable to prevent it. He bore witness to the dismembering of Harold's body . . .''

She stopped suddenly at the look on Marisa's face.

Marisa covered her mouth with her hand, stunned. Although the Normans loved war, her father and brothers had spared her as much as possible the horrors of its results. Now she wished she had not been spared, for the shock of what Brand had witnessed and suffered made her want to retch. She wished her life had not been so sheltered in that respect.

''I regret that I've shocked you, Marisa, and since 'tis not my place to say any more, I will add only this. My brother is a good man—loved by his poeple and respected by his enemies. He is considerate and compassionate, although right now those traits are not easily discerned by a stranger. If you cannot learn to feel affection for him, then at least try to understand what he has sacrificed for the one person he loves more than anyone else—Griffith. Proud as my brother is, he swallowed every last bit of that fierce pride and humbled himself before William of Normandy to ensure his son's future.'' She paused, trying to gauge Marisa's reaction to her words. ''Whatever he may do or say, remember he is motivated by love of his homeland, his people, and— most of all—his son.''

Marisa nodded, trying to assimilate all that this warm and perceptive young woman was telling her. ''You know there is another side to all this, Edyth, although I would suppose few English agree with it, or the bloodbath at Hastings would never have happened.''

Edyth's expression changed swiftly from earnest to unexpectedly bleak. ''Indeed, you Normans believe William merely claimed what was rightfully his. But, as you said, few English, if any, believe he had any right to the throne. Now, what's done is done. There is little we can do to change things since our leaders have been either killed or imprisoned, those few remaining being young and obviously easily intimidated or coerced into cooperation. And so, as Brand is attempting to do, we will make our peace with the Normans as the only alternative to total annihilation. I would like to begin by forging a friendship with you, Marisa.'' She smiled then, to take the edge off her earlier words and show the sincerity of her offer.

Before Marisa could reply, a small dark head appeared in the doorway, his liquid brown eyes peering curiously into the bower. Edyth's gaze followed Marisa's and she beckoned. ''Come in, little one. Come and see your new friend Rollo.''

A small, thin finger slid into his mouth, and he shook his head slowly, his dark eyes going from Rollo, who was now licking up the few remaining crumbs on the tray, to Marisa. The Norman girl opened her mouth to add her encouragement to Edyth's, but before the words came out, the child disappeared.

Marisa managed a rueful smile, even as her gaze was drawn against her will to the great bed where Griffith must have been conceived. ''Perhaps he sensed how I would have massacred the Anglo-Saxon greeting I was going to give him,'' she said.

Edyth laughed aloud. ''I think he would have been very happy, Marisa, that the beautiful lady from Normandy would even attempt to speak his tongue . . . especially since he has been learning yours.''

''Mine?''

''Aye. Brand insisted we all learn the rudiments of Norman French. Griffith speaks Welsh, as well.'' She collected the tray from the speechless Marisa and, before she turned to go, added quietly, ''You will learn one day that my brother is many things he does not appear on the surface. Perhaps you can help bring the laughter back into his voice, the love back into his heart.''

Adela was just leaving the bower, after complaining good-humoredly that she'd not been able to serve her own mistress earlier. ''My lady Edyth would not even allow me to awaken you and serve you the morning meal.''

Marisa smiled mysteriously. "There's no harm done, Adela. 'Twas at my lord Brand's behest."

The older woman narrowed her gaze in thoughtful silence. "He is a considerate one in unexpected ways."

Abruptly Marisa's mood swung. "Oh, indeed he is! That is why he expects me to sleep in *her* bed?"

"But, *chère* where else would you sleep?"

"On the floor."

Adela shook her graying head with a wisdom that comes with years. "For one who dislikes him so, you show an uncommon sensitivity for things that should mean naught to you."

Brand's silent presence in the open doorway put an immediate halt to their discussion. Rollo bounded toward his new master in greeting. "Good morningtide, my lady," Brand greeted Marisa, his voice cool. Putting his hand on the dog's head, he added warmly, "Would you excuse your mistress, Adela, while I take her around the village?"

Dieu au ciel! Marisa thought irately. *He speaks with more kindness to Adela than to me.*

Nodding in deference, the servant cast a meaningful look at Marisa, but the girl was too caught up in her annoyance with her husband to even notice. Then Adela was gone and Brand stood waiting patiently for Marisa. She smoothed her rose-hued, linen bliaut and walked to the door.

"Surely you have a light wool gown that would better suit a walk through Camwright?"

He hadn't meant the observation to sound so critical, but the words were already out of his mouth, and Marisa's cheeks flared with a color to match that of the garment in question. "No doubt you would have me barefooted and loose-haired, like one of those wild-looking Welsh women . . ." Her voice trailed into silence as she realized what she'd said. She proceeded him out the door, scouring her brain for a more suitable subject to cover her blunder, but of a sudden her mind was blank as unused vellum.

As they moved through the yard, Brand answered, "I only meant that you will soil your gown. But, begging pardon, I suppose the daughter of a Norman baron wears silks and fine linen every day and delegates to underlings the overseeing of her dependents. And," came the final dig, "no doubt you were never expected to take up the burden of chatelaine under the loving protectiveness of your all-male family."

Marisa rounded on him, heedless of the others around them, her mouth tightening mutinously, her knuckled fists on her hips. "You think to insult me—to badger me into returning to my father, Saxon?" Her eyes darkened from the heather shade of the flowers that covered the Welsh mountainsides to deepest purple, and Brand was fascinated, against his will, by the animation and color that her ire brought to her face. She was even more lovely when angry.

"Well, let me tell you—you dowry hunter!—that you have come a long way from marriage to the daughter of a crone like Angharad!" In her rising umbrage Marisa ignored a little voice that reminded her of Rhiannon's true parentage. " 'Tis a stroke of luck for you that you married well when you chose to strike your 'bargain.' God only knows what other Norman woman in her right mind would have fallen into so well-laid a trap! The primitive conditions here are appalling compared to Brionne, but I said nothing to demean your home. And now you have the temerity to disapprove of my manner of dress?"

"A stroke of luck, Marisa? Hardly. And I explained my comment concerning your gown. Or do you hear only that which is convenient for you to hear?" The topaz eyes brightened with unconcealed wrath, glittering like cold, golden gemstones. "Primitive as our Camwright may seem to you, 'tis home to me and my people, Saxon and Welsh alike. Perhaps when you reach maturity—if you do not run back to your father or brothers before then— you will realize that home is anywhere you make it, be it even a humble cottage in the weald."

To her mortification, Marisa felt her throat tighten in vexation at his implication that she was childish and would never live up to his expectations. Nay! She would not show tears to him again. Throwing her last shreds of caution to the winds, she shot back, "Whatever you think, I will remain here, if for naught else than to prove that I am every bit as capable as your precious Welsh wife. You may stir my ire until I am incoherent, but you'll not rid yourself of me, Brand Ericson!"

"And I will not stand here and argue with you, you spoiled, empty-headed female!" Without warning, his look became shuttered, blocking out her anger and masking whatever emotions lay behind his leonine eyes. "Go play with yon hound, child. Obviously 'tis what you prefer to shouldering any responsibility." He turned on his heel and strode away, leaving her to her own devices in a yard full of scurrying servants and men-at-arms, who studiously avoided her in the wake of their lord's unusual show of wrath.

Griffith's large, velvet-brown eyes peered up at her from seemingly out of nowhere, and in that moment Marisa could feel only unreasonable resentment toward the child. She turned her gaze away, feeling monstrous but unable to help herself.

"I think you have angered your new husband, my lady."

Marisa started at the deep, Welsh-accented voice of Morgan ap Dafydd, whose lilting words sounded like the singing of bells. His loam-dark eyes crinkled at the corners in a smile that seemed to reveal barely suppressed amusement at what had just transpired.

"He brings out the worst in me, I think," she replied, her own attempt at a smile failing utterly. "He thinks me incapable of anything but romping with Rollo."

Morgan threw back his head and laughed softly. "Marisa, one day you will learn that Brand's only defense against his unwilling attraction to you is his anger."

He began walking toward the stables and Marisa followed along, at loose ends. "I would wager he never fought with—'' She suddenly thought better of bringing up a subject that was rapidly becoming a sore spot.

"Rhiannon? Indeed, I sometimes think theirs was an almost unnatural relationship. They never fought—as far as I know. And every man and his wife argue, perhaps even come to blows occasionally to keep things interesting.''

Marisa stored that enlightening bit of information in a corner of her memory to mull over later. "Are you wed, Morgan?''

The question seemed to take him by surprise, but he recovered quickly. "Nay, my lady, but someday soon I hope to bring my love around to my persuasion.'' Wistfulness flickered in the eloquent eyes.

I seem to bring only sadness or anger with my eternal questioning, she thought. *But how else am I to learn?*

They'd entered the dimness of the barn and Marisa felt immediately comforted by the familiar, tangy smells of hay and horses and leather trappings. "Morgan, would you show me around Camright?''

"I would feel privileged to show you around the lands belonging to Brand, Lady Marisa, but 'tis his place to introduce you to the villagers.''

But Marisa insisted upon saddling her palfrey, to the stableboy's—and Morgan's—obvious surprise, and rode out into the April sunshine with the Welshman. "My father and my eldest brother Eustace raise and train some of the best coursers in Normandy,'' she explained. "I enjoy riding them as much as tending them.''

Neither of them noticed Brand's tall figure standing in the doorway of the falcon house, watching them as they passed together through the double gate in the stockade, Marisa's sun-kissed hair in sharp contrast to Morgan's midnight-black as he leaned over to better hear a remark she made.

The fortress was situated on a steep bluff rising from the south bank of the Wye River. The palisade on the bluff side of the estate was not as high, the cliff being a natural protective barrier to the north, immediately above the Wye. Across the river stood rich forest, and leading from the western gates, with their two watchtowers standing sentinel on either side, ran a lane parallel to the river, thatch-roofed cottages strewn haphazardly along either side of it. The fields for crops were spread out on the south side of Camwright.

Marisa could not take her eyes off the mist-enshrouded peaks of the Cambrian mountains as they trotted westward down the lane toward Wales. Low and broad but rugged, they impressed Marisa with their unusually beautiful grass-covered slopes. Heather bloomed year round in the uplands and gave many areas a perpetually purplish cast.

The villagers who were working around their homes and small garden plots watched them curiously. Children stopped in their play to stare, and chickens and geese scattered before the horses' hooves with squawks of protest, feathers flying as they scrambled for safety. Marisa noticed that a good number of the people of Camwright were fair, a Saxon trait, but that there were obviously mixed marriages in a village so close to the kingdom of Wales, for some of the women were dark-haired, as were their children, and wore their hair hanging free in the manner of their native land. Some even disdained to wear shoes.

At the end of the lane, Morgan stopped and explained of the danger of riding to the south from where they stood. "There is a large bog south of here, my lady, and you would do well to remember to avoid that place. Many an unsuspecting animal—and an occasional human—has lost its life in the sucking quagmire. We'll cross the river and turn into the woods. I want to show you Griffith's favorite place as we circle back to the stronghold."

"Why are you—a Welshman—one of Brand's men-at-arms?" Marisa asked, forgetting her determination not to ask so many questions.

"He once saved my life, and I am bound to him of my own free will ever since."

"But surely you have a family in Wales?"

"Oh, some, but Brand lets me come and go as I please except when I am needed—as when we escorted him to London."

"But what of the bickering, the fighting that is reported to go on between the Welsh and the English?"

"Then I am allowed to choose."

A most unusual arrangement, Marisa thought.

"But Brand is excellent at peacekeeping," Morgan added. "He should have been an earl or a prince."

Marisa looked askance at Morgan, but his expression was serious.

They rode on in silence for a while. Then Marisa became aware of a soft, rushing sound that grew louder as they rode farther east toward the manor estate. "What is that?"

He smiled and said only, "You'll see."

Moments later, just as the strange sound became a low roar, they emerged into a clearing. Marisa forgot to draw breath for a moment at the beauty of the scene before her. A small waterfall cascaded down from a sheer, natural bluff like a shimmering, crystal curtain, foaming as it hit the rocks below and forming swirling eddies that radiated outward into a good-sized pool the lush green hue of the budding leaves above it.

" 'Tis lovely," she breathed, and slid off her mount for a closer look. The clear water at their end of the pool returned her reflection as accurately as the most well-polished metal mirror, creamy sand and multicolored pebbles visible in its pristine depths. Yellow daffodils and white-flowered hawthorn bloomed in a riot of pastels.

Morgan came up quietly beside her. " 'Tis lovely in springtime with the newly blossomed wildflowers. In Cymru—Wales—deep gorges and caves scar the steep slopes leading from the plateaus of our mountains. Clear lakes and sparkling waterfalls such as this, only larger and more magnificent, abound."

Marisa turned to him at his eloquent description of the

home he obviously loved. "I should like to go there some time, Morgan."

His lips curved upward at the corners. "You would, indeed, be something awesome to the Cymry, my lady, with your hair like moonlight and your lovely heather-hued eyes."

Color gently suffused Marisa's cheeks. "Surely, Morgan ap Dafydd, you flatter all the ladies with your nimble tongue."

The deep, masculine tones of her husband's voice responded to her observation. "I sometimes think 'tis a trait of the Welsh, my lady wife, but Morgan is not usually so easily given to flattery."

Morgan and Marisa turned, surprised by Brand's appearance. But only Morgan caught the keen edge of sarcasm in his friend's tone. Brand sat astride the gray stallion, with Griffith riding before him looking very tiny in comparison to the huge animal.

"You feared for your wife's safety, mayhap?" Morgan asked.

Brand said nothing, studying them both and then nudging the destrier forward. "I would never fear for anyone's safety with you, Morgan. 'Tis rather the Welsh fascination for, ah, hair like moonlight and heather-hued eyes that makes me wonder."

Morgan shrugged, recognizing hard-fought jealousy when he saw it, but refusing to rise to the bait.

Marisa, on the other hand, was not nearly so understanding. "If you imply Morgan brought me here for anything but—"

"I imply nothing, Marisa. 'Tis rather that you were evidently so caught up in your admiration for 'the surroundings' that you missed the horn signaling the nooning."

The good-natured Morgan laughed aloud at this revelation, but two spots of color stained Marisa's cheeks. "Perhaps deafness numbers among your failings," she said. "Heaven knows you have displayed enough to me within the past few days. But there *is* a waterfall yonder

and, lovely as is the sound, 'twould be difficult for anyone to catch such a signal from Camwright.''

Brand had the grace to flush slightly at her reference
to what she considered his shortcomings, knowing full
well that she meant his refusal to consummate the marriage. He opened his mouth to retort, and Morgan tact-
fully began to water his horse, when a hare darted out
from the woods nearby and skittered crazily close to
the gray charger. That in itself may not have caused the
beast to spook, but in that same instant Griffith slipped
from the protective circle of his father's arms to give
chase.

Just as his feet touched the ground, Goliath reared unexpectedly and lashed out with his deadly iron-shod
hooves. Brand fought to bring the animal under control
as Griffith's knees buckled from the jolt to his legs. The
little boy froze in terror where he knelt and stared up at
death in the form of the well-trained, striking war-horse.

In the midst of the sudden turmoil, Marisa's voice rang
out, sharp and imperative. *''En arrière, Goliath! En arrière!''*

The beast dropped to all fours on the instant, his mouth
blood-flecked from Brand's furious sawing on the leather
reins.

''Loosen the reins, Saxon, or he will not remain still
for long,'' Marisa recommended quietly. To Morgan,
who'd come up behind her with his sword unsheathed and
upraised in what had been a desperate readiness to strike
the charger before it trampled Griffith, she said, ''Lower
you sword very slowly, Morgan. Very slowly, indeed, or
the child's life may be endangered again.''

Morgan did exactly as he was bid, and Marisa bent to
raise Griffith from his knees. Unthinkingly he turned in
her arms and hugged her tightly, his head pillowed between her hipbones.

Morgan went to retrieve his and Marisa's mounts,
who'd sidled in panic to the edge of the clearing, but
Brand remained mounted and unmoving, staring at his
son clinging to Marisa.

One delicate hand reassuringly smoothed the tumbled raven curls, but her eyes met Brand's, contempt in their midnight depths. ''I suggest the next time you steal a dead Norman's horse, you learn to control it.''

Chapter 5

That night, after the evening meal was cleared away, a few of Brand's men slipped out into the brisk April twilight, presumably for a tryst or some other personal business. Most, however, remained in the hall for a toss of the dice, a game of chess, a match at arm wrestling, or swapping tall tales, seeing who could embellish their story the most convincingly.

One story that did not need any embellishment was that of Marisa's expert handling of Goliath, which had saved the young master from serious harm. "Can you imagine that?" one of the strapping, hard-bitten men-at-arms asked a comrade in wonderment. "That little piece of fluff commanding that platter-hooved brute? God's blood, the animal is battle-trained with a Norman thirst for blood, and my lady gained control of him with only a verbal command!"

"Aye, but with a voice so like an angel that even the wild beasts take heed," answered another.

"If you ask me, 'tis more likely because they share the same devil-spawned homeland—Normandy," grumbled a third.

At the reproving looks of several others, who'd decided to give Marisa a chance, especially after what had happened, he said no more.

Brand moved among his men, talking and occasionally laughing softly at a ribald comment, but for the most part he was even more sober-faced and introspective than usual. Marisa sat talking with Edyth and watching Griffith trying unsuccessfully to ride Rollo around the hall. Every time the boy managed to climb onto the dog's back, the hound would take off like a shot, leaving the bewildered Griffith sprawled among the rushes. Then he would doggedly right himself, sneak up on Rollo, and launch himself again, boy and dog eventually making a game out of it . . . until Griffith won by clutching the shaggy gray fur in his small fists and clinging with stubborn tenacity.

Morgan came to sit with Edyth and Marisa, bringing a small harp and playing haunting Welsh songs for them, his graceful fingers gliding over the strings like a skilled lover's caresses. When he began to sing, Marisa couldn't help but realize he was directing his song to her sister-by-marriage.

Someday soon I hope to bring my love around to my persuasion.

Why, he loves her! Marisa suddenly realized. Even though he politely looked her way many times, it was obvious that the sweet strains of his music, the beautiful tenor of his voice, were tenderly reaching out to Edyth with alluring appeal. At first, Marisa sat enthralled. When Morgan made it obvious for whom he sang, she remained seated awhile longer, fascinated by and also envious of the banked fires within the jet-black eyes, the yearning that permeated every lyric, every note. *What must it be like,* she wondered with a tightening in her throat, *to be so loved by a man?*

From across the room, Brand watched Marisa's captivation with Morgan ap Dafydd's silver tongue and magical fingers, unexpectedly envying his friend his talent. There'd been no need for Brand to woo Rhiannon with song, for she'd been the one to sing and play the harp for him, telling him of the love she'd borne him since childhood, a love he'd felt so certain he returned. . . .

Brand dragged his gaze away from his Norman wife, deciding it would serve her right to fall in love with the Welshman. What ironic justice *that* would be. Morgan and Marisa. An unconscious frown drew his dark brows together at the thought, and of their own volition his eyes sought her fair form as she sat enraptured by the man who really sang to Edyth. Could it be that Marisa was actually smitten by Morgan?

Brand turned away from several men, even as one asked him a question, so preoccupied were his thoughts with his beautiful wife and best friend. He couldn't help but ponder the fact that Morgan ap Dafydd was considered an attractive man, judging from the way the female servants and unattached village maidens twittered and carried on whenever he was about. Could it be . . . ?

He turned and quit the hall, hoping the bracing night air would clear his muddled mind of such ridiculous notions. Morgan was in love with Edyth, so it would do Marisa no good to pine for the handsome Welshman. And it was time his sister was wed. *That would give the wench something to really pine over,* he thought acidly. *She has already stated she could have had any man of her choosing in Normandy. . . . 'Twould only be fair turnabout to have her yearn for someone too strong willed to slip into her silken snare. . . .*

As you have done, mayhap, Ericson? whispered a troublesome imp from the depths of his mind.

A rising wind caught the ends of his hair, now tied with a leather thong around his high forehead, and whipped it into his face—a stinging reminder that he had duties to perform. He was approaching the gatehouse with long, sure strides when suddenly the wind turned icy. An apparition appeared out of nowhere and floated over the ground with eerie ease to block his path.

"Can it be that you flee your pale, sniveling Norman bride, Saxon? Does the thought of what you once had— the thought of one who's very memory you now betray with yon wench—torture you, eh?"

Angharad.

She was supposed to be gone, and at his bidding. By the rood, the crone seemed to appear and disappear out of thin air. "What do you here, old woman? Obviously you have not come to terms with my recent marriage, yet you dare to approach me brazenly when I, as lord of Camwright, banished you yestereve?''

Her small, cataract-glazed eyes in a face that might once have been pretty, gleamed darkly with malice. "And what could you do to me, Brand Ericson, pray tell? The gods have taken my beloved Rhiannon from me. What could be worse since I have no fear of death?''

A chill ghosted over him at her blasphemous words. "Be that as it may, Angharad, for the love I bore your daughter and now bear her son, I tell you once more to get from Camwright. I will not be so magnanimous the next time you—''

"Magnanimous?'' Her cackle of derision was caught up by the breeze and eddied round and round the stockaded courtyard, seeming to bounce off the timbered buildings and palisade and echo in endless stridency. "I do not live here anymore, Saxon, so therefore you have no hold over me. I am of the Cymry and am free to come and go as I please. Remember *that* the next time you issue your grandiose edicts!''

"And *you* remember, old woman, the next time you insult my wife, that this day she saved Griffith's life. Or can you think only of Rhiannon and not her son because, after all, he is not truly of your flesh?''

The weasellike eyes burned with acute dislike, something Brand had never seen in her expression before. But it would take more than the hatred of an old Welsh woman—witch or no—to strike fear into his heart.

"I love the boy as my own, make no mistake about that, Saxon. But I was there in the glade by the pool, and I saw what happened. 'Twas only a paltry show of heroics on her part. She speaks the Norman tongue, so why couldn't she have given the beast a command? Surely you do not think you would have failed to bring that Satan-spawned beast under control when your son's life depended upon it?'' She paused for effect, then added, "No doubt she used some signal unknown to you to rile the horse in the first place.''

Brand rubbed his fingers wearily across his forehead, fighting off an ache around his temples that had been building all night. "As much as it pains me to admit this, Angharad, I did not have the gray under control, nor could I have done so in time to save Griffith from serious injury. By the time Morgan could have come close enough—if he could have accomplished it—to slit its throat, Marisa had already given the Norman command to cease. Although, by all the powers that be, why she should have bothered after the hideously cruel reception she received from you, I cannot say."

Angharad's thinning hair blew about her withered face in the wind, white and wispy like spectral fingers reaching outward. "Bah. You have already fallen under her spell, Saxon, despite her sharp tongue and haughty ways. She knows not what it is to bow before the superiority of her husband, to show compassion for those around her. She shows only her love of self, and that will be her downfall, I tell you, because one day someone will allow their hatred of the Normans an outlet, and your bride will be the easiest target. Mayhap you'll find what remains of her in the bog, or floating facedown in the pool in the glade, eh?"

Brand paled visibly at the monstrous threat, but she was already gone, disappearing wraithlike in a wind-whisked cloud of vapor. *What remains of her in the bog . . . or floating facedown in the pool . . . the pool . . . the pool. . . .* Fear wrapped around his heart like one of Angharad's gnarled old hands and squeezed until—

"Brand?"

Startled out of his morbid, frightening thoughts, Brand swung to face Morgan in the torchlight.

"What is it, man? You look like you've seen one of Angharad's evil spirits."

"Worse . . . Angharad herself."

Morgan began walking toward the gatehouse, knowing Brand had begun his rounds before seeing the old woman. "Tell me about it."

But Brand's thoughts were following another channel.

"Were you aware that she was there—at the pool—this afternoon? She saw and heard everything."

"Well, then—good. 'Tis time she saw Marisa for what she is—spirited and courageous. And of fine enough character to have cared about the life of her rival's child."

Still caught up in his unexpected concern for Marisa's safety, Brand missed entirely the implication of the word *rival*. He made sure all was well and issued orders specifically forbidding Angharad's entry to the yard unless she spoke to him personally, then he turned back toward the hall.

"Sit with me on the porch awhile, Morgan, and we will have a last cup of mead before retiring."

At Brand's signal from the doorway, a servant brought him a flask and two beautifully carved goblets. Before returning to Morgan, he noted that Marisa had retired already. They sat in silence awhile, gazing out into the star-studded, half-mooned blackness of the night sky, each immersed in his own thoughts.

"How could such a sheltered, coddled creature know aught of war-horses, Morgan? I am reluctant to have Edyth give over the keys to such an irresponsible, empty-headed—"

"I would hardly call her empty-headed, let alone irresponsible," Morgan interjected dryly. " 'Tis just your first impression of her. Being the only woman in a family of all men for the last ten years or so, she can hardly be expected not to have been somewhat sheltered and coddled."

Brand grimaced and stared into the swirling dark depths of his goblet.

"She told me earlier that her father and now her older brother Eustace breed and train what are considered to rank among the best coursers in Normandy," Morgan continued. "With her natural curiosity and energy, I can easily envision her learning everything she could possibly persuade the men in her family to teach her."

"Even so, it seems all she cares about is romping with

that great hound of hers and wearing beautiful but inappropriate gowns.''

Morgan smiled in the faint light. "I personally thought she looked quite fetching today.'' Brand threw him a look of annoyance. "But as an observer, it seems to me that she is unsure of just what she is to do. If you remember, you did not take her on the appropriate rounds through the village, so she had nothing else to do but amuse herself. You must make her known to the people of Camwright, else she will have no chance to earn their acceptance. She is too proud to beg you for some responsibility, and you are too stubborn and easily riled of late to take up the challenge of winning her over. You must learn to accept her, thereby setting an example for your people.'' At Brand's dark look, he added with wicked innocence, " 'Twas never your wont in the past to anger so easily.''

Brand set down his drinking vessel with more force than was necessary. "I never encountered such a sharp-tongued, independent, hot-tempered minx before! How else am I to deal with such a firebrand after . . .'' He left his sentence unfinished.

"Rhiannon was completely different. You must accept Marisa for what she is, for what she can be if given the chance. First you must be a husband to her.''

Brand looked up sharply. Could he possibly know? "What do you mean, Morgan?'' he asked softly.

"I would not pry into your affairs, my friend, but 'tis a well-known fact that one can attract more effectively with honey than sour wine. And you've not been very sweet-tempered with your lovely new bride.''

"And you feel free to advise me, being the expert on love with your smooth-tongued love songs and nimble fingers? I do not notice that you have exactly won over Edyth.''

The barb hit home and, seeing the pain that flashed in Morgan's eyes, Brand was immediately sorry for his thoughtless comment. He put his hand on his friend's arm and said in a low, earnest voice, " 'Tis well past time for Edyth to wed, my friend. I will tell her she must choose, for she cannot use her disfigurement as an excuse any longer. 'Tis plain as day that you have loved her for a long time, and I can think of no one who could make her happier.''

Morgan smiled, a gentle curving of his lips that bespoke the love he bore Brand's sister. "I thank you for that, Brand.''

"My lord!''

Adela's voice was soft but urgent as she hurried through the dark yard toward them.

Both men stood at the urgency in those two words and turned toward her. "What is it, Adela?''

She halted before them on the open air porch, twisting her hands in distress, her face creased with concern. " 'Tis Rollo. I—I think he has been poisoned, and Marisa is beside herself.''

"Angharad.'' Brand spat the name with repugnance and turned to stride toward the bower he shared with his wife.

"Shall I fetch Edyth?'' Morgan asked.

"Oh, nay, my lord!'' The anxiety on the older woman's face increased in proportion to the fear in her voice. "The mistress says 'tis the doing of some hate-filled Saxon and will not allow anyone else to touch him. I told her I meant only to use the privy because she would have forbidden me leave the room and fetch anyone else.''

"Give Adela time to return alone, Brand,'' Morgan suggested, "and enter seemingly at your leisure. The lady Marisa will be none the wiser.''

Brand nodded. "Go back then, Adela. Once I arrive, she cannot forbid me to summon Edyth if we need her.''

As soon as Adela was swallowed up by the shadows, Brand turned to Morgan, his eyes glowing with anger. "I will hunt her down and have her put to death for a witch!'' he swore.

"She was Rhiannon's mother, my friend.''

"She was *not* Rhiannon's mother, therefore she is not Griffith's immediate kin, either. How could she stoop to

such unnecessary cruelty when 'twas natural that I would
eventually wed, if for naught else than to provide Griffith
with a mother. They say she drove Rhiannon's father
mad—"

"Nay, Brand. You are not thinking clearly. The story
goes he was driven daft from his grief, and any man who
could not pull himself together for his child's sake would
be easy prey to the selfish machinations of another."

Brand clasped the back of his neck, as if to ease the
building tension there. "Aye, you are right. But this deed
will not go unpunished. She made threats on Marisa's
life moments before you came to me from the hall, and
if she dares to show her face here again, at the very least
I will lock her up for her threats against Marisa. Now
this . . . Things have gone too far!"

As Brand turned and followed the path Adela had
taken, Morgan smiled. He hoped the dog would survive,
but even if it didn't, his death would be a small price to
pay to begin mending the breach between Brand and
Marisa. In showing his concern for the animal that Marisa loved, Brand was unknowingly displaying his own
growing feelings for his wife. It was a good beginning.

Rollo lay sprawled upon the cobblestone floor of the
bower. Beneath him was an old pelt Marisa had evidently
dug up from the bottom of the chest. Brand felt his heart
go out to the girl who knelt beside the huge, weakly
struggling animal, murmuring encouragement in French.
The great head lifted toward its mistress again and again,
only to fall back heavily with each attempt, its strength
waning, the normally clear brown eyes cloudy and disoriented.

Brand glanced at Adela, standing helplessly nearby,
obviously at a loss. At Brand's finger quickly brought up
to his lips in a silent signal, Adela nodded. "Rollo?" he
called softly.

The wolfhound's shaggy tail flopped once, and his eyes
tried to focus upon the man in the doorway, but failed.
Marisa, however, did not even bother to look toward

Brand. "See, Saxon, what your kind have done to the one thing that means more to me than aught except my family and Adela. Small wonder the English gave the battle to the Normans if this is how they fight!"

Without giving him a chance to answer, and never taking her eyes or her constantly soothing, reassuring hands from the hound's body, she said to Adela, "You must find something to make him vomit or he will surely die."

Brand turned back toward the partly open door. "I will fetch Edyth. She knows much of healing—animals and humans alike."

It was then that Marisa turned misery-clouded eyes upon him, the bitterness within the smoky violet depths making him inwardly recoil. "Have you and yours not done enough to hurt him? Do you think I would allow anyone but Adela or myself to touch him now?"

"Then you are even more foolish than I gave you credit for, Marisa, for surely you can trust so gentle a soul as my sister." The compassionate tone of the words dulled the sharp edge of their meaning, and he left before she could answer.

When he returned with Edyth in tow, Marisa's head was resting against the still body of the dog. Edyth dropped to her knees beside them while Brand stoked the embers in the one lit brazier and started a fire in the other. When he murmured something to Adela, she quietly left the room. Marisa looked up at Edyth, failing to notice her servant's departure. "He is dying," she said dully.

"Not if I have any say." Edyth added some finely ground powder from a tiny vial to a small flask of water. "Here, help me. Hold up his head." Marisa did as she was told, discovering as she struggled with Rollo's great head that it was no easy task. Then Brand's firm, capable hands were gently moving under hers to lend his strength, and they succeeded in helping Edyth open the animal's jaws and pour some of the potion onto his tongue. She closed his mouth immediately and Marisa massaged the hound's throat to force him to swallow. Edyth repeated the action several more times.

Just when it seemed their eforts had been in vain, the dog began to heave—weakly at first and then with increasing vigor until he regurgitated the contents of his stomach into an empty bowl. "Good dog," encouraged Edyth. When Brand's fingers withdrew from under Marisa's and they laid Rollo's head back down once again, Brand, to Marisa's surprise, removed the bowl and deftly began to clean up what had dribbled onto the floor.

"Cover him and pray, Marisa. And keep a bowl of fresh water nearby should he rally and want a drink. That is all you can do now."

Marisa nodded, her eyes still upon her beloved pet. "Thank you, Edyth," she murmured.

Brand walked his sister to the door and spoke to her in low tones for several moments. After she left, he closed the door and turned to look at Marisa. Her head lay upon the wolfhound's side, her unbound hair fanned out over the rough gray fur like spun silver webbing. *She has the most beautiful hair I've ever seen,* he thought as his eyes drank in the alluring picture she made. She wore the same night shift she'd worn on their wedding night, and her small body was curled up close to her beloved dog in an attitude of protectiveness, the slender arms gently encircling its neck. Small, bare feet with the sweetest pink toes peeked out at Brand from the hem of the pale shift, and he had the strangest urge to . . .

With a mental shake of his head, he forced his whimsical thoughts to the more sober matter at hand, and hunkered down beside her. "Marisa? You must not put any pressure upon him, no matter how gentle. He may have trouble breathing."

His words penetrated the fog of her misery, and she immediately sat up, the satiny skein of her hair spilling down past her shoulders, one errant tendril trailing across her collarbone to curl impudently about the soft mound of her breast. Brand was hard-pressed to keep from reaching out and entwining that beckoning strand about his finger, drawing her near enough to—

"Make your bed here beside him, Marisa," he said, the gruffness in his deep voice due to his own self-reproach. "You can sleep thusly while remaining near to him should he need you."

The normally melodic strains of her voice were gone now, the sound strangely toneless. "And how can I sleep when he is all but unconscious, his heartbeat barely discernable, his breathing quick and shallow?" She gently forced open an eyelid. "And his eyes. See how huge the centers are? Unmoving, fixed . . . as if he is all but—"

Brand interrupted her without ceremony. "You can do naught else now. Edyth said as much and you must take my word that she knows what she is about. You can best serve him, should he rally, by having your wits about you. And that can only be achieved with sleep."

Seeming to take hold of herself, Marisa nodded and stood up with sudden purpose. She opened the lid of the chest at the foot of the bed and withdrew her bedding from the previous night, making a place to sleep beside the inert Rollo. She covered him first with part of her own blanket and then lay down, as subdued and obedient as a child, an attitude new to Brand in his dealings with her. He felt more capable of handling her impish tricks or even her rash and often unwarranted anger. This suddenly docile, obedient girl reminded him of—God help him—Rhiannon. And for some reason he wanted the other Marisa back, not this unanimated shadow of her former self.

Surely I am undone, he thought in bemusement, as a cold draft of an emotion akin to fear wafted over his heart at the thought of how she would be affected if the hound perished.

He silently watched the woman who was now his wife whisper words of endearment to the dying animal, then lay her head down close to Rollo's, one hand extended from under the pelt to rest on the dog's paw.

Brand contemplated girl and dog for long moments

after Marisa seemed to drift off to sleep. Extinguishing several candles, he doffed his clothing and climbed into bed, only to find that sleep eluded him for much of the night. When at last he slipped into the realm of Morpheus, his dreams were of Marisa—Marisa commanding the mighty Goliath to back down from his unexpected and frightening attack on Griffith . . . Marisa smiling at him in shy innocence at Westminster Abbey . . . Marisa comforting his son after his brush with death . . . Marisa caring for a shaggy, lop-eared wolfhound with infinite tenderness and concern . . . And then Rhiannon's face superimposed itself over Marisa's, animated with joy. *We are to have another child, Brand! Another child* . . . But the small, fragile features, so alight with happiness and wonder, turned pale and waxen and unmoving, frozen forever. . . .

"Brand. Brand!"

He bolted upright, the sound of Marisa's excited voice rousing him from his fitful slumber like an unexpected crack of thunder. It was still dark, just before dawn judging from the blackness around them and the chill in the air as the dying embers in the braziers failed to give off any appreciable heat.

He looked into wide, fatigue-shadowed eyes barely visible by the faint flickerings of a single, worn-down taper beside the bed and, through the sleep-hazed thought processes of his mind, immediately suspected the worst. *By all the saints,* he could only think with a sudden sense of irreparable loss, *she will hie herself off to London once and for all.* . . .

"Rollo seems to be better. He opened his eyes."

Relief swept over him and he spoke with uncharacteristic sarcasm to cover his unwelcome feelings of panic. "Surely you've not watched his every move all through the night?" Brand squinted through the dimness toward the form on the floor still enshrouded by a light cover. He could see nothing from the bed, so he slid down, flinching slightly as the cold stone floor made contact with his warm bare feet, and heedless of his state of undress. In two strides he was squatting down beside Rollo.

"Stoke the fires, Marisa," he said over his shoulder, and put his ear to the dog's side. The heartbeat was stronger and more rapid than it had been hours before, and the respiration seemed to have slowed to a more normal pace. "Rollo?" he queried softly.

The eyes opened and slowly focused. The end of the long tail sticking out from beneath the pelt moved feebly. "Easy boy," Brand soothed, and stroked the dog along his neck. "Light the tapers, Marisa," he said without looking up.

It was quiet for a moment and then he felt her presence close behind him. "What is it now? I need more light." He made to rise, prepared to do what he'd asked her himself, when Marisa suddenly drew in her breath.

In the stillness of the bower, it caught his attention. He spun around and stilled at the look on her face, at the deep blush spreading rapidly upward from the neckline of her gown, over her features, and toward the roots of her halo-bright hair, obvious even in the faint light.

As the cold air enfolded him like the chill of a damp mountain cave, he realized he was naked as the day he was born—and, despite her innocence, Marisa's gaze was riveted to his body in unabashed curiosity and awe.

Chapter 6

For a fleeting moment, Rollo was forgotten as Marisa and Brand stood, spellbound, staring at each other. Despite the telltale hue of her face, Marisa could not take her eyes from Brand's splendidly formed body. And he was caught between the desire to take her in his arms and kiss away her embarrassment, before making her his in every sense of the word, and the urge to walk over to the stool where his clothing lay.

"Surely you have seen a naked man before, Marisa," he said softly.

He may as well have been talking to the wall, for all that she heard him. She found herself fascinated against her will by the play of light and shadow over the broad, rippled musculature of his chest, the light tangle of hair that whorled about his chest and tight abdomen, narrowing to lure her unwilling gaze downward toward his manhood. She hastily skipped over that shadowed area to his long, tautly muscled legs, imposing in their shape and obvious strength, while showing no sign of unsightly thickening or knotting.

This was not a body formed by fleeing battlefields, as she'd so boldly insinuated the night of their wedding. The rosy color of Marisa's burning face deepened at the thought of her audacity then. He could have beaten her, and with good reason, for her blatant insult to his honor.

"Do you like what you see, my lovely wife, now that your hound cannot stand between us?"

His words broke the spell between them, and he turned to stride to the end of the bed and gather his clothing. Marisa knelt beside the dog and covertly watched Brand cover his magnificent nakedness, silently damning the weakness that made her feel disappointed.

"See if he will take some water," Brand suggested as he finished lighting the tapers around the bower.

Marisa reached for the bowl nearby and scooped a bit of the clear, cool liquid into her palm. But when she would have held it to her lips, powerful fingers gripped her wrist and prevented her from tipping the few drops into her mouth. She looked up into Brand's glittering topaz eyes, clearly annoyed. "I will test his food and water from now on," she explained.

"Do not be ridiculous. I will not allow you to risk your life. 'Tis just as easy—and safer—to get his water yourself." He retrieved the full pitcher beside the bed and replaced the water in the bowl. "You can give him his food and water, but I forbid you to test anything given to him by anyone else, do you hear, Marisa?"

"Naturally you would prefer that I feed him, for you would never dream of punishing an Anglo-Saxon—or one of your precious Cymry—for so small an offense as poisoning my dog."

His eyes narrowed. "You are my *wife*, no matter our differences, and I will not have you harmed." *Much as you may sometimes deserve it,* he added in silent vexation. "And he is only a beast."

Marisa touch a few drops of water to the weak Rollo's tongue, and felt her heart soar at his acceptance of the life-sustaining liquid. "Aye, he is only a beast," she murmured so softly that Brand had to strain to hear, "but he loves me." What she did not say unexpectedly affected Brand to the point that he felt a surge of regret—and guilt— because he could never allow himself to love her. He had failed Rhiannon as his love for her had dwindled, and then he had destroyed her. He did not deserve to love or be loved—even though Marisa de Brionne obviously needed that which he dared not give, and he, too, needed that which he dared not accept.

He crouched down beside her, helping to wipe up the water that had dribbled onto the floor. At Rollo's slow switch of his tail, Brand smiled in spite of himself and his dour thoughts. "You will live, you hulking, stubborn hound, in spite of the blunderings of some vengeful soul."

He continued to watch Marisa stroke and murmur to the dog, his thoughts turning to Angharad. If he caught her anywhere near the stronghold again, he would personally choke the life from her.

In the twenty-four hours it took the dog to recuperate, Marisa hardly left the bower. Edyth came with Griffith to check on the animal's progress, and Marisa allowed the little boy to cater to Rollo's rapidly returning appetite with a few tidbits of meat he'd saved from his own trencher. As the dog tested his legs and sniffed around the bower, Marisa laughed with sheer delight at his regaining his strength and curiosity.

By nightfall, she requested warm water for a bath, suspecting that she smelled like Rollo. She luxuriated in the scented water. The cart bearing the bulk of her belongings and some of her dowry had arrived from London, and she'd indulged herself by pouring a generous handful of attar of roses into the bathwater.

Having scrubbed her scalp and hair last, Marisa had just finished rinsing the heavy tresses with Adela's help when Brand entered the room. Adela appeared torn between the desire to continue to wait upon her mistress until she was dry and clothed and the wish to remove herself from Brand's unnerving presence. Marisa was loath to leave the protection of the slatted wooden tub before the unflinching gaze of her husband. What did he want? she wondered.

Brand settled the matter by dismissing Adela when the awkwardness threatened to spoil Marisa's glowing happiness. Rollo came over to sniff at the water as Marisa remained seated, uncertain of how best to get out of the tub and dress while preserving her modesty. She laughed in spite of her situation as the dog lifted one huge paw and placed it over the edge of the tub. "So you want me out, eh, sly devil? Mayhap we should find you a female canine friend."

She glanced at the silent Brand, as if to share in the jest, but his expression remained closed. From the distance that separated them and the shadows that played across his face, Marisa could not make out the interest in the golden-brown eyes that were fastened intently on the animated smile that lit her beautiful face. Gradually that smile faded, as when clouds dancing across the sky blot out the sun, and Marisa told Rollo, "Down, boy."

Staring into the blue and orange ribbons of flame leaping from the nearest brazier, she asked stiffly, "Was there something you wanted, my lord?"

Silence reigned for a tautly stretched moment as she awaited his answer. "Indeed, Marisa. I demand equal time to peruse your attributes as you did mine this morn."

Stunned, she swung back in his direction. "You—you deliberately chose to . . . to flaunt yourself before me this morn, Saxon. I, on the other hand, had no such intentions before you burst into the bower—"

"I beg to differ," he calmly interrupted. "In my concern for the dog—after you startled me out of my bed—I neglected to remember to clothe myself from your untried, maidenly gaze. You seemed to enjoy taking in the sight of me, else you would have averted your gaze as any modest maid would have."

It was true, and Marisa knew it. She turned her head away, giving him a view of her enchanting profile, her wet hair streaming back from the small face. Tears of mortification stung her eyelids and tightened her throat. *Eh bien,* she thought angrily, *I will sit here until I shrivel up like a dried apple rather than strut around before him!*

Then he was standing beside the tub, a length of toweling held out to her like a peace offering, his head turned aside. "Come out, Marisa. I promise not to peek."

His cajoling tone and eyelids squeezed tightly shut in exaggerated earnestness made her feel foolish in raising any further objections. With her arms crossed over her breasts, she stood up with her back to him, feeling completely at his mercy. Immediately the towel was wrapped around her and she was lifted from the tub, feeling for the second time since she'd met him the security of his embrace.

All too soon he set her on her feet on a pelt that had been laid out for that purpose, and, taking her by the shoulders, turned her around to face him. "I want to thank you for saving my son's life, Marisa."

Her eyes widened at his words of gratitude. He'd said nothing until now about yesterday's incident at the pond. "I've been silent until this moment—well, at first because I was too proud to admit that in all probability I could not have prevented the horse from maiming Griffith. And I had convinced myself that Morgan could have accomplished what I might have failed to do." His eyes looked like multifaceted gems, gleaming amber-gold in the light of the tapers. "And then the poisoning of the dog. In the confusion and concern for Rollo, I refrained from mentioning the incident with Goliath until now."

He stepped back from her and turned away, allowing her to dry herself off and slip into her nightgown in privacy.

"What I also wish to tell you is that on the morrow I would like to take you through Camwright and introduce you to each family."

Marisa turned and nodded in acknowledgment. "You are welcome, Brand Ericson, for what I did for Griffith. And I am willing—nay, eager—to get to know the people of Camwright."

He seemed to let out a soft exhalation of pent-up breath, as if in relief at her words. Did he think she had no intention of even attempting to do what was expected of her? The thought stung her to the quick and brought retaliatory words of warning to her lips. "But I cannot open my heart to your people as long as mine remains filled with sorrow because of what was done to an animal innocent of all human injustices and crimes. Be warned, husband, that 'twill be doubly difficult for me to accept your villagers until I discover who was responsible for the deed.''

Brand understood somewhat how she felt, in light of his own love for animals and his abhorrence of such crude, underhanded methods of revenge. But he had no proof that Angharad was, indeed, responsible. And if she were, how would that revelation affect the proud Marisa?

He revealed nothing of his thoughts, saying only, ''You can know nothing of true sorrow, Marisa, until you are of a conquered people.''

Marisa soon discovered the truth of his words—words she had thought uttered only to imply how small would have been her loss had Rollo perished.

They'd left the bower and proceeded through the stockade gates into the village. As they walked along, Marisa saw that many of the people of Camwright wore expressions of stoically borne pain that she had not noticed before—or had not wished to notice. There were widows who had lost their husbands either at Stamford Bridge, Harold Godwinson's glorious victory over the Danes only days before Hastings, or in that last titanic battle itself. A few of the surviving men were missing an arm or a leg, or were disfigured in other, equally hideous, ways.

Despite the bravado Marisa displayed outwardly, she was sickened inside at what she saw, and moved by the suffering on her husband's features when he thought himself unobserved. He took each individual's burden of grief upon himself as their lord, and Marisa knew a burgeoning admiration for this man who loved and cared for his people so deeply and unselfishly.

One couple, Rolfe and Edgiva, exhibited a strange combination of acceptance and resentment toward Marisa. The husband had heard about the courageous deed that had saved Griffith's life, and with awkward sincerity said to her, ''We are grateful, my lady, for what you did for our young lord.''

But as they left the tiny cottage, Marisa heard Edgiva admonish her husband. ''Fool! Do you not know how your cronies embellish their tales until they bear little resemblance to the truth? My lord would have brought the animal under control, and Morgan ap Dafydd was right there to . . .''

The rest of her words faded away as Marisa and Brand moved on, but Marisa could tell from the almost imperceptible pause in her husband's steps, the swift, slight arching of the dark eyebrows in surprise, that he, too, had heard the woman's words. A dark look crossed the features Marisa was beginning to look upon with new interest, in spite of the scar. He glanced her way once, but she pretended she'd not heard the remark.

"I find Rolfe to be a fair man, willing to give me a chance, mayhap," she said. And then her pride came to the fore at the memory of Edgiva's vehement verbal misgivings, and the words were out before she could bite them back. "And at least I know *he* would not be so devious as to strike at me through Rollo."

Brand's expression became more and more grim as they made the rounds of the village. Marisa assumed it was because of something she had done—perhaps the comment she'd made concerning Rolfe. Or perhaps it was the thought that no one would accept Marisa if they all thought as Rolfe's wife did. *He is discovering they are not to be so easily won over,* she thought. *And it cannot please him to know that I will not fully grant my acceptance of them until I know for certain who harbors such a black and vengeful heart.*

Brand, however, was concerned because he suspected someone had poisoned many of his people's minds against her, twisting the story of what had happened with Goliath until it sounded more like Angharad's version. One more reason to get his hands on her scrawny neck. The men, who'd no doubt got the story from Morgan, were being swayed by their wives. The women, in turn, who understandably harbored a natural dislike for a Norman woman, were evidently distorting the facts and adding to the imagined list of Marisa's transgressions.

The last spread of land was larger than most of the others and the home standing upon it was a small hall with several tiny outbuildings. It was almost a miniature replica of Brand's great hall and a few of the assorted structures around it. Brand explained to Marisa that this was the home of Leofric the Blacksmith, a villein who was a step above the ordinary cottar or peasant, with a score or so of acres of his own to farm in addition to his work as a blacksmith. "But Leofric has several older sons by his first wife to help him with the workload," he added.

A dark-haired little girl about Griffith's age ran into a small building that Marisa assumed was the forge.

Leofric emerged shortly, his minuscule daughter pattering behind him. Huge, naked to the waist, and perspiring heavily from the heat of his forge, the man smiled broadly when he saw Brand and Marisa. He was obviously Saxon, for his hair was pale yellow and curled around his great head in a wild abundance. "Welcome, my lord," he greeted, and Brand presented Marisa to him.

There were several children playing about the yard, and their comely, midnight-haired mother, whom Brand introduced as Nesta, was obviously Welsh. She wore a plain light wool gown belted at the waist with a knotted piece of leather. Her dark, glossy hair was unbound and she was barefooted, like her children. She smiled shyly at Marisa, the first woman to have done so aside from Edyth, and Marisa returned the unexpected smile.

"Tell me, Leofric," Brand began, then lowered his voice as they turned back toward the forge. Nesta, leaving the men to their business, invited Marisa into the hall for a cup of mead. As Marisa followed the woman into the dark coolness of the building, she remembered hearing somewhere, long ago, that in Celtic legend, Irish women were always beautiful and courageous warrior queens, whereas in the land of the Scots, the heroines of legend were lovely and mightily proud. And the Welsh—what had she been told? The Welsh women besung by the bards had to be pretty and delicately tender. Yes, that was it, and from what Marisa could tell thus far, Nesta was the epitome of delicateness and sweetness. As the diminutive, raven-haired beauty handed her a cup of drink, Marisa wondered if she had been good friends with her country-woman and former lady of the manor, Rhiannon. Against her will, unreasonable jealousy gripped her in its green claws, until she felt her lips grow stiff from the effort to smile. At first she heard little of what Nesta said to her as she tried to engage Marisa in small talk.

"Come sit, Lady Marisa. You must be tired from your trek through Camwright." She smiled tentatively. "Your silver hair is something to behold. I have never seen the like. Leofric did not exaggerate when he spoke of it the night you arrived."

Touched by Nesta's shy attempts to put her at ease, by her obvious willingness to accept a Norman woman as lady of the manor, Marisa forced herself to respond to the gentle hospitality.

"You are very kind, Nesta, and I appreciate your acceptance."

Nesta smiled again. "I was friend to Rhiannon, my lady, and I hope to be yours. You are very lovely and—I understand—brave, as well."

Marisa lowered her gaze from that of the dark-haired young woman in the face of such frank praise. " 'Twas not so much a matter of my courage, Nesta, as knowing the French command to control the stallion."

Marisa soon found herself warming to Nesta's friendliness. Any kind of friend was, indeed, welcome.

As they left Leofric and Nesta, she told Brand conversationally, "Nesta was very courteous to me and, I might add, sympathetic over the attempt on Rollo's life."

He looked at her askance, his mouth twisting. "Nesta suffered no losses in the recent battles, nor has she lost any children in childbirth. You can hardly expect to gain sympathy elsewhere for the poisoning of a favorite hound when others still mourn husbands and sons lost because of their enemy's thirst for power and possessions. Surely you have been unbelievably sheltered and pampered, Marisa, to expect my people to commiserate over Rollo when many of them have lost so much more."

Stunned into momentary silence as they continued their walk through the bustling village, Marisa reluctantly admitted to herself that he spoke the truth. Yet she also felt she was doomed to spend the rest of her life in Camwright with only Rollo and Adela to care about her.

Still, her resentment flared. "Nesta was lovely to me, my lord," she observed sweetly. "I wonder that, since you obviously have a penchant for Welsh woman, you did not wed her in the wake of your loss."

Under ordinary circumstances, Marisa would never have even thought of saying such a thing, let alone utter it, but ever since the day Geoffrey de Brionne had announced her impending marriage, her world had been turned upside down, her emotions right along with it. With each passing day, things seemed only to worsen. And Brand had implied that her concern over Rollo was frivolous when compared with the sufferings of the people around her. He'd all but said she was unfeeling. Marisa knew she was *not* unfeeling, but perhaps, she silently acknowledged, she *was* frivolous.

Brand stopped dead in his tracks to face her, heedless of the activity in the village around them. "I had planned not to wed again at all, but I began to see that Edyth needed children and a husband of her own, that it was unfair to expect her to mother Griffith when Morgan ap Dafydd loved and wanted her. I never set my sights on Nesta because she was already Leofric's." His eyes were more brown than gold now, as when he kept his anger tightly leashed. "And," he added with emphasis, "I never had a *penchant* for Welsh women. Light-haired, blue-eyed Saxon women interest me equally . . . although I must admit to never having considered a Viking woman."

He turned and continued walking, his strides so long now—as if he could not wait to return to the manor and part company—that Marisa had to run to keep up with him. Not to be outdone, she managed breathlessly, "I was not fishing for a compliment, if that is what you think, Saxon! You told me in very neat terms just why you wed me. But remember the next time you choose to put down

Viking women, that your beloved Harold Godwinson was half Viking himself.''

The horn for the nooning was sounded, and Marisa flounced away as they neared the hall, feeling his eyes boring into her back. She was anxious to see Rollo and not very hungry. Her chest felt tight every time she took a deep breath, and she attributed it to her anger with Brand.

Upon reaching the bower, she flung open the door and was almost completely bowled over by Rollo. Delirious with joy at seeing her after being confined for the morning, the dog raised up onto his back haunches and plopped his great paws upon her shoulders. Marisa staggered backward under the impact. Back in France her brother Eustace had countered such behavior by extending his leg until he could step on the hound's back paw. Rollo would yelp in pain and immediately drop down on all fours. Marisa had thought Rollo's bad habit had been broken, but apparently not.

"Down, you horse!" she croaked, strangely out of breath. After a careless swipe of his wet tongue up the side of one smooth cheek, Rollo obeyed. With a sigh of relief—for Marisa could not reach his back paws to tread upon them—she patted his shaggy head. "Good boy." She held the door open and let him out into the cool early afternoon air. As he happily bounded off, Marisa decided that she could not keep him at her side or under constant lock and key. She watched him romp around the yard, sniffing everything in his path, and decided she would just have to hope and pray that nothing happened to him again.

A dry cough shook her chest with the next deep breath, and she felt suddenly exhausted from the events of the previous two days. She automatically turned to the great bed where Brand slept alone, not realizing what she was doing until she was almost upon it. It did look inviting, and her previous resentment of the memories Brand might still treasure of his nights with Rhiannon seemed rather childish and unimportant to her now. Yet he was still Robert's killer, was he not? How could she ever bring herself to sleep in the same bed with Brand Ericson in light of that fact?

Marisa hauled out the makings for her separate bed on the cold stone floor and decided to sleep for a while rather than eat.

The door opened without preamble, and Brand strained to see into the dim bower. None of the candles had been lit and the braziers were cold. "Marisa?"

Only silence greeted his ears, and he stepped farther into the room before noticing the small form huddled on the floor. He closed the wooden panel quietly and lit several tapers. Taking one in his hand, he bent down to look at his wife and was appalled at the pallor of her face, the bluish circles under her eyes. Of course, she had been up most of the night they arrived at Camwright and then the next with Rollo. Last night was the first good night's sleep she'd had since her arrival. And even of that he could not be certain.

"Stubborn wench," he mumbled as he thought of her obdurate refusal to sleep in the bed. The floor was cold and, from what he knew of Normandy, the climate was milder there. It was milder in most of England, compared to the mountainous region around Wales. She would catch her death if she persisted in losing sleep, not eating, and remaining on the floor in the still-brisk nights. He made to rise, but then something prompted him to stoop down again and put the back of his hand to her forehead. Her skin was alarmingly warm.

That decided matters immediately. Brand replaced the candle beside the bed and pulled back the embroidered coverlet. Carefully removing Marisa from her nest of warm pelts and blankets, he placed her upon the great bed, fearing to wake her and suffer the consequences of his actions. But he needn't have worried. As he tucked the covers around the sleeping girl, she remained dead to the world.

Loading wood into the two braziers and lighting them, Brand soon chased away the chill within the room and went to fetch Edyth. It was then that Rollo pushed open the unlatched door with his nose and searched for his mistress. His keen scent led him almost immediately to the bed, and he rested his head beside her shoulder with a forlorn sigh that became a whimper when the sigh failed to gain Marisa's attention. She stirred and he whined again, louder this time.

She opened heavy eyelids to meet the liquid-brown gaze of the devoted wolfhound. With a smile that seemed to take much effort, she whispered, "Are you hungry, boy?"

His ears perked up.

"Then I will get you something to eat." But her limbs felt leaden, and her chest ached with every breath she drew.

Puzzled, she remained still for a moment, essaying to get her bearings. Then she noticed she was not in her makeshift pallet on the floor, but rather in the *bed*. Extremely annoyed at the thought that someone—undoubtedly Brand—had transferred her here, the last place in the world she wanted to be, Marisa marshaled her strength and flung back the covers. She slid her legs over the side and let them dangle above the floor. It suddenly seemed a long way down. . . .

"Just what do you think you are doing?"

Brand's voice appeared to come at her from far away, and with an effort she raised her head toward the door to meet his gaze. "Someone . . . someone must see to Rollo's food, and besides, I made it clear I would not sleep . . . in this bed. Not under any circumstances."

Edyth and Adela came into the room behind Brand with trays laden with ewers and cloths and medicines.

"The dog has been fed—by me," he added at her look of feeble protest. "Now get back under the covers." He lifted her legs—noting against his will the smooth, shapely calves and daintily turned ankles—and slid them over until she was positioned as before.

The two spots of color that had appeared on her cheeks as if someone had painted them there, deepened in hue in a reaction that had nothing to do with fever. Marisa opened her mouth to retort, but Edyth held a cup to her lips before any sound could emerge, saying, "Drink."

Obediently Marisa drank a warm potion that tasted amazingly like the concoction used in Normandy to loosen up the tightness in the chest—honey and wine and something slightly tart. But she had not given in yet. "I will not sleep here," she murmured.

Brand ignored her as he moved aside to allow Adela to help Edyth undress her and apply a steaming poultice to her chest, then cover her again. Adela moved away and Edyth remained for a moment, smoothing back the errant wisps of curling silver hair that had escaped her braids. "Sleep, Marisa. That is what you need most right now."

Then Brand was before her. "Get—me—out—of—your—bed!" she whispered with what might have passed for a weak attempt at vehemence.

A callused hand touched her cheek and felt the heat radiating from it. To cover his concern, he chided, "Why, Marisa? I am not in it now."

She turned away from him. *You murdered Robert and stole his horse! I cannot betray him.*

"You are my wife, now, Viking firebrand." The softly teasing words were a caress. "And there are no memories of passion spent upon this mattress, if that is what you think. Do you believe me so heartless as to do that to you? The mattress was changed before you ever arrived in Camwright."

But Marisa did not hear his words, for she had fallen into a fitful slumber.

Chapter 7

Marisa felt the constricting bands across her chest eventually ease until it hurt only when she obeyed the overwhelming urge to cough. She fought her way upward from the dark, soothing depths of sleep, as one endeavors to swim to the top of a deep well, only to find that the racking cough hurt her tender throat and chest even more in consciousness. Heavy eyelids opened with an effort, and Marisa was suddenly aware of the thick, humid atmosphere of the bower.

Her questioning gaze met that of the man standing over her, concern darkening his features. She noted irrelevantly that a shock of chestnut hair, gleaming softly with golden highlights in the firelight, fell over his brow. *Such a noble brow,* came the unexpected thought. *Even the scar cannot truly detract from such extraordinary features.* . . .

"Marisa?"

"*Oui?*" The word was a thread of sound.

"How do you feel?"

She shook her mind free of the sleep-induced euphoria, remembering the events of the day before. She tried to sit up, her face mirroring her increasingly lucid thoughts, and Brand hastened to prop her up.

"Thank you," she said quietly, although the thoughtful expression of her slightly narrowed eyes told Brand she was fast overcoming her gratefulness.

It was almost as if they were an average husband and

wife with their calm exchange of niceties, Brand thought as he watched the changing expressions play across her face. *And now she will return to her stubborn, willful self, and all will be as before.*

"Where are Edyth and Adela?"

"I sent them to their beds when your fever broke in the night."

Marisa's eyes widened at this. "Then you—*you* tended me?"

A corner of his mouth twitched at her expression of incredulity. "Aye. And I slept beside you when you were out of danger until shortly before you awakened. But you need not concern yourself, my lady wife, for I did not take advantage of you."

Vague images of the two women and Brand working over her flashed through her mind—Adela heating water until the steam in the room was enough to help loosen and ease the dry cough that lodged in her chest, and Edyth urging her to drink more of the palliative. Then the hazy memory of a warm body beside her brought a blush to her cheeks, and with it the first stirrings of ire at the fact that she had remained, despite her verbal demand to do otherwise, in his bed.

"Well, I thank you again, my lord, but now you may return me to *my* bed."

Any humor that had flickered in the fathomless depths of his eyes disappeared as if it had never been. "Do not act the spoiled child, Marisa. You were taken ill because of your stubborn refusal to sleep where you belong."

"That may very well be, but of a certainty I do not belong in this bed!"

He studied her exquisite features for long moments, noting the hectic color splashed across her cheeks, which reminded him of one of the village children—even Griffith—when about to throw a tantrum, and his lips compressed briefly before he spoke. "You are so caught up in your own selfish whims and fancies, your imagined insults from others, you *tragic* near losses, that you cannot stop to think that things are not always as they appear.''

A cough spasmed through her without warning, and Brand began to regret his harsh words as she grimaced in pain. But she recovered quickly enough to reply with mounting anger, '' 'Tis an imagined insult, then, that you have placed me here—''

He cut her off abruptly with a sharp, negative slash of his right palm through the air, suddenly having had enough of her repeated, childish protestations. ''You obviously did not hear me last eve when I told you about the mattress upon which you lie. The bedding you so vehemently and continually attack as if it were a living thing is not that which I shared with Rhiannon.''

Her mouth had opened to retort when his words finally registered. Her lips silently formed an astonished O.

''I assure you I am no unfeeling ogre, that even we 'Saxon rabble' know something of social amenities. As I said last night, the mattress was changed before you ever arrived at Camwright.''

Recovering her surprise at his thoughtful gesture, Marisa at last got to the heart of the matter. ''There is a much more important reason, Saxon, that I do not wish to share your bed—this or any other.''

He regarded her with obvious skepticism.

''Goliath was raised and trained by my father. He was sold to a . . . a family friend, Robert de Lisieux. By virtue of the fact that you are in possession of Goiliath, I can only assume you killed Robert and stole his destrier.'' She drew in a sustaining breath, determined to get it all out into the open. ''I will not sleep with a murderer.''

If Brand was surprised by her revelation, she could not tell. His face remained expressionless. ''I do not ask a man his name or position when I face him on a battlefield. One either kills or is killed. Therefore, no man who engages in battle can be called a murderer.'' His mouth tightened and his eyes darkened as if in remembered pain. ''I do not know if I killed him. Perhaps I should have let

the man kill me instead, Marisa. Perhaps I should not
consider that he—or possibly one of the men in your family—may have been responsible for the deaths of my
brothers.'' He turned away and moved toward the door.
''I will see that something is brought for you to eat.'' He
disappeared into the yard, leaving Marisa to think about
what he'd said.

Adela brought Marisa a tray of hot broth, fine white
manchet bread, which did not tend to sour or molder as
coarser breads did, and mulled wine. Edyth also looked
in on her. Both women were satisfied with her appetite
and her diminished fever, and removed the boiling cal-
drons of water that had turned the bower into a steam-
bath.

Left alone to rest, Marisa began to feel the beginnings
of guilt at her behavior over what she had assumed was
Brand's lack of consideration. Grim and stern though he
could be, he had not—since she'd met him—shown himself to be thoughtless in his treatment of others. Not even
Rollo, she reflected, when she pictured him allowing the
animal to be carried behind her from London. More important, however, was the fact that she had called him a
murderer. She knew what he said was right, but that did
not make it easier to accept the fact that Robert was
dead—and possibly by his hand.

But what of his own losses? asked a small inner voice.
What about his brothers? In that moment Marisa pictured the anguish that had darkened his eyes and knew
herself to be many of the things he had named her. Yet
how humiliating it would be to apologize to him . . . not
only for what she'd called him, but also for her childish
behavior because of her jealousy of a dead woman.

Marisa closed her eyes in weary defeat. That would be
all but admitting that his feelings for his former wife
mattered to her, and the thought itself was unacceptable
to her. It would mean that she cared enough to let any
feelings he might still have for Rhiannon stand between
them, and that was far from the truth. Or was it?

A black nose planted itself smack in the middle of her

tray, almost sending it clattering to the floor, and roused her from her ruminations. "Rollo," she greeted softly, and stroked the shaggy head as the hound began to make short work of the bits of food that remained. "Where have you been, my wandering Viking chieftain, eh?"

His tail whipped back and forth in acknowledgment, and as Marisa noted his renewed vitality with a smile of contentment, she heard the door creak. She glanced up, half expecting to see Adela or Edyth, but curious dark eyes in a small face met her gaze.

"Griffith?" she asked tentatively, fearing to frighten him away. She had not seen him since the morning before—and he'd still not spoken to her since her arrival. But he remained unmoving . . . and silent.

"Were you playing with Rollo?"

The barest of nods of the little head.

"Please come in, then, and—and would you take this tray away before Rollo gobbles it up altogether?"

The child hesitantly entered the bower, and Rollo turned to see who the newcomer was. Instantly the dog whimpered in greeting, and Marisa could see he was torn between his insatiable appetite and his affection for his new friend. Griffith's face lit up with a smile of pleasure at the dog's attention.

"Please rescue this tray, Griffith," Marisa pleaded, and the boy obediently came toward the bed and snatched the tray off her lap, to Rollo's disappointment. *"Merci,"* she said, switching to French.

He nodded and after removing the cup and bowl from it, upended the empty tray against the wall and turned back to her. It was in that moment that Marisa realized how very much he resembled Brand. Although his hair was ebony and his eyes as dark as Morgan's, his features—the actual structure of his face—were an exact replica of his father's. However, Marisa was by no means an expert on children, and although the Welsh were smaller in stature than the Anglo-Saxons, she could not determine if Brand's son would be as tall as he was.

Aware that she was staring at the boy, she cast about

for some way of getting him to stay awhile. And to speak.
Rollo went over to nudge Griffith's hand, and Marisa had
to smile at how tiny the hand was in comparison to the
wolfhound's massive head. "I would wager you a . . . a
story about the Viking chieftain for whom Rollo was
named that you cannot say 'Marisa,' " she wheedled.

A frown puckered the child's brow, but he said nothing.

"Your father told me you speak some French—and
Welsh, as well. But mayhap the name Marisa is too difficult for you to say."

Again the barest hint of a negative shake of his head.

Marisa thoughtfully tapped her pursed lips with a finger. "Well then, let me hear you say it. Marisa. *Mah-
ree-zah.*"

"Marisa," he murmured in perfect imitation. *"Mah-
ree-zah."* He popped his finger into his mouth and silently contemplated her.

"Magnifique!" she exclaimed in admiration. "You *can*
say it!"

He suddenly moved toward the bed, the expectation
she'd hoped to see in his eyes glowing in unspoken invitation. "Rollo's name. Please, tell me the story."

Marisa turned her head to cough and then get her
breath. When she turned back toward Griffith, she felt
strangely touched at the concern on the minuscule features. "Here." She patted the bed beside her. As he sat
down gingerly at her feet, Marisa felt a vast relief wash
over her at his capitulation. The fact that she felt suddenly very safe and secure upon Brand's bed, now that
he'd exorcised the demons that had plagued her on that
account, added to her sense of well-being.

"Many years ago," she began, "one of the fiercest of
the Viking chieftains landed to raid the coasts of France."
Here she paused and made a comically frightening face.
"The king of the Franks, Charles the Simple, made a
pact with this much feared Viking in an effort to spare
his people death and devastation."

Griffith's eyes widened in growing interest and he

inched closer. "Well," she continued in increasing animation—even Rollo's ears perked up, the discarded tray temporarily forgotten—"Rollo, the pagan chief, promised to wed Charles's daughter, to receive baptism, and to do homage to the king in return for part of what is now Normandy."

"And he is the dog's namesake?"

"Indeed, he is. But the best part is yet to come," she teased with a twinkle in her eye.

"Aye? Tell me, my lady, *s'il vous plaît.*"

That sweet little voice, accented with a mixture of English and Welsh and a French word thrown in now and again out of courtesy, melted Marisa's already softening heart like the wax of a hot-flamed candle. "Well, of course, Rollo also had to vow to keep the peace in his newly granted fief and protect it from France's enemies."

Griffith nodded eagerly, anxious for the rest of the tale.

"As the legend goes, when the proud Rollo was commanded to kiss the royal foot in the act of homage, he drew back in anger, refusing to debase himself."

Marisa paused for effect and Griffith's hand reached out to touch her knee beneath the covers. "Well, then how did they ever seal the pact?"

Laughter danced in Marisa's eyes. "Rollo chose one of his men to perform the deed, and the unhappy warrior seized the king's foot, jerking it up to his mouth and laying Charles flat upon his back!"

The rapt expression on Griffith's face changed into one of pure delight, and childish laughter rang through the room like the tinkling of bells.

"Already a Norman had unseated a king."

Brand's words ripped through the laughter like a razor-tipped lance through parchment. Although Griffith's laughter faded into silence at the sound of his father's voice, only Marisa heard exactly what he said. The amusement died from her eyes, the beautiful smile freezing before it disappeared at the sight of Brand standing in the partially open doorway.

"Father, Marisa told me how Rollo was named—after a Viking chieftain."

Brand smiled at his son and stepped into the room, his gaze moving from the little boy to the suddenly silent Marisa, then back again to his son. "I think you had better let Marisa rest and get well, Griffith, else she will never get better and be able to tell you more tales of the Normans." His slight emphasis on the word *Normans* made it sound to Marisa like something distasteful on his tongue.

Griffith sighed in disappointment, retreating into shyness once more, the light in his eyes extinguishing like a doused hearth fire.

Marisa unexpectedly took pity on the child and offered, "I will tell you more stories, *cher,* another time. Would you like that?"

His solemn little face turned hopefully to her. "Would you, my lady?"

"Only if you call me Marisa."

He slid off the bed and went over to Brand. "Father, is the lady . . . is Marisa my new mother?"

Innocent, spontaneous—the question suddenly hung in the charged air as Marisa unconsciously held her breath and watched Brand's expression with a mixture of curiosity and dread. He tousled his son's dark hair, but he was watching Marisa, his expression inscrutable. "Would you like that, Griffith?"

Startled by his unexpected reply, Marisa felt her mouth fall open with the rush of emotion that sifted through her in the few moments before the boy answered, "Aye."

"Then you had better ask the lady Marisa, for the final decision is hers."

Stunned even further at his having placed the burden upon her shoulders—almost as if he were testing her—Marisa forced herself to answer, "I would never dream of taking your mother's place in your—or your father's—affections, Griffith, but I would be honored to be your 'new' mother."

There! Her eyes challenged the gaze clashing with hers

from across the few feet that separated them. Make what you will of that! Then a fit of coughing seized her and she turned her head aside, mentally cursing the unfairness of having to spar verbally with Brand Ericson when she was at such a distinct disadvantage.

When she had recovered, Griffith was gone and Rollo with him. "If you said what you did only to momentarily placate the boy, then I would warn you that you will only hurt him deeply by your seeming acceptance."

Her eyes flashed at his implication. "I would never do that to a child!"

He strode to the bed and stared down at her, his gaze holding hers unflinchingly. "You've acted in equally thoughtless ways where a beloved pet was concerned."

Marisa had the almost uncontrollable urge to slap his arrogant face at the insult. "Do you think I would not place more importance on a child?"

"Would you? Especially if that child was not yours?"

She drew as deep a breath as she dared without triggering her bothersome cough. "You give me credit for naught! Or"—a sudden thought struck her—"is it that you are afraid to let me come too close to you *or* Griffith? Win his affection and yours as well? Then, of course, you would be untrue to Rhiannon's memory."

Something flickered in his eyes, something so fleeting it might never have been. "I do not want the boy hurt. He still pines for his mother. He needs a woman's love. But it must be sincere, and not just some cruel way to get back at the imagined insults of his father." In a flat, emotionless voice, he added, "And you need not be concerned about winning my affection."

"You are vile! I do not consider an unconsummated marriage an imagined insult. Nor a host of other words and deeds you have said and done to me. Why do you not just send me back to my father, Saxon? Oh, I had almost forgotten: you would lose your precious holdings for Griffith. Well, mayhap I will just hie myself off to London one night while you sleep, and let you suffer the consequences!"

He sat down beside her, a hand on either side of her, pinning her wrists at her sides. His face was inches from hers, and Marisa's heart plunged through her chest from a feeling very different from anger. "So it bothers you that I have not made you mine in the physical sense, does it, my Norman bride? Do you not remember your martyrlike words the night of our marriage? 'Do what you will,' you said as you shrank away from my face."

"I—I was not prepared for your scars," she began, a strange curling heat spiraling through her midsection and radiating outward until her entire body felt fevered from his nearness.

"Ah," he replied with exaggerated patience. "How do you think I saved your father from the fire? I am very human, be assured of that, Marisa. I am as prone to pain and injury as the next man. Surely you must have suspected that I had sustained burns from the deed?"

"I did not suspect aught," she mumbled, trying unsuccessfully to pull free of his grasp.

He transferred both wrists to one callused, long-fingered hand and reached up with the other to trace the line of her slender neck, the sweet slope of her jaw, the shell-like ear peaking out from beneath her unbound, riotously curling hair. "I suppose you thought of little else beside the fact that you were to wed one of the Anglo-Saxon rabble, Marisa. And when you could have had your pick of the young Norman knights and barons all about you."

Suddenly at a loss for words because of the magic his hand was weaving over her senses, Marisa could only stare silently into the golden-brown eyes, impaled by the strange light in their depths, which she was still too innocent to recognize as desire.

"You will not leave Camwright, Marisa, for when you are well, I will teach you what goes on between a man and his wife in the marriage bed." He ran the tip of one finger over the petal-soft lips, noting their trembling. "You will become a very 'willing' wife in every sense of the word, for I suspect there lies a very sensual woman behind the childish, petulant facade to which you retreat when threatened.''

"If I do not leave Camwright, 'twill be because I choose not to, and not because of your imagined hold over me in any physical sense,'' she protested unconvincingly.

His answer was to place his lips upon hers—heated, moist, and infinitely gentle as they teased the corners of her mouth, his tongue tracing the line where they trembled open like a newly budding flower. When he invaded her mouth and their tongues met, Marisa felt her body arch toward him in response, and a shudder rippled through her as his hand dropped to cup her breast for a few glorious moments. He released her other wrist to unlace the ribbons at her throat. He stroked the satiny smoothness of her chest immediately above the valley of her breasts and was startled by her sharp intake of breath as his fingers wandered upward and encountered the small burn just below her clavicle. "Forgive me, sweet,'' he murmured, and, lowering his head from her mouth, laved a gentle circle around the small pink wound with his tongue.

"You . . . you will contract the illness.''

He raised his head and laughed softly. A rarity, Marisa mused, and noted through the gauzelike haze of her growing passion how insignificant his facial scar actually was in the presence of the smile that softened his features. "I am willing, sweet Marisa, to take the chance. After all, *I* had enough sense to sleep upon this nice, warm bed. . . .''

She drew an unsteady breath and Brand heard the faint rattle in her chest. He drew back, feeling guilt and regret at what he was doing to her while she was not yet recovered, at having come this far and finding immense pleasure with her—he, who had at first wished merely to taunt—only to be conscience-bound to end it.

As Marisa discreetly covered her mouth with a small square of cloth and turned aside to cough, the man beside her studied her delicate profile with slow deliberation.

The finely formed features of purest ivory were as perfect as a master sculptor could have wrought, with just the right touch of color on her lips and cheeks to add interest and save the face from paling into insignificance within the silvery halo of hair.

When Marisa turned her gaze to his at last, Brand drank in the lovely eyes still glowing with passion, and suddenly cursed himself inwardly for being a fool—a stupid, witless fool. He had set out to punish her for telling Griffith of things Norman instead of English, and perhaps demonstrating in the process what she was missing by having shown such reluctance to come to him in the physical sense.

"God's blood," he swore softly. He had only managed to fuel the fires of his own long denied passions, to ease one step further into the treacherous web of her womanly beauty and allure. Disgusted with his body's reaction to this foreign beauty to whom he was shackled, Brand hardened his voice. "You need rest, my lady wife, not lovemaking." He stood swiftly, turning away from the bemused Marisa to hide the telltale evidence of his own passion, and strode from the bower.

The ground had softened from the gentle spring rains. As Brand made his rounds of the communal fields, he was well-satisfied with the completed ploughing and planting. Oats, peas, beans, and barley would soon send their tender green shoots skyward, and the individual yield of each villager's garden would add leeks, beets, and cabbage to the vegetables from the fields. The livestock had been put out to pasture and the villagers' workloads would be considerably lighter until after Easter, less than a sennight away, and the May Day festival.

Astride his pony, Brand found his thoughts invaded more and more frequently by blue-violet eyes and the most tempting mouth God had ever fashioned to test a mortal man. He must not allow her to enter his thoughts so easily, for that meant he was affected by her, and he could not have that . . . would not allow himself any semblance of happiness.

He shook his head to clear it of such nonsense. Despite the fact that he would be forced to sleep beside Marisa now—and he felt an increasingly familiar tightening in his loins at the thought of his promise to her—he could only enjoy the physical pleasures. If she acted like a mother to Griffith, so much the better, but she would never come to mean what a wife should mean to a man in the emotional sense. . . . He would never allow it.

Their marriage had been purely political in nature—as were most marriages of the nobility. If Marisa could be a mother to his son, and see to his own needs as a man, as well, then he would count himself most fortunate. That it was not a union of love, as his and Rhiannon's had been, did not matter. He frowned at the thought of his lost wife, although for some reason the guilt and pain that alway accompanied memories of her was not as lacerating this time. . . .

"You're mashing the bean furrows."

Brand looked up, startled—not so much by Morgan's voice as by the fact that he'd managed to approach him unobserved.

"Obviously you have more, ah, interesting things on your mind, my friend, but I also remember a time when this"—he gestured to the newly sown fields around them—"would not have kept you content, when you were eager to do Harold's bidding."

"Indeed, Morgan. That was before the Normans came and I was the King's thane. Now I believe my usefulness lies in my position here at Camwright, in keeping Griffith's heritage secure." He was thoughtfully silent for a moment. "The night of our marriage, my wife implied that I hid here during the great battle, where it was safe." He smiled humorlessly. "Mayhap now I do the very thing of which she accused me but under the guise of protecting my son's birthright."

"Marisa does not know you well enough yet—nor what you did for England."

Brand turned troubled eyes upon his friend. "And it will remain thusly, do you hear, Morgan?" He looked away. "You cannot imagine what hearing about my role at Malfosse would do to an already tense situation. She would hate me all the more, and while she cannot ever have my love—a fit payment for my sins against Rhiannon—perhaps we can learn at least to tolerate each other."

"Then she will wither away to a shadow of herself."

Brand's head snapped around, his dark brows drawn together in a bemused frown. "Wither away?" Within seconds of that spontaneous reaction, his features relaxed. "Once again I have not taken into account your expertise with wenches. By all means, Morgan ap Dafydd, you must tell me how to avoid such a dire ending for Marisa."

Morgan ignored the words weighted with sarcasm. "Do you not feel guilty enough because you failed to love Rhiannon as you felt was her due because of what you chose to take on as your very personal burden? You feel you killed Rhiannon by getting her with child, but I tell you, in all truth you will certainly destroy Marisa. Can you handle the death of two wives by your hand?"

A slow flush crept up Brand's neck and into his cheeks. "You dare much, Morgan, when you delve so deeply into my personal affairs."

"Oh, the death will come about in a totally different manner, but it will come about all the same. You will kill her spirit, and that will truly be a tragedy."

Morgan turned his mount's head back toward Camwright and Brand followed suit. In an effort to get a grip on himself, he breathed deeply of the earthy smell of the damp, freshly turned furrows, for he recognized a glimmer of truth in Morgan's words. "That is absurd. Marisa is the most stubborn, high-sprited female I have ever had the misfortune to meet. Nothing could kill *that* spirit, I assure you."

Morgan lifted a corner of his mouth in a half smile. "Ah, but there you are wrong, Brand Ericson. Marisa is so different from Rhiannon, and you are so caught up in your own guilt and misdirected loyalty, you cannot see what is before your eyes.''

Brand kicked his pony into a brisk trot. ''I have better things to do than listen to your bold—and invalid—criticisms.''

''Give her a chance,'' Morgan said, before he started to drop back, deciding not to pursue his friend too closely in his blackening mood. ''That high spirit needs nurturing, not neglect. She is young and still delights in life and its joys.''

''She is Norman!'' Brand couldn't help but throw over his shoulder as the distance between them widened. ''Why shouldn't she delight in a Norman victory? In being the daughter of a rich count of those very hordes? Why shouldn't she care only for that hulking hound when my people still suffer from real, irreparable losses?''

''This is Camwright, Brand, not Hastings!'' Morgan's voice faded slowly, but Brand heard his final delivery. ''Do not refuse to begin the healing process with the one person with whom you have agreed to spend the rest of your life. You need someone like her, not some meek, lifeless puppet of a woman. You deserve some happiness, some love. Reach out and take it before 'tis too late, or in the end you *will* lose all. . . .''

Chapter 8

Within a few days, Marisa was hale and hearty. She awoke early on Easter Sunday. As she was readying herself for the holiday mass with Adela's help, Marisa unexpectedly asked her faithful servant, "Adela, am I willful and frivolous?"

The woman had been laying out the fine silk bliaut Marisa had worn on her wedding day. She paused a moment and inquired, "Do you want the truth, child?"

Marisa spun around at the blunt question, her arm dropping from brushing her hair, the brush precariously close to slipping from suddenly lax fingers. "Of course I want the truth! If what Brand accuses me of is true, then I would hear it from the lips of one of my own family."

Adela's face softened at the evidence of her mistress's love, and for a moment the wisdom of her years warred with her unshakable loyalty to Marisa, before wisdom won out. "You are young and carefree, *chère*, and while you are capable of running the keep at Brionne, things are different there. Here you are not among your beloved family—doting brothers and father. Your husband is a conquered man, as are his people—wounded spiritually as well as physically. My lord Brand is bitter and with good reason. He was wealthy and powerful in his own right until he stood to lose everything because of a battle waged and won by our people. He sacrificed much—or so he thinks—when he wed you, and you have a challenge

115

before you now.'' She took the brush from Marisa's lifeless fingers. ''Here, let me help you dress, and then I
will plait your hair.''

Her thoughts awhirl, Marisa obediently walked to the
bed and allowed Adela to slide the chainse and then the
bliaut over her head. ''But you did not say if I was willful, as well.'' Her voice was subdued.

Adela emitted the softest of sighs in her effort to choose
her words carefully. ''Willfulness is ofttimes mistaken
for mettle—for backbone. From the little I have been able
to discover about my lord's first wife, she was quite the
opposite—quiet, meek, and very malleable.''

Marisa bristled at the reminder of Rhiannon. ''*Eh bien*,
I am not Rhiannon, nor could I ever be even if I so desired.''

Deft hands gathered the bountiful tresses of palest ash
and began to weave plaits on the sides of Marisa's head,
leaving the back to fall free in the Welsh fashion. But the
girl was too caught up in her own chaotic thoughts to
take heed.

''Most men would love you just the way you are, Marisa, but you must remember that your husband is not
most men. The situation is different—and very difficult.''
She fastened the ends of the braids at Marisa's crown
with apricot ribbon that matched the silk gown's stitching, forming slender loops on either side of her head and
thus emphasizing the regal cheekbones now splashed with
high color, the determined chin, and pert nose. ''It would
not hurt to . . . well, to bow to his wishes in some
things.''

Stormy eyes met Adela's in the polished metal mirror
that hung on the bower wall before the stool upon which
she sat. ''I will not become a mouse!''

Adela shook her graying head slowly. ''You do not
have to, *chère*. Just think about it and perhaps you will
come to understand in time.''

Marisa was halfway to the hall in the bright April sunshine before she realized that the back of her hair was
unbound . . . more like a Welsh woman than the daugh-

ter of a Norman count. She paused, uncertain whether to
return to the bower and give Adela a tounge-lashing or
let it go. She suspected it was Adela's way of beginning
the quest to change Brand Ericson's opinion of her mistress, but Marisa was not at all convinced she wished it
changed.

With a toss of her head, she continued toward the
manor before she saw Brand standing in the great open
doorway, watching her. The color that had suffused her
cheeks in her irritation earlier returned as her eyes met
his. *What must he think?* she wondered angrily. *That I
am attempting to imitate the Cymry women—his precious
Rhiannon—with part of my hair hanging down my back
like some peasant?*

But his words put all thought to flight. "You are, indeed, lovely this morn, Marisa."

Caught between the need to tell him she had no intention of wearing her hair thusly again, and the urge to say
nothing in view of the way the blood was singing through
her body at the genuine warmth in his resonant voice,
Marisa blurted unthinkingly, " 'Twas Adela's doing, not
mine."

He ignored her gibe, taking her by the elbow and guiding her into the well-lighted interior of the hall to break
the fast. His eyes feasted upon the brilliance produced
by a hundred torches and tapers reflecting off her hair as
it cascaded past her shoulders. Unexpectedly reminded
of a shimmering rain shower on a spring day, he had the
strongest urge to reach out and touch the shining silver
spill. But he did nothing.

Marisa noted that, after that one complimentary remark, Brand was unusually silent during the meal. Afterward, he escorted her to the small church within the
sheltering palisade of the stronghold, and stood silently
beside her. She glanced over at him and was caught by
the gem-gold gaze that unexpectedly rested upon her fair
countenance. Flushing delicately, she turned away and
bowed her head.

She was unaware of how very much Brand was reminded of their wedding day—of his first glimpse of her in the beautiful peach bliaut that had flattered her natural coloring and whispered softly with every graceful step she'd taken toward him . . . of the fragrance of roses that had drifted up to his sensitive nostrils then—and now.

When she felt his gaze leave her face at last, Marisa covertly looked over the crowd in the cool, dim interior of the church, and her resentment over the attempted poisoning of Rollo began to be replaced by a determination to win over these Saxons. While still abed, she couldn't help but hear the villagers who came and went from the manor hall with their lambs or two pence due their thane for Easter, and she'd wryly noted that besides her few visitors—Nesta and Leofric, Morgan and Edyth—the only other resident of Camwright to inquire after her had been Edgiva's husband Rolfe. It seemed the few Welsh among them had accepted her—outwardly at least—more readily than the others.

What could she do to prove her good intentions? Her successful attempt to spare Griffith from being struck down by Goliath's vicious hooves had seemed only to add fuel to the fire of their resentment . . . which made little sense to Marisa.

Out in the beautiful, brisk April morning, she made polite conversation with a number of the villagers in halting but simple and sincere Anglo-Saxon. Aside from a few exceptions, her attempts were met with cool courtesy—out of deference for Brand, she suspected—but outwardly Marisa appeared unwavering in her efforts to act the part of lady of the manor. Several times she caught Brand's gaze upon her, an indecipherable look in his eyes, but she merely smiled at him as she did to all with whom she spoke, and turned away to continue on her crusade among the people of Camwright.

Griffith came to stand beside her, shyly inserting his small hand in hers, almost as if he sensed her need for support. She smiled down at him and had bent to whisper something in his ear when she saw a blur of motion out of the corner of her eye and heard a child cry out.

She swung around, relaxing her grip on Griffith's hand, in time to see Rollo standing over one of Edgiva's younger children, hackles up and a low growl issuing from deep within his throat. The child was flat on his back, howling at the top of his lungs, and as Marisa ran toward him, she heard Edgiva's oldest daughter sneer, " . . . that wicked wolf she keeps for a pet. He is trained to do evil, I tell you! He's attacked Alfred!''

Marisa reached Alfred first and saw a stick laying beside his outstretched hand. Instantly, even as she lifted the boy into her arms, she suspected that he'd struck—or tried to strike—the dog. Rollo would never have attacked without extreme provocation, and especially not a child.

''Hush, *mon cher*,'' she crooned softly to the hysterical Alfred, who, she suspected, was not so much hurt as he was shaken. She put one hand to the back of his head and pressed his face gently into her shoulder, heedless of the tears and saliva that were ruining her best bliaut. She felt the warm stickiness of blood beneath her fingers. *Dear God,* she thought, *he's struck his head.*

''Let me have my son!'' Edgiva exclaimed in her ear from out of nowhere. ''Hasn't your hound done enough damage?'' She all but yanked the child from Marisa's arms and stood glaring at her, accusation shining in her eyes. ''Did you train the war-horse to attack my lord Griffith, as well? And did you then interfere to try and insinuate yourself into our good graces?'' Her voice was low, for Marisa's ears only, and the shock of the acute dislike in her vituperative tone scalded Marisa to the quick.

Her eyes suddenly sparked with outrage at the grossly unfair accusation, but Brand's voice rang out over the murmuring assemblage as he strode up to them. ''How badly has the boy been hurt?''

Marisa opened her mouth to speak, but Edgiva was quicker. ''His skull was nearly cleaved in two, my lord!'' Alfred, hearing his mother's dire, exaggerated pronouncement, began to wail all the more loudly.

Brand carefully examined the child's head and then

looked at Rollo, who was now sitting quietly beside Marisa with Griffith's arms thrown protectively around his great neck. His eyes met Marisa's. She could read nothing in that bleak, shuttered look, but intuitively she knew he was assessing the situation, debating what to do with the dog . . . her dog.

He is only a beast.

Surely, despite anything she might have to say, Brand would end the life of any hound that would attack one of his people—and a child yet. She lifted her chin a notch higher, mustering every last bit of dignity she possessed. She would not beg before the people of Camwright.

"Did any of you see what happened?"

Marisa remained silent, awaiting the stream of accusations and falsehoods that must surely come from a people who disliked her so intensely that one of them had already tried to kill Rollo.

Griffith buried his head in the shaggy gray fur. "Rollo is gentle, my lord Father! He would not attack anyone unless Marisa was threatened."

Morgan sauntered over to the long stick lying upon the ground nearby, Rolfe close behind him looking very annoyed with Edgiva. "Or unless he were provoked by a child's cruel teasing." He picked up the stick and, without actually pointing it at Rollo, brandished it a few times as he would a sword.

The dog watched quietly, head cocked, tail switching lazily in the dust where he sat, then turned to lick the salty tears from Griffith's face, unconcerned with Morgan's movements.

"I would guess the boy tried to strike the dog—may have even succeeded—and Rollo frightened him enough to cause him either to stumble backward or begin to flee."

Marisa's hand moved casually to the top of Rollo's head, and sure enough, there was a knot upon the skull the size of an acorn. Still she bit her tongue and remained silent, awaiting Brand's decision while Adela's words went round and round in her mind. *It would not hurt to bow to his wishes in some things. . . .*

"The dog will remain confined to the yard, and when there are children from the village within the stockade, he will be confined to the bower until I deem it safe to allow him loose."

Marisa nodded coolly to her husband in acceptance of his wishes and, without a glance at the people congregated outside the church, turned away and commanded softly, "Rollo, here." He followed her to the bower and, when he was safely inside, Marisa went into the hall alone.

As time passed, she could hear the dancing and singing in the yard, but she refused to take part in such revelry when Rollo had been confined without just cause. Besides, she knew she would not be welcome there. She had done her part as Brand's wife after the Easter mass, and it had ended in near tragedy because of a careless little boy and a hate-filled woman. She occupied herself with the setting up of the Easter feast to which Brand had invited his people in the afternoon.

"Marisa, you will ruin your beautiful bliaut!" exclaimed Edyth.

Marisa turned to her sister-by-marriage and gave her a ghost of a smile. "It matters not. I have others."

"But that is your wedding finery," Edyth said, shaking her head in mock rebuke. "Brand will not be pleased."

"I doubt he even noticed."

"Marisa, 'tis not so," Edyth insisted. "My brother— typical man though he sometimes is—does notice things that many others would not. I saw him looking at you with admiration in church this morn."

"As did I," added Morgan, coming up behind them. "And"—he put his arm around Edyth's shoulders in a possessive gesture that brought roses to her cheeks— "Edyth would be honored to wear your wedding gown for our own nuptuals."

Her own troubles forgotten for a moment, Marisa's face

mirrored her happiness for them. "You are going to wed Morgan, Edyth?"

"If she puts it off any longer, I will be forced to abduct her out of sheer desperation."

"I have never known you to be desperate where any woman was concerned," Brand interjected dryly from behind them.

"Why, Brand Ericson," Marisa said, shocked out of her determination to be cool to him, "what a thing to say before his betrothed!"

Morgan laughed without rancor. "He is just jealous of my harp playing and singing. His bumbling fingers are fit only to wield a sword, and he croaks like the frogs in the bog when he so much as opens his mouth to sing."

All four people laughed aloud at that, and then suddenly the hall began filling with villagers. Marisa and Edyth were separated from the men to oversee the seating of so many people.

By the time the feasting and celebrating were over— well into dusk—Marisa's mouth ached from the wooden smile she'd worn all day and evening. She had given the residents of Camwright no opportunity to see her as anything but content and acting with the dignity expected of a woman in her position, despite their hostility and the incident outside the church earlier.

Her brief interludes of true enjoyment came when she exchanged pleasantries with Nesta and Leofric—she'd begun to accept the fact that Nesta had been close friends with Rhiannon—and Morgan and Edyth. Although Rollo was not allowed in the hall, Griffith visited him in the bower with choice leftovers from unemptied trenchers and returned to assure Marisa her pet was a bit restless, but otherwise in good spirits. *He belongs here, with the other hounds*, she thought once with surprising bitterness. Her mind had gone back to the day she'd romped with the dog in mock swordplay before Geoffrey de Brionne had imparted the totally unexpected news to her

of her impending voyage to England and her marriage to
Brand Ericson.

Only the carefully assessing gaze of Rolfe and Edgiva's
eldest daughter, Maida, reminded her to put aside her
sadly nostalgic thoughts and force a smile to her lips.
She remembered Maida's sneering comment outside the
church, and from the way the girl was watching Brand
constantly tonight, Marisa wondered if the Saxon girl
was half in love with her lord—had possibly even warmed
his bed, which would have been considered an honor to
the daughter of a cottar or peasant.

An unexpected stab of jealousy sliced through her, for
she remembered Brand's words about appreciating blond-
haired, blue-eyed Saxon women. Pale tresses and eyes so
deeply blue as to sometimes resemble violet were different from the yellow-gold hair and light blue eyes of the
Saxon girl Maida.

When Marisa realized she was feeling sorry for herself—something that went totally against the grain—she
lifted her head proudly and began to act with renewed
purpose as if she were enjoying herself. *Think of something else, foolish girl,* she admonished herself. *Think of
how you must apply yourself to learning all there is to
know about your duties as Brand's wife so that Edyth can
wed her Morgan with a clear conscience, knowing that
the manor will be in good, capable hands.*

It worked, but by the time the hall had cleared of the
last revelers, Marisa's footsteps were heavy with fatigue,
mental as well as physical, and she made her way slowly
to the bower in the deepening shadows. Adela had lit the
tapers and stoked the braziers, for it was still damp and
chill from the mountains that stood sentinel just over the
Welsh border. Rollo was ecstatic to see her, even more
so when she let him out. She stood at the open door,
however, to make certain he did not leave her sight. When
he was ready to return, she gave a soft whistle and closed
the door behind him.

Sinking to the settle before a brazier, Marisa felt too
tired to even undress and stared into the shooting flames

and popping sparks that sputtered from the iron vessel. Rollo lay at her feet, as if sensing her fatigue, and a strange, uncharacteristic melancholy settled over her.

Within the dancing scarves of flame, Marisa unwillingly relived the scene after the Easter mass, felt again the futility she'd experienced even as she had tried to draw out some of the villagers, to no avail. She recalled the incident with Alfred and Rollo. The dark, inscrutable look on her husband's face gave her the impression he had been upset with the dog but had refrained from any drastic action out of consideration for her.

Instead of bringing happiness, the thought saddened her even more and, for a brief, joyless interlude in the quiet bower, Marisa knew defeat as never before.

The door opened quietly. Brand stepped into the room and just as noiselessly shut the panel behind him, studying his wife seated before the brazier, still fully dressed. Her whole attitude conveyed defeat.

As he stepped closer, he caught a clear glimpse of her profile as she stared unseeingly into the fire, and suddenly he knew he'd waited too long. It was time to take her in his arms—to his bed—and soothe some of the hurt caused by his unforgiving people . . . and his own insensitivity to her.

Rollo's head came up as Brand moved forward, and the dog unfolded his long legs to stand and greet his master. Automatically, Brand's fingers stroked the animal's head, and he immediately felt the swelling there. So Morgan had been right, and Marisa had probably known, too, for who would know the animal better than the girl? Yet she had said nothing, allowing him to assume full authority in the matter.

He then knelt on one knee beside her, gazing up into her features. "Marisa?"

Slowly, as if in a trance, she pulled her attention from the fire and allowed her eyes to meet his. *"Oui?"*

The pain in her voice, the despair in that one word, brought a pang to his heart such as he'd never expected to feel in his dealings with her, and he reached out to take her hand. Marisa stared sightlessly down at his dark head as he turned her palm over and placed an infinitely gentle kiss thereupon, then held it up to his cheek.

When she would have withdrawn it, he only tightened his grip enough to prevent her halfhearted attempt. "Let me love you, Marisa. Let me show you the joys I should have shown you on our wedding night."

She shook her head, panic surging through her as her lethargy dissolved at his words. "There is no need—you owe me naught. You made a bargain with the King to save your lands to bequeath to Griffith. 'Tis done now."

She stood up, dragging her hand with her, and frantically sought a way to put him off as she retreated a few steps. "You . . . you feel guilty because your people reject me, but I will not have you make love to me to . . . ease your conscience!" Brand opened his mouth to speak, but she rushed on. "Let me sleep on the floor if sleeping beside me unsettles you. I do not mind. I—"

In two strides he was before her, his mouth capturing whatever additional words she might have uttered. She struggled at first, but then realized she was no match for his strength. As his mouth worked its magic over hers, her squirmings stilled and her lips parted under his, wave after wave of shocking tremors rippling through her innocent, newly awakening body.

When he finally withdrew his mouth from hers, Marisa opened her eyes, and Brand's breath caught at the agony underlying the growing passion that darkened the irises to blue-black. "You pity me," she protested in a ragged whisper.

Brand stared down at her, drinking in the beauty that had taken his breath away even as she'd walked toward him in Westminster Abbey. He laughed softly then, to her chagrin. "No, my sweet vixen, I could never pity you. We could have taken the battle at Hastings had we had more like you on our side."

His mouth descended to meet hers once more, and she suddenly clung to him like one drowning in a sea of uncertainty, her self-confidence floundering upon the shoals of the unknown, the unfamiliar in these new and hostile surroundings. As if searching for the solid ground of love and total acceptance, Marisa drank of his strength, his very essence, her pride in dire need of the healing balm of his physical assurances—the sweet brush of his lips, the wondrous warmth and security of his embrace.

When he scooped her up in his arms and carried her to the bed, she made no demur. His lips nuzzled her cheeks, her eyelids, her delightful little nose, and then finally her mouth again. Still locked in the increasingly ardent kiss, he lowered her on the bed and stood quickly to let Rollo out of the room, then began to undress.

Marisa felt such languidness that penetrated to her very bones from his kisses that she hadn't the strength to move a muscle, nor the willpower to take her eyes from his swiftly uncovering form. At the sight of his splendid chest with its broad planes and sculpted muscles rippling in beautiful symmetry, her heart began to beat triple time. Then his slim hips and sleek, steel-tempered flanks and thighs were revealed and, her eyes purposely avoiding the shadowed area of his masculinity, she felt herself melt inside like the dew beneath the onslaught of a gentle morning sun at the need to touch him, to feel his body against hers. . . . He was so beautiful, so tanned in all the places where the spring sun had kissed his skin, the other places burnished by the licking flames of the fire and candlelight.

And then he was beside her, unexpectedly grinning in a carefree, boyish way she'd never seen, which softened his stern features and made him appear ten years younger. "Do you like what you see, my little innocent, or are you disappointed? Do I compare with the Norman guests at Brionne whom you were obliged to assist with their baths?"

As he said the words, a brief frown flickered across his forehead, and Marissa had no idea that it was because he assumed she had bathed other men. Although it was the custom, the thought unexpectedly brought a roaring jealousy sweeping through him. Before she could answer,

before he could succumb totally to the treacherous envy
for those whose bodies her small, beautiful hands had
touched in even so innocent an act, his mouth took hers
again. It moved over the sweet lips and down the silken
column of her throat to rest momentarily at the hollow
where her fluttering heartbeat echoed in rhythm with the
life-sustaining organ palpitating beneath her ribs, and the
scent of roses in springtime filled his senses.

Reeling from his seering kisses, Marisa arched up
against him in wanton abandon when his hand found its
way under her skirts to caress her leg and then slide up
first one thigh and then the other, smoothing, stroking,
bringing her growing desire, the need for release, to an
exquisite pitch. She raised not a murmur of protest when
he slid her clothing up and over her head and allowed the
garments to slide off the bed with a whispered rustle of
silk.

They were both completely nude, flesh to flesh. Marisa
trembled with the growing pressure of her need. Her
hands rode his back, and she had the presence of mind
to be surprised at the silkiness of his skin over the whipcord muscle and sinew. "You are beautiful, Saxon," she
murmured, her sweet, melodic voice husky with passion.

He withdrew his mouth from a coral-tipped, alabaster
breast and smiled at her. "As are you, Marisa de
Brionne. But your beauty is not of this world. 'Tis the
type that makes men mad for want of you."

"And are you . . . mad for want of me?" she murmured, a deliciously wicked look in her limpid violet
eyes, as a liquid sensation centered in that most secret of
places in her body.

"Indeed, I now number among those smitten." And
he positioned himself between her thighs, the heat of his
staff searing her skin and shattering her self-control as
she instinctively arched against him, seeking more.

He found the moist, satiny sheath of her womanhood
and, holding a rigid control over his own desire, gently
entered her. Marisa had been prepared for pain and discomfort, not for the mere prick of a bee sting, and her

legs wrapped around his hips as she joined him in the ancient, primal rhythm that man and woman had shared down through the millennia, working toward that ultimate rapture.

Brand waited as long as he was able, feeling she was so very close. Yet few virgins, he knew, were brought to fulfillment the first time, and when he could wait no longer, he shuddered once, crying out with a wondrous urgency that touched Marisa to the core.

For he did not call out Rhiannon's name in his release. He cried out hers. And that fact completed Marisa's joy.

Chapter 9

Brand gently disengaged himself from the soft body entangled with his in the sleep that comes after satisfying lovemaking. He forced himself to ignore the luring, lingering scent of passion spent, of Marisa's fragrant hair cocooned around them both like a silver-gold curtain. Pushing away to his side of the bed, he covered her sleeping form and arose to extinguish all light but that from the braziers.

Turbulent emotions pulled him back and forth mercilessly, like a piece of driftwood sucked under by an unrelenting undertow and then tossed upward and rushed toward the shoreline by a powerful tide.

What had he done? What Pandora's box had he opened? *By the rood!* he swore silently. *I have never known such—*

"Nay!" he whispered fiercely. "Unfaithful, unworthy traitor! You do not deserve such contentment, such a sense of repleteness."

He looked back at the still form of his wife. No, it was her sensuality that affected him so, the natural wantonness that lay beneath that innocent demeanor. He was allowing her allure to make him forget how unworthy he was of ever feeling love again for a woman, of being loved in turn. He had worshiped Rhiannon as a child growing up and had wed that first love only to discover . . .

With shaking hands he poured himself a cup of wine

and downed it in a few great gulps. *She can have no more. Only the physical act, and she will have to be content with that. 'Tis the least I can do for Griffith. Oh, Rhiannon, do you not see? 'Twas a bargain I had to make for our son. . . . And I owe her at least this for saving Griffith and accepting him so fully. Please understand.*

He felt the night chill upon his naked body, despite the braziers, and returned to bed—to his side of the bed—and tried to sleep, tried to shut out the images of two figures entwined in sweet, joyous intimacy. Eventually the chill left his body.

But not his heart.

Small, dark, rheumy eyes bored into her, and Marisa huddled farther into her cloak, which did not seem to help at all. Wispy, specterlike fingers of white hair reached out for her throat. "So, pale one, you think to take my Rhiannon's husband to bed, do you? And then you will be after his heart—his very soul—when they belong to another." A tendril wrapped itself around the fragile length of Marisa's neck and began to choke the breath from her.

"He is my husband now, old woman," she countered, unaffected by the crone, except for the way she had to labor to draw in air. "He is my husband now, and naught can change that."

The lock tightened, causing Marisa to cough and fight harder for air. Her hands reached up to tug at the constricting threads cutting into her sensitive skin, to no avail. "You will be punished, girlie, but so will others. Innocents will pay the price for your thievery. Those who accept you will suffer because you took my Rhiannon's husband and her son." She cackled evilly, her smile a ghastly parody, revealing many missing teeth and foul breath. The damp chill increased, bringing a musty odor with it, as if someone had opened an ancient tomb and let loose all the decay and corruption trapped for centuries within. "You will pay, I guarantee that, and so will others . . . so will others . . . others . . ."

Marisa's eyes flew open. There was no Angharad before her now, and the pressure that had finally caused black spots to impair her vision had eased and then vanished. She was in the bower, with Brand beside her. . . . She reached over tentatively, only to find that the place immediately at her side was empty.

Her dream forgotten for the moment, Marisa turned her head and saw that he was in fact in bed, but as close to the other side as possible, like a man contemplating suicide at the edge of a precipice. Only the tenderness between her thighs told her that their lovemaking had not been a dream, after all.

The sense of despondency that had settled over her earlier that evening returned in full force. She was, after all, still alone, with only a servant and a dog to care what happened to her, to give her their affection unquestioningly.

Am I so detestable to my husband? Am I so undesirable? Must I pay for being Norman until I am buried beneath the earth in death, or because of the unforgivable error of wedding a man who loved and lost his first wife?

"Oh, Father," she whispered to the inky shadows in the bower, "to what kind of a life have you sentenced me?"

It was the first of May, and Mother Nature had seen fit to give the residents of Camwright a truly beautiful day. A scintillating sun peeped between the myriad billowing clouds at the mortals below, like a mother keeping a watchful eye on her errant children, while the young people of Camwright danced around the village with garlands adorning their necks. In and out of the woods they cavorted, chasing one another, carefree laughter and the sweet voices of youth drifting heavenward.

Marisa went along with the gaiety as much as she could for Griffith's sake. Without quite throwing herself into the revelry wholeheartedly for fear of more censure from the adults of the community, she put up an almost foolproof front. "You look like a beautiful wood nymph,

Marisa,'' Griffith had complimented her after she'd allowed him to pile so many garlands around her neck that she felt weighted down with them.

A smile that rapidly turned into a sneeze was her answer. ''I can scarce move, let alone appear and disappear with the ease of a nymph, Griffith,'' she observed with mock resignation. ''And although the fragrance is heady, so many different flowers make me—make me . . .'' Another sneeze punctuated her words.

Griffith laughed delightedly. ''Do nymphs sneeze, Father?'' he asked as Brand walked up to them and swung his son up into his arms.

Brand eyed Marisa, admiration flaring in the amber eyes before he ruthlessly squelched it. ''I do not know, my son, for I have never had the good fortune to meet up with one.''

A horn sounded, interrupting their bantering and heralding the arrival of unexpected visitors to Camwright. Brand immediately handed Griffith to Marisa. ''Take him inside the stronghold, quickly.''

Marisa let the little boy down, maintaining a firm grip on his hand, and hurried to do Brand's bidding.

''Who would come on May Day?'' the child questioned. ''Today we have fun. We do not—''

But he let his sentence remain unfinished as he watched his father and several of his retainers mount their horses and thunder through the west gate between the wooden watchtowers and around the stockade to disappear eastward.

''Come,'' Marisa urged, Rollo bounding alongside them. ''We will wait inside the hall, and perhaps we will be rewarded with a visit from someone we know.'' That someone, she fervently hoped, would prove to be one of her brothers. It would certainly raise her spirits, even though she had been in Camwright only a few weeks.

The servants were scurrying to and fro, setting up the boards for the noon meal, and as Griffith romped with Rollo and several of the other hounds, Marisa stared into the fire of the large central hearth, wondering if, indeed,

Richard or Raoul—or even Geoffrey de Brionne himself—had decided to honor them with a visit.

At the sound of horses' hooves moments later, Edyth
went to the door, the movement catching Marisa's attention, as well. "Who is it?" she inquired, following
Edyth to the door and peering over her shoulder.

"I do not know, but they look Norman."

Marisa's eyes adjusted to the brightness of the courtyard after the dimness of the hall, and recognition dawned
almost immediately. As the tall, mailed rider removed
his helm, the tawny hair and chiseled features proclaimed
him to be none other than the arrogant Norman who had
accosted them on the trip from London. Fascination
fought with fear for Brand as she watched the men dismount and walk toward the hall. In the instant before
either man at the head of the small party looked up, Marisa unconsciously compared the patrician beauty of her
fair-haired countryman with the more rugged good looks
of her husband, and unexpectedly found the newcomer
wanting—something she was certain she would not have
felt only weeks earlier. And the haughty look about the
visitor, the very way he walked and held his head and
. . . Guilt assailed her as she remembered the times she
had thought Brand arrogant, when true arrogance was
sauntering toward her even as she stood there.

Morgan and several of Brand's retainers followed the
group, and the two women retreated into the hall. "No
doubt Brand has invited them to share the noon meal with
us, Marisa," Edyth opined. She sensed a tenseness in
the girl beside her and put a hand on Marisa's arm. "Is
aught amiss?"

"Oh, Edyth, 'tis the Norman who accosted us before
we reached Camwright. He accused Brand of stealing
Goliath—which he did—but how very audacious of him!
He demanded to see Brand's writ from the King and—"

"Marisa! Have you no faith in my brother? He was
one of Harold Godwinson's most trusted thanes. After
the great battle he marshaled a group of men together
and led that last stand at Mal— Oh, forgive me. Brand

made me promise to say nothing about his dealings with our King Harold.''

Marisa had caught the unadulterated pride in Edyth's first words, and suddenly remembered the fearless manner in which Brand had dealt with the Norman. He had been prepared to fight for what was his by decree of King William, no matter that they had been far outmatched in sheer numbers.

Get hold of yourself, Marisa de Brionne, for you are no coward yourself. If anyone can deal with a Norman, you can.

''Do not worry, Edyth,'' Marisa said unexpectedly, slipping on her most mature, self-confident demeanor. ''We will deal with him.''

But to Marisa's surprise although the tension between the two men was palpable, the Norman who introduced himself as Mauger le Faux was courteous and full of admiration for Marisa. He recognized her instantly, and his Nordic blue eyes lit up with undisguised admiration.

Marisa was relieved that Brand showed no sign of jealousy or offense at Mauger's unabashed attentions to her. Remaining close to Brand throughout the meal and afterward, at his insistence, Marisa knew he was depending on her to catch anything the least bit deceptive in le Faux's rapid-fire French, and she was secretly flattered by his obvious trust. Le Faux pretended to forget Brand's limitations in the Norman tongue, and now and then Marisa broke in with a charming smile to prettily plead her husband's cause.

In spite of herself, Marisa warmed to le Faux somewhat, by virtue of the fact that he was her countryman—and she knew many chevaliers who were naturally arrogant. After all, Rollo's descendants had expanded the original upper Normandy in 911, until in only a century and a half it had become the stongest duchy in France. They had proven themselves to be easily adaptable, converting to Christianity, learning to speak the Frankish tongue and imitate Frankish customs, while contributing their ingenuity and ambition to increase and strengthen their influence and holdings.

And so, while le Faux's men uneasily broke bread with their Saxon counterparts, Mauger himself set out to put at least Marisa at ease and win her trust—something he assumed would be easy enough for a man of his looks and newly acquired wealth. The scar-faced Saxon scum to whom she'd been given in marriage, or so he'd heard, would be no competition for him with the ladies, he decided, even when it came to the exceptionally beautiful wife.

"So your lands march with ours," Marisa said with a smile, when Brand was called from the board by a mishap involving one of the overexuberant and slightly tipsy villagers. "Brand wondered to whom William would grant the adjoining land and village to the north. We are, indeed, neighbors."

"Oui, ma chère, and I regret that I was so abrupt with your husband when we first had occasion to meet. 'Twas probably jealousy on my part." He smiled brilliantly at her and, although Marisa returned it, she felt it did not quite reach his eyes—that he was weighing, considering, assessing, behind that icy blue regard. "I had heard only later of the valorous deed of your husband concerning Lord Geoffrey, and he has earned my admiration since."

Ignoring the French endearment, Marisa answered, "Indeed, Brand has shown himself to be valiant as well as fair and just to all. He suffers the sorrows of his people as if they were his own."

Le Faux stared into the dregs of his wineglass, hiding from Marisa's view the thoughts that might have been discerned in his gaze. Dismissing her praise of Brand, he asked, "And are you happy, Lady Marisa, with this match?"

His eyes suddenly returned to hers so swiftly, Marisa was reminded of a snake striking its unsuspecting prey. But instead of anger at his prying, Marisa felt a hint of nostalgia for her homeland and family—and also pain at Brand's refusal to give her anything of himself except in

the physical sense. Yet she squelched her pain and said
wistfully, "Indeed, I miss Normandy and my family, but
this is my home now and I am content."

At Marisa's invitation to see the other outbuildings
around the stronghold, they rose from the board and left
the hall. Morgan trailed behind like a hound hot on the
scent, and le Faux made no effort to hide his annoyance.
"Do we truly need an escort within the walls of Ericson's
own stronghold?" he asked. "And a barbaric Welshman
at that?"

Morgan's tone was softly incisive, the only sign that
his temper simmered at the deliberate taunt. "We barbaric Welshmen believe every man to be a king in his
own right, so you would do well to guard your tongue,
Norman. After all, the Cymry do not yet number among
those you've crushed."

With a smooth smile of assurance to Marisa, Mauger
half turned toward Morgan and answered, "Time is on
our side, my smug Welsh *king*."

Marisa caught a glimpse of Morgan's flashing eyes but
hastened to change the subject, and he dropped back to
give them more privacy, much as he obviously wanted to
do otherwise.

Strains of laughter floated over from the other side of
the stockade, and Marisa was reminded of the fact that
the people of Camwright were celebrating the day with
wild abandon while she was entertaining Mauger le Faux.
Why had he come today?

". . . the eve after the great battle?" he was saying.
"It's been called 'Malfosse' because of the disastrous
outcome for us. The King would give much to discover
who led that last band of defenders, for—as little as any
of us care to admit it—the man was mightily clever as
well as courageous." He looked at Marisa's profile.
"And most dangerous, if he is yet alive."

*He was one of Harold Godwin's most trusted thanes.
He led the last stand at . . . Malfosse?*

Dieu au ciel! Marisa thought. Was it Brand who had
led the skirmish at Malfosse? If that was true, this man

must not discover it or he would delight in informing King William.

Forcing her lips to smile stiffly, Marisa answered into the expectant silence, "I know naught of such things, my lord. My husband and I never speak of the great battle or things political."

"And yet he rides a Norman courser. Could it not have been stolen in the course of dispatching the unfortunate chevaliers who had fallen in the twilight at Malfosse?"

Now Marisa did wish Morgan was closer to them—or that Brand would miraculously appear to rescue her. "Goliath was a gift from my father. Perhaps you have heard of the horses of Brionne?" she heard herself answer in a glib lie.

"Ah, *oui*, I have indeed, and also those of the de Beauforts. But I find it, ah, shall we say rather odd that Lord Geoffrey would see fit to honor your husband with only one horse—"

" 'Twas part of Marisa's dowry," Brand interjected unexpectedly. "The remainder are to arrive shortly, le Faux."

The steel underlying the courteous tone of Brand's words left no doubt in anyone's mind that the subject was considered closed. As Marisa's gaze flew to his, she saw what was very clearly mistrust in the topaz eyes. Then it was gone.

"What was amiss?" she asked, relieved to have him back, yet hurt by his unexpected and very obvious doubts about her speaking alone with le Faux.

"An overzealous youth flung another into the bog over Maida Rolfesdaughter."

Marisa touched her fingers to her mouth in disbelief. "Is he . . . is he unharmed?"

Brand nodded and turned the party back toward the manor hall. "Walter claims he heard Maida's voice calling to him from the woods, and he followed it until he ended up at the bog. But Maida was not there, only Caedmon, who insisted that Maida had called to *him*." He frowned thoughtfully.

"Undoubtedly too much ale," Morgan commented. "Overimbibing does wonders for getting young men—and women—into mischief . . . although 'tis odd that either one of them would have crossed back over the Wye and then bumbled their way to the bog."

"Aye, Morgan, 'tis indeed most puzzling. But surely Lord Mauger has better things to occupy his time than listening to the woes of the lord and lady of Camwright."

It was a definite invitation to leave and le Faux did not act surprised at the abrupt dismissal. "*Oui*, I have my own men I left behind to keep out of mischief—to say nothing of the motley Anglo-Saxon villagers with their pagan carryings on." His handsome mouth twisted with distaste at the mention of his "villagers."

"May Day is celebrated in Normandy, as well, my lord—if you will only think back to before you came to England—and with equal enthusiasm."

The look Mauger gave Marisa was the first hint that she had managed to penetrate his facade of placid self-assurance. *Be you Norman or Anglo-Saxon?* the silent message seemed to convey, and then he smiled once again. He was a man of mercurial mood changes, Marisa thought.

"Can I expect a visit to Fauxbray?" le Faux asked.

Brand motioned for the stableboys to bring the horses and waited until Mauger and his men had mounted before answering. "Perhaps one day Marisa would care to visit and reminisce about her homeland—with an escort, of course. As for myself . . ." He shrugged eloquently as he let the words die off in an unspoken but definite refusal, indicating he wanted no part of Mauger le Faux.

Several of Brand's men-at-arms escorted le Faux and his party to the northern boundary of Brand's holdings, but Morgan remained at the hall. "It bodes ill, Brand. Since when would any wench in her right mind try to lure one of the village men down to that Godforsaken quagmire? Even the wild animals avoid that place."

Marisa was watching Griffith wrestle with Rollo, her ear half-attuned to their conversation. But Morgan's chilling words caught her full attention. "No one ever goes near the bog?" she asked.

"Never," Brand answered, his eyes suddenly narrowed on her, as if he had just noticed her presence and realized something that had eluded him up until that point.

Marisa dropped her gaze before his, thinking of his silent message of hostility to her when he'd interruped her conversation with Mauger le Faux. "Well, it seems to me," she persisted doggedly, her gaze returning to Griffith and Rollo, "that there are some strange goings-on in your own village of which you are unaware until disaster has struck."

"I agree, my astute wife." The tone of his voice was chilling, and even Morgan cast him a sidelong look. But Brand was not thinking of his wife's possible revelations to the disdainful Norman chevalier. He was thinking of Angharad. Who else would be so bent upon doing evil, and at the cost of innocent lives?

Morgan stood and stretched. "Well, I do not envy you your position as lord of Camwright now that you have a conceited he-ass like le Faux for a neighbor—begging your pardon, Marisa," he apologized with a twinkle in his dark eyes. "You will have enough trouble dealing with the Welsh Princes Bleddyn and Riwallon, if what I heard is true."

Brand raised an eyebrow in interest and then immediately glanced at Marisa. "Will you take Griffith out when you leave, Marisa?"

Stung by his rude dismissal, Marisa summoned Griffith and the dog as she got up to leave. He obviously did not trust her one bit, and it was so unfair that she wanted to scream—to scratch his eyes out while shouting how she'd protected him before Mauger le Faux's sly questioning. But she said nothing.

"You were not very circumspect, my friend," Morgan observed wryly. "Remember I was not very far behind them, and from what I could make out, Marisa said nothing untoward regarding you. Besides, she knows nothing of the night after Hastings. What could she possibly have told him?''

''If memory serves me well, you were too far behind to be able to hear aught.''

Morgan sighed. ''I am telling you that you can trust the girl. . . .''

''I did not dismiss Marisa so that you could regale me with your opinions of my wife and her supposed loyalty to me. Now, what have you heard?''

''Edric the Wild of Herfordshire is planning a revolt against the Normans, and there are some who believe he will enlist the aid of Bleddyn and Riwallon.''

Brand stretched the lean length of his legs out before him, crossing his ankles and scowling at his interlaced fingers. '' 'Twould seem that fate is against me no matter what I do, no matter which way I turn.''

''I will discover all that I can, Brand, and help you prepare for what must come, but—in all honesty—I do not envy you the possible consequences should the uprising indicate that you are not keeping your part of your bargain with William of Normandy. . . . And then there is Madog ap Cynan.''

Brand looked up at his friend. ''I would think he'd be the least of my worries. His violent opposition to Bleddyn and Riwallon should keep him out of Herfordshire.''

''Hopefully so, yet I think you know better than to discount him as a source of trouble.''

Brand mulled this over for a time and then quietly informed his friend, ''I also heard this day that Harald Svenson of Wighton was found with his throat slit.''

Morgan look stunned. ''Harald . . . murdered?'' He frowned in bemusement. ''Surely it could have only been the work of a devil Norman.''

Brand's eyes narrowed thoughtfully, ''I wonder, Morgan. I wonder.''

When Morgan had gone, Brand thought about what the Welshman had revealed. Yet he found that when he should have been thinking of what he could do to discourage the Welsh princes in their plans to join in the uprising in

Herfordshire, or who could have been responsible for the murder in Wighton, he could only envision Mauger le Faux and Marisa walking together and discussing his possession of the gray. If she mentioned Robert de Lisieux, then the Norman would realize Brand had been at Malfosse.

His anger grew until he was forced to acknowledge that there was only one way to find out exactly what Marisa had told Mauger le Faux.

The door crashed open against the wooden wall and the entire bower shook with the force.

Jumping up from the settle with a small cry, Marisa whirled to face the door, certain some drunken villager had somehow managed to get into the compound unobserved and was bent upon ravishing the detested Norman lady of the manor. But it was only Brand.

Fear giving way to anger in her relief, Marisa at first failed to take note of the look of black anger on his partly shadowed face. "How—how dare you frighten me witless like that! Do you take pleasure in—"

"But you have your fearless Rollo, my lady wife," he assured her nastily as a black nose inched its way around the bed from where it had been resting drowsily upon two warm, shaggy paws.

"He knows your scent before you even enter the room, Saxon. Do not ever doubt his courage. Were it anyone else, he would have been at their throat."

Brand closed the door and advanced toward her, ignoring for once the wolfhound who wagged his tail uncertainly and then retreated behind the bed once more. The brazier's glow limned the sweetly formed curves and valleys of her body and turned the edges of her hair to molten silver. With most of the light behind her, her face looked like purest alabaster, her darkly violet eyes huge and glowing in her fragile face. "What—what do you want? What do you mean blowing in here like a frigid north wind and—"

"What did you tell him?"

"Tell him? Who?"

He advanced upon her until Marisa could feel the heat emanating from his body and smell the mead on his breath. *Dieu au ciel,* he had been drinking, and heavily.

"That strutting Norman cock, le Faux, that's who."

"I—why, I told him naught. I am your wife, and I would be loath to denounce my husband—even an English husband—to anyone! I do know of honor, Saxon."

His eyes burned into hers with the intesity of his feelings, for he had begun to think that perhaps she could be trusted, after all, and then to hear her discussing Goliath with le Faux. . . . Bile rose in his throat at the assumed betrayal. "I heard him questioning my owning a destrier—*one* destrier—and—"

"And you did not wait long enough to hear my answer, did you? No, you had to jump in, assuming the worst of me, before I could barely even open my mouth!"

He stared hard at her, trying to ignore the attraction she held for him. If she ever discovered how much he desired her physically, she would, indeed, have a weapon against him. Thank God he was not emotionally taken with her—must never be. "And just what would you have said, Marisa love?" he inquired with mock dulcetness.

Suddenly having had enough of being put on the defensive when she was completely innocent, she ignored his question and attacked, "Let me tell you, Brand Ericson, that I know 'twas *you* who led the English at Malfosse, and I acted as ignorant of the matter as a newborn babe!"

She was rewarded by a stunned look on the handsome features, but had little time to savor her victory before his fingers gripped her arm painfully. "Just where did you hear that lie, Marisa? I was hiding *here,* cowering amid the milch cows in the byre, if the truth be known, remember?"

A rosy hue tinted her cheeks. "I hurled those words at you in anger—I was insulted by your treatment of me at Westminster—but I know you are nothing if not courageous and I said naught to Mauger le Faux!"

His features seemed to relax, and then some of the high color of anger began to fade from his face.

"You are hurting me, Brand."

As if they belonged to someone else, he glanced down at his fingers still wrapped around her slender upper arm, and immediately dropped his hand. "I regret that I have caused you physical injury, although God knows sometimes I want to thrash you. But whatever your noble efforts on my behalf with le Faux—if you can be believed—I was not at Malfosse. I fled the battlefield before that last stand when we all knew the battle was lost. I found the gray just inside the Andredeswald and took him home with me. That is all there is to it."

She must never know the truth, he vowed silently, or she would inform the first Norman who crossed her path, destroying Griffith's future in the process.

Chapter 10

Marisa continued to look up at him, obviously not at all convinced. The sudden, forced nonchalance he only just succeeded in affecting did not fool her for a moment, but the fire in her eyes died. If he was not willing to admit certain things to her, then so be it. Eventually there would come a time, she vowed, when she would find the key to unlock the enigma that was her husband.

She watched him turn and walk to one corner of the bower. He sat down before the small grinding wheel and set the blade of his dagger to it, an odd, unspoken restlessness about him.

Marisa sighed, her gaze drawn to the long, lean fingers moving with deft purpose over the whirling whetstone. " 'Twould all have been so simple—and bloodless—if William had been able to stake his claim without opposition. For, after all, he was the rightful claimant.''

Above the whir of the grinding wheel, Brand inquired with a soft rancor that Marisa missed, ''Indeed, Marisa, and just how is that?''

''William was kin to Edward the Confessor—''

''Through a distant marriage in the family . . . too distant to be acceptable to the English people and the witan.''

''Perhaps, but Edward had promised the throne to William some fifteen years earlier when the English court was graced by a host of Normans due to Earl Godwin's exile. . . . When it was more fashionable to speak French

144

than English because Edward had been raised in Normandy himself.''

Brand scowled. There was no point in rehashing the past, and with a Norman. He merely said, ''There was no agreement that we knew of.''

Marisa was refilling Rollo's water bowl and did not see her husband's forbidding expression as she bent to empty a ewer of clean, fresh water. ''William surely had more right to the throne than Harold Godwinson, the son of a Danish cattle-herder.''

''Tsk, tsk, my lady wife. Do I detect a streak of disdain for the House of Godwin when William of Normandy is a bastard, the son of a tanner's daughter?'' His voice was softly incisive. ''Lest you forget, Marisa, whatever Godwin of Wessex's antecedents, he earned the gratitude of a Danish earl and was given the man's own sister in marriage—the noble Gytha, and then their daughter Edythe was wed to Edward to become first lady of England.''

Marisa stood and began undressing, ignoring the chastising tones quietly lashing her from across the room as the movement of the whetstone slowed. Continuing to voice her thoughts aloud, her attention centered on preserving her modesty rather than on Brand's increasing ire. ''*Oui*, but Harold was sent to Normandy by Edward himself only two years past to strike a bargain with William. He was to ensure the rightful progression to the throne after Edward's death.''

''Sent by Edward? On a mission to ensure the rightful progression to the throne?'' Soft, bitter laughter filled the room before the next words made Marisa wonder at the wisdom of drawing him out. ''Do you really know what happened, Marisa? Nay, of course you do not. . . . You only know the Norman version, which legitimizes William's quest and brands a fallen king a liar and a breaker of oaths. Harold Godwinson only went ahunting. One would hardly approach the Duke of Normandy with an offer of the English crown with a retinue of merely a hound, a falcon, and a few servants.''

"Well, then," Marisa said with the vaguest hint of contempt for so absurd a story when everyone knew the truth of the matter, "how did your honorable Harold end up in Normandy? And why did he swear upon holy relics in William's presence—and that of many others—to help him gain the crown upon Edward's death?"

"Because he was blown off course during a storm," he answered through set teeth. "And tricked into swearing on holy relics—they were hidden beneath the table or nearby somewhere. He was a prisoner of William's, pleasant though it was made to look with the hunting parties and even a war foray into Brittany in which Harold distinguished himself as a soldier. William would not allow him back to England until he had what he wanted. Ambitious Harold was, aye, but he loved England. He would never have sworn to hand his country over to a foreigner—unless he was deceived, or given no choice but to take the accursed oath in order to obtain his freedom. And there is no oath that is binding when taken under duress."

Marisa stared at her husband in disbelief. "Nay! 'Tis a lie." And she turned her back on him in seeming dismissal of his words. Inwardly, however, she wondered if there were any truth in what he'd said.

In the blink of an eye the newly sharpened dagger whistled through the quiet air and sunk deeply with a solid *thunk* in the back of the wooden settle beside which Marisa was disrobing. She spun around, her shed bliaut clutched convulsively to her chest, her eyes rounded in astonishment.

"I may be many things, my fine Norman wife, but I am not well versed in the art of deceit—nor was my king."

Brand rose from the stool and stalked toward her. "Why, Marisa? Why must you continue this . . . this parody of curiosity when you really seek to rub salt into my wounds? You know very well we can never see things the same way." He reached out to jerk the still quivering knife from its place. When Marisa continued to regard him in silence, essaying to divine the truth in all that he had just divulged, he added curtly, "You do grave injustice to the honor of my father and brothers, as well, when you name me a liar."

Anger had lent a harsh cast to his features and made his scar stand out lividly in the firelight, but Marisa caught a glimpse of pain within the topaz eyes that unexpectedly made something in her chest constrict. "What . . . what happened to the other menfolk in your family?" she whispered, the words pulled out of her by some inexplicable force.

He returned the dagger to its sheath and moved to the bedside table to pour himself a draught of mead. "Dead. My father was killed at Stamford Bridge, and both of my brothers at Hastings." All emotion was now gone from his voice, and he threw back his head and downed the mead before turning to face her. "And so, Marisa de Brionne, you may believe you have thrown away your chances for a life of contentment for the likes of me and my people, but at least you have never known the privation of losing almost an entire family while trying to protect the land of your birth. Nor in all likelihood will you ever, by virtue of your birth and origins, be made to grovel before your conquerors to ensure the security of those you love."

Marisa watched him replace the goblet and stride toward the door, catching a glimpse of the anguish that warred with despair in his expression. When he turned toward her at her softly spoken "Brand?" there was only a cold inscrutability masking his emotions. "Brand, I— whatever you may think, I did not betray you to Mauger le Faux. You must believe that, for whatever you are and whatever you have done, I am your wife. You may not think a Norman capable of honorable actions in light of your opinion of William, but my upbringing would never allow me to forsake the man to whom I was given in marriage—unless he were completely lacking in that noble ethic himself."

His eyes roved over her face from ten paces away,

searching for some sign of sincerity, yet revealing nothing of his own thoughts. "I wish I could believe you, Marisa. I would know that I have an ally at my back rather than one more enemy."

When he'd gone, Marisa felt a cold chill settle over her heart. Indeed, he was seemingly alone against a foreign ruler, others of his own station dead and gone along with his king, and then a condescending Norman knight living upon and ruling the adjoining lands—a man who neither understood, nor cared to understand, the delicate balance Brand had evidently sought to maintain between the Anglo-Saxons and the Welsh. Now Brand believed he could not trust her, his wife.

As she readied herself for a bed she suspected she would not share with Brand this night, Marisa thought of how deeply hurt and bitter he was. Yet he was also courageous and just, retaining irrevocably his love of England and all things English. No matter who was right, Norman or Anglo-Saxon, Marisa decided suddenly it did not truly matter. Unexpectedly the path she must take became crystal clear to her. She would win over this man's trust and respect, if not his love, and that of his people. Somehow . . . some way. She would act the part of a noble wife and caring lady of the manor, or perish in her attempt.

"I want his lands."

Mauger le Faux sat his horse at the end of the village he'd renamed Fauxbray and surveyed the land to the south, narrowing his eyes as if to penetrate the trees separating Fauxbray's fields and the Wye River from the village of Camwright nestled along its southern bank.

"I want that defiant Saxon's lands and all else he possesses. . . . "

"Including his Norman wife?"

Mauger cast a sly, sidelong glance at his companion. "Indeed, we would make a most handsome couple—if I decide to wed her after she is widowed. Although"—he glanced ahead again, a frown gathering like a thundercloud across his brow—''I am loath to accept the leavings of a filthy Saxon.''

'' 'Tis rumored that he has not touched her.''

Mauger's mouth twisted unbecomingly. ''No man in his right mind would leave her virgin.'' He skewered the dark-haired man beside him with his pale-eyed stare. ''And how know you this?''

''I have ways.'' Madog ap Cynan flicked an annoying fly from one ear of his small Welsh pony. ''My suggestion would be to win her over, then you will have an ally right within his stronghold.''

Le Faux nodded thoughtfully, prodding his horse forward. ''You told me of the poisoning of her hound. I find that rather an indication of foul play by some hate-filled Saxon. When I was within Ericson's very compound he reported strange goings-on concerning several village youths and a wench over near some bog.'' Madog nodded knowingly, but Mauger did not notice. '' 'Twould seem he has his share of problems—and deliberately caused ones at that. Mayhap we are not the only ones bent upon his downfall.'' He threw an unexpectedly assessing look at his companion, as if to induce him to tell what he knew, but Madog would not admit to anything more.

When Mauger turned to ride back to Fauxbray, the Welshman went off in the opposite direction, leaving the Norman to ponder what he knew thus far and formulate his plans. He had what he considered a valuable, if ultimately disposable, ally in Madog ap Cynan, despite his opinion of the Welsh. Madog and his followers violently disagreed with the policies of the two strongest Welsh princes, Bleddyn and Riwallon. They had enough men behind them to make mischief for Brand Ericson, for they believed he had sold the late prince of all Wales, Griffith ap Llewellyn, to Harold Godwinson. Whether it was true or not did not concern Mauger le Faux. He was interested only in nurturing the mistrust and hatred harbored by the young, rebellious Welsh under Madog and using it to aid him in his plan to destroy Ericson's credibility in the eyes of William of Normandy.

Then, too, he had only recently discovered Madog's very special and personal grudge against Brand Ericson. The Welshman had loved Ericson's first wife Rhiannon for years before their marriage. The fact that within a year or two after the union Rhiannon had, in a moment of despair, confided to Madog that she suspected her husband no longer returned her love, had only added insult to injury. Madog still burned for revenge, blaming Ericson for her death, however indirectly. Even though the girl had pleaded with Madog to say nothing of her discovery—for she loved Brand Ericson deeply and would learn to be satisfied with his affection—since her death, Madog had considered himself released from his promise.

It seemed, Mauger mused as he neared the village, that there was a veritable treasure trove of potential allies whose aid he could enlist in ridding himself of the Anglo-Saxon if he bided his time and nurtured a few friendships.

Marisa threw herself into her role with a vengeance, untiringly making her rounds of sick and injured villagers, learning all that Edyth had to impart concerning the smooth running of the manor, including the established methods of supervising the work in or the care of the kitchens, chapel, barn, stables, kilnhouse for drying grain, cowbyres, the small falcon house, porch, and privy. Finally even Brand had to agree with his sister that Marisa was ready to assume responsibility for the key belt—a symbol of authority. When she met aloofness from Brand's people—which she suspected was due to a reluctance to associate with her—or even blatant hostility, she ignored it, swallowing her pride and ire and doubling her efforts to be efficient and capable, if not always as gracious or enthusiastic as she would have liked.

At night she would fall into bed, too exhausted to be overly unsettled by Brand's warm body so close to her own, though he seemed oblivious to her presence. It seemed to Marisa that she was doomed, for the time being at least, to a life of celibacy after that one night of joyous union, the specter of Rhiannon and all the differences between Norman and Anglo-Saxon looming between them like an impregnable barrier. But Marisa was nothing if not determined, and she stubbornly refused to let her estrangement from Brand daunt her efforts.

May was a time of repairing houses and barns, mending the fences that marked the perimeters of Camwright, attending to the hedgerows and drainage ditches. It was also the time when, to protect their flocks, bands of peasants hiked through the woods to seek out wolf cubs and capture them with poison, staves, pits, dogs—anything that would serve as weapons.

In spite of Brand's reluctance to allow Griffith to venture into the forest, the little boy persuaded his father to permit him to follow well behind the adults, with Marisa and Rollo accompanying him. Morgan reminded Brand that the son of a thane must learn to be bold and enterprising in preparation for leadership rather than hide behind his aunt's and stepmother's skirts. Such was Griffith's enthusiasm, a rare thing since Rhiannon's death, that Brand grudgingly consented.

Brand had arranged a meeting with a Welsh contingent just inside Wales in an attempt to dissuade Bleddyn and Riwallon from joining the coming uprising in Herfordshire. He felt he could not afford to offend the Cymry by putting off the meeting to go searching for wolf cubs with Griffith. "Very well," he told his son, "but one of my men will accompany you."

"You can ill afford a man-at-arms for Griffith's protection during such a hunt," stated Marisa with some exasperation, "and 'twould seem as if you were overprotective of him when others not much older than he accompany their fathers. What harm can be done if we stay near the outskirts of the woodlands with Rollo to protect us?"

Brand arched an eyebrow sardonically. "And 'tis

seemly for the lady of the manor to go along on a hunt with the peasants?''

Marisa's chin lifted. "As far as many of your people are concerned, I am just a Norman woman you were forced to wed, and I doubt that you could be any more concerned than they. I will take care of Griffith. You have my word—which is every bit as binding as yours."

Guilt shimmied through Brand at her words, for iron-ically, his actions lately suggested that she was right in her assumption, although it was far from the truth. He colored slightly and hid his guilt behind an acrid re-sponse. "Very well. But have a care, for 'twould be all the more tragic were I to have wed you for naught if anything befalls my son." As soon as the stinging words were out of his mouth, Brand cursed himself for such an uncharacteristically cruel barb. The color burning Ma-risa's cheeks indicated how affected she was, and Brand knew his wife did not need hostility from him to add to what she was already being subjected to by some of his people.

Marisa turned away. "Come along, Griffith. I will change my clothes and—"

Brand's hand on her arm stopped her. "I regret my harsh and unwarranted words, Marisa," he apologized as Griffith scampered off to find Rollo, and Morgan tact-fully went to see to the saddling of their mounts. "Mari-sa?" She still had not turned to face him. "Forgive me."

His breath caught in his chest when she did swing around, the unguarded pain in her eyes revealing how much he'd hurt her with his cold-blooded pronounce-ment. "There is naught to forgive, Saxon, for speaking the truth." She pulled her arm away and walked regally toward the bower, leaving him to stare after her with profound regret stamped across his features.

She will wither away to a shadow of herself.

Morgan's words echoed round and round in his mind as he watched her until the bower door closed behind her.

* * *

It was well into the afternoon when Griffith led Marisa into the glade containing the waterfall and pool. Laughing at Rollo's antics when a bee mistook his nose for that most delectable part of a flower, Marisa and her young charge fell, giggling uncontrollably, to the grass near the water and watched the hound swipe at the bothersome insect with a great paw, then shake his head several times before ridding himself of the misguided bee.

"Marisa, is Rollo truly a wolfhound—or a beehound?"

Dissolving into gales of renewed laughter, Marisa shook a finger at the boy in mock warning. "One day you will see what yon hound can do, my young lord. I have seen him grab an attacking wolf by the throat and kill him almost instantly."

Griffith's dark eyes grew round with wonder. "Truly?"

"Indeed. But the animal was attacking my brother, Raoul, else he would probably have turned tail and fled." She paused, sobering. "You see, Griffith, Rollo is really a gentle animal, despite his size, but when a loved one is threatened, his bravery comes to the fore."

Griffith nodded, his expression suddenly serious. "Aye, Marisa. Father has told me many times that courage is not necessarily stronger or truer when it is not readily apparent. True courage comes from the heart, he said, and does not need to be bruited about."

Marisa nodded in agreement. "I believe he is right, Griffith."

"And is not my father a very brave man, Marisa?"

Without volition, Marisa nodded. "That he is."

Rollo trotted over to the pond and took a long drink of water, lapping greedily. Griffith watched him, while Marisa stared at the beauty of the waterfall, allowing the muted roar to lull her as the warm May sunshine beamed through the boughs overhead, dappling their prone forms with a latticework of light and shadow.

Drowsily content, Marisa did not hear above the sounds of cascading water the rustling in the foliage across the clearing until Rollo had leaped to his feet, his hackles up and his ears alertly pointed forward.

"Qu'est-ce que c'est?" she automatically queried in her native tongue as she sat up.

Rollo started moving toward the sounds, his growl becoming more menacing until Marisa commanded, *"Ici!* Rollo, here!"

The huge dog paused, obviously torn between his instincts and his mistress's command.

"What is it, Marisa?" Griffith had begun to doze, and Marisa's sharp directive had jarred him awake.

Before she could answer, an old woman emerged from the woods. A cloud passed overhead, blotting out the sun, and the warm air surrounding them suddenly turned chill.

Angharad.

"Grandmother!" Griffith cried, and jumped to his feet.

"What do you here with yon woman, childie, and all but desecrating your mother's grave?"

The little boy froze where he was, uncertainty flitting across his small face as Rollo reached Marisa's side and continued to growl softly from within his chest. "What does 'desecrate' mean, Grandmother?" he asked hesitantly, sensing he'd done something wrong but unsure what it was.

Warning bells sounded like clarions in the back of Marisa's mind as Griffith began to walk toward Angharad once more and Rollo's rumblings increased in volume. "Stay here, Griffith," Marisa ventured, some sixth sense sounding a warning.

"So you'll not allow the boy to see his kin?"

"If that is all you want, why have you not come to see him at the manor? Why do you step out of the trees like some vengeful spirit, frightening me and alarming the hound?" Marisa returned, her own temper surfacing at the crone's audacity. "And what do you mean by confusing him with such a cruelly calculated—and absurd— question?"

The wind picked up and blew streamers of the thin

white hair around Angharad's shriveled face, just as in Marisa's dream only weeks ago. "And you dare to call my question absurd, you *nithing?*"

Griffith gasped softly and Marisa felt her skin crawl. A worse insult in the Saxon tongue could not have been uttered, even Marisa knew. "My beloved Rhiannon lies buried beside yon waterfall, and here you sit with her son, worming your way into his affection until he remembers her not? A curse on you, Norman harlot!"

Out of nowhere a massive gray wolf appeared and walked to the old woman's side. Stunned by all that was happening and being revealed at once, Marisa could only gape at the gigantic beast. It was even larger than Rollo.

"Come to me, Gruffydd . . . come to your grandmother."

Griffith obediently began to move toward her.

Some say she is mad.

Marisa clutched Rollo's thick fur in growing panic. Something was not right here, but suddenly she seemed powerless to move or speak, as if Angharad's curse were already taking effect.

"Come, come to me, childie. I would never harm you . . . come and we will go away from this place, to the land of the Cymry, where your mother's spirit dwells . . ."

Dieu au ciel, Marisa had the presence of mind to think. *She means to take him away—to abduct him!*

She forced her lips to move. "Nay, Griffith . . . please stay with me."

He did not seem to hear her soft entreaty, the hypnotic effect of Angharad's words—her very presence in the now dim, dank glade—drawing him toward her like a magnet to metal.

With every last bit of willpower at her command, Marisa moved forward to stop him, her steps seeming slow and sluggish, as if in a nightmare. Before she went two steps, however, Angharad pointed a bony finger at her and shrilly barked out a command in Welsh.

Marisa knew an instant of panic as the mammoth wolf-beast hunched in preparation for the spring, for she discovered she could not move. Rollo's body tensed beneath her fingers in response just as the other animal launched itself through the air. In her fear for Griffith, Marisa suddenly reacted. She shoved the boy away as Rollo leaped to meet the bounding gray body that came hurtling in their direction, the stench of wild animal permeating the air as the beast attacked in a blur of glistening ivory fangs and eyes reddened with blood-lust.

The two animals collided in midair with a sickening thud before falling heavily to the earth.

Non! Marisa's dazed mind cried silently, concern for the dog overcoming fear for her own life. But no sound came from her paralyzed lips, and the animals landed almost at her feet in a tangle of bared teeth and claws and bloodied fur, struggling ferociously.

"Marisa, he will kill Rollo!" came Griffith's voice from seemingly far away, helping her to break free of her trancelike state.

She looked around for a fallen branch—anything to use as a weapon—but to no avail. In desperation, she began to approach the struggling animals, weaponless, certain that Rollo would lose his life because of a vindictive old witch and her demonic familiar.

The unexpected whine of a projectile spinning through the air penetrated her senses, and Marisa caught the gleam of metal as it flashed past her eyes before finding its mark. Suddenly all was quiet as the struggle abruptly ended.

The wolf lay unmoving, the hilt of a dagger protruding from the side of its neck. Rollo stood panting over it, bloodied but still apparently in one piece. Marisa glanced at Griffith to make certain he was unharmed before falling upon her knees and throwing her arms around the faithful, valiant dog, heedless of the gore coating his shaggy fur.

"You will pay for this, Norman bitch . . . make no mistake about that! This is but the beginning!" shrieked Angharad, raising her fist in a threatening gesture. Then, like a vanishing nightmare, she melted into the forest from whence she'd come.

Marisa raised her head and watched the disappearing form with a mixture of bewilderment and relief. The old hag was of a certainty quite mad, and how Brand could ever have tolerated her presence around his first wife and their son was incomprehensible to her.

"Marisa, you are bloodied," Griffith said anxiously from beside her. "Is Rollo seriously harmed?"

Gently she pushed far enough away from the dog to ascertain the extent of his injuries. "I think not, *cher*— only a few gashes that I can stitch closed with Edyth's help."

Obviously relieved, the little boy looked over at the great wolf lying close by. "I—I do not understand why my grandmother would signal for such a beast to attack you, Marisa." His voice shook slightly as he bravely fought to control his tears.

" 'Twas more than likely an accident. Mayhap the wolf was not trained well enough to follow her commands and—"

"Nay! I saw what she did!" he cried.

Marisa held out a hand to him, her other resting upon Rollo's back as the dog began to lick his wounds, and he fell to his knees beside her, clutching her outstretched hand with both of his small ones, tears now streaming down his face.

It was thus that Brand came upon them, emerging from the woods across from where Angharad had stood only moments before. At the sight of Marisa's blood-streaked face and bliaut, and Griffith sobbing beside her, his heart stopped within his chest.

Chapter 11

"Griffith? Marisa?"

He took several steps toward them before some of the color returned to his face. All three heads turned at the sound of his voice, and Rollo limped toward him in welcome, his tail moving with a vigor lacking in the rest of his battered body.

Marisa watched Brand take in his son's appearance, and then, obviously relieved, his gaze went to Marisa, who had slowly stood up. The apprehension in his eyes was clear, but Marisa's thoughts were in such a whirl of indecision, she hardly noticed.

"Say nothing of Angharad, Griffith," she warned under her breath in sudden decision. "I will tell him."

Then Brand was before them, his hands gripping her upper arms with a firmness borne of some unspoken emotion that made her wince as he examined her from head to foot. "You are unhurt, both of you?" His eyes were on Marisa now, delving into hers as if he would read her thoughts. "What happened here?"

The harshness of his words was due to a mixture of concern and relief, but to Marisa it sounded like an accusation—an implication that she had carelessly subjected Griffith to danger. In the aftermath of the bizarre incident with Angharad and the wolf, it rankled.

She opened her mouth to speak, carefully choosing her words, but Griffith spoke first, rising to his feet. "A wolf attacked Rollo, my lord Father . . ."

"A wolf would not attack in broad daylight, unprovoked. Did you mayhap steal one of her cubs for sport when I expressly forbade you to—"

"If you will examine the beast, you will see 'tis a male." Despite her belief that Brand had every right to be angry in view of how the situation appeared to him, she found her ire rising and was perversely reluctant to reveal Angharad's presence as the cause of the attack. An unholy imp encouraged her to allow him to think the worst—at least for a few moments. "I know better than to toy with a cub—and near its mother, yet—without a weapon to defend myself," she said heatedly. "Most certainly if it involved risk to Griffith."

Brand released Marisa's arms and walked toward the dead wolf, shaking with relief and anger. He mentally acknowledged that his conflicting feelings were a result of more than merely the danger to which his son had been exposed. "Why in God's name would such a beast attack you? What did you do to put my son's life in peril—as well as your own and that of your faithful hound?"

"I do not know. Mayhap he was rabid."

Instantly she could have bitten her tongue—knowing in advance what Brand would say to that. "Then Rollo will have to be killed."

"Nay, Father!" cried Griffith.

"But I see no evidence of it on this beast," Brand said. As Marisa sighed gratefully, Brand removed the dagger from the wolf's neck and wiped it upon the grass. "Whatever happened, you can thank one of the Cymry for saving all of you. From the looks of the hilt, I would say, 'tis a Welsh dagger. 'Tis obvious, however, that your savior wishes to remain anonymous."

Marisa frowned. Who had been hidden in the woods and chose to remain unknown to them, even after saving their lives?

Brand stood up and turned back toward them, scattering her thoughts. "I think from now on you will either take one of my men with you, or you will refrain from going beyond the stockade walls with my son. 'Tis obvious you cannot be trusted to keep him from harm.''

An anger so deep, a pain so cutting from Brand's lack of trust in her rose up in Marisa until she felt she would gag from the sheer force of it. *Tell him the truth and exonerate yourself,* whispered her conscience. The proud, stubborn side of her, however, prompted her, *He does not deserve to know the truth, for he still believes you are empty-headed and foolish . . . incapable of seeing to Griffith's safety.*

While Marisa struggled inwardly with her colliding emotions, Griffith took matters out of her hands. ''Father, I will not allow you to blame Marisa for what happened,'' he insisted with an authority that surprised even Brand. ''Grandmother came here and . . . and . . . and said awful things to Marisa.''

Brand looked from his son to his wife, whose face had colored with guilt at Griffith's revelation. His eyes narrowed. ''Angharad?''

''Aye. She cursed Marisa and . . . and gave the signal for the great beast to attack her. Rollo rose to her defense and then, of a sudden, it was over.'' He looked at the knife in Brand's hand. ''Someone killed the wolf with yon dagger, but never revealed himself. And then Grandmother disappeared, missaying Marisa again, and you came shortly thereafter.''

Brand considered his son's words for a long moment before his frigid gaze came to rest upon Marisa. ''So you chose to lie to me, my lady wife?'' he asked with soft, deadly censure. ''I wonder why that is? Are you a born liar, as is your bastard duke, or were you bent on twisting the facts so that I would have been unable to get to the heart of the matter?''

After all that had happened, Marisa could only stare at him, dumbstruck. But within moments, purging ire swept through her like a riptide, clearing her mind, numbing her breaking heart, and bringing back her wits. Drawing herself up to her full height, small as it was before Brand's tall form, Marisa jutted out her chin with all the dignity and disdain she could muster. "I am not a liar, my fine Saxon thane, nor do I make a habit of twisting the facts. In this case, however, my silence was most assuredly justified. I had every intention of telling you, but you attacked me out of hand. In your mind you labeled me as untrustworthy from the moment you stepped into the clearing and then verbally called me such before your son. By all the saints, Saxon, you *deserved* no explanation!"

It was the second time that day they had exchanged barbs, and for some strange reason it affected her more deeply than any of their previous angry words. Biting back her hurt and fury, Marisa called to Rollo and began to turn away on shaking legs.

"Marisa!"

This time it was no gentle entreaty but an authoritative comand that served only to unravel the already frayed edges of her temper. She turned to face him, her hands in fists, the nails digging into her palms. "Forgive me, Saxon," she said, her voice ringing with sarcasm, "if I did not wish to cause Griffith harm when I brought him here, nor to 'desecrate' Rhiannon's grave by my presence."

She swung around, no force on earth able to keep her there a moment longer, and walked toward the path to the manor, Rollo limping along beside her.

"I tell you that woman is stark raving mad!"

Adela nodded in agreement. "They say she is a witch, as well, with special powers."

Marisa shook her head. "Nonsense. I do not believe in witches, nor in the pagan gods she supposedly worships." She cupped her hands over a basin of warm water and cleaned Rollo's blood from her face. "Nor should you, as a good Christian."

Adela continued to clean one of the lesser cuts on Rollo's neck. "I do not believe in her pagan gods, either, my lady, but a witch worships the devil—which is very much a part of Christianity."

Marisa shrugged it off and dried her hands and face. "Whatever she is, I believe she could be part of the reason many of the villagers will not accept me. And she would have abducted Griffith, of this I am certain." She shed her bloodied garments and donned a fresh chainse of snow-white linen and a pale blue bliaut, for she knew she would eventually be forced to confront Brand, and she wanted to look cool and composed once more . . . and desirable.

Adela looked up at her. "Will you tell my lord of her intentions toward Griffith?"

Marisa nodded without hesitation and knelt down beside her servant. "I must—when he calms down and sees the error on his arrogant ways." She shook her silvery-maned head in disbelief. "He could not believe that the fault was not mine without immediate proof. He accused me of lying, of twisting the facts to suit my own purposes. Can you imagine that, Adela?" Two flags of color pinkened her fair cheeks.

Adela shook her head. "People say and do odd things when under the burden of distress. You said yourself the scene he happened upon would have shocked anyone—especially with Lord Brand being Griffith's father and your husband."

Marisa met Adela's sympathetic gaze for a moment before her glance slid away. "I would that he cared the smallest bit for me, Adela, but 'twas most certainly his concern for his son that prompted him to vent his spleen on me."

The door opened then and Edyth asked, "How is the dog?"

"Poor Edyth," Marisa said with a hint of a smile. "Forever called upon, 'twould seem, to tend my hound."

Edyth returned the smile and stepped into the bower, closing the door behind her. "I love animals, Marisa. Especially the one who saved the life of my nephew and my brother's wife."

The smile vanished from Marisa's face. "Rollo fares well, Edyth. There are only two places that will need stitching. The remainder will heal under the ministrations of his tongue.''

Edyth laughed aloud, ignoring the solemn look on her sister-by-marriage's features as she bent to examine Rollo's cuts. ''Then let us be quick about it, for Brand has called a moot for the entire village.''

''A moot?''

Edyth paused in the threading of her bone needle and looked over at Marisa. ''Oh, forgive me, Marisa. 'Tis a meeting of the villagers—an Anglo-Saxon custom. 'Tis usually for the men of Camwright, but in this case Brand has commanded the presence of all the residents of the village.'' At Marisa's continued silence, she added, ''I believe it concerns what happened with Angharad this afternoon.''

Marisa stood abruptly, and Adela moved to take her place as her mistress moved agitatedly about the bower. ''And, of course, my presence is required?''

''Why, yes, Marisa. You are the lady of the manor, and you were directly involved.''

Marisa swung back in their direction, annoyance marring her features. ''He only wants to put me through some sort of trial, Edyth. He can only wish to humiliate me further before his people for lying to him.''

''Lying to him?''

''Oui. Because of his outright lack of trust in me, I chose not to mention Angharad's presence—only that of the wolf. But Griffith came to my defense when Brand accused me of being careless while his son was entrusted to me. He told all.''

''But surely Brand was only caught up in the moment? He knows that you would never have intentionally subjected Griffith to danger. Certainly he will see that you were angry with his false assumptions—and why shouldn't you have been? You did nothing less than react to his attack.''

''So I did, but in his efforts to condemn my actions, your bullheaded brother could not see it that way.'' Marisa retraced her steps and bent down beside the two women again, stroking Rollo's head as Edyth's needle expertly darted in and out of the jagged edges of the deepest laceration.

"Whatever you may think, Marisa, if Brand has any quarrel with you, he will deal with it in the privacy of the bedchamber and not at the moot. I think you judge him too harshly," she said gently.

"We shall see, Edyth. But whatever he is about this eve, his words of public reprisal will fall upon barren ground." Her eyes met Edyth's, grim determination mirrored therein. "I intend to tell the people of Camwright a few things myself."

The hall was filled with noisy villagers as Marisa paused in the doorway and drew in a sustaining breath. Throwing back her shoulders and lifting her head proudly, she walked toward Brand, who was seated at the high table, the place beside him empty. Their eyes met, but Marisa could read nothing of his thoughts or mood.

Thrown for a brief moment, she quickly recovered her threatened composure as she moved steadily toward her place, the people in the hall gradually falling silent as her presence was noted. Marisa took Brand's hand as she stepped gracefully over the bench, their eyes meeting again, but she feared she would shame herself and her family name if she allowed herself to be distracted by the heavily lashed eyes delving into hers. She immediately withdrew her gaze, and her hand, as she sat down.

Brand remained standing and regarded the villagers before him solemnly. "When any of you have aught that you wish to discuss with your thane, you are free to come directly to me or call a moot." Various murmurs of assent were heard and Marisa noticed many heads nodding in agreement. "Well, now 'tis my wish to apprise the entire village of an incident that involves not just my family, but all of you, as well."

Only the hiss and crackle of the torches lining the wattled walls broke the silence that settled upon them like a heavy shroud. "It concerns the Welsh woman known as Angharad."

Marisa's gaze flew to her husband's face, but from where she sat she could only see his profile. "I would not missay Rhiannon's kin, but I know without a doubt that Angharad ordered a vicious, wild wolf to attack my wife. If it had not been for her faithful hound, Marisa would now be dead—and possibly Griffith along with her."

The murmurs began again, this time louder and more widespread as people leaned over to speak in hushed tones to one another and then look at Marisa. "If you do not believe the tale, you have only to ask my son."

Leofric stood up then, and Brand acknowledged him with a nod. "Where did this happen, my lord?"

"At the pool in the clearing."

"Perhaps Angharad went there to visit her daughter's grave, my lord," said Edgiva, without waiting for permission to speak. "There can be no harm in that. And perhaps the hound known as Rollo went for the other animal first."

"Do you imply Griffith told an untruth, Edgiva?"

Leofric sat down and Edgiva had the grace to blush. "Nay, but everyone knows of the lady Marisa's way with the beast. 'Tis said she secretly signaled the war-horse to attack Griffith so she could appear to save him. Then, too, look what happened to my Alfred," she added indignantly. "Now, mayhap young Lord Griffith was fooled, for he is mighty fond of her."

Marisa felt color creep insidiously up her neck and into her cheeks. *Do not flush, fool!* she rebuked herself mentally. *You proclaim your guilt to all the world by such a lack of control.*

Brand leaned forward on his knuckled fists, staring at Edgiva, his expression stern and disapproving. "And who told you Marisa gave Goliath a secret signal? A small woman ten paces or more away from a huge beast can hardly obtain such results with a flick of her little finger, Edgiva. Or mayhap *you* could?" Soft laughter threaded its way through the crowd. "Nay, rather 'tis Angharad's lies that twist your mind. Are you so afeared of her that you would hate my wife for some truly impossible slight? And with Morgan ap Dafydd and myself as witnesses?"

Edgiva would not give up, however, and opened her mouth to speak again, when her daughter Maida rose beside her and demanded, "And what of Alfred, my lord? Did not the dog attack him?"

As she listened to the exchanges between Brand and the two women, it seemed to Marisa that Brand was too lenient with his people—much more so than her father would have been. But then, she decided, she had no knowledge of the workings of an English moot. To her knowledge, such a gathering was unheard of in Normandy.

"The dog was struck on the head by someone," said Brand, "and the branch beside the boy as he lay on the ground all but proved 'twas he. I examined Rollo's head myself, and he had a knot the size of a large acorn atop it. I do not know of a dog who will not at least attempt to defend itself when attacked. Such a hound would be completely useless for aught. As for Edgiva's statement that Angharad may have been visiting Rhiannon's grave, I expressly forbade her to enter Camwright or the area around it, so she acted against my wishes as thane. She made threats concerning Marisa and, I strongly suspect, tried to kill Rollo by poisoning his water."

Marisa drew in her breath sharply. Angharad? Of course . . . Why hadn't she thought of it before? No wonder Brand had seemed to dismiss her suspicion that one of the villagers had been responsible. He knew—or suspected—Angharad had done it, and for some reason he had not enlightened her.

". . . points to someone having been in the area around the bog very recently." Leofric was speaking again. "I cannot say who it is for certain, my lord, but I have been watching as you bade me."

One of the village youths, Caedmon, stood up in agitation. "I knew I heard a woman's voice drawing me there, Lord Brand. . . . I was not in my cups as some implied! And 'twas Maida's voice.''

Maida turned glittering blue eyes upon him. "I was nowhere near the bog on May Day, you simpleton! No one in his right mind would venture yonder, even for a jest.''

"Aye," Nesta spoke up unexpectedly. "But Angharad knows the area like the back of her hand. She would have no qualms about tricking some unsuspecting lad into the quagmire, in jest or otherwise.''

Brand's eyes narrowed. "Indeed, Nesta. And why not cause mischief and use her influence to have the blame fall upon the Norman lady of the manor who—in Angharad's unstable mind—usurped her beloved stepdaughter's place?''

"Brand?''

He looked down at Marisa, having almost forgotten her presence in all the tumult. "Aye?" He felt the pull of those arresting eyes and forgot all else for a brief span of time.

"May I speak?''

"Of course.''

She stood and faced the restive crowd. "I understand now why my husband forbade Angharad's presence in the village. I believe she is mad. She . . . she would have taken Griffith away with her; you have only to ask the boy and he will confirm my words. When he moved toward her, as if in some sort of stupor, I tried to stop him. That is when the wolf attacked.''

"Lies!" shouted Edgiva, and several other men and women rose to their feet with her. "Angharad would not do these things! She lived within your walls, my lord, for all those years, and you never had reason to suspect her of such vile behavior. 'Tis the Norman woman whom you have wed. She is haughty and self-centered and has brought us naught but trouble since her arrival!''

Marisa did not hear those who rose in her defense, for the deafening roar semed to come from those hate-filled Saxons shouting and raising their fists at her. Brand crashed his fist onto the table so hard that it vibrated and sent several candle holders flying, but Marisa put her hand on his arm as he shouted, "Silence!"

"I have seen all I needed to see, heard all I needed to hear," she stated calmly, the firm pronouncement meant for his ears alone. With all the dignity she could manage, she added, "I pray you will excuse me, my lord, for obviously the words of a Norman cannot be given credence at an English village moot."

She shook off his restraining hand. "I will be in the bower." Stepping over the bench, Marisa left the hall, despair tightening her chest until she felt faint, but with her head high.

Instead of going to the bower, Marisa's steps took her with steady purpose to the stable. No one was about, but she was no stranger to readying a horse to ride herself. She went straight for Goliath's stall, murmuring soothing words to him in French as she entered, and smoothed her hand down the strong, splendid neck. Then, with bridle only, she led him to the door and out into the early twilight.

Stepping lightly onto a low stump, Marisa vaulted easily onto his back, despite her skirts, and headed him toward the gatehouse. The gates stood wide open and, with a careless wave of acknowledgment to the lone man on duty, she kicked the stallion into a canter down the lane through the village toward the west. It was exhilarating to feel the animal's massive strength beneath her, to feel such power at her command, and it was exactly what her battered pride needed.

As they neared the last homestead at the west end of the village, she turned the courser toward the southern fields and leaned forward to speak to him. Immediately the horse's speed picked up until they were surging over the newly sown earth, heedless of trampling the small seedlings, sending their tender, unfurling shoots skyward. The cooling evening air felt refreshing on her flushed cheeks, and strands of pale hair escaped the heavy plaits swinging behind her and whipped about her face as horse and rider skimmed over the ground, soaring to heights beyond the petty concerns of human beings.

With Goliath eating up the distance across the fields, Marisa paid no heed to the fact that they were heading toward the infamous bog. Nor did she particularly care to avoid it. She would deal with the danger when they neared, unless she decided to swing the destrier around and head back.

Goliath himself slowed when he sensed the change in the firmness and texture of the ground as they entered a sparsely wooded area southwest of the fields. As his gallop slowed to a canter and then a brisk trot, Marisa finally pulled him to a halt, noxious fumes rising up from the decaying vegetation and clouding the air like some phantasmagoric pall. Goliath became suddenly skittish, tossing his head and pawing the earth.

"Easy boy," she soothed in French, patting his withers reassuringly. She remained still, held by some force she could not name, as she took in every tree, every square foot of the treacherous morass around them. Who could be responsible for luring Caedmon and Walter here, and to what purpose? she wondered vaguely. If it was Angharad, was she so unfeeling, so brutal, that she would sacrifice the lives of two young men in her plan to undermine Marisa's position at Camwright?

Some say she is mad.

Indeed. A madwoman and a village of hostile people—along with an ambiguous husband—were all but intolerable conditions to one accustomed to respect and authority and love. Marisa shrugged. What did it matter? This was Brand's domain—his to deal with as he saw fit or, at least, as best as he was able. She had no place here.

"But I cannot go arunning back to my father," she whispered to the sighing breeze. For a brief moment, she contemplated the strangely beckoning bog—the depths of that soundless, eternal oblivion that had lured many an unsuspecting animal to its death. Hoofbeats vaguely registered in the back of her mind, but Marisa ignored the sound. Unconsciously she touched her heels to Goliath's sides, but the horse tossed his head and snorted in protest, unwilling to venture farther onto the treacherous, deceiving ground. He whickered softly in warning and pawed the earth uneasily.

A hand on her arm made her start in surprise, and an eerie alarm slithered over her. Marisa looked down into the dark eyes of Morgan ap Dafydd on his pony beside her, relief loosening the pent-up breath lodged in her chest.

"What do you here, my lady?" he asked.

With a brittle laugh, she answered, "Why, I came to see for myself the bog that strikes terror into so many hearts."

"You were doing more than just looking, Marisa, for you didn't hear me come up behind you. When Goliath warned you, you ignored him. What were you contemplating so intently?" His hands reached up to span her waist and help her down.

"Did Brand send you to play protector to me? If so, I can assure you the only ones from whom I need protection are the Anglo-Saxons and Welsh in the great hall at Camwright."

Morgan handed her Goliath's reins and signaled her to follow him away from the quagmire, leading his own sturdy pony with the large, liquid eyes. "You are missing the best part of the moot, Marisa. Or did you not care to hear Brand's defense of you, his dressing down of that shrew Edgiva and those she has influenced? I will wager that, in addition to Brand's tongue-lashing, she gets a sound thrashing from Rolfe when they return to the privacy of their cottage."

Marisa smiled in spite of herself at the thought of Rolfe "thrashing" the domineering Edgiva. "From what I have seen, 'tis more likely to be the other way around." Morgan reciprocated her smile, obviously relieved to get a glimpse of her natural enthusiasm.

"Tell me your secret, our brave Marisa."

"Secret?"

"Aye. Tell me how you know Golliath. . . . I mean, I would like to know how you know the horse so well, how you control him so easily, why you've previously accused Brand of stealing the animal when, as he once told le Faux, the King gave the stallion to him. There is more here than meets the eye, and even if Brand has not found it oddly coincidental, I do. So . . . tell me, Marisa de Brionne, how do you know the fearsome Goliath?"

Marisa hesitated a moment, meeting his sharply discerning gaze, and then complied. " 'Tis no secret. Brand already knows."

"He knows?"

"Oui." She sighed softly with reluctance. "My father and brother—as I once told you—breed and train some of the finest destriers in Normandy. I knew each horse ever born at Brionne during my lifetime, and to whom it was sold."

Morgan nodded his head, having noted the keen intelligence possessed by Brand's wife early on. "And?"

"Goliath was sold to a good family friend, one who had sought my hand in marriage until I made it very clear to Father that I did not wish to wed him." Her expression became sad, wistful, as her thoughts went back in time. "I suppose Brand is right when he calls me willful, because Robert de Lisieux would have made a good husband, and yet I spurned him on some silly pretext. Within the year he went off with Duke William to fight at Hastings. I . . . I recognized Goliath the moment I saw him in London the day we departed, and I knew that Robert de Lisieux was dead."

Morgan was quiet a moment, respecting her sorrow as the shadows began to lengthen with the setting sun and the sweet songs of the birds began to fade away.

"How did Brand come to name him Goliath?" she asked suddenly. "It struck me as odd that both masters should have given him the same name."

Morgan's lips curled slightly in remembrance. "Brand was showing the animal to a very awed Griffith, who remarked that surely such a great horse would be much better than an English or Welsh pony. Brand reminded him that biggest is not necessarily most intelligent or best, and told him the story of David and Goliath. When he mentioned the name Goliath, the horse's ears pricked, and he swung his head around toward Brand. Further mention of the name only served to prove what Brand had suspected—that the horse's name had originally been Goliath.''

Marisa nodded. ''And so, the same name but a new master.'' She was silent for a long, thoughtful moment, and when she finally spoke, her voice was weighted with despondency. ''Brand tells me I know naught of loss or sorrow, but no matter who was right or wrong—Norman or Anglo-Saxon—we, too, suffered losses, however insignificant they may seem to the English.''

Chapter 12

When they were out of the area of scattered trees and dangerous ground, Morgan asked Marisa if she would like to ride back, for the walk would take awhile and it was growing dark.

"You do not mind riding beside a woman on a larger horse?" she teased, coming out of her introspective mood. "Or perhaps you would like to exchange mounts before we are seen by someone?"

Morgan cast one sidelong glance at the enormous warhorse walking alongside Marisa and declined. "Thank you, no. I prefer my own mount, puny as he may seem to you. I am not so clever or skilled as the Biblical David."

Marisa laughed aloud as he cupped his hands for her to swing up onto Goliath, and they rode back toward Camwright, carefully skirting the fields in such a manner that made Marisa feel more than a little guilty at her previous disregard for the newly growing crops. What had she been thinking of?

"Morgan?"

"Aye."

"Will you tell me true if . . . if I can ever succeed in gaining at least Brand's respect and trust?" Thankful for the growing dimness that helped camouflage her heightened color, she went on. "I know I can never win his love, but at the least I would like to prove myself worthy of—"

"Marisa," he interrupted her firmly, "you are every bit

as worthy as Rhiannon—or anyone else—of Brand's respect and trust *and* love." He bent to readjust his stirrup, and it seemed to Marisa that he took rather long to do it. At his next words she knew why. "Brand carries a double burden of guilt—and you are never to tell him what I am about to divulge or he will have my head."

"Well, I have suspected he feels responsible for Rhiannon's death. It's almost as if he is unwilling to allow himself to exhibit affection or accept it from another. Not that he has done much to be unfaithful to her memory," she revealed with unexpected rancor.

"Indeed, he does feel responsible, for she died in childbirth."

"But that happens all too frequently, Morgan, and 'tis no one's fault."

"You are right, but Brand and Rhiannon married very early, when they both felt the full effect of first, young love. Unfortunately, after they'd been wed for a few years, Brand discovered that his feelings had settled back into the old childhood fondness and a love such as he felt for Edyth . . . not the passionate, physical yearning of the body he felt was Rhiannon's due. While Rhiannon's love grew in every way, Brand's altered in nature, and no matter how he fought his demons, he could not undo the transformation of his emotions." In a low voice he added, "He has suffered for it ever since, with Angharad always there to remind him until he banished her from Camwright."

As they neared the village, Morgan made out a rider coming their way. "He comes looking for us, Marisa. Do not tell him what I have revealed, I ask you once more. I only wanted you to know why I believe, as Brand's closest friend, that he needs merely time and support, if you are willing to grant them to him. He must forgive himself before he can forgive you for your imagined transgressions. I also believe that his ofttimes contradictory actions stem from his growing feelings for you, which he fights at every turn." He stared at the approaching figure on horseback, his expression obscured by the waning light. "But he fights a losing battle, Marisa. Of that you can be sure."

With mixed emotions Marisa watched Brand approach on another great steed. Would Brand be angry at her abrupt departure from the hall?

And then he called out, "Morgan! Is aught amiss?" Before his friend could answer, he added, "Marisa, are you unharmed?" He drew up beside them, catching Goliath's lines and squinting into the shadows to assure himself that Marisa was unscathed.

"She is fine, Brand. She and Goliath get along nicely, as you can see, and just felt like kicking up their heels on this fine evening."

"That was a foolish thing you did, Marisa. . . . "

"Foolish, my lord? Hardly. I pray you, do not spoil the tiniest bit of happiness you have caused me at your concern by rebuking me for quitting a hallful of hostile villagers."

He studied her silently for a moment before he answered quietly. "Not exactly a hallful, Marisa. You have friends, those who support you and believe in you. Including your husband."

Their eyes remained locked, a rising moon beginning to banish some of the purple shadows that covered the land. Morgan broke the spell of the moment by adding, "If you consider me one of those hostile villagers, Marisa, I shall hie myself off to the bog with my broken heart . . . and who shall rescue me then?"

Marisa laughed aloud, suddenly acutely conscious of Brand's nearness, giddy from his words. "Only Edyth should be able to break your Welsh heart, Morgan," she admonished. "If you continue to ply me with your sweet talk, I shall be forced to consider you an unfit suitor for my new sister's hand." She glanced shyly at Brand. "What think you, my lord?"

A smile hovered about his lips. "I think I must agree with you, Marisa. At last I may be able to prove his fickleness where women are concerned and persuade Edyth in the process. Unless he minds his tongue, of course."

"Bah," Morgan said in disgust as Brand handed Marisa her reins, and they all turned to head back toward Camwright. "I have been wearing my heart on my sleeve for years now, and only recently have you seen fit to acknowledge my love for Edyth. No one could make her a better husband, Brand Ericson, and well you know it."

The banter continued, Marisa's soft, tinkling laughter ringing out several times in counterpoint to the deeper tones of the men's voices, until they reached the village.

The atmosphere in the bower was different somehow this night—tensely expectant, yet there was no hostility in the air.

Marisa performed her ablutions in the basin of warm water set to the side of one hot brazier, and was thankful the other brazier was not lit because of the increasingly warm weather. She felt more shielded from Brand's enigmatic gaze, a gaze that to her limited experience seemed to combine regret and yearning. She felt shy undressing before him under his warm perusal, especially after his words earlier that evening. Never had he said such a thing to her—*You have friends, those who support you and believe in you. Including your husband. . . .* The remark—the very inflection in his voice—carried a hint of some intriguing message that sent her pulse racing even now.

Brand let Rollo out the door and turned to lean against it, clad only in braies. "Why did you not tell me about Angharad, Marisa?" At her startled look, he amended, "Nay, I know the reason. But you did intend to tell me of her attempt to abduct Griffith?"

She nodded, moving forward to sit primly upon the edge of the bed. "After my anger subsided, I had every intention of telling you. But the moot was called so quickly, I barely had time to help Edyth with Rollo."

He moved around the bower, extinguishing all but the taper by the bed and the brazier. Then he crouched before her, taking her cold hands in his and looking deeply into blue-violet eyes shaded with wariness. Her apprehension unexpectedly tore at Brand's heart. "You saved my son from harm for a second time, and almost lost your own life in the process."

"I love him."

The words were softly spoken, yet with a conviction that made them all the sweeter to Brand's ears. "Look at me, Marisa."

She raised her downcast eyes to his and saw the shimmer of emotion in the measureless, golden depths. "I can never repay you for your courageous act this day."

"There is no need. You think because I am not Griffith's real mother—because I am Norman and was forced into wedding you—that I cannot love your son?" He winced inwardly at her choice of words, although he recognized their truth all too well. "It seems, my lord Saxon, that much of the problem lies in your unwillingness to give me half a chance to prove that I am only human—with wants and needs and the capacity to love as much as anyone else." She withdrew her hands from his and stood in agitation. "As for the rest, I regret that you ever believed I would attempt to take Rhiannon's place in your affection or that of your son."

He followed suit, regret sweeping through him with punishing force. Turning her by the shoulders until their faces were inches apart, he said, "For all my stubbornness—my refusal to look further than your outward beauty—and my cruel misjudgment of you, I apologize, Marisa. I did not recognize a rare jewel because of my prejudice and battered pride. I felt as if I'd sold myself to William of Normandy, but in truth I came out ahead. *I* got the better part of the agreement because I got *you*."

Her eyes widened in wonder at his words, and she realized that his tender admissions were dissolving some of the greatest obstacles that stood between them, the first real offering of peace. "Then I accept your apology, Brand Ericson."

His lips brushed hers with infinite tenderness, lingering at the delicate corners of her petal-soft mouth, moving with featherlike caresses to her fragile eyelids, now closed in growing languor. His strong, long-fingered hands cupped and raised her face to gain better access. "Marisa," he murmured into the hair at her temples. "Marisa,

Marisa . . ." He bent to place an arm under the back of her knees and swept her high against his chest, burying his face in the satin smoothness above the neckline of her nightdress. She smelled of scented soap and a hint of wood smoke and horses, and Brand was hard-pressed to keep his yearning for her under control. This time was to be for Marisa. This time was for her.

Marisa's arms entwined about his neck with growing urgency, delicious sensations warming her from the touch of his lips. She arched her neck as he nuzzled her throat, and her hair tumbled over his arm, almost to the floor, like the silvery shower of the waterfall in the clearing. The laces at her collarbone gently slid apart, seemingly with a will of their own, and further revealed the ivory-sheened skin above her breasts. Brand buried his face in the soft, satiny hollow between those enticing mounds.

He set her down on the bed, his mouth seeking hers once more, his tongue probing the sweet secrets within as her own lips parted in abandon. He traced the softly grained surface of her tongue, the porcelain-hard edge of her small, pearly teeth, gleaming in the light from the single candle. And as their tongues met again, they twined and moved in a rhythm suggestive of what was to come.

Marisa moved her hands upward from his waist, savoring the broad planes of sculpted muscle that covered his naked back and powerful shoulders, noting almost unconsciously how smooth and silky his own skin felt beneath her questing fingers. She cupped his face with her hands, deliberately pulling her mouth from his and turning his head slightly to the right so that her lips could touch ever so gently the scar that branded his left cheek. His eyes, glowing with warm, golden desire, widened at her gesture, and then he buried his head in the glorious mass of her hair as he murmured her name over and over again.

But Marisa was ready for more, and she pressed her hips to his until the evidence of his desire dug almost painfully into the juncture of her thighs, and she moved suggestively against his need. He pulled his face from her tresses and stared down at her, hot longing and devilish amusement in his gaze. "Why, my lady wife," he whispered, "you are most eager this night." He shifted his weight until he was lying at her side, enabling her to help him slip the gown over her head and let it slide to the floor with a whisper of sound.

He stared down at the perfection of her body before him, bathed in the flickering orange-gold glow of the brazier nearby and the feeble light from the taper. He drew in his breath and bent over to capture a nipple in his mouth, teasing it with his tongue until it sprang to life. He sought its twin, kneading with skillful fingers around its periphery even as his lips produced the same response in the roseate bud. Marisa moaned softly with undiluted pleasure and then protest as his tongue left her throbbing nipples to sear a moist, burning trail of fire down her abdomen, hovering just short of the nest of springy blond curls that covered the entrance to the core of her sensuality. In that tense, delicious moment, her murmurs of encouragement resumed and Brand's lips began to nibble at the tender skin of her inner thighs. The silken ends of his golden-chestnut hair tickled the pale, sensitive flesh, his warm breath misting them and causing Marisa a sweet inner pain that spiraled outward, pushing all thought aside save of this man and this moment.

"Brand," she implored softly and, with burgeoning ardor, tugged at the knotted cord that held up his braies. With a soft laugh, he helped her frantic fingers undo the troublesome knot, allowing his hand to linger between their bodies, resting against the throbbing apex of her thighs. "You torment me, *sorcier!*" she complained in breathless objection. Then she was pushing down the garment until she could tease him in the same way, feeling a thrill of satisfaction at his quick gasp of pleasure as her fingers closed around the satin-skinned firmness of his turgid shaft. "Two can play at this game, Saxon," she informed him in softly dulcet tones.

"*You* are the witch," he growled and, kicking off his braies, gathered her even closer to the lean length of him, molding her softness to his whipcord muscle and sinew and reveling in the feel of the woman beneath him, even as he wondered if he could ever get enough of her. Poising himself between her parted legs, Brand quickly searched her face to make absolutely certain that she was ready, and then felt the subtle cruelty of his well-meant gesture, for frustration gleamed in the dark blue pools of her eyes. With a graceful twist of his hips he entered her, slipping into the warm, moist cocoon of her body with such ease that he understood her tears and wasted no time in beginning a pulsing rhythm that sent molten desire streaking through both of them with shattering speed and glorious effect. The tension built and increased with the tempo of love until, on a burst of sensual splendor, they were lifted upward and out of themselves in a mutual, mindless joy that shattered into myriad shards of pleasure, spent before they drifted back to earth, enraptured and replete.

He did not withdraw from her immediately, but rather raised himself up on his elbows and stared down into her face. Tiny beads of perspiration dotted her brow and lower lip, and the flush of passion pinkened her cheeks. Her opalescent eyelids remained closed, the thick tangle of her sandy lashes fanning out over her high, delicate cheekbones, hiding from his gaze the arresting eyes that had captivated him, albeit unwillingly, from the very beginning.

God in heaven, but she was lovely! Here was a woman not only to do a man proud with her looks and regal bearing, but with enough sensuality and joy of the physical union to keep him chained to her bed with a silken tether until he was exhausted—a virtual slave to her, whether he loved her or nay. That thought brought a frown to his face, but he pushed aside whatever feelings of guilt or doubt might diminish the afterglow of their lovemaking. She was courageous and selfless and loyal when it came to those she loved, and he could ask for nothing more in a woman.

Desire rekindled in Brandon once more as she stirred drowsily beneath him, and he knew in that moment that if he could never love her, he would always want and need her, and that would have to be enough.

As it had to be for Rhiannon? a voice inquired in the back of his mind.

I loved Rhiannon, he answered silently. *'Twas the need and desire she never truly commanded.* And had he not hurt the very one who'd loved him so? Nay, he could not give his heart to any woman with a clear conscience . . . not after what he'd done to Rhiannon. Not even to Marisa de Brionne.

Sandy lashes fluttered and slowly raised to catch his slight frown as he battled his demons. "Brand?" she queried sleepily. "Is aught amiss?" Worry shone from the yet passion-darkened eyes, and he immediately sought to banish her fears.

"Nay, sweet. I only want to love you again."

She smiled like a contented cat, that faint uptilting of the corners of her eyes beguilingly emphasized.

"Would you like to be pleasured again, my beautiful Viking?"

She nodded, a mischievous look creeping into her eyes. "Now that you have taught me so well what to expect, I am eager for more."

His mouth sought hers again, their sweat-sheened bodies entwined languidly upon the great bed, still relaxed from their previous interlude. But as their passion grew once more, Brand whispered into her mouth, "I need you Marisa. I need you . . . "

This time, unlike the first all those weeks ago, he did not afterward withdraw to the other side of the bed, but rather pulled her close in a sheltering embrace. Finally they both fell into an exhausted but tranquil sleep.

Marisa awoke with a start as a cold, damp nose was thrust under the bedclothes and encountered her warm, bare arm. Her eyes flew open to meet Brand's amused face above hers. "Lazy wench," he chided softly, "even your hound cannot wait any longer for his breakfast."

Marisa's initial reaction was to counter with a crisp retort, but as the smile playing about his chiseled lips and the unmistakable humor in his voice registered, all the memories of the previous night came back with a pleasant rush, and she felt the heat of color rise to her cheeks. "You gave me little time for rest, Saxon," she murmured, fascinated and suddenly tense with anticipation, as she watched his lips inch closer and closer. All thought fled beneath the fiercely sweet pressure of his mouth on hers.

Rollo's persistent whimper increased in volume until Brand felt Marisa break away. "Mayhap his wounds fester," she suggested, a frown between her eyes.

Brand raised his head to meet the forlorn regard of the shaggy head resting inches away from Marisa's shoulder. "The only place that pains him is his belly, I would wager, and I cannot say that I blame the beast. You have him as spoiled as a lap dog."

Marisa arched a fine, tawny eyebrow. "I would not exactly call his actions yesterday those of a lap dog, Saxon."

"Indeed. If not for our pampered but intrepid Rollo, you would be . . . " His words died off, a sober look replacing the former amusement in his eyes. "And Griffith would have been taken from me." He reached out to scratch the dog's head. "I wonder who's dagger stayed the wolf."

Marisa's eyes narrowed in thought. "Mayhap 'twas someone from the village who dislikes me, but not enough to see me die. Or could it be that this man feared Angharad's wrath had she caught a glimpse of him?" She paused. "There were still many men hunting wolf cubs about the forest, and someone could have seen and heard everything—and even guessed at Angharad's intention to take Griffith with her. Perhaps that brought about the killing of the beast, rather than the prospect of my death."

Brand took her face between his palms. "I think you will have little trouble with my people from now on, Marisa. I told Edgiva in no uncertain terms to show you the respect due my wife or leave Camwright. And—"

"Oh, Brand, no!" The idea of Edgiva losing her home because of Marisa held no appeal for her.

"No? How long did you think I would countenance such hostile behavior toward you?" His eyes darkened in pain for a long moment before he spoke again. "My own resentment was acceptable in my mind, but when I saw it mirrored in the actions of some of the villagers—and especially after the incident outside the church following the Easter mass—I knew I had to put a stop to it. Do not feel pity for Edgiva. If I know Rolfe, he will bring her around, for he has no wish to be banished from his own village because of his wife's vicious tongue."

He pushed away from her and strode from the bed to the door, magnificently naked, to let Rollo out. "Griffith will feed him, so you need not worry, Marisa, and when they see the dog outside, someone will bring our breakfast."

"You had this all planned, didn't you?" she asked with feigned pique, her eyes taking in his bronzed upper body as he worked with deft movements to build a small fire in one of the braziers. The fact that he was pale from the waist down detracted not one bit from the beautiful symmetry of his body. A shiver of remembered pleasure swept lightly over her. He turned to smile at her in answer, and Marisa wondered why she had never noticed the beauty of his smile before. *Because he has had little reason to smile,* a small voice reminded her. "You were very sure of yourself—and my reaction to you, Saxon."

He walked past the partly open door, the early morning sunlight gilding his body, then slid across the bed toward Marisa and buried his face in the silver-blond swath of her hair, forcing her back down beneath him. One leg stretched possessively over her lower body, which was still covered, and Marisa reveled in the gesture. *I belong to him,* she thought.

"I remember well your passionate response the first time, sweet, and was determined to make amends with you at any cost." His voice was muffled, and he nuzzled the delicate curve of a small, shell-shaped ear.

"Brand?"

"Umm?"

"Why did you not tell me of your suspicions regarding

Angharad's attempt to poison Rollo? You allowed me to feel such resentment toward your people.''

He raised his head to gaze down into her eyes. ''I was not certain of her guilt at the time, and I did not want to add to your chagrin regarding the news of my marriage to Rhiannon.'' He seemed to withdraw from her then, very subtly, and Marisa regretted her question, although it had been important to her. ''If it was Angharad who had already spoiled your homecoming, I did not want you to know that she might have been responsible until I was certain.''

''Until you were certain, Brand, or never?''

Instantly she could have bitten her tongue, for evidence of an inward struggle of some kind was clearly apparent in his eyes, and he seemed suddenly to withdraw from her. He pushed himself away, retreating physically as well as emotionally, and Marisa felt her throat tighten.

They had come so far since the night before, and now, she suspected, here was the last—and greatest—obstacle to stand between them: Brand's remorse over what he considered his failings during his first marriage and his seemingly insurmountable guilt. *He will never love me,* Marisa thought with a sense of despondency. *I will have his respect—which is what I desired earlier—and his attraction to me. He said himself that he needed me. But wanting and needing are not the same as loving. Will he ever love me?*

Why should it matter? asked her conscience. *You do not love him, either. Could you ever love a barbaric, foreign Saxon, Marisa de Brionne?*

Pushing aside her jumbled thoughts, Marisa determined to restore the mood they had shared only moments before and cast about for a way to accomplish it. And then, without warning, her empty stomach rumbled loudly in protest.

Brand slowly turned to regard her, a corner of his mouth quirking at the delicate stain of embarrassment upon her cheeks. ''So, you rumble as loudly as yon hound, Lady Marisa?'' His raised eyebrows only increased the rosy hue

of her face. "I wonder who takes after whom in this unusual likeness between mistress and hound. The timing is
uncanny and the sounds rather similar, considering one is
beast and the other is—"

Marisa's discarded nightgown flew toward his head and
wrapped around his face before he could finish his sentence.

A discreet knock on the partially open door caught Marisa's attention, and Brand, disentangling himself from the
feminine garment, told a smirking Adela to set the tray
upon the bedside table and close the door on her way out.
"And now, wench, you must suffer the consequences of
attacking the lord of the manor." Before Marisa could
think to slide off the bed and escape him, his hand caught
her hair, gently but firmly wrapping a thick lock around
his fist, forcing her face very close to his, his intention
blatantly displayed in his expression. "I think I will accept
reparation—only if 'tis properly done," he added wickedly as the other hand cupped her breast, the thumb gently
teasing the nipple. And then his mouth covered hers, and
Marisa knew it would be awhile before they broke the fast.

Chapter 13

Marisa later learned that the villagers would be severely punished if they spotted Angharad, or worse, trafficked with her, and then neglected to inform Brand. If the old woman was caught, she was to be brought to the manor, or killed if she attempted to flee. Brand was obviously taking no chances with the life of his son, his wife, or any of his people.

Marisa mustered up enough courage to ask him why he had tolerated Angharad's presence before Rhiannon's death if she were so conniving and capable of such treachery.

"She never approved of our marriage, for she hated anything that was not Welsh. For Rhiannon's sake, she acted docilely enough. She loved Rhiannon and Griffith and would have done naught to jeopardize their position here. But she never warmed to me, and I in turn never trusted her." He looked up at the tapestry-covered wall before him, seemingly lost in his musings, and a pang of jealousy unexpectedly pricked Marisa at the thought that he was reminiscing about his lost wife. His next words, spoken softly and with the biting edge of self-derision, unexpectedly struck her with empathetic pain like a physical blow. "Angharad told me that I could not keep my filthy Saxon hands from her 'stepdaughter'—or her half-niece—whichever she was." He gave a low, self-deprecatory laugh. "That was so lamentably far from the truth."

Marisa watched the changing expressions on his face as he wrestled with the guilt that seemed to torture him relentlessly. "You did not fulfill your obligations in the marriage bed?"

He shook his head without looking at her and admitted, "Not as Rhiannon wished—or deserved."

In an attempt to wipe the stark anguish from his features, she countered softly, "I cannot believe you did not give her what she needed. Griffith is proof that you did. You are fortunate to have at least a part of her in your son."

He came out of his spoken ruminations then, turning from his contemplation of the tapestry toward Marisa, a look akin to discovery in his eyes as they roved over her face, searching her features as if to be certain she was sincere. "You need not take my part, Marisa."

"And why not, Brand Ericson? You are my husband now."

Marisa took up her role as Brand's wife with renewed enthusiasm, despite a lingering coolness on the part of some of the villagers. Even Edgiva was somewhat civil, although Marisa suspected it wasn't because of a sudden fondness for the Norman lady of the manor.

Marisa also always made time for Griffith. They would take long walks together, accompanied by a man-at-arms at Brand's insistence, and Marisa would delight the boy with tales of the Norman chevaliers' lust for bloodshed and war.

"Since the peasants suffered abominably when they got in the way of knightly skirmishes and ambushes, the Church decreed the concept known as the Truce of God," she informed Griffith one day in June as she taught him some of the finer points of chess out in the warm summer sun of the yard.

"But how does that help the peasant folk?" Griffith asked.

"Wars are forbidden during Lent, on certain saints' days, and every week from Wednesday eve until Monday

morn. The common folk can till their fields three days
out of the week and rest undisturbed on Sundays, but are
wise to take cover on Mondays, Tuesdays, and Wednes-
days.''

Griffith paused over his next move. ''I would not make
fun of your customs, Marisa, but it sounds barbaric to
me. A man cannot work his fields on those three days for
fear of chevaliers thundering through the crops intent on
destruction—or 'glory,' as you called it?''

Marisa eyed the boy with growing respect, for she'd
noticed that he often displayed a maturity beyond his
years. Not only was he bright, but he was also making
her see that the Norman way of life—especially the ways
of the knights—was in some respects barbaric. As far as
she had seen, there was no such scourge in England,
nothing to prevent a man of the soil from working peaceably every day but the Sabbath.

''And how do you choose your dukes, Marisa?'' he
asked. ''The English people chose their king through the
witan in London. The witan represents all our shires.''
His voice lowered with sadness. ''Or 'twas the way of it
before the Normans came.''

Marisa thought about it for a moment, and then, realizing which method was more fair, was hard-put to tell
him the truth. ''Normandy is more like a private estate,
Griffith, to be handed on by the owner to a chosen heir.
Many people did not agree with William's right to be
duke, even though his father Robert made his barons
swear fealty to the boy before he died.''

''Because William was a bastard?''

''*Oui.*'' As more of their customs were brought to
light, it became more and more difficult for Marisa to
view the English as barbarians.

''Marisa, will you teach me to ride Goliath?'' he asked,
suddenly changing the subject.

''Goliath?'' she asked, secretly dismayed.

''Aye. I want to be able to ride like a chevalier! Although,'' he added with someberness in his young voice,

"I would not act so irresponsibly toward the crops of Camwright—or anywhere else."

Marisa regarded him fondly at this very grown-up declaration.

With his next words, however, he unwittingly reminded her that he was, indeed, only a child. "I'll show you our secret place . . . the place Rollo and I discovered beneath the palisade, if you'll teach me," he wheedled.

"You must ask your father first, Griffith," she hedged, hoping that Brand would refuse. "But I will show you what my brothers taught me when my father was not about," she added with a wink to dispel his obvious disappointment.

And so it was that the lady Marisa was caught in the act of brandishing Griffith's wooden sword while she expertly conducted maneuvers astride the fearsome Goliath within the penned enclosure near the stables. As she wheeled the awesome war-horse to and fro and shouted directives in French, demonstrating the animal's ability to strike out with its forelegs on command, Griffith applauded her impressive performance with childish enthusiasm. Rather than being frightfully reminded of his close encounter with those very hooves, Griffith delighted in the learning process, keeping the wooden slats of the pen between himself and the stallion. Firmly seated upon Goliath's back, Marisa controlled him as if she'd been born to the saddle.

"You handle a sword as well as a housecarl, Marisa," he called out in an awe-tinged voice as she swiped at an imagined opponent and then ordered Goliath to finish off the "victim" once he'd been downed.

Nodding to acknowledge his praise, Marisa caught sight of Brand standing not ten paces behind his son, watching her. His disheveled hair shone with gold highlights under the bright sun, and his tunic was casually draped over one shoulder. He'd gone to inspect several sections of fencing surrounding the perimeter of Camwright that had been deliberately broken, and he'd obviously become involved in the physical labor of mending them, for his lightweight chainse clung damply to his upper torso like a second skin. Marisa suddenly felt giddy at the sight. Heady with the sensations that his mere presence could send singing along her veins, she shouted in a teasing voice, "Wipe that sour expression from your face, Saxon, else I may take it into my head to cut you down where you stand!"

She gave a command to Goliath, who trotted toward the stump near the stable, where Marisa dismounted in a quick fluid motion and handed the reins to an anxious, hovering stableboy. The look on the boy's face told her he feared his lord's wrath for saddling the animal and allowing Marisa to ride without telling Brand. " 'Tis all right, Brian," she assured him as she moved through the gate toward Griffith, her eyes on her husband. At first she could not read his expression because of the position of the late afternoon sun behind him . . . she'd merely called out her threat for effect. But now, judging from the tension in his stance, she suspected he disapproved of her behavior.

Putting an arm around Griffith's small shoulders, Marisa guided him toward Brand. "I only wished to show Griffith Goliath's capabilities, my lord," she began with a hesitant smile that quickly faded as she discerned the stern look on his face. She could have no idea that Brand was struggling inwardly to control the fear that had twisted in his gut like a blade at the sight of his fragile wife atop the stallion executing battle maneuvers.

"To ride the beast is one thing, my lady wife, but to churn his battle lust to such a dangerous pitch is another. What if you had fallen?"

Marisa made a moue of dismissal and shook her head decisively. "Oh, Goliath would never attack his rider—he knows me too well. 'Tis only the enemy that—"

"Like my son?"

The excitement in her eyes died, even as it died in Griffith's, at the grim reminder, and Brand instantly regretted his words. "He did not know Griffith well enough, my lord," she answered quietly.

"And I asked Marisa, Father," added Griffith in her defense. "I would have ridden Goliath myself, but she would not allow it."

"I see." Brand fought for self-control. He was hot and tired and frustrated with the deliberate damage being done to the fencing. And then to come upon Marisa brandishing a sword, albeit a wooden one, from the back of the striking Goliath . . . it had almost been his undoing.

"My work was done—at least for the moment, my lord hus—"

"Marisa," he interrupted, "I do not accuse you of shirking your duties. I only question the wisdom of your acting the part of a chevalier. Mayhap you should have been born a man."

Ire flashed in her eyes at his words. "It would have saved you much trial and tribulation, would it not have, my lord?"

It would not hurt to bow to his wishes in some things. . . . Adela's words suddenly echoed in her mind.

"I regret my words, my lord," she said evenly. "Come, I will prepare a bath to ease the ache from your bones. And, Griffith, will you see to Rollo's supper?"

As she took his tunic and turned to lead him to the bower, Brand caught the flash of rebellion in her eyes and smiled in spite of himself.

Marisa quickly discovered that, despite Brand's reserve with her when in public, the rapture they shared in the intimacy of their bower only increased with each passing night. If Brand feared that friends, retainers, and servants alike would think Marisa had supplanted his Welsh wife in his affections, in the privacy of their bedchamber his body was telling her things that his lips would not.

In the beginning of July, Marisa missed her courses for the second month and began to suspect she was carrying Brand's child. She was delighted at the prospect of giving him a son or daughter, yet she was also afraid of how the news would affect him. She said nothing for several days, until one morning as she moved to get out of bed an insidious nausea hit her. Perspiration beaded her face and dizziness buzzed through her head. Lying down, she thought back to what Adela had told her, long before they had ever come to England, about the signs of pregnancy. *Mais non! It cannot be!* she swore fiercely. *It will ruin everything.*

When on the third morning the symptoms recurred, Marisa was forced to acknowledge with a sinking heart that it was no illness.

Brand noticed her indisposure with a sharp eye, and when she sat up in bed for the third morning in a row, only to ask for the chamber pot, the blood drained from his face as the source of her malady registered. Marisa must be with child.

He held her in his arms until the dry heaves subsided, rocking her like a child and crushing her to him as if he could not bear to let her go.

"Brand, Brand, I cannot breathe," she protested, laboring to draw air into her lungs under the press of his great strength. Immediately he slackened his hold and gazed down into her upturned face, his own etched with concern.

"It cannot be!"

Marisa smiled wanly at his words. "We have not exactly been saints in our behavior of late. 'Twas only natural that it would happen."

He gazed deeply into her eyes, already feeling that his life would be only dust and ashes should he lose her to childbirth. He dared not admit what his overwhelming fear forced him to silently acknowledge . . . that he loved her . . . loved her as a man should love a woman—passionately, totally, without reserve; of the body as well as the spirit; not with a gentle, sibling love of brother for sister or with the staunch affection of friend for friend. But with more. Much more.

Ruthlessly pushing aside his vulnerable feelings, he said with a grimness that took her aback, "You will excuse me if I prefer not to lose two wives to childbirth."

Emotion formed a lump in her throat, and she mur-

mured, ''I'm sorry, Brand, to cause you unhappiness.''
Yet the pregnancy was his doing as much as it was hers.
And was it not a natural thing, something to be desired?
The risk was understood and, of necessity, ignored.

Her de Brionne pride rose to the fore. ''But *you* will
excuse *me* if I refuse to shoulder the entire blame for this
unfortunate mistake?''

He said nothing for a moment, caught in the grip of
warring emotions.

''I can always manage to fall from my mare or Goliath.
Or I can take a remedy for such a thing.''

''You will not!'' He held her at arm's length, vexation
creasing his brow. '' 'Twould be murder and we have all
of us suffered enough for our sins.''

''But I would rather rot in hell than live with your
anger until I am safely delivered of child.'' He shook his
head to negate her words, but then another thought struck
Marisa. ''Or is it that you do not want a child that is half
Norman, Brand?''

''That has naught to do with it. He or she would be
mine, as loved as Griffith. Although,'' he added on a
softer note, ''it will undoubtedly be born with sword in
hand—whatever its gender—and shouting commands to
some imaginary destrier.''

Despite his words, he would not touch her intimately
after that, and Marisa felt as if she were made of the
most finely blown glass, inwardly seething with vexation
and frustration. She was not allowed to ride, which was
the ultimate punishment for a woman who loved being
astride a horse. She could not go hawking or watch a
hunt. She was even instructed to relinquish to Edyth many
of her duties as lady of the manor.

''He treats me like a babe,'' Marisa grumbled to
Adela. Chin in hand, she sat at the board one morning
in the main hall, staring morosely at the open side door
that relentlessly beckoned to her.

''He loves you, my lady.''

Marisa remained staring at the sunlight outside until
Adela's words registered. She raised her chin from her

cupped hand and looked at her as if she were undone. "Loves me? I have never known you to take pleasure in such cruel jesting, Adela." She turned to watch one of the female hounds, heavy with her unborn litter, lumber across the hall.

"Lady Marisa, for shame!" Adela said indignantly, an undercurrent of hurt threading her words. "You are overly sensitive, and sharp-tongued into the bargain, for you surely know me better than that. You should be happy that he is so concerned, even if 'tis a bit overdone."

"Indeed, I should be grateful. He treats me with all the care and reverence that he shows yon prized hunting bitch. Delivered of a good litter, her value only increases."

Adela shook her head, sensing the futility of arguing with Marisa in her present mood. "You have only to look beyond your nose, my lady, to see that 'tis more than ordinary concern that shows in his eyes every time he looks at you. He will not admit it, but his eyes tell all, *petite*."

Marisa managed a sketch of a smile for the well-meaning Adela. "Forgive my thoughtless words, Adela, but there are things you do not know. . . ."

"I know more than you would ever suspect regarding your lord's fears, my lady. The servants here have wagging tongues, just as in Normandy."

"What is this about wagging tongues?" inquired Edyth from behind them. She smiled radiantly, her eyes alight with happiness. She was to be married the Sunday after Lammas at the beginning of August. "You look as forlorn as Rollo when he wants something, Marisa."

The young woman had to laugh at the analogy. "Indeed, I do want something, Edyth. I want to go outside and ride or go ahawking, or even make the rounds of the village. I cannot abide this unnecessary and cruel inactivity. I shall go mad if I must behave thusly for much longer."

Adela cleared away the remains of Marisa's breakfast and tactfully withdrew as Edyth put a hand on Marisa's shoulder and sat beside her on the bench. "Marisa, did you know that Rhiannon died in childbed?"

"Aye. Brand told me. And I am so sorry, but it happens all the time. If he didn't wish me to become pregnant, he should not have touched me." Even as she spoke the words, she mentally acknowledged how ridiculous they sounded. Hadn't she been hurt beyond the telling by his refusal to consummate the marriage for so long?

"Marisa, I think you know the answer to that. You are very beautiful and what man would not desire you?"

"Morgan!" she exclaimed childishly to disprove Edyth's point.

Edyth laughed aloud. "I should hope he wouldn't, but that is beside the point. Any man in his right mind who had a wife with your looks and form would be addled not to want to make you his. You are my brother's wife. I see his affection for you growing with every passing day—in spite of himself."

Marisa allowed a soft sigh to escape her lips. "First he accuses me of being spoiled and willful, unable to run a manor, and when I would prove him wrong, he will not allow me to do so."

"Be patient, Marisa. Please try to be patient with him. He carries so great a burden on his back and you can help lighten it if you will only be tolerant of him until he is more like himself again." She reached over to take hold of both of Marisa's shoulders, turning the Norman girl to face her. "I promise you things will be better, especially after the babe is born. Mayhap that in itself will help him exorcise some of his private devils. In the meantime, I have many things that you can help with in preparation for the wedding. Will you?"

Marisa's eyes lit up with enthusiasm for the first time that morning. "Oh, aye, Edyth! What am I to do?"

Soon Marisa was busy polishing the weapons that hung over the western door. Most of them were decorations only . . . swords arranged like the spokes of a wheel, pikes spread out to open as a great fan, and axes forming a great arch over all, blades at the top and handles converging inward. Marisa cleaned with a vengeance, sitting at one of the trestle tables and venting her frustration upon the wood and steel weapons until they shone like new, except for the dents and chips from battle.

They no sooner finished cleaning and polishing the armaments than it was time for the nooning, and the great horn sounded for the midday meal, calling in all those who were in the fields. Brand strode into the hall, his eyes automatically narrowing in the dimness after the bright light of day, searching out Marisa. She looked happy as a lark, directing one of the servants on a ladder as to where to put a sword upon the wall. In impatience, she started up the ladder herself.

"The bracket has fallen, my lady," the boy called down to her. "I cannot replace the sword in its exact position unless another is secured."

"Are you certain?" she called up as her foot touched the third rung. "It will ruin the symmetry—"

"My servants do not lie, my lady," Brand said into her ear, one arm around her shoulder and the other sweeping under her knees to lift her off the ladder and securely into his arms. "You have a most pronounced penchant for disobeying me, Viking. I thought I told you not to do anything strenuous or potentially harmful to you or the child."

Seeing the concern in his eyes, she swallowed her pert reply. "I did not intend to climb any farther," she ventured. "After all, a ladder is not made for more than one person."

Their gazes fused, all else around them receding until Brand realized with a start what he was about and quickly set her on her feet, releasing her as if the very contact burned him.

The color of Marisa's eyes deepened with pain. "Did I mayhap step in dog droppings, Saxon, that you are so eager to release me before all and sundry? Have I need of a bath?"

Brand made a valiant attempt to rectify his error, knowing even as he spoke that the damage was done.

"Nay, my lady wife. Rather 'tis my own odor of sweat and toil that I fear would offend you."

"How little you know me, Brand Ericson, if that is what you think." She proceeded to the high table, vowing silently that one day he would not be able to keep his hands from her no matter who was present.

Brand tried to make up for his attempt to seem indifferent to Marisa with entertaining small talk during the meal. He spoke of the healthy crops and the final mending of the broken fencing, essaying to draw out a silent Marisa. When that failed, he complimented her on the bright array of newly cleaned weapons that lined the wall in perfect symmetry, except for the last sword. "I will resecure the bracket myself, Marisa," he added, watching her face for some sign of softening.

Unable to remain perturbed with him for long, Marisa allowed a smile to curve her soft lips. "Thank you, my lord. We must have everything in perfect order for the wedding."

Unable to keep the warmth from his gaze, he watched her slim, graceful fingers finish her meal, his own meal forgotten as he gave his appreciation free rein. If only he could . . .

The horn sounded, announcing the arrival of visitors to Camwright. His thoughts scattering, Brand stood, stepped over the bench, and strode toward the door, half a dozen of his retainers following at his heels. "Do not quit the hall until I give you my leave—any of you," he ordered.

Marisa saw the poorly concealed terror on Edyth's face. "Normans," she whispered, and then, realizing what she'd said before her sister-by-marriage, hurried to cover her blunder. "Or scavengers from the great battle or—"

" 'Tis all right, Edyth," Marisa said gently, and waited tensely for sounds of someone returning to tell them all was well. Perhaps it was only Mauger le Faux, or even Richard or Raoul—although that was unlikely. She's received a letter from Raoul only a few weeks past, telling her that both he and his brother were very busy keeping the peace for the King and patrolling any areas of England reluctant to accept Norman rule. It seemed rebellion was on the uprise, and therefore there was no telling when Marisa would get to see either one of her brothers.

Morgan returned to the hall before Brand and quickly informed everyone that it was only Eric the Merchant. "News travels fast, Edyth," he told her with a meaningful grin. "He comes with the finest of silks and linens for a wedding that he heard will soon take place."

Edyth left the table and, with Marisa in tow, hurried as fast as she could with her limp toward the great door and out into the July sunshine. "Brand must have told the merchant while he was in London, the sly fox," she told Marisa, her cheeks flushed with excitement. "He had this planned all along, and left poor Morgan in the dark concerning his intentions of 'persuading' me to accept Morgan's suit."

"Poor Morgan, indeed," declared Brand as he approached the threesome with the merchant from Dover beside him. "A bit of suffering only improves one's character. And if anyone's character needed improving, 'twas the puffed up, harp-strumming Welshman's. I only primed him for you by not pleading his cause, Edyth."

But Edyth was throwing her arms around her tall brother, her happiness infecting all. "Thank you, Brand. But I do have Marisa's gown, which she kindly agreed to let me wear, and there is not so much I truly need that you must spend your gold upon me."

"You are my only sister, Edyth. Do not spoil my pleasure, I pray you."

"And, of course, yon blackguard would never give *me* any credit for asking our merchant to visit Camwright," interjected Morgan. "After all, I knew 'twould only be a matter of time before I won him over . . . I merely tolerated his attempts to, ah, improve my character." All four people laughed aloud at his wounded-sounding retort, which didn't fool anyone for a moment.

Eric the Merchant was a large man of middle age, with a girth that bespoke good living and shrewd black eyes that looked as if they were well used to sizing up people quickly. His train was made up of about twenty mules with four boys standing lined up before the animals, which were laden with sacking-covered packs.

"Eric of Dover, this is my wife, the lady Marisa. I would bid you deal with her now, for since my marriage Edyth has relinquished her position as lady of the manor."

Eric executed a rather clumsy bow, which made Marisa smile, and gave her an appreciative grin. "I accept the loss of dealing with the lovely lady Edyth with good grace since her replacement comes so close to duplicating her beauty and bearing."

"And you think *me* silver-tongued," Morgan commented dryly as Eric gallantly brought Marisa's hand up to his lips.

"Thank you, *Sieur Eric*," Marisa returned glibly by addressing him formally.

Demonstrating her ability to deal with an itinerant merchant, Marisa walked along the line of beasts and muleteers, inspecting his wares. Knowing that many merchants would cheat their own mothers to make a good profit, Marisa soon realized that he was fairly honest. His seasonings and spices from the East were willingly traded for dried fish from the bountiful Wye. "We have fine wool, Eric of Dover, to trade for some good wine."

"We have that aplenty, my lady, for the Normans prefer their wine to our mead any day." His rosy cheeks deepened in hue when he obviously realized he may have offended her, but Marisa merely smiled charmingly.

"Ah, indeed, we do," she said.

He pulled a small cask of wine from one of the packs and poured some into a cup for her to sample. "I will take half a score of these casks of wine and after you see our wool, pray come in with your drivers for some refreshment."

Brand watched her with admiration, for obviously she

knew what she was about. She was a woman of many facets, he thought. Determinedly pushing aside the guilt that still lingered on the edge of his conscience over his first marriage, he decided he would relish discovering each of her talents during their life together.

At his insistence, Edyth was examining bolts of silk and linen, shyly asking Morgan his opinion. Morgan rolled his eyes heavenward in supplication. "Deliver me from a vacillating female," he intoned aloud. "Take as many bolts as you wish, Edyth, for 'twill most likely be several years before we see another merchant, the situation being what it is in England."

Marisa caught the bleakness that clouded her husband's eyes and hurried to distract him. "Let us finish this business later. You and your men must be tired and thirsty, Eric. Come, into the hall with all of you."

Morgan had beckoned Brand over to look at several swords made of the finest steel from the Rhineland. Marisa paused a moment when Griffith, who'd been walking back and forth along the train, his eyes as wide as saucers, plucked at her sleeve to get her attention. "Marisa?"

She looked down and smiled at him. *"Oui, cher?"*

"There is something here for you. One of the mule boys told me that 'twas given to him by a Cymry whom he did not know, saying only that it belonged to the new mistress of Camwright."

Marisa took the small, crudely wrapped bundle and slowly untied the twine that held together the ends of the moldy-smelling burlap. Even before it was revealed, unease prickled along her nerves at the feel of the object within, but Marisa shrugged away such unfounded foreboding. "I wonder what it can be," she began. And then the ends of the cloth fell away from their grisly token, and Marisa felt the bile rise in her throat at the sight of it.

Nestled within the surrounding burlap was the lopped off paw of a wolf, or a wolfhound, gray in color and the exact size of one of Rollo's paws. Blood stained the cloth and had congealed where the limb had been severed, the cloying scent of it already drifting upward to her nostrils, adding to the nausea and faintness rapidly overpowering her as her lips silently formed the name "Rollo."

"Marisa!" Griffith cried in alarm.

Brand, who was still looking over the sword blades, looked back to see his wife's face blanch and a sudden spasm of shock whip through her body as her knees slowly buckled beneath her.

In a few swift strides he was beside her, catching her before she hit the ground, and the gruesome gift dropped with a dull thud to the earth.

Chapter 14

"Marisa?"

Heavy lashes fluttered and then slowly raised, revealing disoriented violet eyes.

Brand's concerned face hovering over hers, however, did wonders to bring everything rushing back into focus, and Marisa's gaze regained perfect lucidity. The animal's paw. Some poor dumb creature had lost its paw because of a madwoman's dastardly tricks.

"Marisa, love—are you unharmed?"

The anxiety in that deep voice made her heart swell with pleasure, and the worry shadowing the golden eyes to topaz quickened her pulses. His hand smoothed back stray tendrils of palest blond from her cool forehead in an unconsciously gentle gesture.

"*Oui.*" She pushed herself up to her elbows, ignoring his sudden frown. "I am not given to fainting, Brand. 'Twas just such a shock. . . . Rollo?" she asked suddenly, her fine eyebrows drawing together questioningly.

Immediately an inquisitive black nose appeared on the bed beside Brand's seated form, followed by the rest of the beloved shaggy head and soulful brown eyes. "Rollo, you beautiful beast!"

Laughing aloud at her incongruous combination of words, Brand watched her hug the dog with lavish affection. His rich, carefree laughter was like music to her ears, and Marisa released Rollo's neck to gaze up at him. Years had fallen away and, she thought, he must have looked thusly before his world had come crashing down around him.

"It may comfort you to know that my people were also instructed to watch out for our brave Rollo here." His eyes lit with rare merriment. "There were a few grumbles, but I think he will be safe as long as he remains in Camwright proper."

"Oh, Brand," she whispered, her throat constricted with emotion.

"I am organizing a search party to rout out Angharad, for she must be hereabouts somewhere." His tone was flat, emotionless, as if he were speaking of some rabid animal that had to be found and destroyed. "She cannot continue terrorizing you—and striking fear into the hearts of others who are completely innocent of my actions."

The meaning of his words was not lost upon Marisa. "You speak of our marriage, I know. And you are right, Brand. Your people should not have to suffer because I am a Norman. If I went away—back to Normandy—Angharad would cease her ugly tricks and—"

"And what, Marisa? This does not sound like the fire-brand I wed in London. Do you not remember telling me that had you been English you would have fought for the land of your birth, no matter the threat? Those are not the words of one who would retreat in the face of a challenge." He drew her toward him until their faces were very close. "And, I must admit, I have grown accustomed to your presence—even though the urge to throttle you is ofttimes as strong as the urge to make love to you. Besides, you carry my child."

And without our union you would forfeit Griffith's future.

She pushed that thought aside, however, as his lips firmly molded to hers, and the thrill of anticipation she evinced whenever she was in his arms began to overwhelm all reason.

Yet after a few moments she breathlessly broke away from him. "Brand, we have guests. And the mule boy—he has not been blamed for this, I pray?"

"Ah, Viking, such a soft heart you harbor beneath that beautiful but courageous exterior. Eric is questioning the lad now, but I doubt he had any idea that he was part of such cruel sport. And," he added almost to himself, "my instincts tell me there just may be more involved in this than Angharad alone—although I doubt 'tis any of our villagers."

They returned to the hall, where the muleteer was still being questioned relentlessly by Eric the Merchant. The boy was close to tears as Brand strode up to them, Marisa close behind. She was determined the lad should not suffer, just as she was convinced he'd been an unwitting dupe. "There was no real harm done, Eric," Brand intervened. "My wife is fine now and harbors no ill will toward the boy."

"Indeed, Eric, and—?"

"Gyrth, my lady." The youth knelt at her feet, clutching her hand fervently. "I knew naught of what the bundle contained, I swear it!"

"Of course you didn't," she said gently. "Rise, Gyrth, and join your comrades in a cup of mead and some bread and cheese."

His hazel eyes lit with gratitude and relief at her easy forgiveness, and he rose, bowing awkwardly to her. "Thank you, my lady. Th—thank you."

Eric told her, "He said an old woman or a man disguised as such—for he claims 'twas hard to discern—gave him the package and bade him give it to the lady of Camwright, then disappeared immediately into the woods. He did not think to tell me, and I can well believe it." Eric shook his head in annoyance. "He is ofttimes irresponsible and easily gulled, even by his fellow mule boys." He frowned at Gyrth's retreating form and then turned his gaze to Brand and Marisa. "I truly regret this entire incident, my lord—my lady."

" 'Tis over and done with," Brand answered firmly. "Come. Let us join the others."

"Tell me, Eric," Brand asked later, after they'd partaken of a substantial midday repast, "what you hear about Madog ap Cynan and his followers."

Eric sucked in his large belly and belched in appreciation of the meal, his eyes narrowing thoughtfully. "I have heard only the vaguest of rumors, my lord—that he is restless, eager for a means to stir up Riwallon and Bleddyn against you. But 'tis only hearsay, and even if 'twere true, everyone around these parts knows those two would not cause you mischief."

The tables had been cleared and Marisa and Edyth were outdoors making their final decisions over cloth and foodstuffs to take in trade. Morgan, Eric, and Brand sat alone at the high table. "Aye, but will they come to Edric the Wild's aid in rebelling against the Normans in Herfordshire?"

"That I do not know, but times are troubled . . . anything is possible."

Much later, when Eric the Merchant and his train departed, Brand and Morgan rode together for a final inspection of the fencing around Camwright. "You think there is more to these problems than Angharad?" the Welshman asked, as if reading Brand's thoughts.

Brand nodded. "Think on it, Morgan. I can envision Angharad poisoning the hound and possibly luring Walter and Caedmon to the bog with her tricks, and, of course, she ordered the attack on Marisa the other day. But what of the destruction of entire sections of the fence? And what of the mysterious death of Harald Svenson in Wighton? Or the fact that the youth Gyrth was not certain if the one who handed him that mauled animal's part was a crone or a man? It could easily be someone—Madog ap Cynan— trying to throw us off by taking advantage of Angharad's hatred."

Morgan grunted in agreement. "Mayhap I should go to Wighton on the morrow. Since you've most generously granted me the overseeing of it after Edyth and I wed . . ."

"As part of her dowry, you understand," Brand couldn't help but interject with exaggerated solemnity, and he received an exasperated look in reward.

"As I was saying," Morgan continued, unperturbed, "mayhap I should keep a closer watch on the village."

Brand shook his head and stopped his horse before a newly mended section of fencing. His gaze moved along the wooden reinforcements as he answered, "Nay, I would rather you remain here and keep watch over Marisa—and Camwright," he added. "I will go to Wighton on the morrow and then to Wales to meet with the Welsh princes. I may be gone for several days, and I need someone on whom I can depend while I am away."

Morgan nodded as they started to move away again. "As you wish, but have a care. You'll not have me as a guide and, not being a Welshman . . . "

Brand's level-eyed stare, daring him to insult his capabilities further, effectively silenced his lips, but his dark eyes gleamed with repressed mirth.

Brand left before she even awakened, and Marisa knew only that he would be gone for several days, something he'd mentioned the night before. He still had not made love to her, although he'd been solicitous of her, holding his desire in check, she knew, with an iron will. When she'd questioned him about his destination, he'd merely reassured her that it was routine business and he was to depart the very next day. In Marisa's mind, his abrupt departure not only proved beyond a shadow of a doubt that he did not trust her, it also proved he truly cared not one whit about her.

As the day progressed, despite Edyth's efforts to keep Marisa busy—in the hall in the morning and on rounds in the village in the early afternoon—Marisa's spirits plummeted even as the sun rose higher in the cobalt bowl of the sky. She unexpectedly felt an aching homesickness, even though the residents of Camwright were now somewhat more tolerant of her. The fact that their improved attitude was undoubtedly due to Brand's influence and not of their own free will spoiled it for her.

With Rollo at her side, she was walking toward the manor in answer to the nooning horn when Morgan joined her unexpectedly. "My lady seems under the weather this fine day. Can it be that you miss your husband, I wonder?"

As always, when Morgan chose to tease her out of her doldrums, an involuntary smile tugged at her lips. "He does not trust me, Morgan. He told me naught of his business. He will of a certainty drive me as mad as Angharad with his turnabouts. One day he is solicitous and almost loving—in private, of course—and the next he is cool and aloof, as if we were strangers. I would never betray him—to le Faux, to William, or even to my father. He is my husband!" A flush of anger flagged her cheeks.

"Why do you not go and visit your Norman countryman, le Faux?" Morgan suggested.

"Mauger?" Her eyes lit up for a brief moment at the thought, though Marisa could not tell if he were jesting or not. "And why not? I can ride in a litter—then Brand cannot say I disobeyed him by riding astride—and I can prove my loyalty to him, Morgan!"

"Indeed?"

She turned eager eyes to him. "Oh, don't you see, Morgan? I can actually do Brand a service by visiting Mauger. While he plys me with questions, mayhap I can learn a thing or two myself. . . . I am as canny at playing ignorant as anyone else. Why, I can even win his trust and then lead him on with false information if the opportunity arises. He just may reveal something that would be valuable to Brand."

Morgan was thoughtfully silent for a moment. "Well, he is definitely a threat to Brand's position here at Camwright. Brand is losing some of his influence with the Welsh, and mayhap, well, perhaps you just may learn something of value during your visit."

"*Oui*, Morgan. What if he is up to more than merely giving William faulty information on Brand's activities and disproving Brand's living up to his part of the bargain? I can only guess, however . . . but a visit could do no harm. What say you? Can you give me a good escort if I promise to return by dusk at the latest?"

"He will be furious when he discovers I permitted you to go . . . yet I believe you would be safe in the company of a fellow Norman who knows of your father."

Marisa nodded, in complete accord. "We will say naught until I've discovered information of some use to Brand—if not this time, then the next. In fact"—her eyes twinkled with excitement and deviltry—"I can ride the mare, if he is not to know." At Morgan's raised eyebrows, she added, "I will keep her at a sedate walk, never fear, Morgan, and if Brand does not know of the visit, he cannot discover that I rode astride." She put a hand on his arm in reassurance. "Remember, Morgan, that he once said himself that I could visit Mauger if I so desired."

And so it was that Marisa, with an escort of four men-at-arms, and to Edyth's consternation and disapproval, set out for Fauxbray astride her docile mare rather than Goliath. Edwin, one of Brand's most trusted retainers, led the small party, shaking his head every now and then and mumbling under his breath. But he said nothing about his misgivings to Marisa. If Morgan gave permission, then so be it. Brand trusted Morgan like a brother.

Still, everyone was uneasy. As they made their way toward Fauxbray, they seemed to feel that their every move was being observed. In an effort to push aside her edginess, Marisa drew out Edwin enough to discover that Fauxbray was formerly called Mowbray, and was once held by Thane Waltheof, who had been a good friend of Brand's. It had been a small but prosperous village, and Brand had often made the trip between the two villages to trade gossip and drink a horn of mead with Waltheof. The thane had been killed at Hastings, and his lands awarded to Mauger le Faux.

Once more Marisa felt empathetic remorse for her husband and his losses—in this instance, for the loss of a friend and fellow thane of the late King Harold. Small wonder, she thought, that Brand rarely found anything to laugh about, what with his world in ashes wherever he looked.

When Marisa actually caught a glimpse of the Anglo-

Saxons now living and working under Mauger le Faux, she knew the true extent of Brand's love for the people of Camwright.

"By all that is holy," muttered Edwin, as he, too, took in the tattered clothing that barely covered the bodies of the men and women who lived in the village. They moved about with none of the bustling enthusiasm of the residents of Camwright, as if they were merely going through the motions out of necessity. Even the few children were quiet and subdued, and the sound of youthful voices raised in playful exuberance was missing. Many of them bore signs of beatings, as well, and to look at their faces, at the fear and hatred mirrored in their expressions, was to look upon utter hopelessness.

But the horn had sounded and a flood of hostile-looking Normans soon surrounded Marisa and her men. Marisa, who had not expected a warm reception from le Faux's men, announced in French with cool authority, "I am Marisa de Brionne, wife of Brand Ericson. I am come to pay my respects to *Sieur le Faux.*"

Warily, the Normans guided them to the manor compound, which was smaller than the one at Camwright and heavily fortified.

"I will not leave you alone with him," Edwin objected under his breath when one of the Normans motioned for him to dismount and follow him to the newly constructed barracks nearby.

"I will be fine, Edwin . . . you need not worry," Marisa assured the man-at-arms.

Before either could say anything more, Mauger himself emerged from the great hall, his handsome face lighting with pleasure as he recognized Marisa. Reaching up to help her dismount, his hands lingered at her waist for a moment longer than was necessary. "Lady Marisa! So you have finally honored our humble village with a visit." He smiled with unctuous charm and turned to rap out a curt order to one of his men. Brand's retainers dismounted and were led to the barracks.

Edwin opened his mouth to protest again until Marisa

assured him once more that she would be fine. "Go with
the men, Edwin, and keep the peace among you."

"They will be given refreshment, Lady Marisa, and can
amuse themselves with dice or chess, as they like," he
added expansively when the dubious look still lingered on
the faithful Edwin's face. "But come," he urged Marisa,
leading her to the hall, "I have someone here who knows
you."

Now it was Marisa's turn to look wary. "Someone who
knows me?" she asked, puzzled.

"Oui, chérie. Someone who knew you well in Normandy."

Ignoring the endearment, Marisa suddenly felt as if perhaps she had bitten off more than she could chew, for
settling over her again with unwelcome familiarity was
that same sense of foreboding that had enveloped her in
its chill embrace when Eustace had entered the hall at
Brionne to announce her father's arrival.

Mauger allowed her to precede him into the hall, where,
in spite of the pleasant warmth of the summer day, the
cool interior was well lighted by a fire in the central hearth
and sunlight coming from several small, unshuttered windows. The hall was not without a woman's touch, Marisa
noted. The rushes were fresh and sweet-smelling and everything was clean. She briefly wondered who cared for
the hall, for surely none of those poor, downtrodden souls
from the village could. The sparse furniture—sideboards,
settles and stools—had been polished to a glossy sheen,
obviously with the touch of pride and love. Perhaps the
late Waltheof's wife still resided here?

A man was standing with his back to them. There was
something vaguely familiar about him, but Marisa could
not yet see his face. At their entrance, the man did not
turn immediately, as if he were reluctant to face them.

"Robert? Marisa is here." So intent was Marisa on the
figure near the fire that she missed the informal way le
Faux referred to her and the note of smug satisfaction in
his voice.

As Robert turned slowly toward them, Marisa caught

the fleeting impression of defeat in his sloping shoulders, which he suddenly straightened, and of melancholy in his bowed head, which he raised quickly in deliberate preparation for something that could not be avoided.

With the fire behind him, Marisa could not quite make out the shadowed features, but the empty sleeve that hung limply at his left side, swinging gently with the movement of his turn, caught her attention in a moment of unwilling fascination.

Mauger signaled for wine and then chided, "Such hesitation to meet an old friend, Robert? Come, come—step into the light so she can see you."

"I am not one of your Anglo-Saxon peasants whom you can order about at your whim, Mauger. Even a man with one arm has some pride." And then, "Marisa, how good to see you again."

The words were so bereft of warmth, so at odds with their meaning, that Marisa's blood turned cold in her veins. That voice—once a voice so lighthearted and even-tempered, so filled with hope and, yes, affection—was well-known to her. But there was nothing of those sentiments in the flat, hollow tones of greeting that reached her ears and made her heart dance skittishly in long-suppressed guilt and then fear for the man she had married. For this man had come back from the grave—from Malfosse. This man was Robert de Lisieux. And she had wed the one responsible for that small victory and this man's maiming.

Shock went ricocheting through Marisa, and she closed her eyes for a moment in an effort to quell the wash of chaotic feelings. Yet, hard on its heels, a breath of relief wafted over her. Though maimed, he was alive.

Guilt flickered within her breast because she was bound in matrimony to the man responsible for the complete lack of emotion in Robert's eyes and voice—to say nothing of his disfigurement. Robert de Lisieux, childhood friend and would-be lover . . . husband. Clashing currents of emotion threatened to rend Marisa's very soul as she struggled for control.

So this was what it was like to be sundered in twain by

conflicting loyalties—by what might have been and could be no more. This was but another facet of tragedy in the never-ending repercussions of the conquest of Anglo-Saxon England.

Robert stepped forward into the candlelight and sketched her an abbreviated bow. "Were your eyes closed in relief that you did not wed me, Marisa, or because you fear for the Anglo-Saxon to whom you sold yourself?"

Marisa forced her lips to move, ignoring his question and the bitterness underlying his words. "I bid you good morningtide, Robert."

Mauger took a cup of wine from a pretty, flaxen-haired young woman, who held her head high with pride and unbroken spirit as she set down a ewer and two other cups. He pushed it into Marisa's hands and she gratefully took a few sips, studying the English woman, who was probably responsible for the upkeep of the hall and seeing to the comfort of the guests. "Robert is here on official business for the King," Mauger explained.

"Indeed," answered de Lisieux, "William has found a way for me to be useful, if that word can describe what I truly feel."

"Come, let us sit," suggested Mauger, and the three of them complied, Marisa and Mauger on a carved wooden settle, Robert taking a straight-backed chair across from them. "Come and join us, Godgift," Mauger invited the other woman. She lingered reluctantly, remaining unseated, her eyes not on Mauger, but on Robert de Lisieux.

Marisa found her voice. "How—how are you, Robert?"

He stared at her, hard. "You truly mean that, don't you, Marisa? I detect no pity, only concern for a . . . friend." He looked down into his wine cup, seeking his next words. "That is just one of the reasons why I loved you, although I detect a maturity in you that you did not possess in Normandy." He shrugged, the gesture subtly emphasizing his empty left sleeve, and his gaze met hers once more. For a few intense moments it was as if Mauger was not even there. "I am as well as can be, under the circumstances." But the stoic despair in his expression seemed to cry out to her: *As well as a man can be who lost not only the woman he loved, but also part of his body—his very soul.* Renewed guilt lanced through Marisa.

"Robert, I refused your suit long before you ever went to England with our Duke William," she reminded him gently.

"True, Marisa. I wonder what inducement your father used to get you to wed a Saxon when you spurned the eldest son of a rich and powerful baron of Normandy."

Becoming color shaded her cheeks. "I had no choice, Robert. Eustace was to be wed, and I could not abide the thought of Rohese taking my place."

A smile touched his lips unexpectedly at her admission. She was so like the Marisa he'd once known, and Marisa in turn caught a glimpse of the old Robert de Lisieux on whom she had innocently tested her feminine wiles, with no real intent of ever hurting him.

"Brand saved my father's life," she went on. "Father persuaded William to grant him an audience and then intervened when Brand bargained for the retention of his lands for his son."

"Ah, *oui*. His son by another legitimate wife. 'Tis said he grieves for her yet, lovely Marisa. Had you married me, you would have had no such competition."

Had Mauger uttered such words, Marisa would have known for certain that he was being calculatedly cruel; but there was only a stoic despair in Robert's voice. He had no way of knowing he'd struck at the heart of her problems.

Mauger spoke up then. "While Robert was in the area with his patrol, I suggested he confront the husband you so staunchly defend, Marisa. For at one time Robert owned a magnificent gray named Goliath. He might find the Goliath at Camwright of some interest, especialy since William would reward well the man who could prove who led the bloodbath at Malfosse."

Marisa felt Robert's eyes on her even as her heart caught in her throat at the position in which Mauger had deliberately placed her. "Goliath was a gift from my father. . . ."

"Yet previous to that he was a gift from William," Mauger intervened. "Or at least your husband claimed the first time we met."

Ordinarily a poor liar, Marisa discovered in herself a sudden facility for prevarication. "My father made the gift first to the King, who bade Brand choose those destriers he wished to take as part of my dowry. So, a gift from William or my father"—she shrugged—"'tis one and the same."

"Then how is it that Robert told me your father never named two horses the same?" Mauger persisted.

It was perfectly true, but Marisa merely blinked and answered, as if surely it must be apparent to all the world, "Why, of a certainty no breeder of animals could keep to that custom over the years—no matter how well-intentioned—what with all the animals born, trained, and sold. Goliath is a good name for a great war-horse—too good to use only once in a lifetime of horse breeding."

Marisa looked at Robert, in what could have been a subtle form of mute apeal, and he came to her rescue, just as she had hoped he would. Or so she thought until she saw what new direction he was taking. "He must be quite a man, this Brand Ericson. You look well, you are dressed finely." He paused, bleakness settling once more over his even, patrician features. Unbidden came the comparison of what her life would have been like, had she wed this son of the wealthy Gilbert de Lisieux. "And you look content," he added. "Do you love him?"

The blunt, unexpected question took her so aback that her mouth began to open in surprise before she caught herself. "What does love have to do with an arranged marriage?" she asked defensively.

There was a moment of silence so fraught with meaning that Marisa felt the palpable tension emanating from Robert. His features softened as he said, "I would have loved you, Marisa, arranged mariage or no."

"Oh, come now, Robert," interjected Mauger with su-

perb timing to wreak his havoc on the man's already badly
damaged self-image. "Even had you wed her, you would
still be only half a man after Malfosse. Although," he
added, seemingly oblivious to the gross insult he'd just
mouthed, " 'twould no doubt have been infinitely preferable to wedding a long-haired, uncultured Anglo-Saxon."

Robert's face turned gray, and for one frightening moment, Marisa thought he would spring out of his chair and
run Mauger through with his sword. Robert de Lisieux
would have had every right to do so, as the son of a wealthy
baron of William's, while Mauger, from all that Marisa
could see, was only a newly landed knight, come to England to gain what he could not inherit in his homeland.

The declaration that came from the all-but-forgotten
woman who stood listening to their exchange surprised
them all in its fierce intensity. "The sum of a warrior's
body parts is not what makes him a man," said Godgift.
"Lord Robert is twice the man you ever were, le Faux."
The last words were spat out like some foul piece of food,
and all three turned in surprise to the woman who spoke
them.

She was standing, her long, braided hair framing the
oval of her face. Her eyes looked darkly blue in the light
of the hall, and she seemed to fear Mauger not in the least.

"What she says is true," Marisa said in an attempt to
smooth over the potentially explosive moment, hoping the
woman would not be punished for her audacity. "That is,
in her belief that a man is not less than whole because he
bears battle scars," she hastened to assure Mauger. The
image of her husband's branded face and her first reaction
to it made her conscience writhe as she realized how at
odds with her belief she had once behaved.

"Godgift is so deserving of her name that I cannot find
it in my heart to damage her beauty, Marisa, else she
would be beaten on the spot," Mauger drawled. "She
refuses me my due as her overlord, but I have no wish to
disfigure that lovely body in order to win capitulation. I
rather like the challenge of making her come to me willingly." His words were soft but full of menace, indicating

just how much his pride was wounded, yet he kept his
control before Marisa and Robert. "I would not honor
her, nor stain the reputation of the house of le Faux by
wedding an Anglo-Saxon, although she is of their so-called
nobility and, I believe, Danish. She does hold a certain
appeal for me, though."

Ignoring the slur upon her own marriage to Brand, Marisa smiled tentatively at the woman and asked "Your husband was Waltheof?"

"Aye." Godgift began to busy herself with replenishing
their cups of wine, her color heightening as she approached Robert, and Marisa noted the way he stared up
into her face, as if in sudden discovery.

"My Godgift also refuses to flee to the forest, as many
of her cowardly relatives have done in the face of a new
lord," le Faux continued. "The number of English who
live like wild animals is legion. They hide during the day
and forage and steal at night. But the former lady of the
manor has too much pride. Or mayhap"—he reached out
to touch her cheek as she bent to refill his cup, and Godgift recoiled as if she had been burned—"she longs to
warm my bed but does not dare seem so easily won over."

His laughter grated on Marisa's already taut nerves, and
she stood, politely refusing more wine. She had learned
much, but now it was time to leave. Fear for Brand and
what Robert might do if he came to see Goliath were up-
permost in her mind. "I must take my leave now, my lord.
I thank you for your hospitality." She turned to Robert,
who had also stood. "Although the circumstances are
vastly changed, I am glad we did meet, Robert. Whatever
you do, wherever you go, I wish you godspeed, for what
once was."

He stared at her, drinking in the beauty of her face, as
if committing her features to memory. "Godspeed, Marisa," he murmured, seeming for a moment to forget his
lost arm, his duty to his king, and Mauger le Faux.

Mauger's voice broke the spell. "You will meet up with
Robert again, Marisa. He will of a certainty pay your husband a visit within the next day or two."

"Indeed," Robert said, collecting himself, his voice turning hard and emotionless once more. "I have been patrolling the border between England and Wales north of Fauxbray for the past several days and now must turn south. We will meet again."

A servant approached Mauger, claiming his attention for several moments, and Robert turned away politely. Marisa took her offered mantle from Godgift, and the two women moved toward the door, but not before Marisa noted the black frown that appeared upon Mauger's brow at the servant's words.

"Lady Marisa," Godgift urged in a low voice. "you must tell Thane Brand that Mauger means him harm. There . . . there is something afoot that I do not quite understand, but he means to gain my lord's lands . . . and he seeks to stir up the Welsh against him. . . ."

Robert's approach caused her to bite back anything else she might have said. "Thank you, Godgift," Marisa answered softly. "Rest assured that I will return, if for naught else than to see to your well-being. Send a messenger who can be trusted if ever the need arises." Once the words were out they sounded pitifully inadequate.

Godgift raised lovely, pain-filled eyes to the tall form of Robert de Lisieux, who neared them, yet her low-spoken words were for Marisa. "That is kind, my lady, but there is naught anyone can do. Naught."

Chapter 15

If ever Marisa de Brionne needed to keep her wits
about her, it was on the seemingly endless trip back to
Camwright. In the whirling maelstrom of her thoughts,
she acknowledged that the enormity of what she had discovered at Fauxbray was well worth facing Brand's anger
when he returned from Wales and learned of her visit.
The very presence of Robert de Lisieux . . . the cruelty
and nefarious intent of Mauger le Faux . . . and the fact
that evidently, unbeknownst to a Marisa who'd up until
now gone rather blithely about her business, there were
vagrant Anglo-Saxons at large in the surrounding countryside, choosing to live homeless rather than submit to
Norman rule—all combined to hit Marisa with staggering
impact.

Running through the volatile situation, like a stray but
persistent thread weaving through an unfolding tapestry,
was the fact that she loved Brand Ericson.

Do you love him . . . love him . . . love him . . . ?

Robert's query echoed through her chaotic thoughts in
a mocking litany. *Oui,* her heart answered as they neared
Camwright, even as common sense told her she was a
fool to have ever allowed such a thing to happen. For
Marisa doubted that her love would ever be returned. The
proud, embittered man she'd wed, struggling daily to hold
together his world through any means possible—even
humbling himself before a king he hated—the man she
once called Anglo-Saxon rabble in her ignorance of his

ways, his culture, would forever be tied to his remorse and unremitting guilt regarding his first wife. There would never be room for anything but polite tolerance and perhaps mild, albeit unwilling, affection.

"I must tell him of the visit, Morgan" were her first words as the Welshman met the returning party at the eastern gate.

His dark eyes searched her face as Edyth came up behind him. Marisa could see Adela and Griffith watching from the far side of the yard, as if ordered to remain that small distance away until Morgan had spoken to Marisa.

"What happened?" he asked as he helped her dismount and took the mare's reins.

"Robert de Lisieux—Goliath's previous owner—is alive and coming to Camwright to see the horse for himself."

"Sweet God in heaven!" His expression took on all the darkness of a thundercloud. "That swine le Faux told him of Goliath. How else could he possibly have known?"

"And Godgift warned me that Mauger is trying to stir up the Welsh against Brand, and—" She stopped, choking back her fear and horror. "There is so much I did not know until this morn."

"Come into the hall, Marisa," Edyth urged sensibly, taking her by the arm and leading her forward. "Put some food and mead into your belly to fortify yourself while you tell Morgan what you have learned."

Griffith and Rollo came bounding across the yard then, as if by some unspoken command, and were upon her in a flash, Rollo shoving his nose under her tightly curved fingers to be petted, and Griffith launching himself into her arms. Only then did she manage a smile.

Although Edwin sat and listened as Marisa poured out her story to Morgan, the man-at-arms was unable to contribute much because he'd spent his time with Mauger's men.

"Brand must be told everything, Marisa," Morgan

said, "and if you like, I will do the telling to spare you the brunt of his anger."

She shook her head emphatically. "Nay, Morgan. I thank you, I know you mean well, but 'twas my wish to go in the first place. You can talk of strategy—or whatever can be done to avert disaster and foil Mauger—but please let me tell him first."

"Marisa is right, Morgan," Edyth interjected unexpectedly. "She saw and heard everything firsthand.'Tis her right as his wife to tell him. After that, you can give him counsel and decide the best way to deal with whatever may come of this situation."

Morgan's gaze softened as it settled on his betrothed. "And how can I dispute successfully with two beautiful wenches?" he asked with a sigh of resignation. His expression quickly turned serious. "You must tell him all, Marisa. If you hold anything back in favor of your countrymen, you will never win him over."

Marisa picked at the meat on her hard bread trencher, her appetite diminished because of all that had happened. "That I know, Morgan. That I know."

Later, Morgan and Edyth watched Adela accompany her mistress across the hall to the bower to rest, and the Welshman planted a thoughtful kiss atop his beloved's head. "She has already won his love, though he would never admit to it, but she has yet to win his trust. And that, my Edyth, will be much more difficult."

"She will do it, Morgan. If any Norman can win his trust, 'tis Marisa de Brionne." She glanced up at him, a knowing look in her large hazel eyes, and his lips descended to meet hers in acknowledgment.

Brand entered the bower late that night, silently. He walked over to the bed, signaling Rollo to remain still, and stared down at his sleeping wife in the warm spill of light from a single welcoming taper. His eyes hungrily roved over her fair form, devouring her beauty like a starving man. Yet it was not only her beauty that gave him spiritual succor. There was a strength about her that made her bounce back after every reversal, and he suspected he'd only begun to glimpse the true depth of her resiliency.

She began to toss restlessly, as if in the throes of an unpleasant dream, and Rollo whined where he lay, his eyes upon his mistress's small figure. "Must tell him . . . tell him of Mauger and . . . Nay! 'Tis not the same horse!" Brand reached out to touch her shoulder just as she cried, "Robert! Where is your arm? Nay, he was not there—not there . . ."

"Marisa." Brand sat down beside her and took her gently into his arms. "Marisa?" He put his lips to her forehead, the scent of her pale golden hair filling his senses like an intoxicating wine, despite his fatigue and bitter disappointment.

Her heavy lashes raised slowly, as if the nightmare in whose clutches she was held were reluctant to release her. Sleep clouded her deep blue eyes, making them look like smoky velvet. "Brand?" she muttered groggily.

"Aye, love. 'Tis I."

"Oh, Brand!" She threw her soft, slim arms around his neck, holding on to him as if shielding him from all that she had to say. Forgotten was his cursory leave-taking, all the mistrust and quarreling that had stood between them in the beginning and had only just begun to ease. She loved him, it was as simple as that, and she had to tell him of the danger.

"Brand, I . . ."

"Hush, Marisa mine. I would apologize for my abrupt leave-taking yestermorn. I missed you so."

Brand!" she cried, not hearing the admission that ordinarily would have delighted her. "Why are you back so soon?"

He laughed, the haggard look around his eyes and mouth relaxing as mirth washed away hours of fatigue. "I suppose I do deserve to be treated in kind, Viking."

Her smooth, pale brow pleated in puzzlement. "Whatever do you mean, Brand? You've been to Wales and back already?"

He nodded, the humor fading from his face until he looked older than his years. "I was too late."

"Too late?"

"Aye. 'Twould seem Princes Bleddyn and Riwallon have joined the English of Herfordshire in a revolt against the Normans."

Her eyes widened and she pushed herself away from his embrace, sitting up straight and alert now. "But—but 'twas not a part of your agreement with William, was it, to do aught but keep peace along the border with the Welsh? And you have done that. You cannot be everywhere at once, nor can you control everything the Cymry do!"

"Indeed, my wise wife, I cannot. I suspect the Normans will put down the revolt, and the princes and their followers will hie themselves back to Wales with much booty for their trouble." He stood and gripped the back of his neck as he poured himself some mead from a ewer beside the bed. He let the cool liquid slide down his parched throat to warm his belly and then crouched down to scratch Rollo, who'd stealthily crept up to his master. "But Bleddyn was Rhiannon's kin. Mayhap William will take it into his head that I should have been able to influence him, if not Riwallon."

"Then I shall stand up for you and your efforts to rule justly over English and Welsh alike. He will not take Griffith's future from him, I promise you!"

He was taken aback by the fierce expression in her eyes, the determined set of her chin, the small hands suddenly fisted in her lap. "Why, you *are* on my side, firebrand, aren't you?" he asked in sudden wonderment.

Unexpectedly, her eyes shone with the press of tears that she valiantly fought to hold back. "You have always been too blind to see that, Saxon, but 'tis true. I stand with my husband."

He left off stroking the hound, his eyes locked with hers. But Marisa did not give him time to respond to her declaration. "Brand, I have something to tell you."

He smiled in a way that perceptibly altered her breathing and began to doff his clothing. Marisa had to remind herself of the gravity of her news to keep her mind off the splendor being slowly revealed to her gaze. "Naught else you can say could please me more than what you've already told me, Marisa de Brionne."

She swallowed back her fear, her dread of breaking the magical spell of intimacy that seemed to surround them at that moment. Perhaps he would even . . . She shook her head and looked straight ahead. "Brand, I went to see Mauger le Faux this morn."

He stopped disrobing in mid-motion, the accusation that suddenly appeared in his topaz eyes pinning her to the bed like a helpless butterfly. " 'Tis truly a strange way to prove you stand by your husband, Marisa," he said softly, steel underlying his tone.

In the wake of his almost instantaneous condemnation of her, Marisa's anger began to brew with all the intensity of a newly gathering storm. "I went for a reason." At the sardonic twist of his lips she said with stony emphasis, "I went to find out what he is up to."

His look turned to mild disbelief. "And since when have you set yourself up in my place as thane?"

"You are no longer thane, Brand," she reminded him. "Perhaps, to your own people you are, but the title does not exist in the Norman hierarchy. I went as your wife—your Norman wife—to visit with a fellow Norman. You allow me to do next to nothing, so I took things in my own hands and—"

He was beside her in the great bed in a trice, his face very near hers, his warm breath misting her cheek as he said in a deceptively dulcet voice, "Mayhap I should keep you so satiated from lovemaking that you have no energy for meddling. Mayhap I should give you no time for aught but raising a score of our children, wench. Would that keep you at home and hearth?"

She returned his look levelly, even though he had anchored her wrists above her head, his hand roving up the side of her rib cage to gently cup a breast and almost destroy her concentration. "You are not man enough to

make love to me, Saxon." She forced herself to laugh
bitterly. "You say you are afraid to lose two wives to
childbirth . . . Bah! 'Tis ofttimes a woman's lot to die in
the process of bringing forth new life, and I am willing
to take that chance to give you more sons and daughters." His face turned ashen at her mention of death in
childbirth, but she continued ruthlessly. " 'Tis only your
excuse to remain faithful to your Rhiannon. What would
she think of your reluctance to give Griffith brothers and
sisters? What would she think of your ridiculous coddling
of me, if indeed that is what it can be termed, when your
people are beaten and starved by one such as Mauger le
Faux?"

The color slowly returned to his face as the truth of
her words began to sink in. "I am not frail," she went
on. "I am hale and hearty, and 'twill take more than
bringing a child into this world to kill me. But there is
so much I have to tell you—so much at stake—and you
will only accuse me of some imagined slight because I
went to see what I could discover at the home of one of
your most dangerous enemies?"

He sat up, removing the thong around his forehead and
furrowing the fingers of both hands through his thick hair.
Marisa longed to reach out and smooth the golden-chestnut mane she'd once condemned as barbaric because it
was not of the Norman fashion, but she stilled the impulse.

When he turned back to her, the bleak look in his eyes
took her aback. "You may not believe this, but I am
concerned about you. You are only a woman—and with
child—and you deliberately put your life at risk. I can
take care of myself, Marisa. And Morgan . . . he was to
watch over you, to keep you here and safe from harm."

"Morgan agreed that I could best help you by visiting
le Faux. If memory serves me well, you told Mauger
yourself that I might visit him. I went with an armed
escort and was well-guarded." She paused. "Oh, Brand,
please, please see beyond your own anger. I have so much

to tell you—and mayhap your very position here is in jeopardy!"

His shoulders seemed to slump, and defeat shaded the golden eyes to the color of mead. "What can you tell me, Marisa, that I do not already know? What new treachery threatens us now?"

She tentatively reached out to catch the hand closest to her, but then withdrew her hand in uncertainty, pressing her slender fingers against her thrumming heart. Odd, she mused, how they had shared such intimate touches and caresses in the act of making love, yet now she feared his rejection.

As he looked in surprise at her bloodless fingers before meeting her gaze, she drew in a bracing breath and said, "Robert de Lisieux survived Malfosse."

"Ah, the man I supposedly murdered."

Guilt swept through Marisa at the reminder of her accusation. If she had expected any more of a reaction than his quiet observation, she was disappointed.

He rubbed his face wearily with one hand. "He is fortunate, for I understand 'twas, indeed, a one-sided fray, with nary a Norman who tumbled into that gorge surviving to tell of it." He spoke in a flat, toneless voice, distancing himself from the bloody skirmish, memories of which rose unbidden in his mind's eye, as they had many times in the past months.

She reached out and captured his hand in earnest entreaty. "But he knows you were there, Brand. Mauger told him of Goliath."

He gently kneaded her tense fingers, a vague smile curving his mouth. "He can prove nothing, Viking," he assured her softly. Bringing her palm up to his lips, he lightly brushed his tongue over the cool, sweet surface, his thoughts suddenly on things far removed from battle.

Marisa's next words, however, whipped his attention into proper focus. "Don't you remember what I told you, Brand? Goliath was *his* mount, purchased from my father several years back. He knows all!"

His gaze delved into hers. "He can know nothing aside

from the fact that mayhap I was hidden in the forest beyond that ravine.''

In extreme agitation, Marisa stood abruptly, pulling her hand away from his unnerving caresses. She began to pace before him, her linen shift swirling around well-formed ankles with each turn, molding to her body provocatively with each forward step. ''He is no fool. He is no Mauger le Faux, who would allow his hatred to color his reasoning, his judgment.'' She stopped to face him, her hands on her hips. ''You would have to appear a simpleton—or a madman—to persuade Robert you are less than what you are, Saxon!''

He started to reach for her, then checked himself. ''Robert?'' He arched a dark eyebrow questioningly. Marisa knew what he meant but remained stubbornly silent. ''Not *Sieur de Lisieux* or Lord Robert?''

''I—I knew him very well. . . . I told you earlier that he was a friend of my family.'' She began pacing once more in vexation. ''What does it matter? All he has to do is come here and see his horse!''

''You have such faith in my, ah, bravery, my ingenuity. What makes you think I could even participate in a stand such as Malfosse after having fought in the great battle immediately before, let alone plan, implement, and lead it?''

She rounded on him. ''*Eh bien,* you will not *have* to act the simpleton when Robert comes to Camwright, for you exhibit all the characteristics of such a one by your lack of concern, by your belief that I am so want-witted as not to have guessed.''

Fascinated by the nimbus of soft candlelight behind her silvery head, he reached out and, catching a delicate wrist, drew her to him until she stood between his knees. He ran his fingers through the silken length of her hair, reveling in the texture, the scent, the moon-kissed hue.

''He will report to the King,'' she whispered, distracted by his oddly gentle attentions, the desire in his eyes, his apparent lack of concern.

"What would you have me do, my firebrand?" he murmured. "Destroy the animal?"

"I—I do not know, Brand. But, oh, Brand, *listen* to me!" She made a halfhearted attempt to pull away, but her feet were rooted to the floor. "Brand, there are English living—hiding—in the forest and . . ." His eyes seemed to clear for a moment as they met hers, the message in the amber depths obvious. "You knew—you knew all along. . . ."

" 'Tis my business to know such things. But I am touched that you truly care about the Anglo-Saxons who would rather live out their lives in the wild than under the aegis of one such as Mauger le Faux."

His eyes shone with such grudging admiration, his tone was so warm and loving, that it came to Marisa in a flash that he was deliberately keeping her in the dark about his part at Malfosse to protect her. In the beginning he may have been prompted by his lack of faith in her willingness to remain silent, but now she knew he was protecting her. If she knew nothing about his connection with Malfosse, she could not suffer in any way should his actions be exposed.

She opened her mouth to speak, but he was unlacing the ribbons at her throat, his touch on her flesh sending tingles of sensation shooting along her veins. "You would torture me with the thought of lovemaking when you have not touched me since first you discovered my pregnancy? Can it be that you wish to see to my needs as a woman, Saxon, or have you something else in mind?"

He replaced his fingers with his lips and said softly against the creaminess of her breasts, "There are other ways to pleasure a woman, Marisa love, without endangering either mother or child."

Pleasure seeped through her like a drugging opiate, draining her energy, her ability even to stand, and she sagged against him with a wondrous sense of growing languor. But as their lips met, her passion-dazed mind belatedly remembered Godgift's words of warning. "Brand—Brand, there is one more thing . . ."

"Enough, wench," he said in a dulcet reprimand, dragging his heated lips down the sweet curve of her throat toward her open neckline. "Haven't you brought me enough dire tidings for one eve?"

She tried to shake her head, to penetrate the fog of delicious anticipation that was enveloping her. "But 'tis important . . ."

"Hush, love. Undoubtedly I know of it already. For now, only let me love you."

Godgift's warning about le Faux and the Welsh was temporarily forgotten under his tenderly persistent onslaught.

In the fading gloom of early dawn, two figures could be discerned astride their horses within the deep shadows of the edge of the forest separating Camwright and Fauxbray—one on a large Norman courser, the other on a small Welsh pony. In the silence that still blanketed the earth, only the occasional call of a bird or a tiny nocturnal animal scurrying to its nest could be heard . . . that and the low drone of the men's voices, which softly punctuated the stillness.

"All is in readiness, then?"

"Aye. We need only await for the right moment now. If the timing is wrong, the attempt would have to be aborted, or we would risk exposure." Madog studied the Norman across from him in the crepuscular light.

"And you plan to use the old woman and then get rid of her?"

Madog hesitated, a frown puckering his brow, then nodded. "But no harm is to come to her until after her usefulness to us is served."

Mauger laughed softly. "She has you all running scared, the old crone. Magical powers, indeed. What a superstitious bunch you Welsh are."

"You have never seen that of which she is capable, le Faux, or you would not think to deal with her so lightly. She may be your downfall instead of Ericson's.

"Is that a threat?" When Madog merely shrugged,

Mauger continued, "When Robert de Lisieux sees that horse and reports to William, Ericson will have all he can do to prevent the King from nullifying the pact made by the Saxon's marriage to Marisa de Brionne—even if William does not blame him for failing to prevent Bleddyn and Riwallon from joining the uprising in Herfordshire."

"I would not be too certain of the victory as yet, le Faux. I want his downfall as badly as you, but he has many Welsh friends and informants. It would not surprise me if he knew of my efforts to stir up feelings against him. When we strike the first time, it must look as if 'twas Angharad's doing, otherwise we must bide our time again, and perhaps for much longer."

Le Faux's pale blue eyes slitted. "You must not fail. I give you until Michaelmas. If you have not accomplished at least the first part of the plan, then I will take matters into my own hands."

Madog looked up at the tall Norman, who seemed to tower over him upon his great steed. His eyes were cool, his gaze unflinching. "You cannot accomplish what you wish without my help. Otherwise, William will suspect you of foul play, and I doubt that even the Bastard would approve of such when it involves the son-by-marriage of one of his most esteemed barons."

The only sign of Mauger's anger was the tightening of his hands on the reins. "Perhaps, but I did not come here to second-guess William's reactions to ridding England of one more troublesome Anglo-Saxon." He pulled a pouch from his belt and tossed it to Madog. "You will receive more when you've shown me what you can do." With a deft turn of his wrist, and without another word, he swung his mount's head away from the Welshman and rode leisurely toward Fauxbray.

Madog watched his retreating figure until it was just a blur in the distance. "We will rid our land of this blight, Rhiannon," he promised softly. "First the man who never loved you as you deserved, who was responsible for the murder of the noble ap Llewellyn, and then le Faux. But Angharad shall live, my love, for she is loyal

to you still, and she is of the Cymry. She alone knew of
our love—our child.'' He turned his pony toward a nearby
path heading west. ''Aye, beloved, we will spare Angharad after her purpose is served, and then rescue Gruffydd from Ericson and his Norman wife, I promise you.''

When Madog ap Cynan was gone, there was a soft
rustling in the ferns and wild undergrowth behind where
the two men had spoken. A powerful-looking, gnarled
hand pushed aside the foliage of wild ivy that abounded
in the woodlands, spiraling around the trees and provid-
ing the perfect concealment for one accustomed to living
in the weald. A bearded face appeared with long, dark
hair streaked with silver and tied back with a crude thong,
revealing the seamed flesh that came with age and out-
door living. But the eyes, as dark as obsidian and pos-
sessing a keen intelligence, revealed that he was younger
than his outward physical appearance suggested.

He narrowed those alert eyes thoughtfully and studied
first the distant village and then the path Madog had taken
moments before, weighing, assessing. He reached down
to finger the knife tucked in his rope belt and then turned
his face into the benign morning breeze, toward Camwright, which was hidden from view. He breathed in the
familiar and well-loved scent of the forest in summer;
the myriad smells and sounds assailed his finely tuned
senses. He smiled the smile of one with perfect confidence, of one who shares a very special secret with no
one but the trees and the wind and the wild beasts among
whom he has made his home.

''Angharad.'' He uttered the name in a low voice that
was rough with disuse, and with a sudden loathing that
obliterated the smile from his face and kindled twin red
flames within the dark, omniscient depths of his eyes.
''Angharad.''

And then he was gone.

Chapter 16

" 'Tis as if she diappeared into thin air."

Morgan cast a look at Brand. "Many say she is capable of just that."

Brand grunted and slid from Goliath's back to hunker down beside the evidence of a long-extinguished fire. "You know what I say to that. . . . She has undoubtedly gone into hiding after her latest dastardly deed." He stood once more and gave a low whistle. Several men began to emerge from the woods surrounding them, some leading ponies.

"Enough for today," Brand ordered, his voice dull with weariness and frustration. Two days of searching the area around Camwright and Wighton—even foraying briefly across the Welsh border—had proven fruitless.

"What of the forest between Camwright and Fauxbray?"

Brand set a knuckled fist on one hip, the other hand raking through his sweat-damp hair in unspoken vexation as he stared blindly at the thick barrier of trees and foliage. "I am tempted, yet also hesitant to reveal in any way to le Faux that all is not well within my jurisdiction."

"He would of a certainty demand to know why you are trespassing." Morgan's lips curled downward with distaste.

"There is no doubt in my mind that Angharad was responsible for the attack by the wolf in the clearing, yet

my instincts tell me that there is more here than meets
the eye.''

"Madog ap Cynan?"

Brand nodded and remounted. " 'Twould not surprise
me. There are old wounds there that fester concerning
the death of Griffith ap Llewellyn and Madog's belief that
I led the party that found and destroyed the prince. Now
he has the perfect ally in le Faux.'' He signaled the others to follow, and they headed east along a little-used
path.

"You cannot throw le Faux off the scent when you
continue to flaunt the gray,'' Morgan pointed out.

Brand's brows drew together. "I hardly call riding Goliath upon my own lands flaunting him. You are beginning to sound like Marisa,'' he added in irritation.

In spite of himself, Morgan had to fight an urge to
smile. "We both have a common interest, my friend—
your safety.''

"I am flattered, ap Dafydd, but you both have more
important matters to occupy your thoughts, I would think.
Marriage for you, and the coming child for my wife.''

Brand's seeming lack of concern didn't fool Morgan
for a moment. He knew the Saxon too well. Brand, of
all people, wanted to attract no more attention to himself
than was necessary, yet he would not act the coward to
avoid it.

"You have other horses you can use until Robert de
Lisieux is gone. Do not tempt the fates.''

Brand turned to meet Morgan's dark regard. "The fates
have never been kind to me, Welshman. There is no blow
they could deal me that would be any more crushing than
that which I, and my countrymen, have already suffered.''

Morgan dropped back as the path narrowed to permit
only one horse to follow it. "You could lose Griffith,''
he said softly as he reined in his pony. "And Marisa.''

Marisa was helping with the birthing of a child in the
village when the men returned. As she emerged into the

light of day, rolling down her sleeves and running a palm
across her damp forehead, she almost stepped into the
path of Goliath. "Have a care, wench, else I will be
forced to demonstrate my recently acquired skill with a
Norman war-horse."

She squinted up into the sunshine at the tall man astride
the powerful destrier, suddenly shy at the way his eyes
were caressing her face. Her gown was stained with
blood, and pale wisps of her hair had escaped its sleek
coil atop her head to curl in disarray about her flushed
face. The color bathing her features deepened at Brand's
lengthy perusal. She murmured, "Vivian is delivered
safely of a fine, healthy boy, my lord."

He slid down to stand before her. "And so she is, God
be thanked." He tipped her chin up with a gentle finger.
"You look exhausted, Marisa."

The nooning horn sounded just then, and as the others
filed past or went to their homes, Brand placed one hand
on the small of her back and guided her toward the manor
hall. "I regret, Marisa, that we have found nothing of
Angharad yet."

She looked up into his somber features, her shyness
suddenly forgotten. "I care not for my sake, Brand—
only for Griffith's. If she is gone, so be it. Mayhap she
can find some place elsewhere to live out her life."

How forgiving she is, he thought. *Despite threats and
even attempts upon her life, she harbors no hatred toward the woman.*

Forgetting his vow to refrain from showing overt affection toward her in public, he paused for a moment and
grazed a porcelainlike cheek with the back of his knuckles in an infinitely gentle gesture. "I would that all could
be as forgiving as you, Viking." He remembered her
concern for him following her discovery of Robert de
Lisieux's presence in the area; her ready and total acceptance of the son of another woman . . . a hundred different ways in which she was proving to be not only
forgiving but also loving and accepting and loyal. He had

opened his mouth to speak again when Goliath's great head nudged his shoulder.

Marisa laughed aloud at the stallion's actions, and Brand thought it the sweetest sound ever to have greeted his ears. "He wishes a dried apple or some other tidbit, Brand."

Recovering his scattered wits, he proceeded to guide her toward the stockade, shooting a wry glance over his shoulder at Goliath on his other side. "You will have him as spoiled as Rollo, woman," he admonished with a smile that made Marisa's heart melt like the last patch of snow beneath a gentle spring sun.

They parted at the gate, Brand to oversee the care of a slight injury to the horse's front leg, Marisa to the bower to freshen up for the noon meal. Ravenous, she hurriedly changed her clothing and washed her face. Deciding it would take too much time to replait her hair, she let it fall loosely below her slender shoulders, forgetting in her haste that only a few months ago she had vowed never again to wear it thusly. She could only picture the admiration in Brand's eyes when his gaze alighted on her as it did every night in the privacy of the bower. Her face still flushed from her earlier exertions and excitement, Marisa was hard-pressed to affect a dignified walk.

The meal was accomplished with more merriment than anyone would have expected, given the lack of success of the morning's outing. However, between Griffith's happy chatter and Morgan's merry antics in his quest to entertain his beloved Edyth, Brand could do nothing but allow himself to become caught up in the levity, despite his concern over a multitude of unsolved problems. For a short time, he acted years younger, the burden of his responsibilities sliding from his back like a shed cloak. He leaned leisurely upon his forearms, watching his wife and his son laugh and exchange carefree banter. As Rollo plunked his great front paws upon the bench between them, the tinkling sound of Marisa's laughter enchanted Brand for the second time that day. He relaxed and watched with a heart far lighter than it had been in months.

Then Griffith suddenly asked, "Father, may I go with Marisa when she visits the Norman le Faux again?"

Momentarily taken aback, Brand's expression was enough to make the child wish he had held his tongue. In an attempt at reparation, Griffith added, "I would guard her well, Father, and save you at least part of the escort."

Stepping into the breach, Marisa answered smoothly, "What a brave boy you are, Griffith. But your father needs you here in Camwright every moment. You are too important to accompany me upon so insignificant a visit." Her eyes beseeched Brand to go along, but he could only envision Marisa in the handsome, arrogant Mauger le Faux's company, and an uncharacteristic and totally unexpected jealousy crept over him.

Sudden silence filled the hall.

"There will be no more visits."

He stood, once again mentally shouldering the heavy burden he'd briefly relinquished, and made to leave the board. Marisa's hand upon his, however, stopped him.

"Let me explain, Brand," she began, as Morgan and Edyth quickly diverted Griffith. The other men, finishing their meals, discreetly looked away and began to speak quietly among themselves. For a fleeting moment, husband and wife's eyes met and held, Brand's briefly pain-filled before turning cold, Marisa's anxious and pleading.

Even as her gaze begged for understanding, the stubborn side of her silently made her determined to find a way to return to Fauxbray, even if it had to be on the sly. . . . It was of the utmost importance, no matter what her husband decreed.

The unexpected blast of the horn signaled the arrival of strangers, putting an end to her ruminations. Brand pulled his hand from hers and moved with grim purpose toward the door.

In her concern for her husband, Marisa forgot her temper . . . forgot how cold and accusatory his look had

been before he'd swung away from her . . . forgot her
determination to return to Fauxbray. She could only thank
heaven that Goliath was stabled, for she knew with certainty whose arrival was heralded by the horn.

"Remain in the hall," Brand commanded over his
shoulder before he exited the manor.

"Aye," added Morgan, and with a quick nod at Edyth,
he, too, stood and followed Brand with swift strides.
Several men-at-arms followed suit, buckling on their
swordbelts as they quit the hall.

Marisa's knuckles were white as she gripped the edge
of the trestle table, staring at the doorway.

"You must remain inside, Marisa," Edyth reminded
gently, releasing her from the clutches of the nightmarish
images flashing through her mind.

"Who is it?" asked Griffith, alarmed by Marisa's unusual behavior and the look on his aunt's face.

Marisa turned her worried gaze to the child. Summon-
ing up a wooden smile, she answered, "Just . . . just a
friend of *Sieur le Faux's*, I think." She looked at Edyth.
"I know Brand forbade us to leave the hall, Edyth, but I
must see if 'tis he." She stepped over the bench and
moved toward the door.

"See if 'tis whom?" demanded Edyth as she hurried
to intercept her sister-by-marriage.

"Someone I knew in Normandy. Someone"—her
troubled regard met Edyth's and she lowered her voice—
"who holds Brand's very life in his hands."

Marisa emerged into the July sunshine, willing her eyes
to adjust quickly to the brightness. Brand and Morgan
were not at first visible, but Marisa knew it would be
only moments before they appeared around the corner of
the manor hall with the newcomers.

Hesitating, uncertain, she briefly considered boldly entering the stable and spiriting Goliath away. But where?
Even as she thought it, she acknowledged the impossi-
bility of getting across the yard to the stable and leading
the animal through the gatehouse entrance before anyone

caught sight of her, for there was no safety from prying eyes within the confines of the stronghold.

Besides, Brand would be furious.

Frustration chased across her fine features as she realized there was nothing she could do, and she had to quell an urge to stomp her foot like a child foiled in its game.

She did, however, mouth a most unladylike expletive in French as she stepped forward and caught sight of Robert de Lisieux and his mounted party rounding the corner and coming toward her. To her relief, Mauger le Faux did not number among them, as far as she could ascertain.

Without thinking, she quickly gained Brand's side, her eyes riveted to those of the man who indirectly held the power of life and death over her husband. She would not allow Brand to face him alone.

"What do you here, Marisa?" Brand's low growl drew her gaze from Robert as the Norman pulled abreast of them and signaled for his men to halt.

"He—he was a friend in Normandy, as I told you the other night," came her soft reply. "Mayhap I can—"

"You can do naught because you know naught. . . . Leave us!"

Robert dismounted with unexpected grace, considering his handicap, and approached Brand and Marisa as they continued their low, urgent exchange. Without warning, Marisa turned away from her angry husband and moved forward to meet Robert, a cautious smile brightening her features. "Welcome to Camwright, Lord Robert."

He looked down into her eyes for a long moment and then, recalling himself, answered, "Am I indeed welcome, Marisa de Brionne? I wonder."

Brand approached them, his expression stern and unyielding. "Robert, this is my husband, Brand Ericson. Brand, this is my lord Robert de Lisieux."

In the brief, taut moment that followed, Brand nodded

curtly and asked without ceremony, "What business have you here, Robert de Lisieux?"

"Surely the lady Marisa has told you?"

He shrugged in seeming dismissal. "She told me only that you once knew each other in Normandy and that you seek those who stood at Malfosse. You will find none here who participated in that encounter, but you and your men are welcome to share some refreshment in my hall."

De Lisieux nodded with unsmiling courtesy and signaled his men to dismount and follow him into the hall. Brand, with Morgan and several others right behind him, remained silent, but Marisa could not squelch the low-spoken question, "And what of le Faux, Robert? Why does he not number among you?"

"He would have liked nothing better than to see Ericson brought to his knees, be it by fair means or foul, but I cared not for his companionship."

Grateful at least for that, Marisa nodded, her heart still smashing against her ribs in acute anxiety.

The ruby-red wine of which the Normans were so fond was proffered by silent servants under Edyth's direction. The conversation was minimal and awkward, everyone's thoughts on the gray stallion quartered in the stable. Marisa did her best to put Brand and Robert at ease, but it was a very difficult task, indeed.

"I understand you were a good friend to my wife's family, Lord Robert."

Robert looked up from the swirling, bloodred depths of his goblet and captured Marisa's gaze with his. "I had asked Marisa to be my wife."

Brand had obviously not expected so blunt an answer, and the silence hummed with increased tension.

Before Brand could comment, Robert added, his features twisted with self-derision, "But perhaps Marisa did the right thing, after all. She appears well-treated and seems not unhappy with you. I could have given her love and wealth, but—" He glanced down at the empty sleeve

hanging at his left side and shrugged almost imperceptibly.

It was then that Brand finally allowed his gaze to settle
for a moment on the Norman's missing arm. In obvious
dismissal, he said, "I have heard of men learning to fight
with only one arm. Balance must be adjusted, but it can
be accomplished. It makes one no less a man."

Robert's blue gaze met Brand's, and Marisa wondered
if the statement reminded him of the words of the lovely
Godgift.

"Such things mean naught to my wife, I have
learned." Brand absently fingered the scar on his cheek,
his eyes on Marisa. "Your irreparable loss, Norman, was
Marisa, not an arm."

Marisa's gaze flew to his, the compliment totally unexpected. Tongue-tied at Brand's praise, Marisa felt herself color and lowered her lashes to cover her confusion.

Robert stepped into the silence. "I believe you are
right, Ericson." He stood, his expression turning even
more somber. "Now, I believe you have a stallion that
might interest me. I must ask you to allow me to see it."

It was the moment Marisa had dreaded all her waking
and sleeping moments since her visit to Fauxbray, and
she suddenly felt paralyzed with fear.

"Very well. Your men may finish up here while we go
to the stables."

As the two men left the board and headed for the door,
Marisa at last was mobilized into action. She hurried
after them, despite a low-spoken warning from Edyth as
she approached the great portal and a negative shake of
Morgan's dark head. She was not certain what she could
do, but that she had to be there when Robert saw Goliath
was of vital importance.

Fearing Brand would demand she return to the manor
if he saw her, she hung back as the two tall figures strode
across the yard. When they disappeared into an outbuild-
ing, Marisa approached the door at the end closest to her
and, drawing in a fortifying breath, stepped into the dim
interior.

At first she was guided by the sound of their voices, momentarily blinded as she was by the dim interior after the sunlit compound. Her ears were assaulted by the sounds of animals crunching hay and oats from their feedboxes, the stomp of a restless hoof, the scrape of a swishing tail against the wood of a stall in reaction to annoying, ever-present flies. Her nostrils were stung by the earthy, pungent smell of fresh manure, crisp hay, oiled leather trappings, and, of course, the animals themselves.

The metallic taste of fear coated her mouth.

Straining to make out their figures in the shadows, Marisa was suddenly struck by the fact that she was so desperately in love with Brand Ericson, she would do anything to spare him being discovered as the leader at Malfosse. That the battle had resulted in the slaughter of many of William's soldiers—could even have brought about the death of her brothers and father, as well as the loss of Robert de Lisieux's arm and optimistic temperament—paled suddenly in significance. The full impact of being a part of the victorious Normans, only to be thrust into the heart of the conquered Anglo-Saxons, to actually love one of them and begin to feel his loss and anguish, struck her like a physical blow.

Marisa unexpectedly felt light-headed with the turbulence of her emotions. *Dear God,* she prayed, *give me the strength to help my husband.*

Quietly, she forced her stiff limbs to propel her forward, keeping to the shadows, listening intently to catch the drift of their dialogue. But she was unpracticed in stealth.

"Marisa, you do well to hide in the shadows when we have come here to speak of things which do not concern you."

She froze, dismayed at being caught out of hand. A rush of panic surged through her chest at Brand's admonition, even as she decided that no force on earth would move her from the presence of her husband and Robert de Lisieux.

She fought to control her voice. "I am not of the opinion that a woman should be relegated to healing and embroidery, Saxon. Robert is here on a most delicate mission, and since the animal in question was a gift to first the King and then to you from my father, it concerns me as much as you." Again, the lie sprang easily to her lips.

She emerged into the brighter area around Goliath's stall, her features set in a mask of determination. Brand recognized that look and mentally braced himself for an even touchier bout with de Lisieux. Marisa would not make things easier for him. Why in God's name had Morgan let her leave the hall?

As she moved to stand beside Brand, Robert was silently watching the gray from the opposite side of the partition. The animal raised its head from munching fresh hay and swung toward Brand and Marisa. Marisa reached out to stroke its neck, murmuring soothing words in French.

She looked up at Robert, but the door through which they had entered was behind him, only three stalls away, and the light shining through made it impossible to distinguish his expression.

"Goliath."

Softly spoken, as if from far away, the sound gently echoed through the byre . . . a question, a statement, a plea. With a toss of his magnificent head, the courser swung around toward Robert and a whicker of greeting preceded the thrust of his soft, velvetlike muzzle into the Norman's outstretched hand.

No words were needed. The animal knew Robert de Lisieux like a child knows its parent.

"You chose well when you chose Goliath, Ericson." The war-horse snorted and pawed the stable floor. Instantly Robert produced a dried apple from under his tunic and extended it toward the stallion. "You remember, eh, *copain?*" Goliath snatched the offered fruit and pawed again as he vigorously chomped the treat. "One at a time, greedy devil."

The silence stretched for so long that Marisa wanted to scream in frustration at the injustice of it all. Why didn't Brand say something? Why didn't he deny he had ever been at Malfosse? Why didn't he . . .

She stared up at his set profile as he watched the man and horse across from him. Griffith's future was at stake—Brand's very life. *Dieu au ciel,* she silently demanded, *say something to defend all that you love.*

But it was Robert who spoke first, startling Marisa out of her roiling thoughts. "You must love him very much."

She looked over in surprise, catching his unwavering gaze upon her. He had been studying her as she watched Brand. Had he read her thoughts, her fears?

His eyes never leaving Marisa's face, he continued, "She defended you admirably, you know, Saxon. But, then, Marisa never did anything in half measures. When she gave her affection, her loyalty, it was with all her heart. That is something I doubt I shall ever find in another woman."

His expression was still indiscernible, but he turned his regard to Brand. "You say one arm makes me no less a man, and Marisa said as much when we met in Fauxbray. Mayhap 'tis so, yet, conquered or not, you are far more fortunate than I, Ericson."

He fed Goliath the second apple, stroked his powerful neck, and murmured something indistinguishable into the animal's ear. Then, without a word, he pivoted on his heel and strode from the stable.

At last Brand looked down at the girl at his side. "I fear we will not be apprised of his decision because of his affection for you." Irony laced his words. "Now we will have to wait to see which is stronger—his loyalty to the King or his feelings for you."

Marisa hurried to follow his long strides toward the door, ignoring the bitter, mocking tone of his voice. "But why did you not say something in your defense? *Why?*"

Just before they emerged, he looked down into her emotion-dark eyes. "To say anything in an attempt to defend my possession of the horse would have been to

hint at guilt. Anyone who was there—a leader, a partic-
ipant, an observer—could have caught that destrier. Why
add to a suspicion when I did naught but watch from the
forest and snatch its reins as it emerged from the ravine
in confusion?''

Marisa opened her mouth to protest further when, with
a gentle finger, he lifted her chin until her lips met once
more, to silence whatever else she might have said. ''And
I did not wish to discredit your facile-tongued lie on my
behalf, which he did not question. Unnecessary as it was,
I appreciate your effort, disobedient wench.''

He drew her out into the sunlight and fresh, purging
air. All of Robert's men were mounting up except for
one, with whom the Norman was deep in conversation.
While the other soldier walked over to his waiting horse,
Robert met Brand and Marisa in the middle of the yard.

Marisa noted that the Nordic blue eyes, which had once
twinkled with good humor, were grim but not devoid of
life as they had been in Fauxbray. And then he took both
people by surprise by announcing in stentorian tones,
''On King William's behalf, belated and inadequate as
this is, I nonetheless claim *droit du seigneur.*'' His arm
snaked around Marisa's waist as he bent his tall form to
meet her lips with his.

Stunned, Marisa could not move. But even as she realized what was happening, she could not find it in herself to pull away. This man had been her friend since
childhood, had offered her his heart, and so she allowed
him, in the name of the King and for all that had been
between them as friends, to drink of her sweetness like
a man long-deprived of something vital to his existence.
Her mouth parted slightly under his, but there was not
the building of passion that she would have evinced with
her husband.

The kiss was not overly long, but it was all the more
bittersweet for its intensity. Marisa did not see Brand
stiffen and clench his fists in anger and frustration, for
to attempt to halt the kiss would be tantamount to deny-
ing the King.

When Robert released her, he took his destrier's reins in his one hand and mounted with just a hint of awkwardness. Only then did his eyes fuse with Brand's. Marisa watched his face, searching for a sign of his intentions where Goliath was concerned, her body as tense as Brand's had been only moments before. But Robert's words were for Brand and Brand alone.

"The animal in your stable is not my Goliath, fortunately for you."

Marisa put trembling fingers to her lips in relief and allowed the tears that had been lodged in the back of her eyes to spill forth in profound gratitude.

With a curt nod in her direction, he murmured, *"Adieu, chère Marisa,"* and touched his rowels to the destrier's side as he swung it toward the head of the party.

Chapter 17

Weak with relief now that Robert was safely gone, yet uncertain just how Brand would react to not only her attempted interference but also her willingness to be kissed by him, Marisa slowly turned toward her husband, refusing to hide her relief and thankfulness like some guilty child.

Her head lifted proudly in response to his inscrutable gaze. Just when she thought she could bear it no more, he spun on his heel and returned to the stable. Before Marisa or anyone else could move, he emerged astride an unsaddled shaggy pony and headed toward the path that led to the clearing by the waterfall.

His expression was storm-dark, mirroring his tumultuous battle against anger and jealousy. *Droit du seigneur . . . droit du seigneur . . .* The words mocked him in an unending litany that burned in his brain without mercy. A flimsy excuse for the Norman to take Marisa into his embrace and do what he'd no doubt been wanting to do since seeing her in Mauger le Faux's hall. And she'd let him have his way.

Brand urged the pony on, seeking to escape his thoughts, and disappeared into the forest.

"Let him go, Marisa," said Morgan's voice in her ear. She turned and allowed her misery-clouded eyes to meet his. "He is a proud man and must wrestle with his demons."

"Oh, I know of his *'demons,'* Morgan, and if anyone

245

tells me that one more time I shall hie myself back to London!'' Her eyes cleared as her ire took control. "He goes there to ponder my shortcomings at the altar of his guilt and self-pity . . . the grave of his beloved Rhiannon.''

"You cannot blame him for his jealousy, Marisa.''

"Jealousy?'' She was genuinely puzzled for a moment. "How can he be jealous when he cares not one whit for me except as the pawn in his accursed bargain—possibly his brood mare now, as well—and naught else.''

"Because, whether he will admit it or not, he is in love with you.''

Out of the corner of her eye, Marisa vaguely took note of the others scattering, including Edyth leading a softly protesting Griffith back into the hall. She returned her full attention to the Welshman standing before her. "If he fights any ghosts from the past, they were brought on by his own refusal to admit that he is human, that because he did not feel what he thought his first wife deserved, no other shall have it either.'' She wiped away the teardrops lingering upon her cheeks. "I could have done no less, considering Robert's friendship and what he had denied for Brand's sake.''

"I know, but mayhap Brand cannot deal with this evidence of your affection.'' His arm went around her rigid shoulders, and he motioned to Adela, who was standing near the door of the manor, hesitant to interrupt but aware that Marisa needed comfort and rest. A woman with child did not need such upsets, especially at the beginning of her pregnancy. "Go to the bower, Marisa. Let Adela tend you, and then rest.'' He lifted his dark gaze to where Brand had disappeared into the forest. "Things will be better after you sleep.''

"You treat me like a child, as well, Morgan ap Dafydd,'' she observed, her anger fading at his concern.

"Nay, Marisa, I treat you thusly *because* of my concern for you.''

Shortly thereafter, Adela bathed Marisa's flushed face and burning eyes as she lay upon the bed, for tears had threatened again once she was within the shelter of the sleeping-house. Marisa attributed her emotional state to her being with child.

Edyth came in to see her and offer comfort. "You have been under as much strain as Brand since you first met Robert de Lisieux at Fauxbray, Marisa. You have every right to express outright relief and thanksgiving in any way you can. Brand has much to be proud of in you."

"He has odd ways of showing his pride, Edyth. I know he hides in yon glade because he cannot bring himself to believe that I had any other reason to come to his aid besides my desire to hurt him with the reminder of my past friendship with Robert. A Norman woman sealing a bargain for her conquered Anglo-Saxon husband with the Norman she almost wed. Although Morgan says 'tis his jealousy, I know 'tis only his ridiculous pride."

With knowing glances between them, both Adela and Edyth acknowledged that there was no reasoning with Marisa at this point, and after she was comfortably settled upon the big bed, they wisely withdrew, leaving her to sleep.

When Marisa awoke, she knew by glancing at the time-keeping candle beside the bed that several hours had passed. Sitting up, she caught the wet cloth that had been placed upon her forehead and swung her legs over the side of the bed.

"A most fetching sight—such lovely limbs."

She started so violently that the cloth fell from suddenly slack fingers to the floor. Brand was sitting in a shadowed corner, watching her. Her earlier mood gone, she was uncertain how best to deal with him.

Ignoring her suspicion as to where he'd gone afterward, and her earlier anger, Marisa dropped her lashes and murmured, "I regret, my lord, that I disobeyed you and mayhap caused you distress by my actions earlier today."

As if he had not heard her words, he asked, "Do you know what I discovered while contemplating my sins where Rhiannon was concerned, Marisa?"

Her startled gaze encountered his in wary bemusement. She remained silent.

"That I can barely remember what she looked like. That when I would conjure up dark eyes and ebony hair, a vision of eyes like heather and hair like moonlight blocks out all else."

Marisa bit down on her lower lip, afraid to say anything, and for some reason feeling terribly guilty, although for the life of her she did not know why.

"The anguish, the pain I've suffered because of useless self-flagellation is a dull, dissipating ache that lessens with each day."

"Am I to apologize for that, as well, Saxon?"

There was a long silence before he answered. "Nay." He stood and came forward into the light and, not certain quite what to expect, Marisa tensed. He sat down upon the bed beside her and lifted a callused hand to smooth back an errant tendril of her hair. "I was angry at first that you disobeyed me twice, firebrand, but during my ruminations in the clearing I came to the conclusion that, being yourself, you could have done naught else."

Not certain whether to take his words as a compliment or a subtle admonition, Marisa reminded him, "I have displeased you from the first, Saxon, and I cannot believe that of a sudden you have accepted me wholeheartedly. To ride off into the forest after I accepted Robert's kiss . . ."

"My anger and jealousy were a small price to pay for his denial of his own lost charger." Yet even as he spoke, his lips compressed slightly and his dark brows drew together in an unconscious frown. "I accept the fact that he was mistaken in his observation that you loved me, but I am grateful that you stood by me this day . . . and in Fauxbray."

Marisa's eyes narrowed. "You accept the fact? How martyrlike of you, Brand Ericson!" Ire stirred in the depths of her midnight gaze because of his ready acceptance that she did not—could not—feel genuine love for him. "What would you have me do after all I've had to deal with since our marriage? Fall at your feet like some besotted maiden because you have deigned to throw me a bone as you would Rollo now and again? Or do you feel relieved because you could not return that love if ever I should be foolish enough to allow it?''

''Marisa . . .''

She stood abruptly and opened the bower door at Rollo's insistent whine. Stooping to hug the dog, she buried her face in the shaggy fur for a moment, taking comfort in something dearly familiar and unquestionably accepting of her affection.

When she looked up, Brand was crouching down beside her, and it was with the greatest reluctance that she met his regard. ''You are right, Saxon,'' she said. ''Robert was far off the mark when he declared what he thought I felt for you. 'Twas no doubt the emotion he wished I had harbored for him at one time—perhaps yet a bit of jealousy . . . begging your forgiveness for believing that another perfectly acceptable man could feel love for this spoiled, willful female.''

He gripped her by the shoulders and raised her to her feet, pulling her against him. ''Enough! Let us come to a truce, Marisa. Marriages based on mutual respect and affection have a more solid foundation than most arranged marriages.'' His eyes gleamed with frustration at her verbal sparring and his own suppressed longing, which suddenly sprang to the fore at his memory of her within Robert de Lisieux's embrace. Before she could answer, his mouth slanted across hers in a kiss that effectively cut off any words of refusal she might have uttered.

Marisa responded with all the love within her, her lips parting beneath his like a newly blossoming flower, for in his anger and confusion, he would not guess that she loved him. She was safe to express her feelings for him with her body, though not her words, until perhaps one day the blinders would slip from his eyes.

She prayed that, when that time came, he could return her love freely and openly.

* * *

"My lord?"

Brand straightened from examining a loose shoe on Goliath's hind leg and turned to meet Edwin's anxious gaze. Several weeks had passed in which Brand and Marisa had lived in relative contentment.

"Aye, Edwin," Brand greeted. The man-at-arms looked as if he dreaded what he had to say. "Are you well?" Brand brushed his palms together and leaned one bent arm against Goliath's rump. "Well, speak up, man. I have never known you to fear aught—well, mayhap marriage . . ." Humor laced his words, though the gleam in his eyes was indiscernible in the dimness.

Edwin swallowed and nodded, his gaze sliding to the straw-strewn floor of the stable. "My lord, there is something I must tell you." His eyes met his lord's. "It concerns the lady Marisa."

"Ah, I see."

"My lord," the man-at-arms began in earnest explanation, "I am no spy, no bearer of tales, and I would not divulge such a thing except that 'tis your right to know everything that transpires within your domain and . . . and I believe the lady places herself in danger by her actions."

Brand's eyes narrowed. "I know you are no telltale, Edwin. What is it that concerns you so?"

Edwin drew in a long breath. "The lady Marisa has . . . has been visiting Fauxbray. . . . "

He left off at the look that froze Brand's features. "Indeed."

Edwin's tongue slicked across his dry lips. "No one knows of these visits but me," he hastened to assure Brand. "I know you expressly forbade her to return after the first time, so I followed her secretly on two different occasions . . . at first to see where she went without escort, and then to protect her should the need have arisen."

He colored, for he knew what Brand was thinking by the tightening of his jaw, the clenching of his fist against Goliath. It was not his place, however, to confirm or deny such a thing . . . unless he was asked.

"Know you why she went to see le Faux?"

Edwin's flush deepened. "Nay."

A muscle jumped in Brand's cheek, but he seemed to pull himself together with an effort. "I thank you, my faithful Edwin, for telling me this. Do not reveal what you know of our conversation to anyone else, Marisa least of all. Do you understand?"

"Aye, my lord." He nodded and turned to leave.

Brand watched him disappear into the sunlight and remained unmoving for long moments. His look brooding, he continued to stare unseeingly out into the yard. . . .

Preparations for the coming wedding were in full swing and, taking advantage of Brand's lightening mood, Marisa obtained his consent—reluctant though it was—to be allowed to visit Fauxbray. Brand felt he owed his former fellow thane, Waltheof, at least that much, for Marisa seemed genuinely interested in helping improve the situation within the village. He ignored a niggling doubt in light of Edwin's revelation. If she could in any way influence Mauger—even by imparting false information regarding Brand's plans toward the Welsh, or anything else that might interest the arrogant Norman—Brand would count her commendable intentions well worth the effort. Then, too, Godgift provided an invaluable source of information concerning le Faux's movements.

So Brand hid his trepidation on Marisa's behalf and his knowledge of her secret visits, determined to believe that she visited her handsome countryman for no more than information, and allowed her another visit. Soon her responsibilities at the manor would take up every spare moment before the first Sunday after Lammas, the harvest festival which fell on August first.

A new fortified manor was being constructed in the small but prosperous village of Wighton, where Morgan and Edyth would reside now that he was to hold the village under Brand according to the new Norman system. So, in addition to preparations in Camwright, the neighboring Wighton hummed with extra activity as well. Marisa and Brand had invited to the wedding mass not only all the residents of Camwright, but also the residents of Wighton, for they had no formal church of their own and it was only fitting that they attend. Afterward, everyone would enjoy Brand's hospitality within the great hall.

Benches, settles, sideboards, and tables were cleaned and polished to shining luster under Marisa's direction, bedding and tapestries were aired, hearths swept, servants' clothing cleaned and mended or replaced. The day before the wedding, rosemary added its fresh fragrance to the newly strewn rushes about the hall floor.

When Leofric came to speak to Brand about evidence he'd found of someone prowling about the bog—of strange sounds in the dead of night coming from that direction— the lord of Camwright refused to show his concern before his sister or wife and spoil Edyth's happiness or dampen Marisa's excitement.

"I will get to the bottom of this two days hence, when you are safely wed and ensconced in your new home," Brand told Morgan privately. "But for the morrow, I will allow naught to put a blight upon your wedding day."

Worry furrowed Morgan's brow. "Edyth and I have the rest of our lives to be together, and I am still your man, Brand. If you need my help, you have only to ask."

The day dawned with bright benevolence for Morgan and Edyth's wedding, a shimmering golden ball of sun rising in glorious benediction over the eastern end of the manor hall. The servants and some of the village women who had been recruited to help with the preparation of the wedding feast scurried to and fro in their unceasing efforts to make the celebration one that would be truly memorable. After all, the lady Edyth was well loved in Camwright, and the people had had woefully little to celebrate within the last nine months.

"You are the most beautiful bride Camwright has ever had," Marisa declared as she helped Adela plait and weave peach-hued ribbons through Edyth's dark chestnut hair.

Her eyes aglow with happiness, Edyth laughed aloud.

"And how would you know, Marisa, when I am the only bride from the village you have ever seen?"

"I have the Sight, did you not know that, Edyth?" Marisa smoothed an imaginary wrinkle from the same peach bliaut in which she had been wed only months before. The chainse beneath was russet, in contrast to the pale overgown and the ribbon that laced the dark tresses. The stitching bordering the bliaut's neckline, sleeve edges, and hem was the same umber shade, almost the color of Edyth's hair. Although Edyth had wished to wear Marisa's gown, Marisa had insisted on the changes, the reason known only to her.

"Hmph," grunted Adela, giving the coronet of Edyth's hair one last pat. "The Sight, indeed. You are the furthest thing from a witch of any female I know—except, of course, for the lady Edyth and your lady mother, rest her soul."

Edyth, however, played along. "But, of course, you are a beautiful witch. So, my lady witch, tell me how many children Morgan and I shall have."

Marisa looked thoughtful for a moment. *"Eh bien,* I must consult my familiar. . . . Here, Rollo," she commanded. The wolfhound stood and leisurely stretched his long legs, yawned, and finally padded over to Marisa. She put her nose to his and closed her eyes in feigned concentration. "You are not very convincing, animal. Where is you sense of the dramatic?" Her words caused another burst of mirth from Edyth, with Adela joining in.

"I say she shall have so many children she will have no time to look even sideways at another man," Morgan said from the door.

Startled, Edyth turned toward the open portal, Marisa and Adela following suit. "What do you here?" Marisa asked with what presence she could muster as she straightened from her less than dignified position. "Can you not even wait to see your bride when we break the fast?"

Brand added from behind Morgan, "If we wait until you women are finished with your fussing and primping, Father Aelfwine will be forced to speak over our growling bellies throughout the mass because we will be obliged to skip the meal." But his voice was full of amused indulgence.

"Well, I am ready," Edyth informed Morgan, lively color splashing her cheeks. "I'll not be the cause of such an unprecedented stir at my own wedding." She glided forward, her limp all but unnoticeable as she joined Morgan.

Adela shook her head and began to straighten up the bower, while Brand waited for Marisa. As she stepped out into the bright yard, she missed the admiration in his eyes, for she was dressed in pale gold and daffodil, bright as the sun coruscating low in the eastern sky. "You are lovely this day, Viking."

Marisa shaded her eyes with her hand as they moved toward the hall. "Thank you, my lord, but this day belongs to the bride, and none can rival her radiance."

"Except you."

Tongue-tied for a moment at his compliment, Marisa was shyly silent.

"There has never been a bride in all of England to match you that day in Westminster."

Unexpectedly, Marisa felt the sting of tears blinding her and causing her to stumble. Never had she heard such words of praise from Brand Ericson. His hand beneath her elbow steadied her, and his fingers tightened slightly, as if to reinforce his words.

At the entrance to the hall, he paused and looked down into her misty eyes. "Tell me, Marisa, why my sister does not wear the same gown in which you were joined to me."

"But, my lord husband," she said in a guilty rush, " 'tis the same bliaut." She could not, however, hold his eyes.

" 'Tis altered."

"There is . . . an old superstition in Normandy that 'tis bad luck to be wed in the same gown as another," she lied.

"I do not believe that, Marisa."

She drew in a deep, bracing breath of air and looked him straight in the eye. "Then believe what you must, for 'tis true.'' Removing her arm from his restraining grip, she stepped into the hall. "Ask Adela, if you doubt my word."

After breaking the fast, they all headed toward the small stone church. On the way, Nesta stepped forward unexpectedly from the crowd of villagers to crown Edyth's dark head with a garland of wildflowers. Edyth hugged the Welsh woman in thanks and then continued onward.

Once inside the cool interior, Marisa marveled, not for the first time, that the mass was given in English and not Latin as it was in Normandy. Since it was the Sunday after Lammas, newly baked loaves of bread made from the first harvest of wheat had been brought to the church to be blessed. Then, finally, the brief marriage ceremony was performed.

Marisa watched wistfully when Morgan's kiss of peace lasted long enough to elicit an "ahem" from Father Aelfwine. She lowered her lashes in pained remembrance of the brief, less than gentle touch of Brand's mouth on hers, which had resulted in a bruised lip. She was secretly glad she'd persuaded Adela to alter the bliaut and Edyth to wear the russet undertunic. She had no wish for the union now taking place to bear any resemblance whatsoever to what was between Brand and herself.

As Morgan and Edyth turned back toward the crowd, she glanced up at the man at her side and found herself without warning being gently but soundly kissed on the mouth by her husband. When he drew away, she murmured, "What will your people think?"

"I care not." His gemlike eyes fusing with hers and gleaming with something more than desire, he bent his head again and repeated the tender gesture.

"You cannot fool me, Viking. I know why Edyth was not wed in the exact garments you were, but I intend to remedy a few things."

Before she could react, they were filing out of the church, Brand's strong hand clasping hers, and into the yard, everyone laughing and congratulating the newly wedded couple. Unable to get near Morgan and Edyth at first, Marisa watched the children frolicking, the adults singing and dancing with as much gusto as the youth of the village, and thought again how different this celebration was from that day in April in London. In spite of Brand's words of assurance, she doubted there could ever be anything between them like that which united the Welshman and his shy Saxon bride, and a melancholy settled over her that forced her to pin a smile to her lips, to pretend a gaiety she suddenly did not feel.

It must be my being with child, she reasoned, for a natural, effervescent vitality had always characterized her actions.

After she wished Morgan and Edyth well, Marisa found herself temporarily separated from her husband. For a moment she stood alone, an outside observer. Would she ever be totally accepted by these people? she wondered. Even though she had grown to accept and, yes, love many of them, would she ever truly belong?

"Marisa?"

She looked down at Griffith, who'd come up to her with Alfred at his side. *"Oui, cher?"* She mustered up a natural smile for both of the boys, having forgiven Alfred long ago for striking Rollo.

"May I show Alfred some of Rollo's tricks?"

Griffith's eyes shone with excitement, and Marisa could not find it in her heart to deny him. "Very well, Griffith, but"—she looked at Alfred meaningfully—"you must not tease him."

"Oh, nay, my lady," chimed in Alfred. "Rollo and I are friends now, and I would never tease him."

The two scampered off to find the wolfhound and Marisa's attention was momentarily caught and held by Nesta and Leofric.

Mead flowed freely throughout the early afternoon in the great hall. When at last the meal was served, Marisa was relieved because the drink-induced exuberance of the villagers would be leveled off to near normalcy after their empty bellies were filled. She watched her husband laughing and joking with his people, listening to any one of them who had a question or comment, giving advice when it was solicited. He also readily partook of the arm wrestling and attempts at juggling that were encouraged by the tanner from Wighton, who fancied himself a juggler and acrobat and attempted to impress his new Welsh lord whenever he could.

As if vying for the attention of their people, Morgan played his harp and sang until he was hoarse, while in between songs Brand showed off his considerable dexterity in juggling the Saxon horns made of exquisitely blown glass. "I may sing like the frogs in the marsh," he shouted in challenge to Morgan after flashing a grin in Marisa's direction, "but there are definite advantages to being able to juggle."

"The only juggling worthwhile is that of comely wenches," shouted Morgan wickedly as he began another song, this one a bawdy ballad. Edyth threw him a fondly reproving look, and he winked at her so lasciviously that she laughed, blushed, and turned away, attributing his deviltry to overimbibing.

"Come, my lord," encouraged Bryce from Wighton, "show yon Welshman how nimble you are. Turn a somersault like so . . ." He demonstrated a series of tumbling maneuvers that produced a hearty round of applause.

" 'Twould be less than dignified for the lord of Camwright to perform acrobatics, would you not say, Bryce?" asked Brand with a skeptical lift of a dark eyebrow.

"Give him another cup of mead!" shouted Edwin, one of Brand's retainers. "My lord Brand will do anything— dignified or no—for another draught of Camwright's excellent drink!"

Morgan interrupted his ballad, which was faltering anyway because he'd forgotten some of the words. "Only because 'tis the one thing that loosens his stiff limbs!" he said, and roared with laughter.

That was all the impetus Brand needed. Draining a proffered horn of the potent mead, he prepared to imitate the agile Bryce. Glancing at Marisa, who stood nearby, sudden concern in her expression, he cried, " 'Tis about time someone put that cocky Welshman in his place. He can barely mount that shaggy nag he calls a horse, while *I* have perfected vaulting astride a Norman destrier un-aided.''

"Indeed?" shouted Morgan, jumping to his feet im-mediately to accept the challenge. "Then bring out one of your monstrous steeds and let us see who can and cannot vault atop without a hand up!"

"Mon Dieu," Marisa whispered to no one in particular. "They will kill themselves."

Throngs of villagers spilled out of the great hall to see the contest between the two men. Brian, the stableboy, led forth into the compound one of Brand's great war-horses.

"What of Goliath?" Morgan inquired with bravado.

"I do not wish to push your luck, ap Dafydd. This one is as many hands high as Goliath but has a better temper-ament.''

"Morgan, you have never mounted one of Brand's—"

He turned at the sound of Edyth's voice and kissed her soundly in the middle of her warning. "Fear not for me, sweet wife. I am of the Cymry, fierce, courageous—"

"And drunk!" contributed someone from the crowd.

Loud guffaws and hearty laughter resounded throughout the bailey.

"You first," ordered Morgan good-naturedly, a grin splitting his face from ear to ear.

Brand nodded and, with several sprinting steps, sprang over the side of the animal, only to land awkwardly shy of the middle of its back. Determinedly grabbing a handful of the thick mane, he hefted himself upright and looked triumphantly down at Morgan. "There!"

Morgan shook his head even as several bystanders po-litely applauded their lord. "You call *that* a clean mount?"

"I thought 'twas *magnifique,*" opined Marisa in an at-tempt to discourage her slightly tipsy husband from re-peating the action.

"Aye, and Marisa should know," Edyth added em-phatically.

But Morgan had sown the seed well, and Brand frowned

slightly as he slid from the dun's back and prepared to try again. "Marisa is the one in her cups if she says 'twas good enough," he declared. "Morgan is right. The mounting of the animal was poorly executed."

Dieu nous sauve, Marisa prayed as Brand shook his head once, as if to clear it, and lithely trotted several steps toward the horse. He vaulted to the saddle almost perfectly this time, all things considered. With a smirk of triumph, he looked first to Morgan and then to Marisa.

"Not bad, but I can match it." Morgan moved to where Brand had poised himself for the attempt as the latter dismounted and backed away.

Shorter and more wiry, Morgan had a more difficult maneuver to perform, even had he been absolutely sober and well-practiced at mounting anything but a small Welsh pony. But he was undaunted and, running lightly toward the dun, he launched himself upward toward the horse's back in an exact imitation of Brand. But he fell short, and, his foot catching in the stirrup, he slid down to hang ignominiously with one hand clutching the pommel and his leg looped through the stirrup.

The thunder of laughter greeted his attempt, and immediately Brand and Brian caught the reins of the startled destrier to calm it long enough for Morgan to disentangle himself. "Give up, ap Dafydd. The Cymry were not made to mount war-horses. . . . 'Tis why God provided you with ponies."

Morgan's eyes narrowed with determination. "You attempted twice, strutting Saxon, and so will I."

Edyth clutched at Brand's sleeve, her eyes full of supplication. "And what of your manhood, Morgan?" Brand queried. "You may end up with naught to give Edyth this night—or any other."

Even Marisa laughed at the gibe, although it sounded more like a goad than an attempt to dissuade Morgan.

"Those are words to stop him?" Edyth muttered more to herself than to her brother as she anxiously watched her new husband prepare to mount again.

Just then, the dun decided to present the entire assemblage with a neat pile of droppings, and the crowd roared. Morgan, too, was seized by a bout of laughter and cried, "Now mayhap he's shrunk a hand or so, having relieved himself of such a load.'Twill make my task easier."

And so it was amid the added pandemonium that Morgan sprinted toward the dun and catapulted himself with such zest and exuberant determination toward its back that he went clean over the saddle and landed with a dull thud on the other side of the steed.

Some laughed, and some issued cries of concern at his spill. Brand and Edyth were the first to reach him as Brian led the destrier with its deadly hooves away from the fallen Welshman. His head in Edyth's lap, Morgan opened his eyes and regarded his brother-by-marriage with perfect lucidity. "I bested you, Ericson. I went farther."

Chapter 18

Despite the alarm of many of the wedding celebrants, Morgan had only had the wind knocked out of him. After a few more horns of mead, he was safely carried, with ribald comments, to Edyth's bower, where she shyly awaited him. She, too, had been subjected to much good-natured laughter and twittering among the women who had escorted and prepared her for her husband, but at last they were united and left in peace for the night. In the morning the newly wedded couple would leave for Wighton to begin their married life together.

It was still light—several hours away from sunset—and for many the celebration continued on. Marisa noticed that Griffith and Alfred had been absent from the hall for quite a while, Rollo as well. After a cursory search, a frown of concern settled over her features. Not wishing to alarm Brand unduly, she made several casual inquiries and learned from one of the other village boys that Alfred had bragged to Griffith of seeing an even larger wild dog than Rollo outside the village. Griffith, ever Rollo's champion, did not believe his friend, and the two boys and the wolfhound had gone off in search of this supposed behemoth.

Marisa's blood ran cold, for the only animal—dog or wolf—that she had seen since coming to Camwright that was larger than Rollo was the great wolf that had been with Angharad when the woman had attempted to lure Griffith to her side. *But it's dead,* she reminded herself.

Either way, any possible traffic with the old Welsh witch boded ill for the boys.

Glancing up at the still bright early evening sky, and then over at Brand's happy, animated features as he bantered with his men with a relaxed contentment Marisa had never seen in him before, she decided to investigate the disappearance on her own before sounding a false alarm. Then, if she needed help, she could always enlist her husband's aid.

Now, she thought, *if only I can get Goliath from the stable without arousing suspicions.* . . .

As she began to saddle the horse, Brian stepped unexpectedly out of the shadows with a questioning look. "I only wished to . . . well, I suppose I should tell someone." She sighed in resignation. "Brian," she appealed to him, "I do not wish to spoil my lord's pleasure. I have not seen Griffith or Alfred—or Rollo, for that matter—for a while, and I am concerned. I wish to take a leisurely ride around the perimeter of the village, nothing more."

"But, my lady, dusk is approaching and I do not think my lord Brand would permit you to—"

"Brian," she entreated, "have you not seen how carefree he is this day? He looks years younger. Do not add to his burdens. No doubt I can find the boys and bring them back without mishap. 'Tis more than likely a harmless excursion they've taken. Rollo is with them and he would fight to the death for Griffith." At Brian's continued look of skepticism, she added, "I give you my word that if I do not find them within the hour, I will return forthwith. If, on the other hand, I do not return in that same amount of time, tell my lord Brand what I am about and ask him to come after me."

And so it was that Marisa was able to ride away without interference. The gatehouse guards were inside the hall, and the only others on duty were at the eastern gate on the opposite side of the manor compound. She rode straight into the northern woods, to the clearing around the waterfall, calling out the boys' names. But as she sat astride Goliath in the quiet glade, only the rushing sound of cascading water greeted her ears.

She sat for long moments in temporary indecision, wondering where two boys and a wolfhound would wander in their escapades.

Innocents will pay the price for your thievery . . . I guarantee that. . . .

Angharad's words in Marisa's dream came back to her in a flash of revelation. Where would be the most likely place for two innocent boys to have a mishap, whether Rollo was with them or not? *"Dieu au ciel—the bog!"*

In one smooth movement Marisa swung the charger's head toward the west and touched her heels to its sides. The path was wide enough, but at the relentless, desperate pace she drove the horse beneath her, leafy branches and vines from the trees that canopied overhead whipped against her face and neck, scratching and bruising tender skin, snagging and renting her jonquil-yellow silk bliaut. At most, a quarter of an hour or so had passed, and if she hurried—if her luck held—she could still intercept the boys and bring them back to the village before Brian sounded the alarm. *Please, dear God, let them be safe!*

Once far enough west of the village, she emerged from the forest, forded the Wye River, and raced the gray south toward the infamous quagmire. Gooseflesh rose on her body at the very thought of returning there once again, for one visit had been quite enough. Yet her pace slowed not the slightest, for even if Angharad were uninvolved, the bog was a dangerous place for an adult, let alone for two children and a dog.

The stench of decay stung her nostrils, and Goliath's pace slowed as the stallion balked at the change in the ground beneath him. Bending over his neck, she urged him on in French but could not induce him to take up the same distance-eating gallop he'd maintained earlier.

"Griffith! Alfred!" she called, finally giving in to the war-horse's instincts and allowing him to slow to a walk. No answering call was sounded. "Rollo!" she called out. Nothing.

Or had she heard the faint sound of voices? she wondered as she gingerly circled around the worst areas. Goliath snorted and stopped, pawing the spongy ground in protest. Marisa patted his withers in reassurance. "Easy, boy. You must help me find them. I know they are here." She dismounted and led the courser by the reins as she strained to hear the vague, disjointed sounds she'd thought she'd detected only moments before. She called once more. "Griffith! Alfred! Rollo!"

The soggy ground sucked at her feet and made walking difficult, and Marisa had no idea which sections of the morass were safe and which were not. Dead trees, their barren, skeletal branches reaching skyward in seeming supplication from their watery hell, protruded everywhere, even deeper within the bog where Marisa knew she dared not venture. The stumps and trees gave no indication as to the solidity of the earth or the depth of the swamp in which they were entrapped.

Where were they? she thought in growing panic.

As she strained to hear noises—any kind of sound in the eerie stillness—Goliath whickered and tossed his head in warning. Suddenly a large, shaggy body came hurtling in her direction, almost unrecognizable from the mud that covered its coat.

"Rollo!" she cried in joyous relief. His tail waved back and forth in vigorous welcome, spattering her gown with mire. She stooped down beside the dog and rubbed him behind the ears. "Where is Griffith, boy? Where is Griffith?"

He whined and sniffed the air, then pulled away from her and started to trot away, only to return, waiting, his ears pricked forward and his head cocked. Marisa took up the gray's reins and began to lead him toward the dog. Rollo barked sharply in response and trotted away again, looking back from time to time to make certain Marisa was still following.

The scene that later greeted Marisa was the stuff of which nightmares are made. Alfred clung to what little remained of a submerged tree stump, surrounded by the murky greenish water of the swamp. Griffith was attempting to make his way toward his friend but was repulsed each time by the sucking, shifting ground beneath his feet.

Marisa watched his latest retreat in silent horror, noting the extreme frustration and fright on his small face. Yet he called to his friend, "Hang on tight, Alfred. We will get you out of this, never fear."

His words, his determination, the set of his small jaw, all unexpectedly reminded Marisa of his father, and with a surge of pride she began to step forward. Alfred called in a shaky voice, "Look, Griffith, there is someone in the trees yonder. . . ."

Rollo bounded toward Griffith with Marisa and Goliath following, just as an unholy and unwelcome apparition stepped from the trees to which Alfred referred . . . a contrast of dark skirts and white hair . . . of small, milky eyes, pale, withered skin, and surprisingly youthful—eerily so—ease of movement.

"Rollo, Marisa!" Griffith cried joyously. He hugged Marisa tightly, then attempted to marshal his courage and push away. "Marisa, Alfred saw the wolf, the same wolf that was killed in the clearing. . . . He saw it in the bog and tried to follow."

Rollo's low growl of menace put a stop to his words, and both he and Marisa turned toward the old woman slowly advancing toward them. She seemed to literally skim over the sodden ground, and the look upon her wizened features was triumphant.

"So you have come in search of your grandmother, Gruffydd," she crooned in Welsh, completely ignoring Marisa. "Come to me, now. We will go away from this place."

Marisa put a hand upon the boy's shoulder. "Stay with me, Griffith."

Rollo's growls deepened, his bared teeth warning Angharad to come no closer.

The wind picked up, in a place where it had been absolutely still, the stagnant air almost suffocating.

"Leave this place, Angharad," Marisa commanded with calm authority, "and I will say naught of your presence, for Brand wants your capture badly."

Angharad's ferretlike eyes never left her grandson. "Come away, I say to you, my Gruffydd. You do not belong here with your weak father and his harlot, this *nithing*."

An involuntary shiver rippled through Marisa at the crone's use once again of that comprehensive insult and condemnation in the Saxon tongue—a word that labeled the recipient as worthless, bereft of rights, no longer a member of any kin, society, or even the human race.

"Lady Marisa!"

Marisa dragged her gaze away from Angharad's and trained it on the child stranded in the bog. The terror in Alfred's voice, the look frozen across his small features—both acted as a catalyst for Marisa to pull herself together. Shrugging off the eerie feeling caused by Angharad's presence and the possibility that she might have to physically fight for Griffith, Marisa allowed her faith in Rollo, and the very real chance that Alfred might perish, to galvanize her into action.

"*Rollo, garde l'enfant—garde Griffith!*" she ordered in French so he would be certain to understand. The dog placed himself between Griffith and Angharad, his great dark eyes never leaving the latter's face.

"Lady Marisa, I am *sinking!* I think the stump is moving."

"Easy, *cher*. We will get you out safely. Just do not move. Remain still as you can, *n'est-ce pas?*"

Casting a desperate look about for something—anything—that would act as a line, Marisa caught sight of a long-dead hanging vine wound through the naked branches of a barren tree on what looked like solid ground. She hurried over to the tree and had to spring upward several times before she could catch one end, but it pulled easily enough from between the lifeless boughs.

After securing it to Goliath's saddle, she moved swiftly back toward the edge of semisolid ground, only to hear a menacing snarl issue from Rollo.

"So, you think to stop me with yon hound, Marisa de Brionne?" As Marisa glanced over, the gleaming blade of a knife caught a stray shaft of the weakly penetrating sun. "The Cymry are trained to use daggers as easily as any other weapon, stupid girl. Will you watch me bury my knife in your beast's throat as easily as some unseen cur did to my Lucifer?"

Marisa felt an icy prickle of fear upon her scalp and down her neck, but she continued to loop the vine around her shoulder and bent elbow until she could wade as far as possible into the brackish miasma toward Alfred and then throw him the slack. "My Rollo is shrewder than you give him credit for, Angharad," she called over her shoulder with seemingly unshakable conviction. "He will not sit idly while you run him through. . . . *Prends garde, Rollo!*" she ordered as she stepped into the slime-covered water.

The dog jumped to all fours and began prowling around Angharad, all the while growling low within his deep chest. He never remained behind her for long, however, the intelligent eyes going from Angharad and the dagger in her hand to Griffith and back in wary surveillance.

Feeling as if she were in the grips of a bad dream, Marisa pushed each leg forward, fighting her skirts, the water, and the impeding muck beneath it.

"My lady!"

Genuine panic was taking over now. "I'm coming, Alfred. Be a brave boy, now, and do not move."

Between the snarling behind her and the terrified voice of the child before her, Marisa was torn in two directions while the low keening of a chill wind swirled around them. It was terribly frustrating to be unable to make swifter progress through the swamp. . . .

Suddenly from Griffith's "No!" and the sounds that increased in pitch and ferocity behind Marisa, she knew that Rollo had tangled with Angharad. Marisa hazarded a glance over her shoulder and, to her horror, saw Angharad's knife glinting from the faithful dog's side . . . and now the woman was picking up a bough with which to strike the wounded animal at the first opportunity.

"Leave him be!" shouted Griffith as dog and woman circled each other like mortal enemies, a trickle of blood wending down the wolfhound's mud-matted coat. Just as the boy ran forward in an attempt to knock the branch from Angharad's grip, it came slamming up against the limping, stunned dog's ribs and threw him staggering sideways, knocking into Griffith and sending the boy sprawling.

"Angharad!"

The entire swamp reverberated with the hate-filled, hoarsely projected word. All eyes went to the owner of the commanding voice . . . except Angharad's. Her arm raised to strike the death blow at the dazed dog's head.

"Nay!" screamed Marisa.

Then three things happened simultaneously. As Marisa's cry went streaking through the clearing, a figure from the forest sent his own dagger whizzing through the air to bury itself in Angharad's back. The crone crumpled slowly, a look of surprise stamped upon her age-furrowed features. At the same moment a rope came snaking through the air out of nowhere and landed atop the water within Alfred's reach. And Brand emerged upon the scene from the edge of the woods near Goliath and rode straight toward the shocked Marisa, mud flying as he brought his horse to a skidding halt.

Flinging himself from the suddenly skittish stallion's back, he cast a quick, assessing look over his shoulder toward Griffith. The old man from the forest assured him, "The lad is fine. . . . See to your wife and the other child."

Brand waded into the slime-coated water toward Marisa and caught hold of her around the waist. "Are you unharmed?" At her nod, he directed, "Get back to firm ground, Marisa. I'll see to Alfred." She did as she was bidden, too shocked to argue and certain that Alfred was now in capable hands.

Falling to her knees upon the spongy earth that edged the bog, Marisa fought sudden fatigue and overwhelming relief that Griffith was unharmed and Rollo . . . . Her eyes widened as she took in the strange old man squatting beside the hound and ministering to him with oddly gentle hands. How much more could one animal survive? she wondered, trying not to acknowledge that the blood flowing from Rollo's side boded ill.

Pulling herself to her feet, she turned to watch Brand coax Alfred to cling to the rope as, hand over hand, he drew the boy toward him. She swung back toward the strange little group several yards away. Nearing Griffith, she reached out to enfold him within her embrace, his mud- and tear-streaked face turned up to her beseechingly. "Will Rollo die, Marisa?" he asked in a tremulous voice.

"Nay, Gruffydd," answered the old man. " 'Twill take more than the puny knife of that scheming succubus lying upon the ground to kill such a noble-hearted beast. Fetch me some mud from over yonder for Rollo's wound, lad."

Griffith did as he was bid—anything for his beloved Rollo. Out of compassion Marisa approached Angharad where she was lying upon the ground, wounded. The old woman had managed to turn her head to stare malevolently at the stranger, her dark eyes burning with hatred, blood dribbling from the corners of her mouth and one nostril. "Drystan the Accursed," she hissed with soft virulence. But the man ignored her.

"Angharad?"

The sound of Marisa's gentle query made the other woman's head jerk back convulsively in an effort to avoid the younger woman's touch. "Does not your name mean 'loved one' in the Welsh tongue? Yet you are so full of violent hatred. . . . I wonder at the mother who once named you thus."

"She is the devil's spawn—her mother a witch who

undoubtedly burns in hell,'' Drystan said with contempt.
''The name was ill-chosen.''

'' 'Tis not over yet, coward,'' Angharad told Drystan
with a chilling parody of a smile. For one last, fleeting
moment her dark, rheumy gaze held Marisa's. ''Old
scores will yet be settled, Norman whore, and your
treachery will be repaid in kind.'' Her eyes closed then,
and with a last, thready sigh, she gave up whatever soul
she possessed.

''Is Grandmother dead?'' Griffith asked in a hushed
voice when he had given Drystan the oozing muck he'd
collected in his small hands. His gaze went from the man
crouching over Rollo to Angharad's still form, Alfred all
but forgotten for a moment.

''She was never your grandmother, child. What she
has done this day—and that other at the clearing—should
not have the power to hurt you, nor ever cause you
shame.'' Griffith gazed again at the stranger with the
beautiful, lilting Welsh accent who reached into a pouch
at his side and produced dried leaves and crumpled them
into the mud before applying the mixture directly to the
wound in Rollo's side.

''Who . . . who are you, my lord?''

''Indeed, who are you, for we owe you much,'' added
Brand as he came up behind them with a very subdued
Alfred in his arms. He let the boy slide down to stand
upright on his own two feet, keeping a steadying hand
on Alfred's back as he waited expectantly.

At Drystan's silence, he pressed, ''You killed the wolf
in the clearing earlier this summer, didn't you?''

Drystan nodded and stroked Rollo's chin.

Marisa straightened and stepped over to Drystan and
Rollo. Stooping down to caress the dog's great head, she
murmured, ''Then I owe you my life, Drystan, for had
you not intervened, I surely would have perished.''

A half smile softened the melancholy cast of his features, and his keen, black eyes met hers. ''You would
not have perished with Rollo fighting for you. Surely he

would have won the struggle. . . . I but put it to a quicker end.''

He stood then and, glancing at Brand as he ruffled Griffith's sable locks with affection, said, ''Have a care, for Gruffydd's sake, if not for your own. An old but unrevealed enemy of yours, a Welshman with a malady of the soul, tossed the rope today to save Edgiva's son, but he would as soon see you and your Norman wife killed and Gruffydd in his possession.''

Brand's eyes narrowed. ''Why did he not reveal himself?''

''He will in time. Beware, he plots with the Norman whose lands march with yours.'' Drystan turned toward the forest from whence he had come before adding, ''The dog must be transported on a litter. He should not walk for several days.''

''But who *are* you?'' Brand pressed.

The old man paused before asking softly, ''What can it matter?''

''A great deal. You saved my son and my wife this day and one other time, as well. I would know who you are, wise one.''

He turned to Brand, his face a study in bleakness, and said in Welsh, ''Wise? Nay, that I am not. . . . I am sorrow.''

''Why did you bother to save the boy?''

Madog ap Cynan took another draught of mead as he sat at a badly scarred table in the small wooden cottage he called home. ''Because I wanted to, Hywel.''

The man across from him shook his head. ''You gave our presence away. Even though we were hidden in the forest, Drystan knew we were there. He is more canny than the wild beasts among whom he abides. And,'' he added slyly, ''le Faux will not be pleased.''

Madog slammed down his carved drinking horn with such force it cracked, and the little mead left within dribbled out the bottom. ''I care not what pleases him! He only uses us, nothing more. When we have served our purpose, then he will betray us or attempt to dispose of us in some heinous scheme that only he could dream up.''

''Now Ericson knows of the danger . . . He—''

Loam-dark eyes burning with some indefinable emotion knifed into Hywel's. ''We do not know what Drystan told Ericson . . . or even if the Saxon believed the old man. There is no reason why any of us could not have been in the area of the marsh. Part of it is on Welsh soil.''

The other Welshman paced back and forth, frowning in contemplation. ''We will have to watch our step now, Madog,'' he warned, then stopped to look at his surly companion. ''You may do well to sit and brood about a foiled plan, but 'tis so because of you.''

Madog raised his hooded gaze to Hywel. ''Edgiva was friend to Rhiannon, and she has Cymry blood running through her veins. How could I stand by and allow her son to die?''

''The pale-haired one would have saved him.''

''I am not so sure, with her beloved hound's life threatened, as well as what appeared to be Gruffydd's safety.''

''Well, a fine mess we have now! What will you tell the Norman?''

A humorless smile pulled up one corner of Madog's mouth. ''Why, the truth—as far as I deem wise.'' He stood and fetched another horn before drinking deeply. ''Angharad lured the boy and Marisa to the bog. We undoubtedly could have taken them both then and there except for Drystan's unexpected appearance. But at least Angharad is dead. That should please the cur.''

''But he will say that you botched the job, that we could have killed Drystan and taken them anyway.''

Madog's dark brows raised in mock consternation. ''Why, Hywel, I do believe you are afraid of Mauger le Faux. So afraid that you cannot think straight.''

Hywel spun away. ''Bah! I only wish for you to exercise more caution next time, for it may be the last chance we get.''

"We have time aplenty until Michaelmas if we wish to go along with le Faux's plan. And if we do not, we have even more time to implement a similar scheme without him and rally more support against Ericson than le Faux is aware of. It only remains for us to lie low. Now that Angharad is out of the way, or so Ericson will believe, there is no threat to Gruffydd or his Norman wife. There will come a time when his guard will relax, no matter what the old man told him. And we will be ready."

But Hywel had one question for which Madog had no answer. "Just who is this Drystan? I know he is a recluse, has shunned human companionship for years, but exactly *who* is he?"

Madog shrugged, his eyes narrowed in thought. "No one really knows. No one, mayhap, except Angharad. If that be the case, the secret died with her."

Chapter 19

Dusk was approaching as the tired, happy villagers drifted away from the all-day revelry in the hall and toward their respective homes. Most allowed curiosity to show on their faces, but it was Edgiva and Rolfe who rushed up to the returning party at the sight of their son sitting before the lord of Camwright on his huge dun-colored destrier. The look upon Brand's face was unlike the relaxed and smiling mien he'd exhibited during the wedding and the celebration afterward, and Marisa, who followed on Goliath, held Griffith before her and kept glancing back at Rollo's makeshift litter being pulled behind the great war-horse.

All of them were wet, muddied, and bedraggled.

"Alfred!" Simultaneously, Edgiva and Rolfe cried out the child's name and ran forward to intercept Brand.

"Hold right there," he directed. "Alfred is fine, but you will spook the stallion." He smiled faintly at Rolfe. "God knows he's been put to the test with Morgan's clumsy attempts to mount him this afternoon." He carefully handed Alfred down to Rolfe and dismounted.

Alfred clung first to his father and then threw himself into Edgiva's waiting embrace. "Mother, Father—Angharad was at the bog and—"

"And what were you doing at the bog, childie?" Edgiva admonished sternly.

His look turned sheepish. "Well, I—I was trying to

find the wolf that has been lurking about to prove to Griffith that he was larger than Rollo."

"The wolf?" Rolfe looked up at Brand.

"Undoubtedly one of Angharad's tricks, for no one else has seen such a beast. I wouldn't be surprised if she somehow made Alfred think that he, indeed, saw such a creature, only to lure him and Griffith to the bog."

"Well, I *did* see him, Father, but when I gave chase I ended up in the—" He paused uncertainly, knowing he would be punished for disobeying the order never to go near the marsh. "But the lady Marisa waded into the water to rescue me while Angharad tried to kill Rollo and take Griffith away." He took a deep breath and rushed on before anyone could stop him. "And then Lord Brand sent Lady Marisa out of the water and saved me himself."

Edgiva looked her son over carefully. "Are you unharmed, Alfred?"

He nodded. "Aye, Mother, only wet and hungry." He turned to see Brand helping Marisa and Griffith down. She walked back to Rollo's still form upon the litter. Alfred broke free of his mother's encircling arms and ran to stand beside Griffith. He squatted down beside his friend and regarded the hound solemnly. "Will he live, my lady? He is the bravest dog in all of England."

"I hope so, Alfred. You must say a prayer for him."

"I will, my lady."

In the deepening shadows, a movement behind Marisa caught her attention. It was Edgiva, with Rolfe behind her. "You saved my Alfred's life."

The statement was free of rancor. Rather, it was disbelieving.

"Nay, Edgiva. I only made the attempt. 'Twas my husband who saved your son's life."

"But if I hadn't come upon the scene when I did, Marisa would have done the same."

Edgiva glanced over at Brand and then back to Marisa. Suddenly she was kneeling before the Norman girl, clutching at her sodden skirts. "I owe you more than I can ever repay for risking yourself for my son—and after the way I have treated you, after the way I have thought ill of you and let everyone in Camwright know it.''

Marisa put a gentle hand on the older woman's head. "Rise, Edgiva. You owe me naught.'Twas Brand who—''

Edgiva raised eyes glistening with tears to Marisa. "But you would have performed the rescue. You knew not that Brand would appear to take over. I can see by your clothing that you were nigh up to your shoulders in that treacherous slime for my son. I am forever in your debt. And I regret that I ever believed Angharad's evil, vicious lies where you were concerned.''

"Do not speak ill of the dead," Marisa said quietly, bending to take Edgiva by the arm and raise her to her feet.

"Dead? Then 'tis what she deserves," muttered Rolfe. He awkwardly took Marisa's hand and pressed it to his lips in gratitude. "My wife has learned a valuable lesson. In Angharad's efforts to turn everyone against you through Edgiva, Angharad surrendered any loyalty to my wife and her kin. Alfred would have been carelessly sacrificed to obtain her selfish wishes.''

A growing crowd had been gathering around them and murmured comments spread through the onlookers like ripples in a pond.

"I will say this only once," Brand informed them. "Angharad was evil and twisted. It took Rhiannon's death to bring out the worst in the woman, but I believe that a deep-seated treachery lurked within her throughout her life. It needed only some incident to bring it out into the open." He put one arm around Griffith's shoulders and took Marisa's hand. As he started for the manor, Brian came at a run to take the reins of the two horses. "Please, good people, take yourselves to your beds and be thankful that worse did not happen.''

Rollo was resting quietly upon the makeshift bed he had shared with Marisa on the stone floor of the bower in their first days in Camwright. Marisa was soaking in a warm bath before one of the braziers. Her hair pinned high upon her head, she lay back against the wooden slats and allowed her eyes to close wearily.

Brand reclined in bed and watched her every movement until she had finished washing. Attar of roses had been added to the water to soften her skin, and the scent drifted over to him like an aphrodisiac, beckoning, luring, tempting him mercilessly. It was all he could do not to lift her from the fragrant water and carry her, dripping wet, to the bed and make her one with him physically.

But he did not dare. Old fears and painful memories were still powerful enough to stay him, badly though he wanted to bury his arousal in the sweet sheath of her.

"I regret I took it upon myself to try to find Griffith and Alfred before telling you, Brand."

Her quiet, unexpected words rolled over his already stimulated senses like soothing, warm water.

"I had never seen you so relaxed, so content, and I did not want to spoil your pleasure if 'twas merely a matter of rounding up two stray boys and a dog." She raised her head and met his regard, the elegant line of her throat accented by the few tendrils of damp hair that hung and curled gently downward toward her gleaming shoulders. "By the time I realized they could be at the bog, I felt there was no time to be wasted, that I dared not take the time to go back for you."

"Yet you had the foresight to tell Brian of your plans, therefore ensuring that soon I would come after you."

"Then you are not angry?"

"Nay, Viking. Only proud . . . and very fortunate to have you for my wife."

Something in his voice caused a tingling warmth to radiate toward every nerve ending in her body, and it had nothing to do with the temperature of the water in which she sat.

When she made to rise, he was there before her, spreading out a pelt beside the tub for her to step upon and then holding out a length of toweling in which to wrap her. As he lifted her from the tub and set her down, he let her slide slowly down the length of his hard frame before her feet touched the ground. The sensuality of the movement ignited a spiraling heat in her midsection, and Marisa suddenly felt weak for want of him. Then he was vigorously toweling her dry, and she wondered at the reversal of his actions. Brand pulled the few pins from her hair and allowed it to come tumbling down about her shoulders like burnished silver, before carrying her to the bed and tucking her in. He doused the tapers and flambeaux that lit the room, then slipped beside Marisa, gathering her to him and imprisoning her within his loving embrace, his chin resting upon the fragrant mass of her hair.

"Good night, my sweet Marisa," he murmured softly into her ear, and was rewarded with a soft *"bonsoir"* before the exhausted girl slipped into peaceful slumber, her earlier arousal forgotten in her extreme fatigue.

As the moments passed, Brand held her to him like a man drowning, his arms entwined about her slim form as tightly as possible without causing her pain or waking her. At last he knew beyond a doubt that he had misjudged her from the very first, never giving her a chance because of his obsession with his guilt over Rhiannon. He'd caught glimpses on countless occasions of her bravery, her loyalty, her capacity to love and give of herself, to defend to the death those she cared for, and to finally accept his blinding, excessive fidelity to his dead wife. Without outward rancor—at least for the present—Marisa had been willing to accept what he would give her.

He closed his eyes and unashamedly allowed tears to seep from beneath the long, dark tangle of his lashes to lay upon his cheeks. God, what a fool he'd been! Now she carried his child. If only—if only she could safely have the babe and not . . . He threw up a barrier against the insidious thought. She would not die; he would not *let* her die. She was young and strong and just stubborn enough to give him healthy sons and daughters and scoff at his fears for her. Marisa de Brionne was full of life and laughter and would not give that up without a struggle . . . until she had no more breath in her body with which to fight.

"Oh, firebrand," he murmured into her hair, "I do love you. God in heaven, how I love you—fully, with everything I have to give. Do not leave me, ever, my love, my life. . . ."

Marisa struggled for breath. Green, brackish water was filling her mouth and throat and lungs. Angharad's gnarled fingers were upon her head and pushing her down, down into the murky depths of the bog, the water choking the breath from her, slowly cutting off her vital link with life.

She moaned softly and turned in her sleep. The constricting pressure was suddenly eased and her eyelids fluttered open. She was in bed with Brand, safe within their bower. She turned her head slightly to look at him. One arm was still lying across her ribs. He must have inadvertently tightened his hold upon her in his sleep. Her heart constricted with love as she gazed upon his peaceful countenance. He was so much a part of her now. Someday she would win his love. Someday . . .

In the candlelight she noticed the trace of moisture upon his cheeks, partly dried but still evident. Her brow knitted in a frown. Why had he wept? What had affected him so that his bronzed cheeks still held telltale signs of tears?

There arose an instinct within her to assuage and to shield, an instinct so strong and sure that Marisa thought she would die of it. *Let me love you, Brand,* she cried silently. *Let me love you.* But she knew he would not allow her body to fuse itself with his for as long as she was with child.

She cautiously pushed herself up on one elbow and studied the face she had come to love so well, then slowly, but with accelerating force, an idea took shape in her mind until it would not be dismissed. If he would not make love to her in the way she craved above all else, then she would take the initiative—and in such a way that would leave no room for objections. Indeed, she mused, a smile curving her beautifully molded mouth, no room for objections at all.

Slowly, gingerly, Marisa removed Brand's arm from beneath her breasts and eased herself toward the side of the bed, pausing every few seconds to regard his peacefully sleeping features. If he awoke now, all would be lost. But he continued to sleep, and Marisa silently blessed the potent mead which, no doubt, contributed to his deep slumber.

Free at last, she landed lightly upon the cool stone floor. A glance at Rollo assured her the dog, too, slept undisturbed. She moved soundlessly to the table on Brand's side of the bed and carefully lifted the flask of wine from it. Marisa clutched the vessel to her chest and felt the erratic vibration of her heart. Glancing over at her sleeping husband once more, certain that he could hear the wild tattoo beneath her ribs, she returned to her side of the bed and eased onto it until she was beside him once more.

In that moment, Marisa dared nurse a flicker of hope that her plan would succeed. Even though Brand's reaction might be less than enthusiastic at first, she dismissed the thought of failure.

He turned onto his back and flung one arm upward. Marisa held her breath, but he did not awaken. She slowly reached out and pulled back the light coverlet with careful and tantalizing deliberation until the light of a full moon shining in from one of the several unshuttered windows bathed his long, sleek form with its lambent glow. A shaft of desire hurtled through her at the sight, sending the blood singing along her veins.

She leaned toward him and pressed her warm lips lightly to his ear. Her tongue leisurely traced its perimeter, her breath, moist and heated, searing the tender skin.

"Umm?" Brand murmured sleepily.

He turned his head toward her in a natural response to

the sensual invasion, and Marisa's lips left off their plundering of that most sensitive place, descending to glide across the curve of his cheek and the slight cleft of his chin. Dragging her tongue upward, she worshiped the corner of his mouth, his eyelids, the soft skin at his temple. Brand smiled in his sleep until Marisa's mouth returned to his and inadvertently nudged him out of his exquisite dreams.

His thick lashes fluttered and raised, and Marisa drew back slightly to gauge the look in his eyes. Even in the dim light she could make out the glint of passion in the desire-drugged depths.

Satisfied that he would have difficulty in putting a stop to her play now, she let him speak before continuing her sweet assault.

"Marisa . . ." He frowned vaguely, recognition beginning to dawn in his eyes. "What do you think you are doing, wench?"

"Tsk, tsk . . . Such an intelligent man and he cannot even divine what his wife would have from him."

His eyes widened in sudden comprehension, and a host of contradictory emotions chased across his features. "*I* do not want it," he began rather unconvincingly. "There are other ways to—"

"But I *do* want it, *mon cher,* and not some 'other way.' "

She bent over him then, touching her lips to his, her loose, silver-gold hair trailing over his belly and chest until it enveloped their heads in a shimmering curtain of intimacy.

"Marisa, please," he began halfheartedly as her actions sent his desire soaring to dizzying and dangerous heights.

"Brand, please," she began in gentle mimicry, her mouth nuzzling the satin-skinned scar on his left cheek that now seemed small and insignificant to her. She followed the length of it down beneath his jaw and then began to trace it with her small pink tongue. Brand attempted to sit up, but Marisa cautioned, "Ah, ah, ah

. . . I would not have you spill the wine and spoil my game.''

"Wine?'' he repeated uncomprehendingly. What with the last vestiges of grogginess that still lingered, the surprise at her having taken the initiative, and the very real effects of Marisa's relentless seduction, Brand could only object verbally, and not very convincingly.

''You cannot do this. . . . The babe—''

''Will be fine, Saxon. Relax and allow me to love you as I have longed to for many weeks.'' She sat up, tossing back her magnificent moon-gilded mane. ''Besides, Saxon, you are my prisoner of war right now, and I may do anything I deem fit.''

His lips twisted faintly with irony. ''That we are all your prisoners—every man, woman, and child in England—is blatantly obvious.''

''Nay, Saxon, that is not the war I speak of. This is our private war . . . of love.''

Before he could answer, Marisa's lips touched his once again, the heady fragrance of roses surrounding him as effectively as a drugging philter. In a burst of swiftly fleeing sanity, he tried to sit up a second time, but she leaned into him firmly, her tongue blazing down the column of his throat and back up again to send shooting heat through his loins and producing a treacherous languor within him. It robbed him of his determination with devastating success.

Brand tried to twist away with a groan of protest in one final, feeble attempt and failed to do anything but renew the vigor of Marisa's onslaught and evoke a soft whine from Rollo. ''Hold still, Saxon. You disturb yon courageous hound.''

Brand sighed, closed his eyes, and gave in to the pleasure that was rushing through his body, reasoning that there wasn't much else he could do, for already his awakened desire left no doubt in his mind that he could never merely lie still and foil her assault on his senses. Marisa would win this night.

When he felt a drop of cool liquid hit the hollow at the

base of his throat, he started, heavy lashes lifting as he
sought to make out what his minx of a wife was doing to
him now. Calmly Marisa held the small flask of wine,
umber-hued in the dimness of the bower as the liquid
dripped through the air to hit him with soft pelts remi-
niscent of a spring shower. Before he realized what she
was about, Marisa had lowered her lips to lap up the
precious wine from the hollow where it had pooled over
his throbbing pulse. "It tastes much better with the added
flavor of your body." She raised desire-glazed eyes to
his, black as midnight, and added in a husky voice, "I
never thought a Saxon could improve the taste of Norman
wine, but it seems I was wrong."

Brand writhed in an agony of need as Marisa continued over the lightly hair-whorled chest, teasing his paps
until they sprang alive with the touch of her lips as she
lovingly kissed the trickling wine from his increasingly
taut body.

"You torture me, Marisa," he said raggedly.

" 'Tis no more than you deserve for depriving me of
what is rightfully mine."

"Cease this outrageous behavior, wench."

"Nay. You will not put a stop to my play now."

"You—you have my word I will not put a stop to
aught."

She raised her eyes from just above his flat, hard belly,
looking like a tawny she-cat as the moonlight beaming
through the window above and behind her formed a nimbus about her head. Fine, downlike body hair was
brought into faint relief from the muted glow limning her
slender form. "I will not risk it."

"Am I to have no part in this, then?"

"You have made it very clear in the past just how little
a part you would have in our mutual loveplay, and I do
not—cannot—trust you to have a change of heart now. I
would show you what you are missing."

Despite his words assuring her that he would do no
such thing now, Marisa remained firm. She slid down his
body as smoothly and effortlessly as silk. The contact

with and faint friction between soft, smooth skin and fluid muscle against that of crisply haired chest, taut belly, and limbs over iron-thewed muscle and sinew acted to stimulate both of them to the breaking point.

When Marisa allowed the wine to puddle inside his navel, so heart-wrenchingly close to the turgid staff of his arousal, Brand moaned and allowed his fingertips to feather over her shoulders and back, lost in exquisite, undiluted sensation, and unable to lie still beneath her ministrations any longer.

And then she was greedily drinking the wine from that small indentation and pressing downward, around his heated, pulsing manhood, up and down the sleek, solid thighs and back up again until Brand felt so strongly the need to bury himself deep within her that his arms encircled her shoulders, urging her upward, while Marisa resisted his attempts to hasten their joining.

"Marisa, do you want me to beg?" he cried out. With a secret smile of satisfaction, she glided herself once more up over his rigid body, allowing the softly mounded nest between her thighs to linger against the evidence of his need for a long, teasing moment before finishing her ascent.

Then their mouths were meeting once again, savoring the taste that was uniquely each other's, mingled with that of wine, as Marisa levered her body over his and impaled herself upon him, wickedly imitating that first slow, exquisitely agonizing descent over his body with her own, sheathing him so deeply she thought surely he was touching her heart.

"Brand, I love you," she whispered against his mouth, and his eyes flew open to lock with hers even as their bodies naturally began that primal, urgent thrust and retreat that has forever bespoken love without the need of uttered communication. He rejoiced in the words that once would have caused him pained memories, would have conjured up a guilt as useless and destructive as the failure of man and woman to carry on in a world turned upside down, failure to continue to pit themselves against adversity, bloodied but unbroken.

"Please, if you have any feelings in your heart for me, do not refuse me *this* again, or I will surely wither away and die." She reached out to replace the almost empty flask upon the table, but her reach fell short and the vessel dropped to the floor with a clatter that only vaguely disturbed the peaceful interlude in the room.

"Marisa, Marisa," he murmured into her mouth, his breath caressing her porcelainlike cheeks and brow as he worshiped them with branding kisses before burying his face in the fragrant tumble of her hair. "Marisa mine," he whispered, still unable to say the words he knew would bring her untold happiness and security. But something yet held him back. The last vestiges of old, useless fears, vague uncertainties . . .

His hands stroked and caressed up and down the satiny sides of her rib cage, down to the sweet indentation of her still-small waist, and then up to cup the sides of her soft, pale breasts, thumbs gently intruding between their straining bodies to tease her nipples. The action added the final impetus for that shattering implosion that crescendoed within her and made her cry out his name in abandon, her head thrown back, her body convulsing with the ultimate ecstasy.

As Brand felt the silken cocoon of her contracting around him, he allowed his own need to burst forth, to rock him with a wondrous splendor he'd known only with Marisa, spilling his seed deep within her womb, where grew the child he so wanted—and whose birth he so feared.

Turning to his side, he cradled her to him lovingly, cherishing her with his body, sheltering her with his strength, pledging himself to her with his thoughts. His lips touched her hair as he stared into the night shadows. *I love you, as well, my precious wife. I love you, as well.*

Chapter 20

August passed all too quickly for Marisa. Basking in Brand's obvious, if unspoken, adoration, she felt peace and blissful happiness slip over her as the child within her grew and made its presence felt through delicate, featherlike flutterings from within. Many a night Marisa fell into a deep, contented sleep, satiated from Brand's gentle yet intense lovemaking, his hand resting protectively upon the slight swell of her abdomen.

She did not know if he had succeeded in ridding himself of the uncharacteristic fear that had gripped him at the news of her pregnancy, but Marisa was content with his acceptance of her love and his own ardent response, albeit unvoiced. Though he didn't declare his affection verbally, Marisa knew with increasing certainty that he had strong feelings toward her . . . strong enough to send a surge of pure, unadulterated joy sweeping through her whenever their eyes met, their bodies touched.

She was also aware of an increasing acceptance by the villagers. No longer was she ignored by many who had been under Edgiva's influence, but rather she was treated with respect and admiration, and it warmed her heart.

At the same time, Brand's guilt began to slip silently away, banished by his final acceptance of its utter futility, by the realization that Rhiannon's death was not his punishment for failing to feel the depth of emotions toward her he had felt had been her due. He knew now that one could no more control one's feelings of love or hate than one could prevent the sun from rising, the seasons from changing.

Acknowledging Marisa's trustworthiness where he and his people were concerned, and her love for Griffith, Brand began to relax as he'd not done for several years. He went about his business with new confidence and purpose. He would apply himself even more vigorously to the healing of old wounds and the adapting to Norman rule. Angharad and the threat she posed were gone; only the warning from the strange Welshman lingered to echo faintly in his memory from time to time, blighting a burgeoning bliss in the knowledge of the treasure the fates had bestowed upon him in the form of Marisa de Brionne.

All remained quiet through August after the incident at the bog. Morgan reported all was well in Wighton, despite the remaining mystery surrounding the murder that had occurred earlier that summer.

For the rest of the month Brand allowed himself to become immersed in the harvesting of the remainder of the wheat and other crops. Then as August turned to September came the overseeing of the threshing with wooden flails and the winnowing of the grain from the straw and the chaff. For the first time he could remember, Brand enjoyed taking a more active role in the agrarian concerns of a successfully run village and manor. He suspected that even had things been unchanged, even if Harold Godwinson were yet alive and ruling England, the lure of serving his king while reliable retainers oversaw matters at Camwright and his other holdings would have lost much of their appeal. Marisa's presence alone would have been enough to anchor him as nothing else had ever done in the past.

Most assuredly he was bewitched by a woman with eyes as dark as blue-violet irises and hair that made a man lose all thought save touching it, wanting to bury himself within its glorious fragrance and texture. The sound of her laughter soothed his heart like a warm, healing unguent. Her touch revitalized his bleeding soul like no stimulant he had ever known. Surely, he'd always thought, no man had ever been blessed with a wife such as his childhood love, Rhiannon . . . thus the reason for his unremitting regret and guilt at his inability to sustain what he had once considered love. Yet now, even more, Brand stood in awe of the fact that he had unwittingly acquired a beautiful, desirable, and most important, thoroughly loving, loyal, and courageous wife. What, he often wondered, had he ever done to deserve such a miracle? It remained only for him to admit his all-consuming love, a love of the body as well as of the soul, something very different from what he had felt for Rhiannon. For now he could acknowledge that, although he had loved his first wife, he had not been *in* love with her. But that was over and past, and somehow he knew even now that Rhiannon had accepted what he was capable of giving her and that had been part of her beauty. If she had suffered inwardly, he never knew it, and to pine for what could never have been, to berate himself for the rest of his life, was useless.

So now it was left only for him to tell Marisa of his love . . . and tell her soon.

"Oh, please, Marisa! Can I accompany you to Fauxbray?"

Marisa tousled the dark hair and shook her head, her eyes meeting Brand's over Griffith's head. "Then who will watch over Rollo, *cher?* He is not yet fully recovered and someone must keep an eye on him."

The boy's expression turned crestfallen with disappointment. "Rollo can remain in the bower, Marisa. I have time to exercise him before you leave, and then he can take a long nap while we are gone."

"Nay, son."

Brand's firm pronouncement effectively silenced the boy, but in his dark eyes Marisa noticed a fleeting spark of rebellion that was totally alien to the child, and she mentally determined to speak of it to Brand when she returned.

Edwin and three other men-at-arms were to accompany Marisa to Fauxbray, and as they mounted and stood waiting before the eastern gate of the manor compound, Brand crushed her to him, lifting her completely off the ground as his lips soundly met hers. "Hurry home, wench," he murmured for her ears alone, "for I hunger for you already." The gold in his eyes became more pronounced as if in affirmation of his words. "And have a care in that cur's company. If he but touches you . . ."

Marisa slid down and pushed away from him, self-conscious at his behavior before his men. "He has never touched me before, Brand. I go only to glean what information I can and to see how I can encourage Mauger to treat the people of Fauxbray more fairly. Robert witnessed Mauger's cruelty firsthand, and I would add to his report to my lord William. If naught else, my father can perhaps put in a word to encourage the King to warn Mauger he does naught but incur the hatred of the people whom he rules. Even William knows that honey attracts more effectively than soured wine."

"William is in Normandy. He has other troubles within his duchy."

"He will have his hands so full of English rebellion he will have no time to keep his Norman barons under control, if he does not heed the warnings of those who have seen firsthand what is happening in Fauxbray, as well, I suspect, as other places. I can do no less than at least attempt to ease matters for both our people."

"Sometimes 'tis difficult to remember that you are Norman, Marisa de Brionne," he said as he helped her to mount her mare.

"I am human, Saxon. I cannot tolerate the abuse of any people, especially at the hands of one who shares my heritage. Besides," she added with a lift of her chin, "they are my people now."

But the worry that replaced the earlier yearning in his eyes did not diminish with her confident words. "So be it, firebrand, but hurry back to me, for I'll not rest easy until you are safely back in Camwright." He stepped back to watch them file out through the gate, his hand shading his eyes from the bright September sunlight, until they turned north and disappeared from sight.

Mauger le Faux greeted Marisa with the same hateful arrogance that had characterized his actions since she'd first encountered him on the way to Camwright after her marriage. The sun gilding his tawny head unexpectedly brought to mind Robert de Lisieux when Marisa knew him in Normandy. But the very way he sauntered toward them, the innate cruelty that compressed the lines of what could have been a handsome mouth, that glittered coldly in what could have been blue eyes sparkling with humor and genuine warmth, reminded her of just how treacherous an adversary le Faux could be.

Godgift appeared from the dark interior of a small stone church nearby and a look of dislike twisted her features. At first Marisa was surprised, but then she realized that, indeed, the woman must have some important news to divulge. In an effort to deceive Mauger, Godgift would give him no opportunity to suspect she harbored anything but distaste for another Norman. Yet even as this thought swiftly registered in Marisa's mind, Godgift deliberately allowed her features to relax into complacency as she felt Mauger's eyes come to rest upon her, and her ruse worked.

"Come now, Godgift. Surely you can receive a countrywoman of mine with more civility than you showed only a moment ago . . . and especially in light of your new willingness to share, ah, the more intimate aspects of a relationship between a man and a woman?"

Her cheeks flamed, and as she averted her head a moment to collect herself, Marisa thought she noted a faint, purplish bruise along the curve of her jaw. "How goes your harvesting, Mauger?" Marisa asked, intentionally directing the conversation to safer ground.

He shrugged in dismissal, although Marisa detected an undisguised gleam of disgust in the cold eyes. "Come inside"—he motioned toward the manor—"and have a goblet of wine while we discuss more pleasant things than the poor crops at Fauxbray.''

Marisa placed a hand upon his arm for emphasis. *''S'il vous plaît*, could we not walk through the village? I have not seen all of Fauxbray and 'tis such a beautiful day. We will not have many more, I suspect.''

He sighed with annoyed impatience before reluctantly capitulating. ''Very well. But, Godgift, you must accompany us, as well,'' he added as the woman swung to return the hall. Her expression turned sullen for his benefit, but then her eyes met his and she quickly smoothed her features into a look of blandness.

Mauger complained about everything as they made their way through a village that was the complete opposite of the bustling Camwright. According to the Norman, most of the men were out in the fields, so Marisa could only judge by what she saw of the women and children left behind. It was very quiet and few of the females of Fauxbray were visible. There was no one drawing water at the well, no one tending the garden plots near each cottage or homestead, no one exchanging gossip with neighbors as they went about their daily tasks. And the children . . . Whereas in Camwright one could always hear happy laughter and shrieks of delight as they played, often chasing one another among their homes when they were free of their chores, here there was silence and very few little ones about at all.

Marisa glanced at Godgift during one of Mauger's malicious diatribes concerning the laziness of the Anglo-Saxons with whom he had been saddled, but could discern little from the stony features of the silent woman. Once, when their eyes did meet, Marisa thought she saw a flicker of pain pass through the attractive blue eyes, but it was shuttered almost immediately by lowered lids.

'' 'Twould seem to me, Mauger, that you would benefit more from kindness than cruelty,'' Marisa observed softly, not wishing to alienate him or all would be lost.

He snorted dersisively. ''Kindness? Since when is a lord kind to his serfs? They are—''

"They are all freemen, not serfs!"

For one fleeting moment the hatred that distorted Godgift's features was so intense, so unexpected in a countenance deliberately kept expressionless, that Marisa felt a chill rush up her spine.

Not so Mauger. "Freemen—bah! They are what I say they are, for I am lord and master here now, and they will do my bidding or suffer the consequences. No people who allowed themselves to be defeated deserve anything but contempt. Surely you grow soft, Marisa de Brionne, living with that Anglo-Saxon husband of yours."

"And what if it had been we Normans who had been defeated at Hastings?" she asked.

Mauger stopped and stared at her, shocked. "Normans defeated? Why, 'tis—"

In that moment a stick came arcing through the air toward them, and a puppy chased after it with short, uncoordinated strides and playful yelping. The stick landed right in front of Mauger and Marisa, and before anyone could say or do a thing, a little girl about Griffith's age charged around the corner of a cottage directly across from them. "Fetch, Will! Fetch it!" she cried with childish enthusiasm.

Marisa heard Godgift's sharp intake of breath as Mauger stooped to snatch up the stick and raised it to strike the child.

Marisa reacted instinctively and bent to scoop up the little girl before the switch could be applied, pretending not to have noticed Mauger's intent. "There, there, *cher enfant,* what are you about?" she gently chided.

Rounded eyes stared up at her, the finger stuck in the child's mouth reminding Marisa of Griffith when first she'd come to Camwright.

"Hilde?"

A woman old beyond her years stepped from the interior of the cottage, blinked in the bright sunlight, and halted in mid-motion when she saw the three adults before her, the child held in Marisa's arms.

"How dare you allow your brat to name a cur after my lord King, Margaret of Fauxbray?" Mauger demanded.

His incensed query brought about an instant change in the woman. She began to wring her hands, her eyes darting about as if in search of someone. "I—I cannot control her, my lord," she began piteously. "When—when my Michael comes home, he will take her in hand, I swear . . ."

"Your Michael is long since dead, stupid woman," Mauger pronounced callously. "When will you ever get it through that addled head of yours and begin carrying your load?"

Marisa glanced at Godgift, but the latter was staring at the woman in the doorway of the cottage. Marisa's gaze followed the Danish woman's, and she was shocked at the ch·nge in the woman called Margaret. Her eyes focused unseeingly toward the east, her hands falling limply to her sides.

She is mad, Marisa thought suddenly as she eyed the disheveled hair, the tattered clothing, the streaks of grime spread over her suddenly blank face. Pity washed over her with such force it was all she could do to prevent herself from going to the woman and offering comfort. But the little urchin in her arms who'd been inspecting her face so intently reclaimed her attention as her weight began to make Marisa's arms tingle.

"Did you kill my papa?" Hilde asked innocently.

Instinctively, Marisa hugged the child to her, emotion choking the very breath from her throat. "Nay, Hilde.'Twas not I."

"Then where is he?"

Fighting for control, knowing the little girl would take no comfort from a less than convincing performance, Marisa answered, "He is in heaven, *chère*, where no one can ever harm him again."

The puppy suddenly barked and Mauger flung the stick at it, striking it in the ribs and causing it to squeal with the unexpected pain and cower in terror at his feet. "My dog! I pray you, do not hurt him, my lord Mauger,"

Hilde pleaded as she pushed herself from Marisa's embrace and slid to the ground.

All the while, Margaret had not moved from where she stood staring into the distance, daughter and adults forgotten in the place to where her mind had retreated.

Marisa felt sick inside, and when Mauger demanded, "Come, Marisa, let us finish the rounds you seem so intent upon making. I grow weary of this nonsense," she demurred.

"I—I feel faint, Mauger," she lied. "Let us return to the manor."

In truth, it was fury that made her want to slip her fingers around Mauger le Faux's throat and squeeze until his body stilled forever. The pitch of her anger actually made her feel faint, and so the pallidness of her features convinced Mauger that, indeed, she was feeling unwell.

"Pray change his name, child," Marisa whispered to Hilde as she bent over one last time toward the puppy and its mistress. "Why not name him Harold after your brave king who fought with your father?" As she straightened, only Godgift saw the momentary flash of ire that revealed Marisa's true dislike of Mauger le Faux.

Assured by the presence of Edwin and his companions' horses tethered near the manor hall, Marisa entered and spent some time with the man who was beginning to become so abhorrent to her that she was hard-pressed not to reveal her revulsion. When one of Mauger's retainers summoned him to the door of the hall, Godgift moved to replenish Marisa's goblet.

"You must tell Brand to beware of Madog ap Cynan."

Marisa smiled pleasantly and nodded in feigned reaction to Godgift's gesture of offering.

"Remember, Lady Marisa, the name Madog ap Cynan. He conspires with Mauger to bring your husband's downfall. Madog is to do the dirty work so Mauger will appear blameless. You must tell him to beware. . . . "

She drew away as Mauger turned and strode back into the cavernous room.

"You are feeling better now?"

Marisa nodded. "I am with child and am yet subject to bouts of queasiness."

He picked up his refilled goblet and held it up in a mocking, toastlike gesture. "To your clever husband, Marisa."

She touched her cup to his, inclining her head sightly in inquiry.

"Not only has he succeeded in outwitting Robert de Lisieux concerning the destrier he stables within his stronghold, but now he has succeeded in sowing his accursed seed within your belly."

Squelching the temptation to fling her wine in his face at his sordid besmirching of the act of love that had resulted in her pregnancy, Marisa merely replied, " 'Tis expected of a wife, Mauger, and also, if you will recall, the union took place at the behest of King William. Brand Ericson may be Anglo-Saxon, but he is not the villain you would make him."

"But, Marisa, do you not miss Normandy? Here we are, you and I, stuck in this wild border region among hordes of miserable English and the even less civilized Welsh." He sat down upon a settle and stretched his legs before him, staring sullenly at his crossed feet.

"Are you regretting your part in the conquest, your newly granted holdings?"

He looked up at her, an indefinable look in his eyes as they traveled up and down the length of her body, his gaze narrowing slightly as if he would see through her clothing. "I regret only that I am stuck *here*. I would not even consider bringing a Norman woman to this Godforsaken place until I have these curs whipped into proper subservience."

"You would do better, as I said before, if you were kinder. Even," she added quickly at his black look, "if you secretly detested them to the end of your days. If you can prove to my lord William that you can rule profitably, your holdings will be increased, I would wager. Who can say how much land you could eventually acquire? But you must show some compassion, some consideration, even if 'tis not genuine.''

His eyes met hers as he weighed the wisdom of her words. "We could do this as lord and lady of Fauxbray, Marisa de Brionne. And Camwright as well."

He rose to his feet and walked leisurely over to seat himself upon the bench beside her. "If something were to happen to Ericson . . ."

A warning sounded in her mind as sharply as the horn signaling the nooning, but Marisa met his gaze unflinchingly. "That is unlikely. He is highly thought of and has many friends among the Cymry, as well."

His face very close to hers, he shrugged and murmured, "But no man lives forever."

"I must go." If she remained any longer, his lips would be touching hers and she feared that her inability to hide her revulsion would ruin everything.

"Oui, in a moment." And then his lips were touching her gently upon the cheek, her lowered lids, her mouth.

Marisa put her hands against his solid chest and pushed him away, sensing suddenly that he was playing cat and mouse with her. "His . . . his men might see," she began, casting about for some way to extricate herself from her predicament without completely alienating him.

But he pulled her into his arms, none too gently, and soothed in a deceptively dulcet voice, "They are occupied with other things. . . . " Before she could think of anything else to deter him, his mouth was pressed firmly against hers, his lips working to part hers to taste the delights within.

"My lady?" came Edwin's query from the open door.

Marisa tried to pull away, hoping that the man's eyes would take a few moments to adjust to the dimness of the hall, but Mauger's arms were suddenly steel bands around her body, imprisoning her firmly in their viselike hold. Even as she fought to draw breath in his bruising embrace, it came to her in a flash of realization that he was deliberately compromising her . . . and before Brand's men.

"Lady Marisa, are you prepared to depart?"

She heard the soft *clink* of Edwin's sword as he stepped into the hall, proceeded toward them a few steps, then halted.

An indicting quiet enveloped them all before Marisa decided she'd had enough of Mauger le Faux's calculated maneuverings. Throwing caution to the winds, she fought to raise her hands to encircle his throat when, without warning, he dropped his arms and rose from the bench as if he'd been scalded. Looking deceptively sheepish, he cleared his throat uncomfortably. "By all means, my lady, you must return to Camwright if you are expected."

Thunderstruck, Marisa stared up at him for a long moment, astonished at the man's facility for duplicity.

But Edwin was not easily deceived, especially in light of what he knew of Marisa de Brionne. "Are you unharmed, Lady Marisa?"

His words galvanized her into action, and her hand came up in a sudden movement, striking le Faux full upon the cheek. He never flinched, but rather allowed a subtle smirk of triumph to hover about his mouth. "By all means, do that again, Marisa, to better convince them of your innocence." The words were softly spoken, but not so low as not to be heard by Edwin and possibly the men behind him.

Dragging her gaze from his, she turned toward the faithful retainer who had hazarded much by implying she'd been at risk at the hands of their host. "Indeed, Edwin." She looked at Mauger, her irises black with suppressed outrage. "I thank you for your 'hospitality,' *Sieur le Faux.*" Despising the weakness that sent hectic color sweeping across her cheekbones, she stepped over the bench and walked stiffly toward the door.

Her thoughts whirled, her mind heedless of the gently rocking gait of the horse beneath her, the sweet songs of the birds in the surrounding forest, the mote-laden rays of late afternoon sun that penetrated the trees to dapple the men and horses before her with woven patterns of light and shade.

Of one thing Marisa was certain: Mauger le Faux had arranged to have Edwin enter the hall. . . .

Insects hummed and droned, a soft breeze sighed through the boughs that canopied overhead, a small rabbit darted across the path and caused the lead horse to shy slightly, yet Marisa remained oblivious to all of these things. She was convinced of the importance of maintaining her ties with Fauxbray, yet she feared not only Brand's reaction should Edwin inform him of what he'd seen, but also her own aversion to exposing herself to Mauger le Faux's unwelcome advances. Then again, perhaps Edwin or one of the others could remain present within the hall itself during her visits. . . .

Her musings were brought to an abrupt halt as the man before her suddenly slumped forward and then toppled from the saddle to the ground, his pony prancing sideways in alarm. A shout went up from the man behind her. Marisa made to turn around to see what was happening, when unexpected and violent movement ahead of her caught her eye. As she watched in silent horror, Edwin, in the lead, was set upon by several Welshmen who appeared out of the woods on either side, grim-faced and fierce-looking. They surrounded him on the narrow path. Before Brand's man-at-arms could even unsheathe his sword, he was sent tumbling sideways in a haze of blood and metal blades flashing. Down he slid to hit the earth beneath his plunging pony.

The man directly in front of Marisa had met the same swift and bloody end.

By sheer willpower Marisa forced her head toward the sounds coming from behind her. The other two men were engaging more Welshmen, and as they fought on the crowded path, the clashing of metal on metal sang savagely, blasphemously through the stillness of the forest. Her heart thrumming in her chest, fear clawed its way up through her body to constrict her throat, preventing the scream that had lodged there from being vocalized.

And then an arm snaked out from seemingly nowhere, despite the skittish sidling of her mare, and strong fingers closed over her mouth and nose, cutting off her air, causing the world to recede after a moment of valiant struggling.

Darkness descended.

Chapter 21

Griffith kicked halfheartedly at a stone in his path as he made his way to the clearing that still remained his favorite refuge, despite the wolf attack on Marisa. He'd wished to accompany the small party to Fauxbray, for he felt certain now, with the self-confidence of a child who'd blossomed with nurturing and encouragement, that he could help protect his beloved stepmother in his father's stead. Instead, he'd been relegated to walking Rollo and, much as he loved the animal, it rankled.

He kicked the same stone with even more vigor as he encountered it once more along the path, his steps quickening with agitation. In his need to be alone he'd even refused Alfred's request to accompany him, telling his friend that he had no wish for company. There were times when a man . . . or a boy . . . needed to be alone.

Brand trotted his pony into the compound and dismounted with less than his usual catlike grace, seeking— needing—a glimpse of the woman whom he'd grown to love so profoundly. He was hot and tired and irritable. He needed the immensely gratifying sight of his beautiful Marisa, the soothing sound of her melodic voice. . . .

Brian emerged from the stable before Brand could even inquire of the man-at-arms at the gate if the group had yet returned from Fauxbray. "Has my lady returned?" Brand asked the youth.

"Nay, my lord."

Brand frowned thoughtfully. " 'Tis past time they were back at Camwright." He ran the fingertips of one hand along the scar that seamed his left cheek, his eyes upon the manor as if he would see through the very walls to the palisade on the opposite side and the path that led east and then north to Mauger le Faux's lands.

"And where is Griffith?"

"He went to the glade, my lord, and would not even let me go with him!" Alfred exclaimed from behind them in a petulant voice.

As if on cue, Rollo began to whine loudly from within the bower, the sound of his nails scratching the closed wooden portal, indicating his eagerness to be freed and sounding suddenly eerie in the late afternoon stillness.

Brand absently tousled Alfred's hair and, tossing the pony's reins to Brian, strode toward the bower and let the wolfhound out. Still unable to bound about with his usual exuberance, Rollo nonetheless displayed his happiness at being released with an energetically switching tail, then he began moving toward the gate. "Rollo, here!"

The animal paused at his master's command, but whimpered from deep within his throat and continued on a few steps before returning to sit at Brand's side and regard him with soulful brown eyes.

"What is it, boy?" The hair on Brand's neck prickled instinctively. Something was not right here.

"He wants to go to Griffith, Lord Brand," volunteered Alfred.

"So 'twould seem," Brand mused aloud as the dog left his side and once more padded toward the gate. He raised narrowed eyes to the clear September sky, gauging by the position of the sun how long Marisa had been gone, and then he made a sudden decision.

"Thomas!"

"Aye, my lord," answered the gateman.

"Take John and ride posthaste to Wighton. Tell Morgan I need him—as quickly as he can get here."

As the two retainers made ready, Brand sent Alfred

back to his home and entered the hall for a quick, revitalizing horn of mead. He then returned Rollo to the bower in the process of fetching his swordbelt. At the dog's whimper of protest, he soothed, "Not this time, my stalwart friend. Marisa would never forgive me if I allowed harm to come to you while you still heal from Angharad's knife." When the hound whined even more loudly, as if in disagreement, Brand reluctantly but firmly closed the door behind him.

Adela approached him as he signaled Brian to bring him Goliath. "Can I do aught, my lord?" In spite of her obvious determination not to show undue worry, Brand could read it in her eyes.

He gave her a half smile, which, because his own senses were tingling in warning, failed utterly to impart reassurance. "Aye, Adela. When Marisa returns"—he unconsciously emphasized the word *when*—"tell her that I have gone to fetch Griffith, no more. Do not alarm her, and if you must, by all means begin the evening meal without us."

She nodded and watched him mount the massive gray. "Hurry back, my lord, for I fear . . ." Her words died off in midsentence, what she could not say hanging heavily in the air, fraught with unvoiced meaning. Their eyes met in apprehension and unspoken communication before she turned away, unable to control her silent tears any longer.

The weald seemed unnaturally quiet to Edwin, bereft of the natural trilling of the birds and the soft, scuttling sounds of small creatures going about their business. Only the buzzing of bothersome flies—or was it in his head?—the snort of a horse . . .

Edwin tried to lift his head at the thought of a horse nearby, but the pain that sharded through the hollow between his shoulder blades from the dagger still lodged there was enough to cause his head to hit the ground again. He tasted blood, but realized with something akin to relief that it was from a cut in his mouth, and not stemming from internal injuries. He had to get to Camwright, he silently acknowledged through the mists of pain. Even if he had to tie himself to a horse's back to ensure remaining atop the animal, it was imperative that he tell Brand what had happened. That was even more important than the preservation of his own life.

With superhuman effort he tried again to lift his head, bracing himself, waist up, on bent elbows. The world rocked and a wave of agony engulfed him with such force he thought he would faint. Only by sheer determination did he remain conscious. Dragging his upper torso around to one side, he ignored the stabbing pain of a broken right leg and caught sight of his pony standing nearby, nervously twitching its tail and stomping its foot in agitation. Through a distorted blur he could make out the other men sprawled helter-skelter across the path, and one horse unmoving on its side, but there was no sign of the lady Marisa.

Edwin tried to gather enough saliva inside his dry mouth to whistle, but in vain. He rested his forehead against the cool forest floor once again, gathering what remained of his strength and willpower. Maybe he could rasp out the animal's name. His mouth formed the name, but only a whisper emerged. Frustrated beyond measure, he tried again. *"B—Bones . . ."*

The pony's ears pricked forward at the sound, and instantly it turned its head to meet the bloodshot stare of its owner. Well-trained in obedience, the animal moved toward Edwin, sidestepping the fly-infested bodies of the dead in its path. When it stood before its master, Bones bent his neck and nudged Edwin's shoulder, inadvertently sending pain shooting through the downed man's back. He groaned, took as deep a breath as he could, and brought himself up to a semisitting position, the black, mindless depths of oblivion beckoning him once more.

"Nay," he rasped, as if to keep unconsciousness at bay with his verbal denial, and blindly reached out, groping for what looked to him like the reins. Bones threw back his head in protest at the pull exerted on the bit in his mouth and stomped a hoof, narrowly missing his master's hand as the fingers fell slack and slipped to the ground once again. *Nay, fool,* Edwin thought in self-disgust, *the stirrup.*

He heaved himself with his remaining strength closer to the pony—to almost under its belly. He barely had time to mentally thank God the animal hadn't sidled away before he passed out again, the stirrup dangling tantalizingly out of reach above his outstretched hand.

Brand sat astride Goliath in the middle of the clearing, his senses absorbing the familiar sights, sounds, and smells. A host of disordered emotions went shooting through him in the wake of memories, good and bad, juxtaposed alongside one another . . . time he had spent here with Griffith and Rhiannon—happy times, especially with his son's carefree laughter drifting on the breeze over the softly rushing sound of the sparkling spill of water in the background. Shared glances communicating mutual love for and parental pride in their offspring, even as Rhiannon's body swelled with another child.

Then his gaze came to rest upon the small cairn of rocks that marked her grave, and his memories took a different turn as the door to the past swung slowly shut once and for all: Marisa de Brionne's sweetly feminine voice turned sharply authoritative as she stayed a fierce war-horse, murmuring soothing words to a distraught Griffith after an attack upon her person by a monstrous he-wolf . . .

He shook his head to clear it, studying the area around the crystal-clear pool and the periphery of the forest for signs of Griffith's presence. That his son had come here was certain, for Griffith had left an easy trail to follow along the pathway. But where was he now?

Brand dismounted and squatted down to better examine the grassy verge around him with all the skill of a native Welshman. There had recently been several others present besides Griffith, Brand concluded, as he plucked a broken blade of grass and twirled it absently between his thumb and forefinger.

Then his gaze fell upon the wooden dagger he'd carved for Griffith himself, half-hidden in the grass. He picked it up. The toy weapon weighed next to nothing as it rested upon his open palm, and uncharacteristic fear seized him in its unyielding grip. Griffith had been abducted by someone, someone who had covered the evidence of his presence well but not well enough to mislead a man trained to track, trained by one of the Cymry themselves.

An old but unrevealed enemy . . .

Madog ap Cynan was the only one who wished him mischief, as far as he knew. The Welshman was hot-blooded and, from what Brand had heard, resented his influence with the Princes Bleddyn and Riwallon. Yet the man and his followers had never dared attack Brand or his family directly. So why would he have taken Griffith? What grudge could he harbor that would cause him to stoop to such baseness?

"By the rood," he whispered into the silence, his face turning ashen as suspicion struck. Could it be that Madog was somehow in league with Mauger le Faux? Now that Griffith was in their hands, could Marisa not be their next target?

His flesh crawled with an instinctual sense of disaster, for Marisa was either still within le Faux's stronghold or somewhere between Camwright and Fauxbray.

Apprehension racing through him, he sprang to Goliath's back, fatigue forgotten, and urged the mighty steed down the path to the manor.

Something dangling above his right ear caught Edwin's attention as he came to. It was the stirrup swinging gently with each movement of the pony standing patiently over him.

The incessant droning sounded like a roar in his ears; his tongue felt thick and dry, seeming to fill the entire cavity of his mouth. What he wouldn't have done for a drink of water.

He marshaled his energy and reached for the stirrup, concentrating on Brand's doubts regarding Marisa and

Mauger le Faux rather than on the agony of his wounds,
the limbs that were like dead weight and refusing to co-
operate with his mind's commands.

He'd recognized Brand's newfound, burgeoning love
for his beautiful bride. He knew also of the hatred his
thane harbored for the arrogant Norman. There would be
hell to pay for Marisa de Brionne—if she were ever found
alive—should the sly, facile-tongued Norman plant even
the tiniest seed of doubt in Brand's mind . . . enough
uncertainty to shatter the tentative, embryonic peace of
mind that Brand Ericson had begun to attain at last.

His right hand touched cool metal and Edwin slid his
fingers through the rung and closed them around it with
a death grip. He pulled, agony tearing through his back
with the strain on lacerated muscle. The pony started
slightly and then stilled, as if sensing it was of utmost
importance that he remain quiet.

Black spots appeared before Edwin's eyes, and for a
heartrending moment, he feared he would faint again.
The pain in his broken leg added much to his burden,
and he silently vowed he would attend mass with admirable regularity if God but gave him the strength to somehow drape himself over Bones's back.

He increased the pull on the stirrup with the remainder
of his ebbing strength, forcing his thoughts once again
to Brand in an effort to block out the pain. He feared
Brand would be fair game for Mauger le Faux's machinations, especially if Brand doubted the lady Marisa's
real motives for secretly visiting Fauxbray. But only he,
Edwin, had seen and understood the cunning, the deceit
in le Faux's eyes. The others had been behind him as
he'd entered the hall. . . .

Edwin slowly dragged his body forward, blood vessels
standing out at his temples from the strain, the inches
seeming like leagues. He had to get to Camwright, to tell
Brand of the ambush and warn him of le Faux's duplicity.

He was close enough to Bones's side to attempt to get
up on his back. Edwin raised his head, and to his weary
gaze the side of the animal looked as formidable as a

sheer mountain escarpment—and just about as easily
scaled. His lashes lowered in temporary defeat. How in
the name of all that was holy could he do it?

"Easy, my friend. Let me help you." A strong arm
went around his shoulders, carefully avoiding the hilt of
the dagger that still protruded from the wounded Saxon's
back.

Edwin relinquished his hold upon the stirrup and
looked up at his savior through a fog, yet he caught the
impression of long dark hair streaked with silver and
onyx, omniscient eyes. God had heard his promise and
had come to take him to Camwright Himself. In the wave
of relief that overwhelmed him before he succumbed to
blessed unconsciousness, Edwin briefly wondered why
God spoke with a Welsh accent.

Just as Brand forded the Wye to approach the south
bank, he heard the infinitely welcome sound of the horn
signaling several horses approaching the nearest gate of
the manor. A surge of hope flaring within his breast, a
prayer of thanksgiving upon his lips, Brand thundered up
the bank, along the central lane of Camwright, and then
into the compound hard upon their heels, Goliath prancing and curvetting almost uncontrollably with the acute
sensitivity of a finely trained destrier primed for the challenge of battle. But Brand could have wept with crushing
disappointment as he looked down into Morgan ap Dafydd's loam-dark eyes instead of Marisa's.

'You could muster up at least some kind of welcome
since we dropped everything to leave Wighton and—''
Morgan's words died aborning as he saw that Brand's
face was drawn with alarm.

"What is it, Brand?" Edyth asked.

Brand sliced a look at Adela, standing in the doorway
of the manor, wringing her hands. The negative shake of
her head made his heart twist within his chest. He slid
from Goliath's back and tossed the reins to Brian, saying
tersely, "I will need him very shortly, so do not stable
him." To John and Thomas, he added, "You two, as

well, grab a cup of mead, a chunk of cheese, and fresh horses. We ride for Fauxbray forthwith.'' He strode into the hall, ordering a young page, ''Bring me my battle jerkin.''

''What *is* it, Brand?'' demanded Morgan, his face taking on an expression as grim as his friend's.

''Marisa went to Fauxbray this morn and is still not returned.''

Morgan frowned. ''But surely you sent along an escort?''

Brand donned the offered leather jerkin with mail rings stitched over it and also downed a cup of mead. Seeming not to have even heard Morgan's question, he continued his thoughts aloud. ''All along I suspected le Faux, and with good reason, but now I'm sure Madog ap Cynan is also involved. If the Norman has imprisoned Marisa, then 'tis Madog who has Griffith. They are in league, I am convinced.''

''Now wait a moment, friend. How do you know any of this for certain? You summoned me to—''

''To search for Marisa. I thought if she were being held captive in le Faux's stronghold, I would need every man I could muster to free her. But I have just come from the clearing. I knew Griffith went there. And here is irrefutable evidence that he was taken against his will, abducted from practically beneath the shadow of my own palisade walls.'' He slipped the toy knife from his belt and tossed it to a nearby trestle table.

''But could he not be somewhere else? He could have dropped that dagger anywhere. . . . ''

Brand's piercing gaze halted any other words Morgan might have uttered. ''I made him the knife and a sheath to go with it. He wears it securely at his waist. I tell you, Morgan, he lost it during a struggle, although the signs of nefarious intent were well covered. See for yourself if you must, but make haste. I wager Madog not only has Marisa and my men, but also knows exactly what happened to my son.

"Now hurry, else you will be left behind and of no use to me when I meet le Faux face to face."

The Welshman shook his head. " 'Tis not necessary. I trust your judgment. When do we leave?"

Morgan and his small group were already mounted when Brand strode from the hall out into the sunlit yard, dressed for battle, looking more Cymry than Saxon in his leather and mail vest, his long chestnut hair held down by a leather thong tied around his forehead.

He moved toward Goliath, his features set, implacable. Touching his foot to the stirrup, he froze in mid-motion at the unexpected sound of the horn once more.

The hope that momentarily lit his heretofore impassive features declared to all the world his love for Marisa de Brionne. But as everyone held a collective breath for a fleeting moment, the only sound that greeted their ears was the *clip-clop, clip-clop* of a single horse—one lone, overburdened animal.

For the second time in less than an hour, Brand knew bitter disappointment. The pony who came into view, surrounded now by several of Brand's men-at-arms from the east gate, held the mysterious old man from the woods and a second man slumped forward against the animal's neck and held secure by Drystan himself.

" 'Tis Edwin!" someone shouted, and instant pandemonium broke loose.

Morgan was off his pony in a flash, close on Brand's heels as the latter ran to ease Edwin from Bones's back.

"Tell the lady Edyth," Morgan ordered as Brand lowered Edwin gently to the ground, carefully cradling his head and shoulders.

"Have a care with his back, Brand Ericson," Drystan cautioned, "for I pulled a Welsh dagger from it."

As if in answer, Edwin's eyelids fluttered and raised, a moan of pain slipping from between his lips.

"His right leg is broken. It must be set right away."

Brand stared into the older man's face, held by something vaguely familiar in his eyes. "What happened? Did you see aught of the lady Marisa or my other men?"

"Dead."

At Brand's suddenly blanched features, he clarified, "The three men are dead. There was no sign of the lady. I believe she was taken prisoner."

Brand's gaze lowered to the faithful retainer in his arms, then locked with Drystan's. "Ap Cynan?"

"Aye. But le Faux is not blameless. Ap Cynan supposedly does only the dirty work, yet he harbors his own grudge, I know. He acts for his own purposes, not le Faux's."

Brand's grip upon Edwin tightened involuntarily and he groaned softly. "Forgive me, Edwin," he murmured to the stricken man.

"My—my lord . . ." Edwin began in a hoarse, halting voice. "Lady Marisa—Lady Marisa and—le Faux . . . I saw them." His eyes closed as he collected the tattered shreds of his strength. "—saw them together—a trick . . . beware the Norman . . ." And he fainted before he could further elucidate.

"Help me get him into the manor," Brand said, mystified by his man's ramblings.

"Where is Gruffydd?"

As Brand relinquished Edwin to several other men, he raised his regard to meet Drystan's, bleakness clouding his eyes. "Gone. Abducted from the clearing by the waterfall not long ago."

Drystan's mouth tightened, his dark eyes lighting with twin sparks of hot anger. "And so he would abduct a woman and a child. He is not of the Cymry when he commits so heinous a crime in the name of a love he once bore a woman he could not have."

Brand stared at the older Welshman, suspecting he was half mad and his rantings nothing more than that. He would be foolish to give credence to the words of a deranged recluse. He stood as Edwin was carried into the hall, ignoring Drystan's reference to Madog's motives.

"We ride to find and bury the dead. Then we go to Faux-bray."

"You will find no answers there, Saxon." Drystan slid from the back of Edwin's pony.

"I thank you for bringing Edwin home, old man, but I have matters to settle with Mauger le Faux. My own faithful retainer just bade me beware, and you tell me I will find naught at Fauxbray? There is more to this situation than meets the eye. I should have realized that only a cur such as he would dare to abduct and then . . ." He let his thought go unspoken, even the oral expression of the deaths of Griffith and Marisa too shattering to bear.

"You hate le Faux, and with good reason, but I tell you once more the fate of your wife and son lies with Madog ap Cynan. . . . ''

But he fell silent, for Brand was already striding toward Goliath with grim purpose.

Just before twilight Godgift slipped from the hall and hurried down the village lane toward Margaret's cottage. She threw a furtive glance over her shoulder once or twice, praying le Faux would remain occupied with the village wench he'd taken to using in an attempt to appear insouciant over Godgift's stubborn indifference to first his advances and then, finally, what had become rape.

She closed her eyes for a moment in an effort to block out the image of Mauger le Faux looming over her flaccid form as she'd forced heself again and again to remain absolutely still during his brutal invasion of her body.

She held a wrapped piece of bread and chunk of cheese within the folds of the skirt of her overgown, knowing Margaret ate next to nothing in her unnatural preoccupation and seemed unconcerned as to whether little Hilde ate or not. Even the child seemed to be down to skin and bones, and it made Godgift's heart ache because her mother didn't care anymore. She might as well have been dead, as Mauger had cruelly stated on several occasions, for not only was she a burden to the village in Mauger's eyes, but she was also incapable of caring for her only child. Godgift prayed daily for a miracle—for Hilde's sake—while, at the same time, secretly wishing the child had been hers.

It was unnaturally quiet as she approached the cottage. There was no sign of Hilde or the pup she'd found and adopted. The fine hair on the back of Godgift's neck prickled, and she hesitated briefly before raising a hand to knock upon the half-open door.

There was no answer.

She called softly, "Margaret? Hilde?"

Nothing. Or wait, had that been a muffled sob?

She pushed the panel open fully and stepped inside, taking a moment to let her eyes adjust to the dark interior. She fumbled with a battered tinder box on a small, crude table and coaxed a flame from the wick of a worn-down candle.

"Margaret?" She strained to see better in the wavering candlelight. "Hil—" The word lodged in her throat.

She stepped forward woodenly, her horrified eyes taking in the sight of Margaret's form sprawled across the bed, her skirts drawn up around her waist in a grotesque parody of a woman who'd just raised them for her lover. Or her murderer.

Godgift felt bile rise and sear the back of her throat at the sight of the woman's slit neck, the knife still clutched within her outflung hand. The pallet was streaked with ruby-red blood, as was Margaret's overtunic. Had she taken her own life, or had it been made to look like suicide?

A whimper caught and drew her attention away from the grisly sight, and Godgift suddenly remembered the little girl. There in the corner by the small stack of kindling huddled Hilde, the puppy clutched convulsively to her chest, her knees drawn up in a protective attitude.

"Hilde, child," she murmured, and moved to stoop before the stricken little girl. Dried tears streaked the small, pale face, and she stared up at Godgift in mute

terror, her breath still coming in soft, uneven gasps. The
puppy whimpered softly and stilled.

Godgift gently smoothed back the child's hair, then sat
down beside her and took her onto her lap, puppy and
all. She rocked her back and forth, her lips pressed to
her forehead, murmuring all the while words of comfort
and assurance. When Hilde began to relax and then succumb to the soothing, healing balm of sleep, Godgift
made a decision.

She got to her knees, her strength and stature serving
her well as she struggled to keep her balance and refrain
from waking the sleeping child. She need not have worried on that account, however, for Hilde remained within
the protective haven of exhausted slumber. She moved
toward the door with her precious burden, the bundle of
food still clasped in the fingers of one hand, and peered
out into the lane. An unexpected blast of the horn heralded the arrival of a good-sized party of armed riders,
but rather than trying to make out who they might be,
Godgift took advantage of the diversion.

Drawing in a deep, fortifying breath, she stepped out
into the late summer twilight and, moving around toward
the back of the cottage, slipped into the forest and away
from Fauxbray, she swore silently, forever.

Chapter 22

"What could possibly be of such importance as to merit charging through my gates thusly?"

His tall form and fair hair delineated by the light from the hall behind him, Mauger le Faux looked sinisterly like Lucifer to Brand. A fallen angel, his inherent evil almost but not quite hidden by his malignant male beauty.

"Where is Marisa, le Faux?" he demanded bluntly, ignoring the Norman's question.

"I assumed she returned home like a good little wife, in view of what—'Edwin,' I believe his name is?—witnessed."

"Do not play games with me, Norman," Brand countered with quiet menace. "I would know what happened to my wife and son."

Mauger raised a sandy eyebrow in exaggerated astonishment. "I know naught of your brat, but"—the corners of his mouth curved upward insinuatingly—"I know much of your wife."

Before anyone could move, the sharp report of flesh cracking against flesh reverberated in the deepening dusk around them.

Brand's men stepped protectively toward him while le Faux's guards drew their swords.

"Stay your hands," the Norman commanded sharply. His eyes never left Brand's features, which were taut with fury and the last remnants of sorely pressed self-control.

"The truth is painful, is it not, Ericson? Yet you seem

to be a sensible man. Think. Why would she be so eager
to visit a fellow Norman if she were content with you?
How many times has she sought me out? Three? Four?
And how many have you known about?'' he added slyly.

Only with the greatest difficulty did Brand refrain from
running him through where he stood in the doorway of his
hall, not even deigning to invite him in as even the mean-
est courtesy dictated. Spinning through his mind in a litany of impending disaster were Edwin's words: *Lady
Marisa and le Faux . . . I saw them together.*

''For the last time, I ask you *where is she?*''

Mauger shrugged carelessly. ''Hiding, mayhap, from
her fear of your wrath when you discover her infidelity. Or
perhaps,'' he added with the barest hint of relish, ''she
hides from your scarred face, your village of pathetic rabble . . . even your Cymry whelp.''

Restraining hands gripped Brand's arms but, tightly
strung though he was, ready to choke the life from the
man standing before him, Brand held himself in rigid
check.

''Come away, Brand,'' urged Morgan in his ear as Brand
shook off the well-meaning hands of those nearest him.
''You'll get naught from him.''

''So it seems, Morgan,'' Brand said after a long, assessing moment. His murderous impulse quelled temporarily, Brand's next words were calm, yet the steel timbre
of his voice held enough promise of retribution to make
Mauger le Faux's eyes widen slightly in surprise. ''You
have not seen the last of me, Norman. We *will* meet again,
man to man, weapons drawn. I promise you that if harm
comes to my son or my wife, you will wish you had perished at Hastings.''

He moved to swing away when Mauger's reply challenged him. ''You dare to threaten me, Saxon swine? Why
wait until we meet again? Why not settle this now? To the
victor goes all.''

Brand's eyes met the Norman's, clear topaz coldly clashing with opaque blue that glittered with derision. The vir-
ulent hatred shining in those pale orbs would have given

a lesser man pause, yet Brand shrugged negligently, the
gesture one of insulting dismissal. "I have a task of much
greater magnitude at hand, le Faux. I can contain my eagerness to tangle with you for a while longer."

He turned and strode to Goliath, his men right behind
him.

Torches were being lighted around the compound, and
as Brand easily vaulted astride the great horse, his tight
pull on the reins and the tension that vibrated through him
were communicated to the mighty destrier. The gray drew
back onto his hindquarters, rising up magnificently, his
great hooves slashing the air.

Le Faux and his men stared wordlessly at the Saxon
seemingly so at ease atop the awesome Norman courser.
The fluid play of powerful equine muscles and sinew
melding into splendid body lines was thrown into burnished relief in the torchlight. The animal's frenzied shriek
echoed through the stronghold and village beyond in an
uncanny forewarning, as if the stallion sensed that Marisa
de Brionne, only daughter of the man who had raised and
trained him, was in mortal peril.

Marisa awoke to a hammering headache, chilled to the
bone and stiff and sore, as well. That they were in the
mountains she determined by the cooler temperature and
the wind that whistled around the thin walls of the shelter,
presaging the onset of autumn.

Essaying to determine where she was, she lay very still
upon a crude pallet—bound, gagged, and blindfolded. She
vaguely remembered hearing masculine voices speaking
Welsh in flashes of awareness while she had bounced
across the back of a pony. From the little she could discern, and considering her limited knowledge of the language, she guessed she was being kept away from any
villages. Rather, she was most likely in a little-used or
deserted cottage where Brand was unlikely to find her.

Brand. He would come for her, she assured herself.
Surely he'd been aware of her abduction soon after the
fact, for he knew at what hour she usually returned to

Camwright. The images of falling men and bloodied weapons brandished on the sunlight-speckled path flashed before her mind's eye, and tears pricked her eyelids for Edwin and the others. Why would anyone wish to take her captive? Angharad was dead and, evil though Mauger le Faux was, he would not dare do anything so boldly untoward . . .

A soft whimper caught her attention from across the dark room. Marisa halted her racing thoughts, trying to hear more, but only silence greeted her ears. She rubbed the side of her face against the rough cover beneath her, trying to work the gag from across her mouth. It had loosened slightly from the trek through the forest and into the mountains, and she scraped her tender cheek raw in her efforts to free her mouth of the stifling rag.

Just as she slid the gag from her lips, another quiet sob broke the stillness. *"Qui est là?"* she whispered in French, reverting to her native tongue in her agitation.

"Ma—Marisa?"

Dieu au ceil, she thought. *It sounds like* . . . "Griffith?"

"Aye," he whispered back.

"Oh, Griffith, what do you *here?*"

She heard a faint shuffling sound, as if he were shifting position before he answered. "They . . . someone I could not identify, for I did not see them before they blindfolded me, took me captive in the glade while you were in Fauxbray. But they are Cymry and I understood everything they said."

"Do you know where we are or what they intend to do with us, Griffith?"

"We are in the mountains, well into Wales, I think. But, Marisa, they wish me no harm, so the one called Madog said. He told one of the others that I belong in Wales with him, that I should have been his son and not Father's."

His revelations made little sense to Marisa, but when he spoke softly again, his words scattered her confused thoughts. "And then the one called Madog said they would demand ransom for you before they . . ."

"Before they what, Griffith? Do not be afraid to say what you heard."

"I am not afraid, Marisa." But the sob that followed as he drew in his breath belied his words.

"Come, Griffith, you can tell me. Whatever you heard, it does not mean aught will come about. Your father will come to our rescue—and Morgan . . . is he not Cymry? He knows these mountains like the back of his hand and will surely aid my lord in his search."

Seemingly somewhat mollified, Griffith finally let out the words that caused him such distress. "They will demand ransom for you, Marisa, before they kill you."

Fear shimmied down her spine for a split second before Marisa got hold of herself. "That is nonsense, *cher*. Brand will be here before they can even make the demand. Have you no faith in your father?"

An unreassuring silence followed her query, and Marisa finally closed her eyes in an effort to ease the pounding in her head. Vague snatches of conversation from the men evidently outside guarding the hovel and the steady, low-pitched moan of the wind came to her, eventually lulling her into an exhausted and troubled sleep.

"We cannot even track in the dark," Brand stated bitterly. "Griffith will be lost to me."

"And what of Marisa?" Morgan asked.

Silence followed, punctuated only by the sound of moving horses.

"Surely you do not believe le Faux?"

Brand turned toward his friend, his set features highlighted and shadowed alternately by the whimsical moonlight. "Surely you heard what Edwin said?"

"Bah! The man was half-delirious with pain. . . . He could have meant any number of things."

"Whether he meant what le Faux implied or no, my primary concern is for Griffith." He could not bring himself to tell Morgan of Marisa's clandestine visits to le Faux. "Would an enemy not kill the next in line for my holdings?"

Morgan sighed. "Then we can begin our search at first light. I have a feeling our friend Drystan may be of more help than you credit him."

"What do you know of him?"

"Only that he is a recluse—has been for years. He shuns human company and is said to be mad, but I do not believe it from what I saw this night."

Brand shot him a thoughtful look.

"But of one thing I am certain. He and Angharad were mortal enemies, and clever and evil as she was, he survived all these years to triumph in the end. The rumors go that she did everything within her power to rid Wales of him." He was silent a moment. "I could possibly understand what makes one man shun others, but I have no idea why Drystan has been in the area of Camwright and Fauxbray so consistently if he is Cymry."

"You do not think he is half-witted?"

"Does he act half-witted or mad? From what you related to me the morning after the wedding, he is not only clever and fearless, but also extremely skilled with a knife. And he has a penchant for being in the right place at the right time, thank God!"

An old but unrevealed enemy would as soon see you and your Norman wife killed and Gruffydd in his possession.

If the old man were right, then Griffith was not so much in danger of losing his life as Marisa, Brand thought.

He is not of the Cymry when he commits so heinous a crime in the name of a love he once bore a woman he could not have.

Could it be that Madog ap Cynan had once loved Rhiannon? For what other reason could he carry so terrible a grudge? And if it were true, then, indeed, Drystan was right. Ap Cynan would not harm Rhiannon's son, but he might very well wish to see dead the woman who took her place.

Marisa! his heart cried out in anguish. *My beautiful, courageous—and traitorous!* screamed a voice he wanted to ignore—*Marisa . . .*

As they approached the eastern gates of the manor,

Brand advised his men to get some sleep. "We ride for
Wales on the morrow at first light."

When he and Morgan entered the great hall, an unexpected sight met their eyes. Edyth and Drystan were deep
in conversation at the board, two horns of mead and the
remains of their evening meal still before them.

" 'Twould seem marriage has rid my sister of her shyness, ap Dafydd," Brand opined dryly. "She has captivated the mysterious Drystan." But they moved forward
as one, even as Brand spoke, both eager to hear the old
man out.

Drystan looked up first, his keen senses seeming to per-
ceive their presence even before he outwardly acknowledged it. "I told you that you would find no answers at
Fauxbray. Are you ready to listen now?"

"Aye, Drystan. Can you help me find my wife and
son?"

The older man nodded his dark head. "I believe I know
where they—or at least one of them—are being held."
Brand's eyes widened fractionally. "You have wasted much
time already, Saxon, but as I told you at the bog, I do not
believe Madog will harm the boy. 'Tis you and your Norman bride he seeks to destroy."

"We can leave immediately if you believe you know
where they are hidden. If you can just tell us, Morgan
knows Wales as well as—"

A vigorous shake of Drystan's head halted Brand in the
middle of his sentence. "I will take you there myself.
There is no time to lose."

"But I do not expect you to embroil yourself in my
troubles, old man . . . much as I am indebted to you,"
he added. "You have already come to Marisa's and Griffith's rescue, as well as that of Edwin, but now there is no
need to further endanger—"

Drystan rose and stepped over the bench. He stood before Brand, his black eyes boring into the younger man's.
"I would endanger myself as many times as necessary to
save Gruffydd—and also the lady Marisa." He glanced
over to the corner of the hall, where Edyth had gone to

minister to the sleeping Edwin. "Your man will live, but I have much in my past for which to atone."

Brand clasped the back of his neck and threw back his head as if seeking the mental impetus needed to spar with the older Welshman. "No man can carry such a heavy burden that he feels he must take it upon himself to be the savior of another man's wife and son and retainer and—"

"I have other reasons."

"What other reasons? How do I know you speak the truth if I know naught about you? Perhaps you will lead us astray. 'Tis possible that you only think you know the whereabouts of my wife and son."

"I may be called accursed and coward and fool by some, but I am no liar. I know where they are, and your lady wife's very life is endangered with every moment you detain me here."

"Why do you not tell him, Drystan?" Edyth inquired gently, as she moved to Morgan's side.

"I am Drystan the Accursed. Did you not hear Angharad call me such before she died?"

"Do not speak in riddles, Drystan. I think your secret, whatever it may be, festers like a mortifying wound," interjected Morgan. "Perhaps 'tis time to unburden yourself, and," he added, "we will all be more at ease with one another if you clarify the mystery surrounding your identity."

Drystan looked at Edyth and, as if through some unspoken encouragement, let out a pent-up breath in resignation. He nodded at her and turned his gaze to Brand. "Gruffydd's welfare is of the utmost importance to me. The lady Marisa loves him as her own and would give her life for him. Edwin is a brave and loyal man. I could have done no less for them." He sighed and looked into the flickering flames of the central hearth, his eyes suddenly moist with unshed tears. "But in the end, it always revolves around Gruffydd." His voice began to break with misery and remorse before he looked back at Brand. "I am sorrow—did I not tell you that, as well? I am the lowest of the low, deserting my wife and child in my own consuming, selfish grief, as I allowed the contrivances of a cruel, vindictive woman to set me to flight.''

Brand frowned and glanced at Morgan, but the Welshman was studying Drystan's anguish-etched features.

"I am sorrow—I am accursed—I am a pathetic coward. I am all these things and more. . . . I am Rhiannon's sire.''

Drystan guided them through the black September night on a borrowed pony, driven as strongly as Brand in his quest to find his grandson and Marisa de Brionne. He knew the area even better than Morgan, having lived in the mountains and forests for years. "If we can reach them before the sun rises, there is a good chance the lady Marisa will be yet alive. We must pray that Gruffydd is with her,'' he'd said as they left the safety of Camwright's gates.

They pressed on relentlessly, the moon and stars obliterated by dark, scudding clouds, the smell of rain on the breeze. The five men—including Thomas and John—knew that, although the inky skies that gave off no light could have been a severe hindrance, in this case they proved to be a blessing, for Drystan needed nothing more than his sense of direction and his instincts to lead them soundlessly into Wales. The cover of absolute darkness was to their advantage under his guidance.

No one spoke, and Brand had much time to think—and worry about the success of their mission in view of the fact that the Cymry most likely keeping watch over the two captives were undoubtedly chosen for their ability to function in the night as capably as during the day. And who knew how many there would be? Could five men successfully overpower a greater number and then spirit away a boy and a woman before anything was discovered amiss? As capable and fearless as Brand was in battle, he felt panic crawl insidiously through his gut at the sheer delicacy of the strategy. There was more involved here than the ability to wield a sword or throw a lance.

Yet he comforted himself with the thought that both Morgan and Drystan were very skilled with a dagger and the old man had directed Brand to bring his longbow. Used normally for hunting, it would be an asset in a silent assault on guards.

Brand shifted in the saddle, willing himself to concentrate on assault and probably hand-to-hand fighting rather than on the stunning revelation of Drystan's identity or—even more naggingly persistent—Mauger le Faux's superbly sown seeds of doubt regarding Marisa.

Feeling more like a serpent than a man, Brand inched his way over the wet ground beneath the camouflage of the underbrush before dawn, thankful that the light rain misting the earth decreased the crackling and crunching of dried leaves and dead scrub. In the predawn blackness, through the lowest branches of a towering evergreen under which he'd finally settled, he could dimly distinguish the outline of a small structure.

Now that he was actually here, the alien feeling of alarm that had threatened his levelheadedness had been replaced by cool composure, his every instinct, every sense, narrowed down to absolute concentration on the task at hand. Brand Ericson was ready to kill—even to sacrifice his life if need be—to ensure the continuance of the same for Griffith and Marisa.

"Do not move until I give the signal," whispered a voice in his ear.

Having sensed Drystan's quiet approach, Brand did not move a muscle in reaction to the man's words, except to allow a muffled "aye" to emerge from his throat as softly as a leaf floating on a zephyr. Then the Welshman was gone, vanishing as silently as he'd appeared.

Brand could make out six guards in all, unless his eyes were playing tricks on him. If one of the rescue party could take two of them immediately, the other four could be picked off before they knew what hit, by either Morgan and Drystan with their daggers and—if Brand left his cover and stood—by his arrows. They had agreed that surprise through silence—no singing of steel against steel in swordplay—was the best method in case Madog should be in the area to either execute Marisa or separate Griffith from her. That is, if they were within the cottage.

It seemed to Brand that the men keeping watch were less vigilant than he'd anticipated, probably because Madog did not expect anyone to search the mountainous area around them so soon and at night, let alone be led directly to the clearing itself. Yet there was no fire to attract attention. Pray God their guards were down, he thought, for it would make the task of the rescuers easier.

The pale, tentative edge of the sun spread its first glow across the horizon, turning the umber shade of early morning to dim gloom in the clearing around the hovel. As one of the Welsh sentries paused directly in front of the low-branched fir tree under which Brand was hiding, Brand lay down his longbow, deciding to jump the man when Drystan gave the signal—the cry of a skylark.

Even as the thought ran through his mind, the call sounded, so natural that none of the men dimly outlined in the still-shadowed glade even raised a head in suspicion.

In the next instant, the two guards on either side of Brand slumped to their knees before hitting the ground, and Brand nimbly levered himself to a crouch and sprang from the shadows toward the guard before him, slitting his throat from behind with his own knife. Several muffled thumps and a soft groan punctuated the stillness of the new day, and Brand's heart lightened perceptibly at the obvious success of Drystan's plan.

He wiped the blade of his dagger across the dead guard's sleeve and made a dash for the hovel. *By all that is holy,* he prayed, *let them both be here.* Flinging the door open, he flattened himself against the wall for an instant, dagger still clenched in his fingers, eyes straining to pierce the chill, lightless room.

"Griffith?"

"Father? Is it you?"

At last Brand made out the small, huddled form of his son, obviously alive and hopefully well. He crossed the room in three strides and crouched before the boy. "Are you unhurt, Griffith?" His knife slipped through the bonds around small wrists and ankles before he removed the blindfold. "And . . ." The words lodged in his throat, numbing dread overtaking him suddenly, for he had not discerned anyone else in the room.

"I am here, Brand," answered the voice he had feared stilled forever. "Did I not tell you, *cher Griffith*, that he would come for us?"

Brand rose and moved to the pallet against the opposite wall. He removed the blindfold and cut the ropes that bound her before helping her to sit up. "Are you well, Marisa?"

"*Oui,*" she answered, leaning toward him.

"Not here," he ordered tersely, avoiding her outstretched arms and pulling away just as Morgan came striding through the door.

"They are here?"

"Aye, and both unharmed. Are the guards—?"

"Dead. All of them."

"Then we must leave—now."

Morgan nodded, scooped up Griffith, and threw him over his shoulder. "Not a peep out of you, boy, else we will all end up trussed and blindfolded at Madog ap Cynan's behest."

When Brand helped Marisa to her feet, her knees buckled from stiffness. He caught her and swung her effortlessly up into his arms, her head cradled against his chest. Once outside, he glanced down at her and, as she looked up at him, was staggered for the hundredth time by her vivid features, the dazzling smile and dancing eyes, the sweet scent of silver-gold hair. In spite of her ordeal, in spite of the bruises and scrapes she sustained, she still had the power to heat his blood. The feel of her in his arms once again caused myriad emotions to go coursing through him, immense relief only one of many. Yet he found himself willing to give her up to Morgan and rather unsubtly asked for Griffith to ride with him.

"What? Do not be so unimaginative, Saxon," the Welshman exclaimed in a low voice as they made their way through the forest to where the horses had been con-

cealed and tethered. ''Think of the ways in which you can
console your lovely wife while spiriting her away beneath
ap Cynan's very nose!''

There seemed no alternative than for Brand to lift Marisa sidesaddle onto his sure-footed pony and then seat
himself behind her.

They rode like the wind for the border, although the
descent from the foothills slowed them somewhat, as did
the extra burden of Griffith and Marisa on the small horses.

''You should have brought Goliath.'' Marisa leaned her
head as far back as she could and smiled up at Brand in
the growing light.

But his golden-brown eyes were cool and distant, and
he could not prevent the answer that sprang to his lips.
''Always something Norman, Marisa, is it not? I wonder
that you did not just hie yourself back to London and your
father long ago. But then again, mayhap the solace you
found in Fauxbray was more than enough to make up for
any lack on my part.''

Chapter 23

Marisa's tired yet loving smile turned into a faint frown as Brand's gaze left hers. Her eyes remained trained on his face for a long, puzzling moment before she lowered her head against his chest. Deciding that he was only tired and relieved, she remained silent, dismissing his sharp sarcasm as a result of the enormous strain under which he must have been since Griffith's abduction and her failure to appear in Camwright the previous afternoon.

She fell asleep as trustingly as a child, despite the fast clip of the pony, content in the security of his arms.

The sounding of the horn at Camwright woke Marisa near noon to a clear, brilliant day in a world washed clean by the rain. They emerged from the path through the weald toward the eastern side of the stockade.

As they rounded the western end of the hall, Edyth emerged, anxiously taking in the party before a smile of jubilation transformed her face. "Thank God you are all safe!" she exclaimed as Morgan handed Griffith down to her and then dismounted before kissing her soundly.

"Marisa said Father would come to us. She had more faith in him than did I," the boy murmured with a frown.

"Nay, child," Edyth reassured him softly. " 'Tis just that ofttimes an adult is better at concealing fears."

"What's this?" Brand inquired coming up behind them. He swung his son up over his head to sit upon his shoulders as they moved toward the hall. "No frowns or fretting on an empty belly. Let us eat, for I am ravenous, and then you can tell us what happened.'' He turned slightly toward one of the gatemen. ''Morkere, secure the eastern gates and post extra men in pairs—armed—at both entrances and around the perimeter of the village.''

Morgan and Edyth exchanged glances as Marisa was left standing alone. The hurt in her eyes was unmistakable, and before either Morgan or his wife could move, the observant Drystan walked up to her, the other men handing over their horses to Brian and another youth before following Brand into the hall.

''Drystan,'' she murmured, her brow smoothing at his gesture, ''you had something to do with our rescue, didn't you?''

''Just a bit,'' he said.

'' 'Just a bit,' indeed!'' exclaimed Morgan as he and Edyth fell into step beside them. ''He led us right to those devils.''

Marisa's eyes misted with emotion as they met the man's dark, unfathomable gaze. ''Then I am forever indebted to you, my lord.''

''I am no lord, Lady Marisa.''

''You are lord of the forest, Drystan. And once again you saved our lives.''

Edyth ushered them into the hall and directed the servants to put out the noon meal. ''What is amiss with my brother and Marisa?'' she murmured to Morgan when she finally sat down.

Morgan's mouth twisted wryly. ''He believes Marisa played him false with le Faux, the fool.''

Edyth looked from the unsmiling Brand to his quiet, weary wife and then back to Morgan. ''Played him false? And with le Faux? Never!''

At first the talk around the board was low-toned, as if the men were aware of their lord's displeasure, yet none could discern the cause save Morgan.

''Tell me, Griffith, exactly what happened when you left the stronghold,'' Brand urged as they ate.

Griffith complied and then relayed what he'd heard concerning the identity of his captor and their plans for Griffith and Marisa. ''He said I should have been his son, not yours.''

Brand's eyes narrowed and he turned to Drystan. ''That is what you meant just before you told me I would find no answers at Fauxbray. He loved Rhiannon, didn't he?''

Drystan nodded. ''Since before you even knew her. He nursed a secret, festering resentment toward you, which turned to hatred as the years went by. For some reason, it did not ease after her death.''

Brand sat lost in thought until Morgan asked, ''And what happened to you, Marisa?''

Marisa's gaze met Brand's and it seemed to her that pain flickered in his eyes before his look turned harsh and un-yielding. What was amiss? she wondered in frustration. ''We were attacked along the path leading to Camwright, by Welshmen, I think, for the air was thick with flying daggers.'' She shuddered in remembrance. ''The man riding before me was felled and I heard shouts from the two behind. And then Edwin was killed.'' Her face paled at the thought of the valiant men who had accompanied her only to lose their lives.

''Rest easy, Marisa,'' interjected Morgan when Brand offered no words of enlightenment. ''Drystan brought Edwin safely back to Camwright, and although badly wounded, he will live.''

''And what happened then?'' Brand asked.

Marisa looked at her husband, needing the comfort of his arms about her, yet sensing he was, for some inexplicable reason, angry with her.

''I was knocked unconscious and remember only snatches of riding through the woodlands and then into the mountains, slung across a pony like a sack of grain.''

''The child, Marisa,'' interjected Edyth, her face a study in solicitude. ''Is the child . . . ?''

Marisa smiled tentatively at her sister-by-marriage and then looked again at Brand. For a fleeting moment his look softened and registered concern.

''The babe is fine.''

She missed the tightening of Brand's jaw, despite her

reassurances. "There will be retribution for this collusion between le Faux and ap Cynan, but first I think we need rest while I devise my revenge. No one abducts my wife and child and lives very long to boast of it."

The hall was silent for a moment, his words lingering heavily in the stillness. Then Drystan stood to take his leave.

"We owe you much, Drystan. Will you speak to Griffith alone?"

The older man shook his head. "I think you should tell the boy when you feel the time is right."

Brand nodded and stood. Stepping over the bench, he went around to the Welshman and placed his hands upon his shoulders. "You are welcome at Camwright anytime. If you ever decide to dwell among men once again, I pray you will consider living here." He paused. "Have a care, Drystan, for Madog may suspect your involvement."

The Welshman nodded. "I can take care of myself, Brand Ericson, as I have for over a score of years. Do not be concerned." After bidding Griffith, Marisa, and the others farewell, he walked out into the sun-drenched afternoon.

"Do you wish me to remain here, Brand," Morgan asked, "in case of retaliation from Madog or le Faux?"

At the mention of le Faux, Band slanted a look at Marisa, who was halfheartedly pushing the remains of her meal about her trencher. "Nay, Morgan. I believe you may be needed more at Wighton should Madog suspect your participation in the raid. Take your men and see to your own now."

Morgan nodded.

Marisa stood then and excused herself. "I am very tired." She moved to give Edyth a hug before she exited the hall, her chin held high in spite of her bewilderment with her taciturn husband.

Rollo nearly overwhelmed her in his excitement at seeing her. Only his still tender side prevented him from completely bowling her over.

"So you missed me, *copain*, eh?"

The wolfhound's nose insistently nudged her hand for the tenth time, and Marisa bent to wrap her arms around his neck, burying her face in the thick, coarse fur and weeping softly. So many emotions were churning within her breast that she failed utterly to repress her tears.

Rollo stood patiently, then finally sat down, his tail swishing softly upon the smooth stone floor when his mistress gave no indication of rising. Then even his tail stilled, his head drooping in canine empathy.

At last Marisa rose and shed her rent, soiled bliaut and chainse. She washed her face and slipped into bed, sleep overcoming her in spite of her troubled thoughts.

The door to the bower opened softly and Brand entered, motioning to Rollo to lie still where he'd plopped down beside the great bed. He, too, shed his soiled clothing and, after washing his face, lay down beside Marisa. But, unlike his wife, Brand found no comfort in sleep. It eluded him as images of Mauger le Faux and Marisa flashed before his mind's eye time and time again.

Edyth had had Edwin moved to the other bower and Brand had looked in on him. Nesta was with the wounded man-at-arms, but he was sleeping and Brand didn't have the heart to wake him and fire him with questions. So the doubts grew and magnified in his mind, and his agitation built itself up into a roaring conflagration of wrath toward the girl at his side. His fatigue and irritability did nothing to help matters.

At last he'd fallen deeply in love, body and soul, only to be betrayed. The old guilt crept insidiously into his heart. It was probably no less than he deserved after failing Rhiannon. But that did not make it any easier to bear.

When at last Marisa opened her eyes, Brand was sitting across from the bed, cleaning and polishing his dagger, clad only in braies. She pushed herself to her elbows and the light coverlet slipped down, revealing the creamy swell of her breasts. The movement caught Brand's attention and he looked up at her, the light from several tapers gleaming off his burnished hair.

Marisa sat up and, under his cool but intense regard, pulled the cover to her chest. "Did you not wish to sleep?"

"Indeed, my lady wife, but I could not under the circumstances."

"You are worried that Madog and his followers will attack Camwright?"

An eyebrow quirked sardonically. "I would that I had so little to fret about."

A chill passed over her, for here, she suspected, was the crux of the matter. And it obviously had nothing to do with weariness or relief.

"You have your son back safe and sound, my lord, so what can be amiss?" she queried through suddenly dry lips.

Brand gave the blade of his dagger a final swipe with a cloth and laid it down. He stood and stretched, the action throwing the superb bone structure and musculature of his tall, streamlined body in flame-limned relief. "I thought you were many things, Marisa de Brionne," he said when he'd relaxed once more, "but not a traitor. Not truly."

She bristled, suddenly remembering all the old antagonism between them . . . his refusal to see her as anything but a spoiled, irresponsible child. "Not truly? Just a *bit* of a traitor? In small ways that could really do no harm?"

"You might say that." He began to pace the chamber, his agitation apparent in the tightness of his usually lithe gait. "At first I considered you willful and frivolous and much too interested in things Norman. I believed you showed little interest in accepting my people and then accused you of telling Mauger le Faux about Goliath while he visited Camwright." He stopped pacing at the foot of the bed and turned to face her. "But I was wrong on all accounts."

"How magnanimous of you to admit it. If I am exonerated from such an unflattering list of shortcomings, why then are you so angry with me?"

"Because I did not seriously consider the fact that you would play me false with a devil like Mauger le Faux— Norman or no."

Marisa's mouth fell open in astonishment, and before she could gather her scattered wits, he continued. "Tell me, my beautiful wife, if the child you carry is mine?"

His words hit her like a slap in the face. *"Your child?"* she whispered, stunned. "How could you think otherwise?"

"How could I not if I'd had my wits about me?"

High color flamed in her cheeks. "Because I never visited Fauxbray until after I told you of the child."

"How do I know when you really began your visits, Marisa? Your *secret* visits? And how could I doubt the word of two men, one a trusted retainer?"

"Two men?" she asked warily, sudden unease creeping over her.

He leaned forward on knuckled fists atop the great chest, his eyes burning into hers. "I had it from Edwin and le Faux himself that you and he had been intimate."

Her modesty forgotten, Marisa let loose the coverlet and without warning sprang toward him, her right arm swinging and catching him off guard. Her small fist struck him full on the jaw.

For a moment he looked so angry that Marisa thought she had gone too far, but he merely caught her wrist and pushed her off her knees, sending her sprawling backward upon the mattress. Instantly he came around the bed and pinned down her shoulders with his hands as he sank into the mattress beside her.

"You are such a fool I should not even deign to tell you this," she cried, "but I will—for your own sake and that of our child's. I went to Fauxbray to discover what I could about his plans, to learn from Godgift what I could about your Welsh enemies."

"And what did you learn, my beautiful little informer, eh?" The mockery in his voice singed her pride, yet she continued.

"That Madog ap Cynan was conspiring with le Faux to bring about your downfall and—"

His laughter cut her off, a sound devoid of warmth, his breath fanning her face. "We all know that, Marisa. You are not as clever as I thought if you can only come up with something you could easily have guessed from your abduction.''

"If we were lovers, why would Mauger allow Madog to abduct me?"

"Because you were duped, Marisa. That is the irony. You were duped by le Faux, for he cared naught for you."

"And I cared naught for him!"

"Then what did Edwin see at Fauxbray yesterday that made him say, 'I saw them together—Lady Marisa and le Faux. Beware the Norman'?"

A host of changing emotions flitted across Marisa's delicate features as she remembered Mauger's kiss. Then her midnight-blue eyes turned even darker with burgeoning ire at his lack of faith in her and her love. "Edwin did walk into the hall when Mauger was kissing me." Pride demanded she say no more, for she would never beg him when she had shown no interest in any man since meeting him. Despite their bad beginning, she had never given him cause to mistrust her.

"So you admit to being lovers." A fierce, heretofore unknown jealousy shot through him like an arrow from a longbow, and he knew a fleeting urge to throttle her.

"If you think Mauger le Faux's kissing me against my will made us lovers, then I cannot change that."

The gem-gold eyes turned deepest topaz with his rage. "You would do well to dwell upon that kiss, for 'twill be your last. Whether he be Norman chevalier or no, Mauger will die, as will Madog ap Cynan. Remember that kiss, my lady wife, and let me give you something with which to compare it." His lips slanted across hers with punishing force, and Marisa struggled to twist her head away. But one of this callused hands came up to grip her hair firmly while a powerful leg was thrown over her lower body to pin her to the bed.

Marisa determined not to respond to him, yet as soon as she was unable to move from the strength of his body over hers, she noticed a change in his kiss. His lips and tongue teased hers unmercifully until her mouth fell open

and their tongues entwined and said everything that words
could not. Marisa felt the familiar, wondrous languor steal
through her lower abdomen and then extend out to her
limbs until they tingled with arousal.

He drew away abruptly, leaving her breathless. She
could only stare up at him, noting with some satisfaction
that he was breathing heavily—that he, too, was not unaffected. "A token, Marisa, to measure against that which
you shared with le Faux yesterday."

He rose from the bed, pulled a chainse over his tousled
head, and left the bower.

Brand took his evening meal in the hall alone, for it was
rather late. One of the serving girls took a tray to Marisa.
Griffith would more than likely sleep through the night.
The guards were still heavily posted and would continue
to be so until Brand decided how best to go about ridding
England and Wales of Madog ap Cynan and Mauger le
Faux.

His thoughts took a different turn. If King William decreed Brand should lose his holdings as part of his punishment for killing a chevalier, Brand could always take
Griffith into Wales and disappear. He had many friends
among the Cymry.

As for Madog, Brand was almost certain he was responsible for the death of Harald of Wighton and the gruesome "gift" given Marisa by the boy from the merchant's
train. It would have been easy to make Brand suspect Angharad of those incidents to throw off his suspicions. And
le Faux had probably been in on it with him. If le Faux
wanted Brand and Marisa dead, the perfect ally would be
Madog. With Madog doing the dirty work, the King could
not blame Mauger for the deaths of Geoffrey de Brionne's
daughter or her Anglo-Saxon husband. And Madog could
have hidden behind Angharad's hatred toward both Brand
and Marisa . . . until she was killed.

Yet two voices continued to vie for supremacy within
him. One told him he'd been duped by a beautiful face,
and the other told him he was a fool to believe Mauger le

Faux's sly innuendos about a young woman who'd shown her loyalty and love over and over again.

But what of Edwin's words? Besides Morgan ap Dafydd, he was Brand's most trusted man, and his warning had not been merely the ravings of a delirious man.

Brand pushed away the half-eaten meal and took his horn of mead with him to stand in one of the open doors of the hall, resting his shoulder against the door frame. As he stared out into the clear, balmy night, he realized just how much he was indebted to Drystan—how fortunate he was to have safely retrieved Griffith and Marisa and Edwin, as well. That he had lost three other good men was lamentable, but a part of life. Yet they would be avenged, all of them. Whether Marisa had committed adultery or not, her honor would be upheld. He would never admit to le Faux that he believed his maligning of Marisa.

He raised the horn to his lips and took a long, sustaining draught.

If you think Mauger le Faux's kissing me against my will made us lovers, then I cannot change that.

Perhaps Marisa had spoken the truth when she said that Mauger's attentions were unwanted. But could he ever be certain? Surely there had to be a way to discover the truth. Surely . . .

Suddenly the answer came to him. So simple, so obvious . . .

He set down his horn on a nearby table, pushing aside his shame at the need for proof, and stepped out into the star-studded night.

Marisa paced before the bed in unconscious imitation of her husband. Her movements were like a caged she-lynx—frustrated and jerky as she pivoted on her heel each time she came close to either of the wooden walls of the bower.

"How could he believe such a ridiculous lie?" she asked no one in particular as Rollo lay with his head on his paws, his doleful eyes following her progress to and fro. "He knows I love him, want his child, yet he accuses me of adultery with a snake in the grass like Mauger le Faux!''

The more she paced, the more agitated and outraged she became. ''I will not live with his animosity as I had to in the beginning.'' She turned to face the faithful dog, her hands on her hips. ''One person can take only so much, Rollo. He put me through hell and now he would do the same once again for who knows how long!'' Misery seeped into her heart and threatened to rob her of her determination as she thought of leaving the man she loved so deeply. Yet what other choice did she have?

Marisa walked over to the tray upon the bedside table and shoved some of the cheese and bread into her mouth. ''I will need my strength, Rollo,'' she explained to the hound between bites. ''If I can get to London, someone will help me get to either Father or Richard or Raoul. But I will not remain here.'' Hot tears cascaded down her cheek at the thought of leaving what had become her home, what she had fought for with such vigor and determination, only to be forced to turn her back upon her new life, her new family and friends.

She stuffed the remainder of her supper in a small bundle with an extra dagger Morgan had given her. She'd asked him to teach her how to throw it, but they'd only managed to get in two lessons before his marriage to Edyth. Finishing the cup of wine, she replaced the stopper and put the flask in with her knife and food. Then she collected her mantle from a peg on the wall and stooped before her beloved Rollo.

''I—I cannot take you, Rollo.'' He cocked his head and switched his tail where he lay. ''If I am set upon by thieves or vagabonds, you would in your weakened state be killed for certain.''

Rollo sat up and licked the tears from one cheek before Marisa pushed his head away and buried her face in his shaggy neck. ''And Griffith loves and needs you. I cannot take you from him.'

The dog whined as if in protest, but Marisa was adamant. ''I love you too much, *copain,* to expose you to danger. You belong here with Griffith. You must help him reach manhood, to be as strong and courageous and wise as his father.''

She pushed away and stood up, fighting for control. If the dog sensed that something was wrong, he would not tolerate being locked in the bower without howling and scratching at the door. And Marisa needed absolute silence and secrecy.

''And so you hate me enough to shun our bed, Saxon?'' she whispered to the shadows. ''I am so abhorrent to you that you will not even deign to sleep anywhere within the bower?'' She dashed away the unwelcome tears, acknowledging that that was truly the catalyst that would drive her from Camwright and out into the night. If he had at least returned to the bower for the night, they could have argued, even come to blows—anything to indicate there existed a willingness to communicate, to try to surmount this new barrier between them. But it was not meant to be, for the door remained closed and no sounds came from outside.

She scratched Rollo behind the ears once again and said, *''Adieu, cher Rollo. Soignes-toi bien.''* She opened the door, scanning the yard through eyes narrowed against the darkness, and slipped out into the night.

Brand entered the smaller bower where Edwin lay asleep upon a small bed. Nesta had returned to her home at Brand's insistence earlier in the evening. Now Maida, Edgiva's eldest daughter, watched over him.

Brand entered so quietly that she started when he touched her arm. ''How does he fare?''

''Well enough, I suppose, my lord. He's done naught but sleep since I arrived, although Nesta said he awoke once and recognized her.''

He nodded. ''Go stretch your legs, child, and see what you can glean from the kitchen. I'll stay with him for a while.''

She coyly smiled her thanks in obvious anticipation of receiving more from her handsome thane than a smile or kind word, but his eyes were on Edwin and his thoughts seemed suddenly far away. Maida exited the bower with a wistful sigh.

Brand gently examined what he could see of the splint Drystan had put on Edwin's right leg, for the man was on his stomach because of his knife wound. He uncovered Edwin's upper torso to see how Drystan had bandaged the puncture between his shoulders. A neater, more efficient-looking job of binding and setting he'd never seen. Was there anything the Welshman could not do?

Edwin stirred slightly as Brand took the stool Maida had vacated. The man-at-arms frowned in his sleep, either in pain or in the throes of an unpleasant dream.

Brand murmured his name as he pulled the stool closer and leaned forward. "Edwin, can you hear me?"

At the sound of Brand's voice, Edwin's eyes slowly opened. "My lord . . . the lady Marisa—?"

"She is safe, Edwin. Do not speak. Save your strength now."

"I—am not so unmanned as—that."

Brand laughed softly. "Irascible as always. How do you feel?"

"As if yon gray destrier mistook me for the enemy."

Brand smiled at Edwin's humor, and his spirits rose at the prospect of discovering exactly what Edwin had meant when he'd spoken of Mauger and Marisa. He offered him some water, carefully raising the man's chin and holding a cloth underneath it to prevent it from dribbling onto the bed.

When Brand allowed Edwin's head to rest, cheek down, against the feather mattress, the man-at-arms surprised him by saying, "I—do not remember what—I said to you since I—was brought back to Camwright, my lord, but of two things—you must be apprised."

Brand nodded and leaned closer again.

"Le Faux is even worse than he appears. He made it seem as though the lady Marisa and he were lovers. He . . . hurt her, would not let her go when she struggled against his kiss. I saw this, although mayhap the other men

. . . had not so clear a view . . . and did not hear his sly words to her after she'd slapped his face . . . words intended to make it seem as if they . . . had kissed before.'' His eyelids began to droop from the effort of speaking just when Maida returned.

Brand felt as if he'd been kicked in the stomach at Edwin's revelation, at what he'd said to Marisa in his false conclusions and pigheaded anger. ''Sleep now, Edwin, so you may be up and about soon.''

The other man nodded almost imperceptibly. ''Beware le Faux. I do not trust him.'' Softly spoken, the words were no less clear or dire-sounding in the stillness of the bower.

As Edwin's lids lowered, Maida moved closer and stood uncertainly at Brand's side. He stood up, nodded to her, and strode from the room.

Chapter 24

The door to the bower that Brand and Marisa shared flew open, causing Rollo to jump back to avoid being struck. Brand loomed in the doorway, taking in the room with a single, sweeping glance and acknowledging with a sinking sensation in the pit of his stomach that it was empty. The dog whined and tried to push his way past his master, but Brand backed away quickly and shut the door before Rollo could worm his way through.

She could not be far, Brand reasoned, the fine edge of panic shearing his senses. She would never leave the village without her beloved hound. She was upset with him, and with good reason, and was probably trying to work off her anger somewhere about the compound. . . .

But no one had seen her—not the gatemen, the guards, the stableboys who were fast asleep but would have heard anyone entering the stable. Nor had the hastily roused servants seen her, or, most certainly, the men who were still sleeping soundly around the perimeter of the great hall.

He returned to the bower, another thought creeping insidiously into his mind. This time as he approached the sleeping-house, Rollo could very definitely be heard whining and scratching insistently at the door. Brand opened it more carefully this time and commanded, "Back, Rollo."

The dog obediently backed away from the wide-swinging portal and greeted Brand with a sharp, deep-throated bark.

"Where is Marisa?" he asked the animal.

Rollo barked again and trotted toward the open door. Brand followed him into the yard and watched him sniff around. "Take me to your mistress, boy," he said softly. "Take me to Marisa."

By the time Brand had spoken to Edwin, Marisa was well on her way down the bluff that buttressed the north side of the manor. She'd painfully squirmed her way through the hollow beneath the stockade that Griffith had told her about, and she was now sliding down the scree-strewn cliffside, trying to be as quiet as possible. Fortunately, she was guided by a three-quarter moon that bathed the area with its silvery radiance.

At the bottom of the bluff, she did not stop to nurse her cut and bleeding hands and knees, but rather raced along the Wye until she was well past the east gate of the manor. She then forded a shallow section of the river and was swallowed up by the dark forest.

Guided by instinct alone, Marisa headed east. Briefly she considered going to Mauger le Faux for a horse, then dismissed the idea in view of what Brand had said about le Faux's collusion with the Welshman who had been responsible for her abduction. She could not trust Mauger le Faux, and so her only hope was to keep to the forest until she was well away from Camwright and then perhaps steal a horse to get herself to London. It was an almost overwhelming challenge, but her one hope was that, since she was Norman, she perhaps would be aided in her quest by fellow Normans granted holdings in Wessex or patrolling the area. And if she encountered Anglo-Saxons, she spoke their tongue fairly well now and could throw herself on their mercy.

On the other hand, a good part of William's army had been made up of mercenaries—Bretons, Angevins, French, and Flemish—who had no real loyalty to William or anything Norman. These men would not necessarily be sympathetic to a Norman woman traveling alone. There were also deserters from both armies, scavengers and homeless Anglo-Saxons who now made their homes in the weald. Of a certainty they would not look upon a Norman woman with understanding.

As Marisa plunged blindly through the woods, her earlier anger and determination began to be replaced by doubt and fear. What chance did she have of ever reaching London alive? She should have demanded of Brand to be escorted back to her father. Surely after what he believed to be her perfidy he would have complied . . . except that he probably would have been unwilling to give up what he had won for Griffith. "My life would be a living nightmare," she whispered to the wind, "with Brand so near and yet so distant in heart and mind."

As she reached the path between Camwright and Fauxbray, memories of the slaughter of three good men assailed her and caused the sting of tears to prick her eyes. She stopped before she crossed the river to continue her sojourn east and leaned against the bole of an oak, catching her breath and essaying to organize her chaotic thoughts.

What was she to do?

Just as Rollo led Brand to the depression beneath the stockade, the horn sounded from the watchtowers at the western gates, an eerie sound in the dead of the night, and the hair stood up on the back of Brand's neck. He squatted down and examined the hollow for a moment as Rollo began to scratch at the dirt with his front paws. "No one but a child could fit through there, boy." He shook his head in disbelief, knowing that the hound would not lead him astray where Marisa was concerned, then straightened. "We will attend to this as soon as I see who comes to Camwright at this hour."

As he strode toward the gates, they swung open to admit Morgan and several of his men. "By the rood, Welshman, have you nothing better to do than cavort back and forth between Wighton and Camwright in the middle of the night?''

"You know better than that, friend. I could not shake a feeling of impending disaster and thought mayhap I could do more good here at Camwright."

"As it happens, you are right. Marisa has slipped through a depression beneath the palisade and fled. Come.'' He motioned for Morgan to dismount and turned, the Welshman all but tumbling from his pony in his haste to follow his friend.

"Why would she wish to leave?'' Morgan asked, suspecting he already knew the answer.

"I accused her of adultery with le Faux."

"You . . . you did what?''

"You heard me. We had words and I said things I had no right to say to her.''

"By God, you are an even bigger fool than I gave you credit for.''

"You are so right for once, ap Dafydd.'' Brand squatted down before the hole under the palisade. "Look."

Morgan examined the hollowed out dirt and wood. "Who could have done this? They had to chip away at the wooden stakes, for they go well beneath ground level.''

"Angharad.''

"Angharad? That's absurd!''

Brand straightened. "Not as absurd as it sounds. Think of the times she seemed to appear out of thin air.'' He turned away. "Come, we have our work cut out for us and not a moment to spare. You are a godsend, Morgan, for only a Welshman can track in the dark with any degree of success. Will you help me?''

"You are a lackwit to even ask.''

Marisa silently cursed the bright September moon and the fates that had led her to the widest point on the otherwise narrow path connecting the two villages. To leave the obscurity of the woods to cross the wide, silver ribbon of track would be to expose herself to danger, especially in light of the fact that she had been hearing soft, rustling sounds that she feared might not be the movement of nocturnal animals or the light breeze sighing through the trees.

Well, she could not remain where she was until morning, cowering in the shadows like some frightened hare. The longer she remained, the greater was the possibility that Brand might discover her absence and come after her. Or that she might encounter someone else even more unwelcome.

Dieu au ciel, she thought, *am I doing the right thing?*

But it was rather late for second thoughts and, dragging in a deep breath of the clear night air, Marisa glanced up and down the path. Determining that it was deserted, she stepped out of the cover of trees. But she had taken no more than five steps when an arm snaked out from nowhere and pulled her up against an unyielding form, a hand covering her mouth to keep her from screaming.

Sudden fury washed over her at the fact that she had been foiled in her pitiful attempt to escape before she had even left the boundaries of Brand's land, and she fought to free herself from the firm grip as she was dragged backward toward the woods from whence she'd emerged.

"Easy, Marisa, else you'll unman the lord of Camwright," murmured Morgan ap Dafydd from nearby, the unmistakable lilt of humor in his words.

"Aye, Marisa," Brand added softly, his lips at her ear, "or would you prefer to be Mauger le Faux's captive?"

The query was a warning, certainly not meant to incite her anger, but incite her it did. As his grip began to relax, she bit down upon the fleshy pad between his thumb and forefinger and managed to free her mouth from its gag. Jerking around in his arms while they were still on the moon-bathed trail, she brought her knee up toward his stomach. It fell short of its mark and caught Brand in the groin.

He immediately released her and doubled over with a grunt of pain.

Marisa was too furious to feel more than a prickle of contrition. "Mauger le Faux? Of course I would rather be his captive than yours, you hulking Saxon! You've been so intent on catapulting me into his arms, I decided to take you up on your challenge." She canted her head to one side, her eyes narrowed like a hissing cat's. "Now if you and yon Welshman will step aside and allow me to pass—"

"There is no way on this earth I will allow you to go to *him*. You are my wife, Marisa, and you will come home with me." His ire was increasing not because he believed her capable of betraying him physically with le Faux, but because after all that had happened, after all that had been revealed, she would still prefer to seek shelter at Fauxbray than remain with him.

They stood there on the brightly lit path, oblivious to anything else, glaring at each other.

"You'd best continue this discussion elsewhere," Morgan said into the quivering silence. "If we do not leave now, neither one of you will live to have another disagreement."

Marisa took advantage of Brand's momentary distraction and spun around toward Fauxbray. She sprinted out of Brand's reach, but she was not quite fast enough. In desperation, knowing Morgan's keen tracking senses in the weald, Brand made a lunge for her. She heard the movement and saw him out of the corner of her eye, but did not elude him quickly enough. He caught her skirt as she skipped away, and the rending sound as Marisa fought free was magnified by the unnatural stillness.

Brand sprang toward her once again, knowing they must at all costs heed Morgan's warning, and caught her about the waist. She lost her footing and pitched toward the earth, but Brand managed to twist his body so that he took the brunt of the fall.

They both scrambled to their feet, Brand still smarting

from the blow to his groin and Marisa fighting for breath after having had the wind knocked out of her.

"Get back to the trees," Morgan cried, but it was too late. Even as Brand drew his sword, apparitionlike figures suddenly emerged from the forest on either side, surrounding them swiftly and silently. Madog ap Cynan's grim features were harshly discernable in the ghostly play of light upon the path as he contemptuously surveyed his prisoners.

"So 'twould seem you cannot even content your second wife, Ericson, so diligently does she flee your bed."

Brand pushed Marisa behind him as he faced Madog, and Morgan flanked her other side. His lips compressed into a tight line at Madog's words. "You will die this night, Welshman, for daring to abduct my son and my wife."

"You *killed* your wife, Saxon scum. You killed Rhiannon as surely as if you had choked the life from her."

Brand paled at the Welshman's words, feeling the healing wound of his guilt being torn asunder as ap Cynan's words struck with barbed impact.

"When she discovered she could not have the kind of love she craved—nothing beyond that of a sister—she came crying to *me*. And I gave her everything that you could not. *Everything!*"

Brand took a step forward, brandishing his weapon.

"Ah, ah, ah . . . Stay where you are, valiant warrior. 'Tis a shame that you were not as good a husband as you were purported to be a fighter for your ill-fated king."

"Why don't you have done with words, Madog, and fight Ericson man to man?" said Morgan. "I hardly call cutting a man down in cold blood behavior worthy of a Cymry." Morgan's voice was cool and casually mocking, but there was no mistaking the brittle edge of menace to the challenge.

An unexpected realization, however, began to dawn upon Brand. "Was the child Rhiannon was carrying when she died yours, Welshman?"

"Aye! And you let her die along with the babe. Now I will kill you and your Norman harlot and have your firstborn in reparation."

Warring thoughts spun through Brand's brain as he tried to assimilate the stunning revelation. Madog and Rhiannon? *Their* child? If it was true, how much useless guilt and remorse he would have been spared had he only known. . . .

"Lay down your arms, ap Cynan," a new voice commanded, "and order your men to do the same. I do not care to hear a Norman woman so named by a filthy, savage Welshman—even if 'tis true."

Madog turned as Mauger le Faux sauntered toward him, at least ten of his men mounted behind him, longbows strung and pointed at Madog's contingent. So engrossed were they in the scenario taking place before them that Madog's men had failed to hear the approach of the Normans.

"Stay out of this, le Faux, lest you dirty your hands and have to answer to your bastard king."

"Two insults in as long as it takes to draw breath? Surely even you have gone too far . . . to say naught of the way you thwarted our little plan." In a lightning move le Faux slapped aside the Welshman's sword with the flat blade of his own, the metallic *clang* vibrating through the clearing, and ran him through where he stood.

Two of Madog's men made a move toward Mauger and were instantly felled by swiftly released arrows.

As the stunned Madog sank to his knees, le Faux wiped his blade on the felled man's shoulder. "You are either very stupid, ap Cynan, or incapable of following orders, for you were to leave Marisa unharmed and hand her over to me. I have since discovered you intended to kill her." He clucked his tongue and shook his tawny head in mock regret. "That was your fatal mistake, for you should have guessed I would take the daughter of one of Normandy's wealthiest barons to wife, even if she was already breeding by her dead Anglo-Saxon husband." He smiled evilly. "Your usefulness has been served, Welsh dog, for William shall now be apprised that your rebels were stirred up against me by Ericson. The evidence will be found here . . . his body with yours.''

He looked up at Brand, who stood silently in the moonlight, coolly assessing the situation. ''Now, Saxon, I would take up the gauntlet you so carelessly cast on your last visit to Fauxbray.'' He threw a glance toward one of the Welshmen nearest Madog. ''Get him out of the way, savage, else I'll cut him up for food for the dogs.''

As the man dragged his dying leader aside, Brand said, ''I will gladly cross swords with you, le Faux, but not until Marisa is safely out of harm's way.''

Mauger nodded slightly. ''Very well. Let yon Welshman of whom you seem so fond escort her over to my men, for she will be mine after this child's play, have no doubt.''

''I would rather die of an arrow through the heart than ever go to you, Norman.'' Marisa's use of the word *Norman* emerged as an insult.

''Do as he says, Marisa,'' Brand ordered softly, then more loudly added, ''But Morgan stays at my back. I will not allow one of your men to cut him down from behind.''

Marisa stumbled toward Mauger's men, fear for Brand constricting her throat and making her movements awkward.

The two men began their deadly match. Barely were the first movements of thrust and parry joined when one of Madog's men, Hywel, tried to slip back into the forest. In the blink of an eye, a watchful Norman fitted an arrow to his longbow and sent it streaking through the air, putting an end to the Welshman's stealthy retreat.

A strangled sound nearby caught Marisa's attention. She pulled her horrified gaze from the two men fighting in the middle of the cleared area and saw one of the Normans drop from his destrier, the dagger of an unseen assailant protruding from his throat.

Pandemonium broke loose. Norman horses began to

toss their heads and dance sideways in agitation. Several other men slipped to the ground. The remaining Normans dismounted and sent their mounts sidling out of the way. Razor-sharp blades grated, sliding from their scabbards, as the Normans looked to defend themselves from this new threat.

Madog's men, however, took advantage and melted into the trees. Only the bodies of their leader and three unfortunate comrades remained as evidence of their presence. The sounds of new fighting filtered into the narrow clearing from within the shadows where they had fled.

Marisa retreated to the edge of the trees and trained her eyes upon her husband battling it out with her countryman. Hordes of Welshmen suddenly swarmed from the living wall of trees across from her. Then, in the midst of everything, Drystan was at her side, leading her even farther from the fray.

"Come, my lady. Let me take you back to Camwright and safety."

"Drystan," she breathed, unable to comprehend the change of circumstances.

"Aye, child. Do you think I would allow your brave husband to die for naught—for *less* than naught?" He inclined his head in Mauger's direction.

"But . . . but who are they?" she asked as her gaze was drawn to the Welshmen who were now attacking the startled Normans.

"They serve Prince Bleddyn, kinsman to Griffith through his mother."

She strained to make out his features in the moonlight, but a man's shrill scream drew her attention back to the bloody skirmish taking place before them.

"Come. Brand Ericson was not given his name for nothing."

She stared at him as if he were undone. "I cannot—*will* not—leave him!"

"Go, Marisa, for the love of God," rasped Morgan as

he passed by, his sword clashing with that of one of the Normans. "Get her out of here!"

But still Marisa refused to leave. "I'll not desert him now!"

"You are not safe here, my lady," the old man warned her.

"I care not about safety, Drystan. I will not leave Brand while his life hangs in the balance."

Having previously seen evidence of her intrepid nature, of her courage when a friend or loved one was in danger, Drystan understood her need to be near Brand. Saying no more, he allowed her to remain at his side in the shelter of a large beech tree.

Brand was holding his own, even gaining the upper hand, until one of the Welshmen made to attack Mauger. Two of the Norman men came to their leader's rescue and then turned toward Brand, making it a grossly uneven three to one.

Seemingly without effort, the Saxon dispatched one of them, his muscles bulging and straining, his blood-covered weapon flashing again and again in the moonlight.

Then Mauger's retainer buried his sword blade in Brand's upper left arm, sending blood rivering down to his hand, dripping from his fingers to darkly stain the earth beneath him. He jumped back from Mauger's wicked blade, perceiving another Norman coming up from his right side, but he was unable to turn swiftly enough to avoid the man's weapon.

In the blink of an eye, before Drystan could prevent her, Marisa acted without thought and darted toward Brand. She flung her body between her husband and the interloper just as Morgan appeared from nowhere and intervened as a decoy to Mauger. Pain jolted through her as, despite Brand's attempt to shove her back, she caught the tip of the sword in her shoulder, taking the thrust meant for him. With the last vestiges of strength she possessed, she heaved herself out of the way of the struggling men before sinking to the ground, unconscious.

Instantly Drystan lifted her and carried her to greater safety.

"Marisa!"

Brand's cry was wrenched from him, echoing through the predawn, the sound of a shattered soul, a battlecry for a cause that he took up with new ferocity.

The last he saw of Marisa was her still form being borne away by Drystan. In that instant he lost all reason, acting only on his battle-trained instincts. Like a Viking *berserkr* of old, blocking out the pain in his left arm and the growing heaviness of the sword in his right, he revitalized himself into a frenzy. Wielding his weapon mercilessly, he first cut down the man who'd struck Marisa; then one by one he dispatched the Normans all around him until at last he knocked Morgan out of the way to get to le Faux.

With two hands, he heaved his sword up and around, thrust and counterthrust, meeting his opponent's again and again. Ephemeral impressions—the coppery stench of blood; the earthy, pungent odor of sweat and fear; the gleam of spittle upon the men's cheeks as they panted and strained against one another—mingled with the cries of the wounded and dying.

Brand fought with such mindless lack of fear or caution that slowly, under his relentless onslaught, Mauger le Faux began to weaken. He was oblivious to the dissipating struggle around him as the Welsh, under their fearless leader Bleddyn, gained the upper hand and began to retreat back into the forest. Brand continued to drive Mauger le Faux without mercy. Then, in a slashing movement that came with all the speed and precision of a striking eagle, he severed le Faux's head from his body and ended the struggle.

Crouching, he spun around, ready to continue his quest to avenge his beloved Marisa's death . . . until he realized that it was over.

Brand slowly straightened to his impressive height, exhaustion washing over him in a ravaging wave. Yet it was nothing compared to the anguish that filled his heart as his gaze settled upon Drystan leaning over the inert Marisa. He could not bear it. He could not go to her and look upon her pale, lifeless form, for there would be no recovering from this loss.

A hand touched his shoulder, and his pain-filled gaze met that of the great Bleddyn. "Do not sorrow, for she is not dead, Ericson, only wounded. Love her and care for her well, for Drystan tells me she cleaves to Gruffydd as if he were her own. We could not ask for more."

As Bleddyn disappeared into the trees, Brand could not even conjure up the words to thank him. Not dead? He moved as if in a trance across the corpse-strewn clearing, his arm throbbing but his heart bouncing against his ribs in a surge of delirious hope that he dared not acknowledge.

Then he was kneeling beside her, his sword slipping from numb fingers. He looked up at Drystan, who nodded and moved away.

"Marisa?" he queried hoarsely, noting the contrast of the long sweep of sandy lashes with the pallor of her cheeks.

Her eyelids raised, and relief swept along his veins at the lucidity in the beautiful indigo eyes. "Brand . . . you are . . . unharmed?"

He smiled, his eyes brimming with love. "Aye, firebrand, 'tis only a flesh wound."

"Take me home, Brand—to Camwright." Her lids fluttered closed.

Brand looked up in sudden panic at Drystan, who was talking in low tones to Morgan. The recluse came closer and squatted down beside him. "She is in need of rest, Brand Ericson, that is all. She will recover, I promise you."

Brand raised the back of her hand to his lips, tasting the delicate flesh beneath his fingers before he heard the sound of an approaching horse. He looked up to see Morgan leading one of the Norman stallions toward him. "He is not as handsome as Goliath," the Welshman informed him wryly, "but for a hulking Norman beast, he will do."

Brand mounted the animal, and Drystan carefully handed up Marisa. "Take her home, my son, and tell her all that is in your heart."

Chapter 25

Griffith lay dozing in his grandfather's lap in the stillness of the bower. Rollo rested beside the bed upon which Marisa lay, his great head on his paws, but his eyes alert and moving from his mistress to Brand and then to Drystan.

"I acted the coward where my beloved Efa was concerned, and because of my folly, Angharad's lies drove me away," Drystan was saying.

Marisa glanced at Brand, who stood at the end of the bed, one foot braced against the carved chest, an arm resting across his knee. "But surely you could have done naught if Efa was dead," she began in sympathy.

The older man's countenance turned almost savage in its intensity. "I was so eager to escape the room, to run away from my grief, that Efa's eyes were barely closed in death before I fled. I never even knew I had two daughters."

"Two?" Brand's forehead creased in puzzlement.

"Aye. Twins. The first was stillborn, and then Angharad told me that Efa was dead. In my mindless panic I never guessed that there could be a second child, born alive. I ran out into the night like a man possessed."

"Rhiannon," Marisa murmured softly.

"I never knew I had a daughter—a living part of my Efa—until many years later, when I came upon the girl picking wildflowers near another village, miles away. She

355

was the picture of my wife, and I knew then what Angharad had done.''

Marisa shifted slightly in bed, pain marring the smoothness of her brow. Instantly Brand was beside her, rearranging the embroidered pillow behind her shoulder. ''But why would Angharad ever do such a thing? She was Efa's half sister.''

''Angharad was once very beautiful and accustomed to getting her way in all things. She had boldly offered herself to me—had even said she loved me—on many occasions. She suggested we run away together, I suppose because I was wed to Efa and she always coveted that which belonged to Efa—first her husband and then her only child.''

''So much pain and sorrow over love,'' Marisa observed quietly.

''But so much to be gained in the discovery of a great love.'' Brand's voice was rich with promise as his eyes caressed her face, and Marisa's heart stumbled in its steady cadence at the tenderness in his gaze.

Brand pulled his eyes from Marisa's fair countenance to regard the Welshman. ''So you shunned the company of men until now. A self-inflicted banishment.''

Drystan nodded and touched his lips to Griffith's dark head. ''I deserved no better. I became one with the animals of the mountains and the forests, and slowly nursed my hatred of Angharad until it burned like a living fire within me.''

''Why did you not make yourself known to Rhiannon then, Drystan, when you realized what Angharad had done? You would have been welcome here in Camwright, infinitely more so than Angharad.''

Candlelight caught the gleam of moisture upon a weather-roughened cheek. ''How could I explain to my daughter what I had done in my supreme cowardice? How could I explain my refusal to face and suffer my grief? She would have denied me, and with every right.''

Brand shook his head emphatically. ''You did not know Rhiannon, old man. She would never have denied you.''

More silent tears cascaded down Drystan's face, a testament to a need for cathartic release that had been long held in check.

"You are welcome to remain here near your grandson for the rest of your days, with the opportunity to lavish all the love and attention upon him that you could not give to Rhiannon."

Drystan's dark eyes met Brand's with gratitude, and he stood with Griffith still secure in his embrace. "I am glad I was always in the right place at the right time, Brand Ericson, for from the moment I saw the lady Marisa place herself between Gruffydd and Angharad in the glade that first time, I knew she loved my grandson as her own." He looked at Marisa, a gentle smile lighting his somber features. "You are, indeed, a gift from the gods, my lady, with your silver hair and midnight eyes, your fiery spirit and valiant heart. Our Saxon here could not have done better, not even with my own daughter." He let himself out before Marisa could acknowledge the touching compliment.

Brand regarded his wife, noting the soft color that had appeared in her cheeks at Drystan's praise. "It will be my never-ending delight to continue to learn about every facet of Marisa de Brionne." Surprise registered in her eyes at his statement. "I did not know Rhiannon as well as I thought, and I will see that I do not make the same mistake with you, Marisa." He took her hand in his, turning it palm up to tenderly place a kiss thereupon. *And by not being honest with Rhiannon, by assuming so much without confronting her, I was foolish and self-destructive. . . . That will not happen with us.*

"Will you forgive my accusations, my vile behavior toward you when I suspected you and le Faux?" he asked.

Her smiled acceptance of his apology made Brand's heart constrict with joy.

Marisa shivered lightly as he returned his attention to her hand. His lips touched each fingertip in turn, then moved to graze the delicate hollow at her wrist where her pulse beat steadily.

"You will be my undoing, Saxon, with your magic."

His eyes met hers, gem-gold with the promise of much to come. "One with so fiery a spirit and valiant a heart can surely wait until her shoulder has mended."

She pursed her lips ruefully. "I guess I will have to tie you to the bed in your sleep, my lord husband, for I cannot endure such torture until my shoulder heals."

"You have no choice, pouting wench, for even the intrepid Marisa de Brionne must yield to her body's limitations. . . . A kiss is all you'll get for now." And before she could answer, his firm, smooth-textured lips gently coaxed hers into submission.

Several days later, Marisa stood in the doorway of the manor, admiring the play of muscle and sinew under the burnished flesh of her husband's bare torso as he rode Goliath around the compound, practicing wielding his sword from astride the horse, Norman fashion.

Marisa laughed delightedly when he nearly unseated himself after one particularly zealous overhead circling of the heavy blade. Drystan smiled behind his hand while Griffith applauded his father with childish pride.

"Morgan was right when he said God gave the Welsh their smaller ponies for a reason," Marisa called out. "I suspect He also gave the English their ponies for the same reason."

Brand dismounted with catlike grace, tossing the reins to Brian, and strode across the yard to stand before his wife. "And, of necessity, He gave the Normans their monstrous chargers to match their inflated opinion of themselves."

Marisa opened her mouth to retort when one of the gatemen interrupted their banter. "My lord, someone comes across the Wye—a woman and a child."

Brand immediately squinted toward the watchtower, as if to see the newcomers as they rounded the open gate, although it was yet too soon.

"Brand?" Marisa's voice immediately drew his attention back to her. He turned and frowned at her effort to walk at her normal gait, forgetting in her eagerness to join him that her shoulder wound prevented her from moving as quickly and gracefully as was natural to her. "Brand, I believe I know who it might be."

" 'Tis the lady Godgift, my lord!" shouted another guard.

Brand touched her cheek lightly. "Return to the hall, my love. I will bring them inside."

Fighting the natural urge to go to the Danish woman and the little girl she suspected was Hilde, Marisa nodded and slowly turned back toward the hall.

It was then she realized he had called her "my love." *Could it be?* she thought as her blood began to sing through her veins, the sound of the endearment still echoing in her ears. She continued on into the hall, deliberately pushing aside thoughts of herself and Brand in the face of the arrival of Godgift and the child. Their having fled Fauxbray did not bode well.

Brand left the compound and hurried toward the river with long strides, reaching the steep bank just as Godgift struggled out of the river, her skirts leaden with water and her back bent with the added burden of Hilde and the girl's puppy in her arms. The child was not asleep, Brand realized as he slid down the more gently sloping end of the bluff to help them; Hilde stared sightlessly into space, unmoving.

"Here, let me take her," he said and lifted the little girl from Godgift's numb arms, helping the woman up the bank with his free hand.

"Thank you," she said quietly when they reached level ground. After drawing in several deep breaths of air and shifting the small dog to her other hand, she apologized. "I would never burden you with the responsibility of the child and myself under ordinary circumstances, my lord, but le Faux's men will search for us and, as you can see, Hilde is in shock. I—I cannot take her back there!"

"Hush, Godgift. Let us get you to the hall and the

child to bed. You can tell me what happened then. And,'' he added with grim satisfaction, ''you need not fear le Faux's men. . . . They are gone.''

Surprise and then relief registered in her eyes. She nodded and followed Brand through the gates of the compound and into the great hall.

The noon meal had been served and Hilde had been persuaded to take a few bites of food before being put to bed in the bower Griffith now shared with Drystan.

''I think Griffith will help Hilde emerge from her stupor, Godgift,'' Marisa suggested over the remnants of the repast.

Godgift's mouth tightened as memories of life under Mauger le Faux assaulted her. ''I would have stayed, Lord Brand, for my people, but when I saw what he'd done to Margaret, and in the child's presence . . . the fiend!''

''You may make your home here, Godgift, and Hilde, too.''

But Godgift looked at Marisa for approval, as well, and the warmth and acceptance in the lovely eyes convinced her beyond a shadow of a doubt. Her lips curved upward slightly, a weary sketch of a smile. ''You have my eternal gratitude. Fauxbray will never be the same again. There are too many bad memories for both Hilde and myself.''

''But where have you been for the past sennight?'' Marisa inquired, curious as to where Godgift had stayed since the day she and Griffith had been abducted.

''With the English who make their home in the weald.''

Marisa turned her gaze to Brand. ''Can we not take these people in, Brand?''

He returned her look, defeat mirrored in his eyes. ''There are too many of them, Marisa. I can help them with extra grain during good years and perhaps when the vegetable crops are plentiful, but there is little else I can do.'' His look turned even bleaker. ''Besides, there will always be those who refuse my help, who maintain that I sold out to the Normans."

Marisa bit her lip in vexation.

"Do not forget," Godgift reminded them sensibly, "there will always be a Norman overlord in Fauxbray. Mauger le Faux is dead, but someone else will be sent in his place."

"There may be an investigation," Brand added grimly. "Not only will there soon be a new overlord of Faux-bray—for I sent a messenger to London—but we may all of us be sent fleeing into the weald if William does not believe my explanation of what happened here."

"He will believe it," Marisa said with finality, the hue of her cheeks deepening with the force of her resolution. "He has no reason to doubt the word of a de Brionne."

Brand smiled in spite of himself. "Mayhap, once again, I misjudge the capabilities—the fierce determination—of my wife."

October came gently upon the land, easing over the countryside as effortlessly as a smoothly worn gauntlet. The trees nearby sported their autumn finery of yellow and gold, orange and scarlet, rust and brown, though in the distant mountains the hardy evergreens and heather remained unchanged year round.

In Camwright, things continued much the same. Yet there hung an air of tension, of expectancy over all.

Brand traveled to Fauxbray several times to oversee any matters that needed an overlord's attention and to provide extra provender as needed to help the villagers survive the coming winter. What he saw and heard at a village moot in the deserted manor hall troubled him deeply, but the most he could hope for was that a fair-minded Norman would be granted Mauger le Faux's holdings. He could by no means offer even that possibility as consolation to a people starving for hope for a brighter future.

When the horn sounded to announce the arrival of visitors to Camwright, apprehension streaked through

Brand's body like a fire through dry timber. Not only could this visit herald new difficulties in the form of a high-handed liege for the neighboring Fauxbray, but also likely as not an inquiry into the death of le Faux.

Brand had heard from the moot held in Fauxbray that the men Mauger had left behind had disappeared shortly after that fateful night. Surely after seeing their dead leader and comrades strewn about the pathway to Camwright, they would have gone straight to London to gain an audience for the grisly tidings they bore. Yet Edwin had informed Brand that the character of many of those "retainers" was questionable, as unprincipled and avaricious as that of their leader. And so Brand had no inkling as to whether the remaining men had become scavengers or informers.

Now, it seemed, he would discover how much more had been revealed to William of Normandy than in his tersely worded missive.

Marisa and Griffith had just returned from a walk through the village with Hilde, and Brand had been examining a wounded hunting falcon. As he emerged from the falcon house, the rumble of hoofbeats shook the very ground, and he knew with a sinking certainty that the moment he'd dreaded was at hand.

Marisa hurried toward him, shooing the children into the manor, and rejected Brand's attempt to persuade her to follow them. "Nay, Brand. I will face this with you."

He looked down into her face, searching for the words that would send her fleeing to the safety of the hall, then realized that there were none. There would never be any such words with Marisa.

They stood staring at each other with equal determination until a vaguely familiar voice advised, "Pray, do not banish Marisa to the hall, for she will surely find some way to jump back into the thick of things, despite any warnings to do otherwise."

They both looked up into the handsome features of Robert de Lisieux. He sat on his horse calmly, only the quirk of one corner of his mouth suggesting his amusement at Marisa's obstinance.

Marisa drew in her breath in shock, and then realized that if the new lord of Fauxbray were to be anyone besides her very own brothers, Robert de Lisieux would be the next best choice. He had already proven his magnanimity, and for that they were indebted to him.

"So we meet again," Brand greeted softly.

The Norman dismounted and approached them. Hilde, who had remained with a curious Griffith in the yard and was standing between the three adults and the door of the manor hall, gave a small whimper of distress and stood rooted to the ground in fear.

"Take them into the hall, Marisa," Brand said quietly. She seemed about to comply when Godgift appeared at the door of the hall.

"Hilde!" she cried, and swiftly emerged into the compound to scoop the frightened little girl into her arms. As she turned back toward the building, she met Robert's intense gaze and paused infinitesimally before lowering her lashes and hurrying back into the shelter of the hall.

At the question in Robert's eyes, Brand enlightened him. "Godgift fled Fauxbray with the child the day before Mauger's death. Hilde, the little girl, saw her mother raped and murdered by le Faux—or by one of his men—only hours before their escape. No doubt your coloring, height, and the sword at your side reminded her of your countryman and the horror of what happened that day."

The blue of Robert's eyes darkened with outrage before he signaled for his men to dismount. "May we seek refreshment within your hall, Ericson? We have much to discuss."

While Brand explained what had happened between Mauger le Faux's nefarious scheming and Madog ap Cynan's festering grudge, enough mead was passed around for an entire village. After supper some of his men became engaged in games of chess and dice, even armwrestling. Others had gone outside to talk of horses with their Norman counterparts and ask questions about the huge, impressive destriers that had contributed to the downfall of Harold Godwinson and his forces. As much as Marisa knew of the animals, there was nothing quite like one soldier speaking to another about matters of horseflesh and battle.

Robert had removed his swordbelt and ordered his men to do the same while in the hall, out of consideration for the child Hilde. He sat back in a settle now, watching Godgift and Griffith coax Hilde into playing with her puppy, Will.

"What is to be my punishment, de Lisieux, for killing one of William's chevaliers?" Brand ventured at last.

After shooing Godgift away to tend to Hilde, Marisa had remained near the head of the table and was supervising the clearing away of the remnants of the meal. At Brand's blunt query, her attention was instantly diverted from her duties as chatelaine to the concerns of a devoted wife.

"William has been in Normandy since the spring, and earlier on I had sent a detailed report to him on this area. I recommended that he either take action to bring le Faux into line or repossess his newly granted fief. His reply, which was a while in coming, said to oust le Faux myself, by his writ, and take over Mowbray. I believe that was the original name of the village?"

"Aye." Brand softly let out a pent-up breath. "Mayhap I underrated the fairness of your duke, Robert de Lisieux."

Marisa joined them, bringing a freshly filled ewer of mead. "Then you will be our neighbor, Robert!" she exclaimed with a smile of relief and happiness.

He regarded her with an odd light in his eyes, as if in acknowledgment—and acceptance—of what now could never be between them. "Aye, Marisa." His gaze left her face and moved to the woman and two children laughing over the antics of the enormous Rollo and the minuscule Will. "Do you think I could persuade the lady Godgift to return to Mowbray? As former lady of the manor, she would be my natural choice, if she will have me, for I glimpsed her quiet courage and love for her people even under le Faux's abuse.''

"So long as you accept Hilde, for she is like the child Waltheof and Godgift never had.''

"Easily done, Ericson. Easily done.'' He stood and slowly approached the threesome sitting amongst the clean, herb-scented rushes on the floor.

Marisa went to stand behind Brand, her hands resting upon his shoulders. "Brand, do you think Hilde is ready to—?''

She never finished her question, for just then Hilde looked up at the man whose eyes were filled with tenderness and, forgetting her fears, pulled on his left sleeve to make certain she had his undivided attention. It was done with childish spontaneity, the acceptance of his handicap without question, as only an innocent child can do. "My lord Norman, will you be angry because I named my dog Will?'' Her anxious gaze searched his face and he squatted before her, a large, strong finger gently tracing the delicate features and smoothing away the crease of a frown that tracked across her small brow. "I named him for King William,'' she added, her expression clearing as a ray of pride shone through.

"*Eh bien,* I believe my lord William would be honored that you named your puppy after him.'' His gaze met Godgift's and she gave him a smile that transformed her features.

"Will you, both of you, come to live with me at Mowbray?'' he inquired gently, "for I will have need of both a wife and a child—and,'' he added quickly, "a brave hound to guard our hall.''

Hilde contemplated him with childish thoroughness, then looked at Godgift, whose cheeks were stained a delicate pink. "May I sleep on your proposal, my lord?'' she asked in imitation of what she'd heard Marisa teasingly say to Brand on many occasions.

For the first time in months, Robert threw back his head and laughed heartily, Brand and Marisa joining in as they came up behind him just in time to hear Hilde's query. "Of course, *chère*. You must always sleep on important decisions."

The braziers burned brightly, casting a roseate glow over Marisa's ivory skin, turning the satiny swath of her hair to palest gold as she sat upon the bed, her shift down about her shoulders to bare her mending wound to Brand's gentle examination.

"I do not know if I like the idea of having a former suitor of yours for a neighbor," he said into the peaceful silence.

"And you do well to worry, Saxon."

His fingers paused in their soothing massage. "Just what do you mean by that, wench?"

"I mean that what I need rather than your needless fretting is to be safely in your arms until I am withered and gray, until you are too ancient ever to look askance at another woman."

His eyes filled with emotion as he turned her to face him. "I have not looked askance at another woman since you first walked toward me at Westminster. You took my breath away then, my Marisa, even as you do now." His lips caressed her brow. "You've made me whole, as I've never been before, and I love you more than my life."

Her eyes widened. "You love me?"

"Indeed, Viking. Surely you must have suspected, with your woman's instincts. I have loved you ever since you got poor Rollo sotted with my breakfast wine." He stilled while she adjusted her legs under the cover, and a grimace marred the classic beauty of her features as she twisted toward him too quickly. With infinite gentleness he pushed an errant strand of glossy hair back from her cheek. "I loved you when you pitted yourself against Goliath to save my son, and I knew you to be everything I stubbornly refused to acknowledge."

"In that case," she said with dry humor, "I am glad I did not have to intercede with William for you and wound your pride."

He shook his head. "It mattered not." At her look of

surprise, he added, "All that truly mattered was that you and Griffith remained at my side. I had already decided to take you both to live with me in Wales if things had turned out for the worst—if I had been sentenced to death for having killed le Faux. Land, titles, wealth to pass on to Griffith—none of that was of any importance compared to your safety, and our being together—always."

Marisa shook her head in disagreement. "I would never have allowed you to leave your home, Brand Ericson. I would have gone to the King myself to plead your case, for you are the sword of your people."

A frown of bemusement drew his brows together.

"*Brand*—the Anglo-Saxon word for sword," she mused. "Drystan said you were not given your name for naught, and now I understand what he meant."

"And what, pray tell, is that?"

"You were the sword, the strength of your people at Hastings and then at Malfosse, and you will always be so—a symbol of valor and hope from which they can draw courage, as they must."

"Ah, my wise Norman wife, whose silver tongue matches her glorious hair. You must promise never to throw yourself into the path of a sword again, for truly a part of me died in that clearing when I thought you had perished."

Marisa closed her eyes and settled more comfortably within the haven of his embrace. "Then I give you my word that I will not, for you will need every bit of your strength to keep me happy for the rest of our lives."

His voice rich with laughter, he said, "You are an insatiable baggage, Marisa de Brionne. Can you think of nothing else but making love?"

The sweet curving of her lips revealed a secret satisfaction. She turned her body and pressed it to his with all the yearning acquired during a month of abstinence. "No, my lord. Not at the moment."

Epilogue

Brand downed a horn of mead and poured another. He lifted it to his lips and a voice from behind him chided, "You'll do her no good so sotted you cannot see straight."

He paused in mid-motion, acknowledging the wisdom of Morgan's words, yet feeling a driving need to hold at bay all the mixed emotions roiling through him with frightening force.

He replaced the horn upon a nearby table and began to pace the hall agitatedly, the walls seeming to close in upon him in his frustration. His eyes kept going to the time-keeping candle with its marks for each hour.

"Eight hours, Morgan. . . . Eight hours!"

" 'Tis hardly enough time for the birthing process, Brand."

Brand slued around to face his friend, the lines of strain around his eyes and mouth attesting to the toll exacted by the past hours. "And how is it that you are such an expert on these matters?"

Morgan yawned and stretched before scratching Rollo behind the ears. The dog was at loose ends—unable to be with his mistress and pointedly ignored by his distracted master. "You forget that I have several younger brothers and sisters."

Brand grunted and moved to the doorway, staring out

into the blue-black vault of a crepuscular sky. He breathed deeply of the clear, cold air and wished Drystan were there. The old man had said he would stay nearby when Marisa's time came, but he had not yet returned from an all-day outing with Griffith. Strange, Brand mused.

"It always takes longer for the first, friend. Sit with me and we'll cast the dice."

Brand threw a glance over his shoulder. "Surely you jest, Welshman. I can think of naught but Marisa."

"How does she fare?" inquired Drystan, as if conjured up, from the east entrance of the hall.

Brand swung around, relief easing some of the tightness that had invaded his chest. "I do not know, Drystan. Adela will not allow me in there."

Drystan lowered a bundle of herbs and roots he'd gathered to a table and moved to wash his hands in one of several basins set aside for that purpose. Griffith, who had entered with him, went over to Rollo. "God's blood," Drystan muttered, "but women can be ridiculous. Just wait until I enter that sacred bower. They will set up the screeching of an invaded hen coop," the older man predicted.

Morgan laughed aloud and Brand's lips twitched.

"You may accompany me if you like, Brand," Drystan added as he dried his hands.

Uncertainty flitted across Brand's features and then was gone. If he could do battle, he could face Marisa's suffering with an equal show of bravado. "Brand?" It was Edyth.

His head snapped around to meet her hazel-eyed gaze, so like his own.

"Adela says the babe is ready to be born, but Marisa . . . Marisa has lost much blood and her strength is ebbing. . . . She calls for you."

The color drained from Brand's face and a terror clawed through him like none he'd ever evinced upon a battlefield.

"Adela says that mayhap your presence would help."

Before she could finish, he was pushing his way past her, Drystan close behind him.

"This is women's work, Welshman!" Adela exclaimed indignantly. "I will let no man deliver my Marisa's child."

"I know more of birthing than you think."

"Oh, aye, of bringing forest creatures into the world, but this is a *lady,* and no wild hermit will touch my baby."

Brand's words dropped like heavy stones into the sudden quiet. "Then you will be removed bodily, woman. This is my village, my manor, and *my wife.* If Drystan says he knows much of birthing, then no woman's superstition will prevent him from assisting Marisa."

But with infinite patience and gentleness Drystan sought to reassure the distraught woman. "I was not here when my own daughter bled to death and perished. I would make it up in the only way I know how . . . by helping the lady Marisa, who means so very much to all of us."

Adela fought her fears, biting her lip to stop the tears of vexation that threatened.

"You may remain here, Adela. I will need you."

And so, while Brand held Marisa's hand and tenderly dabbed the beads of moisture from her face, Drystan worked quickly to turn the babe into the easiest position for birth, with Adela and Edyth helping. Awed by his skill, the two women learned much from this wise and gentle man who had become so valuable to all of them.

Mouthing words of endearment and encouragement while he valiantly fought to hide his deepest misgivings, Brand was rewarded with the sudden cry of a healthy child emerging into the world.

" 'Tis a girl," Adela said proudly.

Marisa turned her head to regard her husband, a shadow darkening her eyes. "I so wanted to give you a son, Brand."

He brushed back the damp strands of her silken hair

and raised her hand to his lips. "And I wanted you to give me a daughter just like you." His smile told her he spoke the truth, and Marisa sighed contentedly.

Adela cleaned the babe and showed it to the parents. "Lay the babe upon the lady Marisa's breast," Drystan advised, and without further ado the woman complied.

"She has your fair hair, Marisa." Brand touched a tiny fist, and instantly the fingers curled around his larger one, clinging with surprising tenacity. "She will soon be riding Goliath and brandishing a wooden sword. . . . Woe to any who would dare approach our village with less than friendly intent." Laughter lurked in his eyes, and Marisa returned his smile.

Brand looked up at Drystan, who was washing his hands. The Welshman nodded a silent assurance that everything was fine, and he and the two women quietly took their leave.

As Marisa looked from the child to her husband, a sudden thought struck her. "Why, Brand Ericson, you look terrible!"

"And you never looked more beautiful."

She gave him a dazzling smile in answer, and Brand thought that, as long as he lived, he would never see so breathtaking a sight. "Thank you, my lord. But what shall we name her?" Marisa's eyelids suddenly began to droop.

Brand shrugged. "We have time to name her later, firebrand. Why don't you rest while I hold my daughter?" Carefully he took the baby into his arms, staring down at her in wonderment, feeling no less thrilled than the first time he'd held Griffith.

"I like Morgana—after your stalwart friend."

"Morgan? Why, if you do such a thing, that cocky Welshman will be singing praises of your moonlight hair and your heather-hued eyes until the end of his days!"

Marisa laughed softly and met his gaze. Within those splendid blue-violet eyes, Brand saw his future, fraught with challenge and full of promise. Suddenly all his demons were exorcised. Every last trace of his guilt slipped from his shoulders, as smoothly and surely as a discarded mantle.

He leaned to touch his lips to hers in an unspoken promise of love and laughter. ''Very well, then, Viking. Morgana it shall be.''

Author's Note

Malfosse ("evil ditch") was an actual historical occurrence. It happened much the way I have described, according to historians. No one knows who led that last stand by Anglo-Saxon housecarls (the king's trained corps of men) the evening of October 14, 1066. I gave my character Brand credit for heading the last resistance that felled a good number of Norman horsemen under (according to one source) first Eustace of Boulogne and then Duke Wiliam himself. Although in *Brianna* I hinted that it might have been a secondary character in the story, Robert of Wessex, who was responsible for rallying a group of Englishmen at the forest's edge, there was never any positive reference—only rumors to show the good and valorous side of a man who was also twisted by hatred and a perverse need for vengeance against an innocent young woman. Rather, I would like to think that that courageous, unknown leader could have been a survivor very much like Brand Ericson.

Also, I took the liberty of having William of Normandy attend Brand and Marisa's wedding at the beginning of April 1067, when, in fact, he had returned to Normandy one month before.

LINDA LANG BARTELL

From the moment she picked up *The Wolf and the Dove*, LINDA LANG BARTELL knew she was irrevocably hooked on historical romances. She says, "Here was an outlet for my love of history and my incurable romanticism. I became an avid reader of historical authors of the seventies while I taught high school French and history. It wasn't until my husband Bob and I moved from our hometown of Cleveland, Ohio, to Michigan that I decided to try to write my own book—and, to our delight, also conceived our daughter, Heather Lauren. That first manuscript is in my basement, but my second one sold, and the rest is history.

"I still love to read historical and general fiction, but I don't have the time I once did, because of my writing, research, and family. I love sports and dancing and am inspired in my writing by music . . . anything from Tchaikovsky to Van Halen."